William Robertson

The Kings of Carrick

A Historical Romance of the Kennedys of Ayrshire

William Robertson

The Kings of Carrick
A Historical Romance of the Kennedys of Ayrshire

ISBN/EAN: 9783337348571

Printed in Europe, USA, Canada, Australia, Japan

Cover: Foto ©Andreas Hilbeck / pixelio.de

More available books at **www.hansebooks.com**

THE

KINGS OF CARRICK

A Historical Romance of the Kennedys

of Ayrshire

BY

WILLIAM ROBERTSON

Author of "Historical Tales and Legends of Ayrshire," &c.

SECOND EDITION

LONDON: HAMILTON, ADAMS, & CO
GLASGOW: THOMAS D. MORISON
1890

PREFACE.

THE history of the Carrick division of Ayrshire during the last six hundred years is largely that of the Kennedy family. The present Marquis of Ailsa is the seventeenth in direct lineal male descent from a certain John de Kennedy, who, so far back as 1357-8, was confirmed by David II. in all the lands belonging to him. And that this John de Kennedy was descended from the more remote De Carricks, hardly admits of any doubt.

It goes without saying that a family that can look back across five or six centuries of continuity must necessarily have a story that is worth the telling. Vastly important centuries in the history of Scotland, they necessarily evolved men meet for the times; and inasmuch as Ayrshire during all that long period shared largely in the alternating fortunes of the centuries, it is beyond any reasonable doubt that its sons were men of character and of intrepidity.

It was a Kennedy who stormed the grey Keep of Dunure, and drove thence a Norse baron who had long held it in his safe keeping. A Kennedy was one of the hostages for

David II. in 1358. With one of the Douglases, a Kennedy for some unknown reason incurred in 1431 the ire of the Sovereign, and was kept in close custody in the Castle of Stirling after his fellow conspirator—if, indeed, they were conspirators—had regained his freedom. A Kennedy was Bishop of Dunkeld in 1438, Bishop of St. Andrews and Chancellor of Scotland in 1440, and was appointed one of the Regents of Scotland during the minority of James III. ; and left his memory savoury in the halls of learning, in that he founded the College of St. Salvator in St. Andrews, in the year 1450. A Kennedy formed one of the retinue who attended Margaret of Scotland on her marriage to the Dauphin Louis in 1436. A Kennedy, the parson of Douglas in the beginning of the 16th century, was accounted worthy to occupy a place in Gawin Douglas's " Palace of Honour," and himself courted the muse to some purpose when he wrote the " Flyting of Dunbar and Kennedy." A Kennedy, the first Earl of his race, was slain on the field of Flodden. The second Earl was Ambassador to England in 1515-16. The third, a pupil of the celebrated George Buchanan, was one of the Lords of Secret Council to James V., was taken prisoner at the rout of Solway in 1542, is said to have been converted to the Protestant faith by Cranmer, and was successively a Lieutenant-General of horse to Queen Mary, an extraordinary Lord of Session, one of the nation's deputies at the marriage of

Queen Mary to Francis the Dauphin of France, and Lord High Treasurer of Scotland. The fourth Earl was with Queen Mary at Langside, though, sooth to say, he is better remembered as the King of Carrick who roasted the Commendator of Crossraguel in the black vault of Dunure. The fifth Earl was Treasurer of Scotland in 1599. The sixth was prominent in resistance to the designs of Charles I. in 1638, and was one of the three ruling elders sent to the Westminster Assembly of Divines in 1643. The seventh was the only Member of Parliament who in 1670 voted against the Act for punishing Conventicles.

The records of the family might be still further continued; but these are sufficient to show that the house of Kennedy has produced many sons who have done the State some service.

Naturally, their position in Ayrshire has never been questioned. They have contributed largely to its history, and to some extent have made it what it is. This it would not be difficult to show, were this the proper place to discuss the nature of the influence they have wielded.

It was, perhaps, unavoidable that the Kings of Carrick should have come into sharp contact with the families whose rights or whose prejudices they disturbed, or who were jealous of their broad acres and all but unlimited power. In the work which follows the author has selected a period in what was perhaps the greatest of their feuds, and the most brimful of interest. And what renders this particular feud the more notable is, that it was essentially a family quarrel, the Cassillis Kennedys opposed to the Kennedys of Bargany.

John Mure of Auchendrane, who figures prominently in these pages, was not the last of his race. The family existed till the eighteenth century, when it went out in the person of a poor and distressed man. Arrested for debt, he was preparing to accompany the bailiff to the gaol of Ayr. The officer, touched by his situation, offered to accept the dule tree of Auchendrane—the tree of mourning, an exceptionally fine plane tree—in payment of the debt. "What!" said the last of the Mures, still proud in his poverty, "sell the dule tree of Auchendrane! I will sooner die in the worst dungeon of your prison!" And to prison he went.

"The Kings of Carrick" is best described as a revised edition of "The Kennedys," which found such favour with the public of the west country that a second edition has been rendered necessary.

CONTENTS.

CHAPTER IX.

CHAPTER X.

CHAPTER XI.

CHAPTER XII.

CHAPTER XIII.

CHAPTER XIV.

CHAPTER XV.

CHAPTER XVI.

CHAPTER XVII.

CHAPTER XVIII.

CHAPTER XIX.

CHAPTER XX.

CHAPTER XXI.

CHAPTER XXII.

CHAPTER XXIII.

THE
KINGS OF CARRICK.

CHAPTER I.

PREPARING FOR THE ENCOUNTER.

THE old House of Cassillis stands on the banks of the river Doon, on the very border of the Carrick division of Ayrshire, three miles distant from the Capital of Carrick, Maybole, and seven from the town of Ayr. And here, for centuries, dwelt the great heads of the family of Kennedy—a race of feudal chiefs, who came into prominence with the battle of Largs, and who were so dominant in the south-west of Scotland that their power passed into the immortality of that terse, doggerel verse which holds its own while more refined and artistic productions pass into oblivion—

'Twixt Wigton and the town of Ayr,
Portpatrick and the Cruives of Cree,
No man need think for to bide there,
Unless he court St. Kennedy.

The Castle itself is one of the old square peels which were wont to stud the country side. Its heavy, solid walls, twelve and fourteen feet in thickness, proclaim that it was built for purposes of defence and of defiance. Protected behind by the river Doon, which runs some thirty or forty feet beneath, it was originally surrounded otherwise by a deep-cut moat which, save by the guarded drawbridge which bespanned it, effectually prevented sudden attack or untimely surprise. The moat has long since been filled up, the last faint trace of it obliterated, and the piping times of peace have transformed

2

the castle into a quiet country mansion, which looks out in front over a placid smiling rustic park to the uplands which dominate it above, and which culminate in the fairy-dancing heights of Cassillis Downans, and on the other three sides over fertile fields and plains and undulating woodland, which suggest not a hint of the stormy times, which, when the power of the Kennedys culminated in the virtual Kingship of Carrick, wrought deep their impress even on the natural surroundings of the venerable pile. The Doon meanders quietly past, opening up in its sinuous course a series of charming prospects, and lilting the same melodious cadence which of old charmed to slumber lords and ladies and retainers bold and grim.

Within, the castle is rude in style and appointments, to modern ideas. The steep stone stairs lead up to turrets and recesses, to fairly spacious chambers and lofty passages, to secret places and points of vantage; and down to dungeons dark and damp, whose unresponsive walls have often heard the yells of the frantic captives, and the last faint moans of the dying. Every chamber, every room, is redolent of history and tradition; there are niches built up in the walls which are said by the believing to contain the bones of the skeletons of unfortunates who, centuries ago, came within the vindictive scope of the old Earls; and a lofty pillar, around which the main staircase winds, is said to contain a narrow flight of steps leading down to the very foundations, and finding its exit in close proximity to the river.

A thousand eventful scenes have been enacted within these walls. Imagination calls up the long silent revel and shout and song of the armed retainers; it hears afresh the war cries of the defenders as they rushed to meet the enemy in the gate; it fills the lofty halls with gay companies dancing the quaint old Scottish dances with courtly dignity, and in garb more æsthetic and picturesque than modern fashion can boast; it surrounds Cassillis with forest and plain, where the deer roamed and the huntsman chased; it sweeps away all the innovations of the centuries and leaves us alone with a period when Ayrshire history was in the wildest of throes, and when future destinies were being carved out with steel by men whose highest ambition was their own aggrandise-ment and self-glorification. Other mansions and keeps stud this westland, where history-making has not been idle, and where associations and memories cluster thick, but none of them all is more saturated with story or more begirt with romance than this square, turreted peel by the banks of the Doon. Generation after generation of Kennedys dwelt here in semi-regal, semi-barbarous splendour. Many a foray was' directed hence; many a warrior went out from beneath the shadow of the peel to fight in fray whose very memory has perished; many an intrigue was planned by men who planned only to execute. Scenes of joy and of sorrow, of war and of bloodshed, cluster round the spot and rush in eventful cur-rent across the mind of the thoughtful visitor.

Not the least interesting feature in the scene of which Cassillis House is the centre, is the dule tree, a magnificent, regularly proportioned plane, whose heavy boughs and gnarled branches bespeak an antiquity at least as venerable as that of the Castle itself. It is a tree among a thousand. About half-a-dozen of its compeers are spared to keep it company; one of them, at least, wider in girth, several of them raising their heads further into the blue; but none of them all for shapeliness and beauty can match the dule tree, which stretches its branches right over the old gateway, and all but brushes the walls of the keep. They have been com-panions—plane tree and castle—during centuries of change. They have grown old together; yet to this very day they stand as strong as they did long ago, when the Kennedys trooped out from the ramparts of the one, to battle, or gathered beneath the friendly, drooping shade of the other, to mourn their comrades who had fallen victims to the rough

times in which they lived.   It was here the men of Cassillis
gathered when the sad news of melancholy Flodden reached
the west country; it was here they mourned their chief and
their comrades who had fought and fallen on the luckless
field.   It was from one of these gnarled boughs that an irate
Lord of Cassillis, a century later, hanged the gipsy laddie who
had dared to tamper with the affections of his spouse.   So
says tradition, at any rate.   It is not a pleasant task to dis-
sipate a legend which has haunted a country-side for a couple
of hundred years; but a strict regard for truth compels the
admission that the story is an invention of the enemy.   In
presence of the tree, however, let no man sweep off the
cobwebs which make the credulous respect it, and the rustic
gaze on it with as much awe as admiration.

It is not necessary to tell in detail the history of the
Kennedys.   Their first recognised progenitor in Ayrshire, was
a doughty captain who stood by Alexander, when he beat
back the Norsemen on the shore at Largs.   This worthy, with
an eye to the main chance, did not still his exertions with the
fray itself.   At its close, he pursued all the way along the
sands of Ayrshire, from Largs to Dunure, a Norseman who
held in possession a strong walled castle by the sea; nor did
he rest until he had dislodged the Norseman from his keep,
and installed himself in his place.   By conquest, by policy,
by marriage, this worthy's successors gradually extended their
sway until the whole southern part of Ayrshire, and a great
part of Galloway, owed them allegiance.   In the course of
time, like most monopolists, they quarrelled among themselves, separating into two recognised factions, the one headed
by the Earl of Cassillis, the other by his kinsman, Kennedy
of Bargany, whose house was by the Girvan, and who, at the
period of his greatest strength, was able to muster at his call
no fewer than nine hundred retainers, staunch and true.
Cassillis was more powerful than he.   His lands were broader,
his resources more extensive, his followers more numerous.

But, on the other hand, he had fewer extraneous friends, fewer of the smaller lairds and gentry at his call. His rule was iron; he brooked no equal, no interference; and while, at the period to which we refer, and at which our tale opens, he was, taken singly, the dominating force of the south-west of Scotland, his rival was better able to enlist in his cause the "wee" lairds, whose pride was in the inverse ratio of their importance, and whose jealousies were as broad as their acres were contracted. The two rival factions were thus fairly pitted against one another, with the result that for many years Carrick was decimated by fratricidal conflict.

Of these smaller barons the most notable was John Mure of Auchendrane, a feudalist as untamed and as unquenchable as the fiercest warder of Border story. Auchendrane had the advantage of a military training in the wars of the Continent, where he had achieved some distinction as a commander; but he was rather more of a politician than a soldier. Sharp and penetrating in his instincts, he read the men by whom he was surrounded much better than he could have read a book. He had sounded all their shoals and depths; he knew the mainsprings of their actions; and there was not one of them that he could not, and would not, turn to account when it suited his own purposes. He was cruel and vindictive; he never forgot an insult or an enemy; and he was as tenacious as a sleuthound in following up the track of his vengeance. Still, he preferred, wherever he could, to work behind the scenes. It was for him to plot, for others to execute; and many a blow that was struck at the Earl of Cassillis was directed by a hand that itself remained invisible. A family feud was life and death to him; and so deeply had he sworn to prosecute the war upon the Kennedys of Cassillis, whose domains "marched" with his own, that with all their bravery and recklessness of danger, these Kennedys gave his strong tower a wider berth than they did that of even the bold Bargany himself.

Kennedy of Bargany consorted with Mure. The latter was his adviser and his father-confessor to boot, and he seldom set about any undertaking without first taking counsel of Auchendrane.

It was the opening year of the seventeenth century. For a score of years and more the two branches of the Kennedy family had been at feud; but never, during the whole period, had the conflict been more religiously carried on than now. Neither side gave the other cessation. The Earl of Cassillis hardly dared to ride abroad beyond his own domains. The town of Ayr was all but a sealed book to him, for Bargany was omnipotent there, and the burghers followed his standard to the fray. The retainers of the two factions had fallen foul of one another at Maybole, those of Bargany getting the worst of the struggle; and in revenge Thomas, the laird of Bargany's brother, had waylaid the Earl of Cassillis while on his way home from Craigneil, a strong tower of his in the extreme south of the county, in the valley of the Stinchar, and all but succeeded in taking his life. The tide of fortune was ebbing and flowing alternately; and Carrick was divided into two hostile camps which hated one another with all the characteristic ferocity and tenacity of old friends who had taken arms in opposing causes.

The Laird of Bargany was in Ayr; and thither had repaired Mure of Auchendrane, Mure of Cloncaird, the Master of Stair, and other adherents of the Bargany faction. It was the depth of winter, and the old town was wreathed in snow. But within the comfortable town house of the laird the frigidity of the elements found no analogy. The ale cup was as generous as the host himself; and the company were jocund as they recounted their deeds and pledged one another for the future.

"We have been too long in the clover," broke in the impetuous Bargany, who had begun to chafe over the time spent in the burgh town, "for the last ten days and more we

have done little but eat and drink and sleep, and curse the
Earl of Cassillis; but we are no nearer the end with it all, so
far as I see, nor are we likely to be until we throw off this
laziness and begin business again."

"That is so," assented Mure of Cloncaird, "we are quite
going to rust idling our time away here and doing nothing,
while Cassillis, for all that we know, is getting ready for
action, and moving heaven and earth besides, to prejudice the
Privy Council against us. If we don't bestir ourselves, and
that speedily, every mother's son of us will be put to the
horn before we know where we are."

"We are a great deal more likely to be put to the horn,"
replied Auchendrane, "for doing too much, than we are for
doing too little.   Still, the Earl has the ear of the Chancellor;
there is no denying that."

"I should imagine he has," assented the Master of Stair,
drily, "for he is married to the last Chancellor's widow—old
enough to be his grandmother."

"Old enough to be his mother, anyway," said Bargany,
"but whether he has the ear of the Chancellor, as Auchendrane says, or not, this is no life for me to be living.   It is
the powerful who grow more powerful and are most regarded
in these times; and unless we show that we are a force in
Carrick that has to be reckoned with, who knows whether
Cassillis may not some fine day get all our lands forfeited to
the Crown and then to himself, because, as he puts it, we are
troublous and tumultuous?"

"What a pity your brother Thomas missed his chance at
the Earl the other day, Bargany!" observed Cloncaird in a
regretful tone.

"The devil is good to his own," was the reply.   "Yet, I
don't know how they missed him.   Sometimes I begin to
think there is treachery in the air, though, if there were,"——
here Bargany paused for a moment, and completed the sentence by bringing his hand down with a resonant blow on the

table. Resuming, he continued, "Thomas, with Dalrymple here, and a dozen of our men, hid in the ruins of an old farm house by the wayside near Craigneil; and if Cassillis had only come when they expected his coming, and were looking for it, nothing could have saved him. But something kept him so long that they began to think he was not coming at all, and they grew careless, I suppose; and, when at last he did pass them, it was at a flying gallop. They fired their muskets at him, and chased him, too, but he fled like the wind. Is not that so, Dalrymple?"

"Yes, that is exactly as it was," replied the Master of Stair. "I fired at him myself; but I never saw horse gallop so in my life. He was out of sight before we got fairly after him."

"Cassillis will not forget that, young man," observed Auchendrane, addressing the Master of Stair; "and he will take his revenge when he can get it."

"I daresay he will," assented the Master of Stair; "he will take his revenge—when he gets it."

"Everything comes to him that waits," resumed Auchendrane, "and the Earl is not invulnerable any more than we are. From all I can see we shall have chances and to spare, before long, for he is arming his men afresh and training them to warfare."

"Yes," assented Cloncaird, "that is true. One of my fellows saw five hundred and more of them at Maybole last week, being drilled by Sir Thomas Kennedy of Culzean."

Bargany laughed, "The less we say about Culzean the better, when Auchendrane is here. You and he," he continued, addressing Auchendrane, "are sworn friends?"

"Sworn friends!" echoed Auchendrane with an oath, "yes, sworn friends. The King himself saw to that, and put it so to me, that I did not dare to refuse to sanction the marriage of my son James with his daughter. He pressed me at least so sorely, through the Earl of Abercorn, that I gave way. That marriage ties my hands so far as Culzean is concerned, though, between ourselves," he continued, sinking his voice, " if it should be the will of Providence to take Culzean home to Himself, it would matter very little to me how He did it. Cassillis would be deprived of his right hand man, and Carrick would be none the poorer."

" They tell me that the Earl and his brother, the Master, are friends again," remarked Cloncaird.

" I think not," replied Auchendrane. " The Master of Cassillis would die for his uncle of Culzean, but between him and his brother there is no love lost yet."

" Corbies winna pick out corbies' een," rejoined Bargany ; " but whatever may happen when it comes to the push, the sooner we know what we are to expect the better. In any case, I must be off home. Ayr is too relaxing in these days when there is work to be done ; and so I am resolved to seek the banks of the Girvan, and put my house in order for the fray. Who knows that the Earl is not now marching on Bargany ?"

" And if he is," observed the Master of Stair, " your brother Thomas will keep his hands full if any mortal man can do it."

" Yes, I believe he will, but, all the same, home I must go."

" Be careful, Bargany," advised Auchendrane, " you have too many men in Ayr to go home so quietly that the Earl will not hear of your coming."

" Let him hear," was Bargany's reply, " let him hear until his ears tingle with the tidings. I mean to go, despite my Lord Cassillis and all his power. I have sixty men in Ayr with me whom I can trust to the last drop of blood in their veins, and I can muster as many more of the men of Ayr who will never see me with my back to the wall. With a hundred and twenty followers, I shall pass Maybole under the walls of the tower, and let my Lord Cassillis come forth and dispute my passage if he dare."

Bargany's resolution was loudly applauded by Mure of

Cloncaird, and the Master of Stair. Auchendrane alone, wary
old soldier, doubted the expediency of the proposed action,
but his advice was over-ruled; and shrugging his shoulders,
he deferred.

"Very well," he said, " so be it. But remember, Bargany,
what I tell you. You have too few men to do your turn if
the Maybole garrison is strong, You are going to run a risk
that is not warranted by anything you can hope to gain, and
you are about to risk your own valuable life and the lives of
your men for no good purpose under the sun."

" I am going to establish my right, sir," retorted the impetuous Bargany hotly, "to walk or ride from one end of Carrick
to the other whenever I may see fit. If the Earl interfere not
with me, I shall not interfere with him. If he try to stop me
his blood be on his own head—and my blood, too," he added,
"if he slay me. So cease your advice and your protests,
Auchendrane. We shall leave you at the Doon if you prefer
to escape the risk."

" I shall see you through," was Auchendrane's reply, spoken
in quiet but firm tones, " I shall see you through, if ever you
get through at all."

" And if I don't," laughed the mollified Bargany, "you can
see what remains of me through. As for your protest against
my riding home to Bargany, we'll discuss that when we reach
the banks of the Girvan. Meantime, we must make our
arrangements for the journey all the same."

With Bargany thus resolved, and scorning secrecy, the news
of his intended departure created the utmost sensation, first
in Ayr, and then in Maybole. Cassillis felt that he was
openly challenged, and he was in no way loath to respond.
Without loss of time he quartered three hundred men in and
around Maybole, and by the aid of his spies kept himself
familiar with every movement of the enemy. Bargany did
not attempt to hide from himself the gravity of the task
which he had undertaken. He saw to the appointments of

his immediate followers; he enlisted the services of upwards of fifty of the war-loving burghers of Ayr, and by the aid of Auchendrane he added to his force twenty of the vassals of his friend.

The day of his departure was fixed beforehand, and all was excitement in the rival capitals of Kyle and of Carrick. The Earl of Cassillis left his home by the banks of the Doon, and repaired in person to Maybole to direct operations. Here he found everything in readiness. His retainers, under the trained oversight of his uncle, Sir Thomas Kennedy of Culzean, were ready for the combat, and as eager as they were ready.

"When does Bargany leave Ayr?" was the Earl's first question as he dismounted at the door of the Castle and shook hands with Culzean.

"Two days hence," was the answer.

"And is everything ready to give him greeting?"

"Everything," replied Sir Thomas, "we can give account of him, I think."

"Yes, I think we can. What force has he at his back?"

"Not more than a hundred and thirty men at the outside, with Mure of Auchendrane, the Master of Stair and Mure of Cloncaird in addition."

"Is Auchendrane with him?"

"Yes."

"The old villain!" ejaculated the Earl angrily, "Carrick will never be at peace so long as that man lives. It is he who has put Bargany up to this; it is he who draws the strings that make the puppets dance."

"You forget, my lord, that you are speaking thus of a sworn friend of mine, the father-in-law of my daughter."

"I forget nothing of the kind, uncle. You pretend to believe in the old fox; but, for my part, there is not a man in this whole west country whom I distrust so much. Sworn friend and all as you are of his, I would not like to trust you over-much to his tender mercies."

" That may be, my lord ; but this is a subject on which we are not likely to agree. I admit he has no great friendship for you ; but then, you have no great friendship for him. Besides, he is sworn to back Bargany at all costs, and he will not try to rid himself of his oath."

" Well, well, uncle, we can discuss this another time. We have more serious work to attend to ; and the sooner we set about getting everything cut and dry the better. So let us get to business at once."

Entering the Castle the Earl and Sir Thomas Kennedy discussed how best they could stay the march of Bargany, and inflict a crushing blow on his bid for supremacy in Carrick.

" We shall leave nothing to chance," said the Earl, " we shall choose our own ground for the combat, and, if Bargany escape his deserts, it will not be my fault. Were he once out of the way the enemy would be as weak as ditch-water, and therefore, whatever betide the rest, see that every man who marches out from Maybole is warned to make a target of him. This must be Bargany's last ride."

CHAPTER II.

THE TRAGEDY OF THE BROCKLOCH BURN.

THE snow drove pitilessly down as Bargany and his followers moved out from the town of Ayr. So heavy was the drift that, to use the suggestive language of the old chronicler, no man could see a lance's length ahead of him. Auchendrane, fully alive to the dangers of the march, again counselled Kennedy, if not to abandon his intention, at least to seek his home by a less dangerous route ; but the hot-headed chief of Bargany refused to listen to his advice, and ordered his men to advance.

Ayr was in a turmoil; and amid the pelting snow the town's folk gathered in the streets to bid the marchers God-speed. They accompanied them beyond the burgh bounds, and saw them out into the bleak, white-coated country without; and then, not without serious misgivings, they retraced their steps, to hope and to fear and to speculate on the result.

With Auchendrane, Bargany rode at the head of the company. Both were well mounted, as were also the large majority of the force. The remainder, composed chiefly of the burghers who were at Bargany's call, were on foot, armed for the most part with muskets, with short swords by their sides, or bearing long Scottish lances, which, many years previous, had done good service on the field of conflict. It was but a small company that plodded that weary day through the storm. The wind whirled up the snow in thick flying drifts, and rendered the march fatiguing in the extreme; indeed, so exhausted were the footmen when the Doon was passed, and when, three miles distant from Ayr, they began to ascend the steep, rough road which lay along the shoulder of Brown Carrick Hill—though it was white enough then—that Auchendrane for the third time approached Bargany, and urged him to change the direction of his march.

But no chilling winds that ever blew could daunt the resolution of the leader.

"It seems to me, Auchendrane," was the reply, "that you have some reason or other that I do not know, for trying to dissuade me from this enterprise. I have told you already that, come man, come devil, I will ride home this day. I have not come out to seek Lord Cassillis' harm, and I shall pass on my way quietly and in peace if he will but permit; but never shall it be said that Bargany turned his back on danger, no matter when or where. I tell you again, as I have told you before, that you can go home if you like."

"I do not understand you, Bargany," replied Auchendrane,

" I have told you already that I will see you through, but I would be no true friend to you, did I not point out your dangers. You have not, I tell you, enough men here to enable you to force your way past Maybole."

" And again, I tell you, Auchendrane, that if I am in life, by the blessing of God, I shall sleep in Bargany this night."

" You are more likely to sleep among the snow, Bargany. You know that Cassillis is in force at Maybole, that his men out-number ours by three to one, that they are fighting on their own ground, are well equipped, and will come forth fresh and warm to their work, whereas ours are cold and benumbed, and their hearts are beginning to fail them."

" That I do not believe," replied Bargany, " the snow may benumb the fingers, and chill the blood of a brave man, but it can never daunt his courage or affright his heart."

" You are wrong, Bargany. A chilled body and a chilled soul often go together. Why not seek the other route to the valley of the Girvan ? It is a better road than this, and Lord Cassillis might look for us until to-morrow's daybreak ere he would find us."

" He will not need to seek us so long, Auchendrane, so cease your advice. If you don't relish a skirmish, Auchendrane lies over there among the trees, and as I have told you already, you had better seek your fireside, than go into a combat faint-hearted."

Auchendrane bit his lip at the renewed imputation ; but knowing how dangerous it was to cross Bargany when his blood was up, he subsided.

And so they rode on. Between them, as they toiled up the steep, lay the plain between the Doon and the Ayr. The latter river, save at its estuary, was invisible, hidden amid dark pine and beech woods ; but the former, as it roared down its channel directly beneath, wrought a dark streak into the otherwise white country. Out to sea lay the sullen ocean, dark, too, and wintry, as became it on such a day.

The horizon was foreshortened, and the aspect rendered all the more inhospitable. Above rose the undulating slope of Carrick, finding its loftiest altitude in the modest summit of Carwinshoch.

Now and again they encountered heavy snow-wreaths, but these they surmounted in stubborn, taciturn fashion. They were getting hardened down to the fatigue, and were plodding on in that sullen, dogged style which the wayfarer acquires who has twenty-five good miles ahead of him, and knows that, come wet, come dry, he must reach his destination by night-fall.

Auchendrane kept his eye ahead. He imagined that the Earl of Cassillis would not be so oblivious to tactics as to ignore the sending out of spies; and, aware of the gain that might result from their capture, he was ever on the outlook. Nor was his foresight in vain, for, rounding the corner of a thicket, at a spot where the road took a sudden, sharp, angular bend, he descried, slowly approaching, two horsemen, who, as the cavalcade appeared to view, drew rein, and stood still. The appearance of Bargany's men took them, evidently, by surprise; they remained where they were, neither advancing nor retiring, but looking upon the cavalcade which, with snow-muffled tread, had stealthily and secretly stolen upon them. Following their example, Auchendrane and Bargany called a halt, for they knew not whether the men were spies or the advance guard of a larger body who might be close at hand.

After a brief consultation, Bargany ordered out three of his best mounted troopers, and, putting them under the orders of Mure of Auchendrane, they rode forward to meet the horsemen who had so suddenly been taken aback. Their movement converted the temporary lethargy of the strangers into instant action. They at once wheeled their horses, and putting spurs to them, rode off. Ere, however, they had well gathered weigh, Auchendrane was after them. His horse was better and speedier than those of the pursued, and he gained rapidly

upon them.   Stride by stride he shortened the distance, until
he reached within fifteen or twenty yards of them, when he
commanded them, as he drew a pistol from the holster of his
saddle, to halt.   The command fired them with fresh energy
to effect their escape, and they lashed their horses to their
topmost speed.

"Stay," shouted Auchendrane, "draw rein at once, or you
will never draw rein again."

The pursued paid no attention to his call; on the contrary,
the more loudly Auchendrane demanded their surrender the
more anxious they were, and the greater efforts they put
forth, to make good the order of their going.   Over the rough
road they went, men and horses, helter-skelter.   Mure drew
nearer and nearer.   Anew he threatened, but the fugitives
were deaf alike to his threats and his calls, and plied whip
and spur the more vigorously.

Auchendrane was in no mood to be trifled with.   He did
not know that the followers of the Earl of Cassillis might not
be in force hard-bye, and that each striding effort of his horse
might not be bearing him on to his own undoing.   So, ceas-
ing to parley, he took aim and fired.   The shot was wide of
its mark.   A second shot grazed the side of one of the fugitives, though without wounding him seriously, and a third
whizzed past between them, bringing them into uncomfortably close quarters with the leaden messenger.

The fugitives drew rein and slackened the speed of their
horses.   In an instant Auchendrane and his troopers were
alongside of them, the troopers with muskets unslung, waiting
but the word of command to shoot them dead in their tracks.
But it was not Mure's purpose so to dispose of them; and he
sternly ordered them to wheel about and ride towards the
force under Bargany, which was still awaiting the issue of
the chase.

The men, who were indeed spies, were at once taken before
Bargany, who subjected them to a rigorous examination of

the purpose for which they had ridden thither. One of the two refused to answer, but the other was more fearful, or more compliant, and purchased his life at the cost of all the information he could impart. The tidings he conveyed bore out the fears of Auchendrane. The Earl of Cassillis was advancing from Maybole at the head of a strong force of his retainers for the purpose of giving battle to Bargany.

The spy who had chosen to encounter the chances of death rather than break silence to the detriment of his master was sent into Ayr under charge of two of the burgesses who undertook the duty of escort, and who, sooth to say, were only too glad to have such an excellent opportunity to return home ; the other, Pennandgow by name, Bargany took with him, " for he was of blood to the laird of Auchendrane," and might prove useful as an informant.

Resuming their march, they pressed on, the snow drifts whirling the faster as they ascended the hill, and the path becoming the more rugged and the more tiresome. They went cautiously, Bargany having learned from the communicative Pennandgow that the Earl of Cassillis had left Maybole more than an hour before, and had taken up his position a little way ahead. And this proved to be so ; for, as the party under the Laird descended towards the bed of the Brockloch burn, which, turbid and befouled, ran across the highway, they discovered that the enemy occupied the heights on the other side. No sooner did the Bargany men discover the foe than they raised a shout of defiance, which was taken up and rolled back to them in increased volume by the retainers of Cassillis.

At the advice of Auchendrane, Bargany called a halt and took counsel with Mure of Cloncaird, the Master of Stair, and Auchendrane himself. The last named would fain have tendered words of warning, but the blood of the younger men was hot and fiery, and they counselled instant advance ; and the most that Auchendrane could accomplish was to persuade

3

Bargany to send forward a flag of truce, and demand the right to pass along the highway unmolested. This duty was undertaken by the Master of Stair, who, affixing a long white scarf which he wore about his waist, to the point of his sword, rode across the burn and leisurely walked his horse up the bank on the other side.

The Earl of Cassillis perceived him coming, and, with Sir Thomas Kennedy of Culzean and Kennedy of Pinwherry, advanced to meet him. The Master of Stair was in no way abashed. He doffed his head-piece as they neared one another and saluted them politely. His salute was returned with equal formality.

"Well, Dalrymple," said the Earl in friendly tones, "you come, I am afraid, on an evil errand."

"Not so, my lord," was the reply, "I come on no evil errand. All I come to say is that I have been deputed by the Laird of Bargany to crave your lordship's permission to ride homewards, for him and his followers, to Bargany."

"Does Bargany ask it as a favour or as a right?"

"Favour, my lord?" replied the Master of Stair; "what favour can it be to ride along the King's highway? We ask no favour at your hands. We have the right with every leal subject of his Majesty to walk or ride along his Majesty's highways, whenever and wherever we choose, and that right we do not intend to cede, even to your lordship."

"If that is all that Bargany wants," responded the Earl, "why are all these men with him, why march in battle array, and why take up these positions for attack?"

"Look above you, my lord," was the Master of Stair's reply, "and you will find your answer. You have come out here to oppose us in the exercise of our rights, and can you expect that we will stand idly at ease when you are ready for attack? That would not be consistent with reason."

"Hark ye, Dalrymple," said the Earl, "Bargany has not come here on any such peaceful errand. I know all his ongoings in Ayr. I know why you have brought with you so many of the men of Ayr, armed as is not their wont when they are on a peaceful errand; and I see yonder among your troopers one of my men whom you are keeping a prisoner. Bargany has come here prepared to fight his way through if he can."

"That is as your lordship shall take the responsibility."

"I am willing to take it, Dalrymple."

"Very well, my lord; then I shall return and say that you will not let us pass undisputed."

"That will I not, sir," replied the Earl; "if you advance, you do so at your peril, and God do so to me and more also if I do not make Bargany rue his attempt. And hark ye, Dalrymple, look well to yourself. That flag you carry protects you, else you had never left my presence but to die. I have not forgotten how you, with Thomas Kennedy, shot at me hard by Craigneil within those few days; and I give you fair warning to beware henceforth how you cross my path. Do you understand, sir?"

"The Master of Stair," replied Dalrymple in tones as unbending as those of Lord Cassillis himself, "can take care of himself."

"Then let him do so," was the Earl's reply, as he turned and rode back to his men.

The Master of Stair returned to Bargany and communicated the results of the interview.

"Just as I expected," was Bargany's answer; "if I had thought it would have been otherwise, I would hardly have sent out the flag of truce. But now, Auchendrane, you, Cloncaird, and you too, Dalrymple, I call you to witness that the Earl of Cassillis has denied to me, as one of his Majesty's lieges, the right to ride along one of the highways of the realm. There remains nothing else than to make good that right if I can."

The party then, headed by Bargany himself, began in

compact array, slowly, and feeling their way, to descend to
the channel of the burn.   The road was rough at best, and
with the snow lying thick, it was all the worse; but the
nature of the road was one of the least of the difficulties, for
no sooner had they reached the level of the burn than the
Kennedys of Cassillis opened fire on them.   The distance
was not great, but the inaccuracy of the fire-arms was; and
though shots pattered down thick, neither man nor horse was
at the outset seriously wounded.

But when the advance continued, and the enemies came to
closer quarters, Auchendrane, upon whom, as a tried leader,
the ordering of the attack was laid, divided the force into
three divisions.   One of these, which he himself headed, rode
up the line of the burn with the object of turning the right
flank of Lord Cassillis; the second, led by Bargany, attempted
to carry the heights above by a headlong rush; and the
third, mainly composed of the footmen and of the men of
Ayr, remained as a reserve, with instructions to cover the
attack of Bargany and to harrass the enemy by a continuous
fire into his ranks.   No better leader could have been selected
than the Laird of Bargany to lead so desperate an enterprise
as that which he attempted.   Indomitable of will, of courage
and physical strength unsurpassed, loved and trusted by his
followers, hesitation was not a quality that ever interfered
with his determination.   If the slope could be carried at all,
he was the man to carry it.   Calling on his troops to follow,
he dashed up the heights, and, though met by a steady fire,
which emptied some of the saddles and sent riderless and
wounded horses plunging down the glen, he succeeded in
gaining a footing on the heights above, but only to find his
further advance barred by a strong triple line of the foe,
behind whom stood the Earl himself, calm and passionless,
and giving his orders |with a coolness and an equanimity
fitted to impart to his retainers the utmost confidence in their
chief.

Undaunted by the overwhelming odds, Bargany dashed at the men of Cassillis, who, with shout and battle cry, advanced to meet him. A terrible hand-to-hand conflict followed. Like some giant warrior of old, Bargany cleaved his way through the ranks of the enemy, overthrowing a horseman with each successive sweep of his long sword, and leaving behind him a passage through which his men pressed on. But the nearer he came to the Earl, the more closely the foe hemmed him in, until at last he was compelled to turn on the defensive and to gather his followers into a small, serried circle. The Earl encouraged his retainers to the onslaught; though, in truth, they needed no such encouragement; for they fought with resolution and with courage undaunted.

Auchendrane succeeded in crossing the burn, and in attacking the enemy on the flank; but he too was met by a force superior in numbers, and failed to hold his own. Driven back, step by step, though he grimly contested every foot of the field, he was utterly unable to render the Laird any assistance; but Mure of Cloncaird, who was in command of the reserve, seeing the straits of his leader, hurried forward to his relief. He fell upon the Cassillis men in rear; and Bargany, seeing his opportunity, redoubled his exertions and his blows, and succeeded in clearing himself of the enemy. The fray now partook of a more open character; for Bargany, with a strong force, held the centre of the position, while on the right Auchendrane was still doing his utmost to harrass the enemy.

Thinking to bring the conflict to a close by a bold attack on the Earl himself, the gallant chief of Bargany made herculean efforts to reach him; but ever as he did so his way was blocked by fresh combatants who surrounded him on all sides and who, but for the heroic exertions of his followers, would have speedily compassed his destruction. The sight of the dead and wounded who littered the ground, nerved the combatants afresh; and they struggled and fought with a tenacity worthy of a better cause and a nobler field.

Among the followers of Lord Cassillis was a yeoman of the name of John Dick. Aforetime he had been a vassal of Bargany, but a change of residence had also involved a change of leadership, and he was now fighting against a chief whom he had loved, and for whom, not long before, he would willingly have sacrificed his life. As Bargany rode hither and thither, he encountered his old retainer. His arm was uplifted to slay him, but remembering even in the height of the combat that Dick had fought under his own banner, he forebore. His clemency was ill-rewarded, for as Bargany, always struggling, rode on, Dick, couching his long lance, took steady aim, and hurled it with all his force. The blade was but too well directed, for the point of the lance struck Bargany on the right side of his neck, inflicting a ghastly wound. Bargany turned in an instant on his assailant, but Dick was beyond the sweep of his arm. The gallant leader struggled hard to retain his seat in the saddle; and when he felt that he must succumb, he dropped the reins on his horse's neck, and yielded himself to the inevitable. Two or three of the Cassillis faction rode towards him, with the intention of completing the work which Dick had begun; but Mure of Cloncaird interposed, and placing himself between them and their intended victim, shielded him manfully.

Bargany's share in the contest was over; yet he was not destined to die in the hands of the enemy. For the gallant horse which he bestrode, as if conscious that his master stood in need of aid, extricated him from the struggling mass of humanity ere he fell prone to the earth, and bore him away from the scene of his last conflict. Nor was it until he had been carried by the way over which he had charged so nobly, that Bargany fell from his saddle, and lay insensible amid the snow.

With the fall of Bargany the fight was practically over. The Earl's purpose had been achieved. His most potent rival in Carrick he had seen wounded, as he rightly conceived, mortally; and though struggling rivals still strove in angry encounter, the fray was all but terminated. Auchendrane, failing to turn the right flank of the enemy, had, by this time, reached the scene of the main combat, and, under his direction, an orderly retreat was made. A few shots were fired from both sides in parting; but each was so anxious to carry off its own wounded that no attempt was made to prolong the fray.

It was with heavy hearts that Auchendrane, Mure of Cloncaird, and the Master of Stair sought the cold couch on which Bargany was lying. They undid the steel helmet which he wore on his head, and loosened the collar of his iron-fronted jacket, and, lifting his head from the ground, exposed him to the chilly, snow-particled wind, which still blew a pitiful requiem over the scene. They bound up, with such rude bandages as they could command, the wound in his neck, from which blood continued to flow, and without loss of time improvised a horse litter on which they laid the dying chief. It was with sad hearts that they set about the return journey to Ayr. Nature's aspect was of the dreariest, but it was none the less in keeping with the melancholy cortege. All the way the blood dripped slowly from the wound, and one might have tracked their path by the crimson spots upon the snow. Behind them came a series of similar companies. Over a score of Bargany's followers bore traces of the fight; some of them, grim pictures of conflict, with battered helmets and blood-begrimmed faces, sitting erect in their saddles, and enduring their sufferings with the stoicism of Scotsmen; others, more hardly hit, hanging limp and senseless across their saddles, supported on either side by sympathetic hands. And behind them rode the company of the dead, eighteen in number—men who had fought their last battle, who would never again hear the call to arms, nameless warriors who had sacrificed their lives in a cause in which they had no direct interest, and with which they had, in any possible results, nothing to do.

A weary two hours' march brought them to the town of Ayr. For the second time that day the streets were thronged with an excited crowd; but how different the excitement of the night from that of the morning! They had cheered Bargany and his followers, as with high hearts they had ridden up the winding High Street, and old men had sighed for their age and their unfitness to join the band; women had wished them well; and the youth of the town had cheered them till the high-walled houses gave back the echoes. But now as the cavalcade, with its dead and wounded, rode along, wailing took the place of cheering, and weeping and silent anguish the place of enthusiasm, and oft repeated God-speed.

Bargany was at once conveyed to the house which he had left hale and strong, and full of blood and of courage, in the morning, and laid upon his bed. Medical aid was in readiness; but as the doctors unrolled the bandages and looked at the wound, they gave no hope of recovery. All they could do was to recall the wounded man's senses, and to bring back to consciousness the spirit of the departing warrior.

"Where am I?" was Bargany's first words, as he slowly emerged from his unconsciousness.

"You are in your own house in Ayr," replied Auchendrane tenderly, "and among friends."

"Ah, Auchendrane, are you here?" responded Bargany. "Tell me, am I dying?"

Auchendrane did not reply, and the others turned away their heads. Bargany rightly interpreted their silence.

"How long have I to live, doctor?" he asked in faint tones, but endeavouring to rally himself. "Do not fear to tell me, for I do not fear to die."

"You are very sorely wounded, sir," was the doctor's reply.

"I know that; I feel that. I am very faint. But I have something to say before I go. Raise me up, Cloncaird," he said to Mure, who stood by, with his namesake of Auchendrane, and the Master of Stair, "raise me up so that I can speak to you."

Cloncaird complied with his request, and propped him up in bed with pillows.

"I feel that I have not much time to waste," resumed Bargany, "but I want no priest to shrive me. I have lived without the Church, though not without my God, and I mean to die without the Church. Tell my brother Thomas what I say, and listen to it all of you. There will be joy in Cassillis House this evening; let it be short-lived. Slacken not one single effort because I am gone, but let my death be a fresh stimulus to exertion. You can strike the Earl of Cassillis at many a point; do it, but do it warily. Do not be head-strong as I have been to-day. If I had taken your advice, Auchendrane, I would not have been lying here now."

"Everything is preordained," replied Auchendrane. "What is to be, is to be. No man may escape his destiny."

"That is quite true, but let my death be a warning how you guide yourselves in the future. I foresee a long, weary struggle ahead of you; husband your resources, your energies. Strike when you can do it safely, and strike hard and home. Above all things, be true to yourselves and to one another, and Carrick will bless the day that breaks the power of the tyrant."

Holding out his hand, Bargany bade farewell to his friends in succession, and then calmly laid his head down on the pillow from which he had raised it. Life was strong in him, and it was not until the Tolbooth clock had pealed out with dismal monotone the hour of midnight that his spirit took its flight to that land where beyond these voices there is peace.

CHAPTER III.

AUCHENDRANE INSPIRES TO VENGEANCE.

WINTER had given place to spring, the grass grew rank and

green by the vault in the quiet churchyard of Ballantrae,
where Bargany, the victim of the fray by the Brockloch Burn,
lay at rest, and the trees of the great Dalrymple forest were
putting out their buds, and getting ready for the warm
breezes and the mellow suns of June. Another Laird was in
Bargany, Thomas Kennedy, a counterpart in most respects
of his brother, but a stronger man mentally and better under
self-control. He had ridden in the cavalcade which wended
its way from Ayr to Ballantrae, behind the banner of Revenge
whereon was inscribed the old motto, "Revenge my cause,
O Lord," and when the days of the mourning were ended, he
had, as in duty bound, taken up the quarrel where his brother
had laid it down.

The Earl of Cassillis had said that the death of Bargany
would break the back of the conspiracy against his supremacy.
But Bargany was not dead. The title had only passed from
one man to another, and he who now bore it was a more
dangerous foe than he who had laid it down.

The Earl had not been idle. Strong in Court influence, he
had succeeded in obtaining from the Estates of the Realm an
inhibition against Mure of Auchendrane, Kennedy of Bargany,
and their associates and followers, which forbade their bearing
arms; while he himself held a special permit to arm in his
own defence against their wiles and machinations. Mure and
his friends practically, as Cassillis knew, set the inhibition at
naught; they were armed to the teeth, and ready to take
advantage of the first favourable opportunity which offered
itself, for revenge.

The one point on which the Earl and his kinsman, Sir
Thomas Kennedy of Culzean, differed, was in their estimate of
the character of Auchendrane. Sir Thomas tried to think
well of him, and succeeded. He accepted Mure's sworn
friendship as genuine, and continued to maintain intimacy
with him, visiting him at his house, and receiving his visits in
return. The Earl read him on different lines. He could not
trust him, and he never pretended to trust him.

They walked together by the banks of the Doon, the Earl of Cassillis and Sir Thomas Kennedy. On the rising ground above towered the Castle, at their feet danced the river, the sun lighting up its wavelets as it swept along in its bed. The winter snows were all melted on the hills above Loch Doon, and the heavy floods which a few weeks before had roared adown the tortuous pebbly channel, had ceased. The dule-tree was becoming gay in its light foliage, and everywhere around nature breathed of the vernal influences. The sun shone on the grey walls of the keep, and lighted them up until they shook off their baldness and their grimness, and looked as soft and reposeful as a pleasant dream.

It was a day—if days had anything to do with it—to banish heartburnings and thoughts of revenge ; but the times were out of joint for the cultivation of the finer feelings, and the Earl of Cassillis was not the man to seek his ends otherwise than by the approved methods. For more than three centuries his fathers had wielded the sword ; by the sword they had maintained their position, and kept their acres— why should he lay it down ? Sir Thomas Kennedy was otherwise minded. By nature he was not a man of strife, though he never fled from it, or behaved himself otherwise than nobly in the fray. He would fain have seen the swords of Cassillis hung up to gleam, or to rust, in the armoury, and the muskets applied to no other purpose than the chase ; and many a time, as opportunity offered, he sought to implant in his kinsman the same motives by which he endeavoured to control his own actions, and regulate his own conduct.

" Why should there be this ceaseless strife ?" he asked of the Earl as they strode along the narrow footpath by the river's brink. " It was, indeed, an ill-omened day when you rode forth from Maybole Castle to meet Bargany. Had you let him pass to his home in peace, instead of slaying him, there would have been no need for these ceaseless precautions. Your horses might have stood unharnessed in their stalls, and

your followers might have rested by night without their
swords by their bedside, and their muskets for pillows."

"I must defend my position, uncle," replied the Earl, "it
was not I who was to blame for Bargany's death. Bargany
brought disaster upon himself. He might have gone home
quietly if he had liked, but he did nothing of the kind. He
marched out from Ayr in battle-array, with his own men and
with half a hundred of the men of Ayr to boot; and if I had
refused the conflict and allowed him to march with all his
men under the very walls of Maybole Castle, the victory
would have been his. As it is, it was mine. Bargany brought
his own death about, not I; besides, it served him right, for
he had done nothing else for months before his death than
plot against my life, and against the cause which you and I
represent."

"That may be all very true, my lord," responded Sir
Thomas, "all very true, but you take these things too
seriously. You assume that Bargany was worth the crushing
with all your might. Why, what could he have done to have
shaken the position of the Earl of Cassillis?"

"Not much in himself, uncle; but you forget that he did
not stand alone any more than his brother does to-day. He
was the head of the insurgents, of the freebooters—for they
are nothing better."

"Admitting all that," responded Sir Thomas Kennedy, "the
result of that fight at the Brockloch but proved what I say,
that neither Bargany alone, nor Bargany and all his crew,
could shake the position of Cassillis. You can afford to be
generous—why not try it, at any rate?"

"No, thank you, uncle," replied the Earl, "I can try many
a thing that I don't think of trying, and that is one of them.
Let things take their natural course. Everything is fore-
ordained."

"Only within certain limits. A man can manipulate a good
deal of his own foreordination, it seems to me. At any rate,
you need not let other men foreordain for you."

"Well, uncle," was the Earl's reply, "I can't discuss these things with you. They are sophistries that you and the Abbot of Crossraguel can settle for yourselves. As for me, I mind my own gait, and I go my own courses. Providence has given me the Earldom of Cassillis; and, if it be His will, I will see to it that it loses nothing in my hands. I look at things from my own standpoint, and, so far, I am justified. Besides, the Privy Council have justified all that I have done. They have forbidden Bargany to carry arms, and Auchendrane, and all of them who were at the Brockloch, and given me permission to arm to the teeth, if I like, against them."

"Quite so," rejoined Sir Thomas. "Then there is all the better reason why you should be strong in mercy. You drive them into traitorous schemes; and murder and stealthy assassination will follow as naturally as the Doon runs to the sea."

"I cannot listen to any more of your advice, uncle," the Earl said, with just a tinge of heat and resentment. "I neither can nor will slumber so long as Auchendrane is awake and plotting, as I know he is doing. I am sorry that it should offend you that I so estimate Auchendrane. You have given his son your daughter in marriage; but for all that, I swear it that if he had opportunity, he would wreak his vengeance on you as fast and as remorselessly as he would upon me. Do you think that John Mure is the man to obey the injunctions of the Privy Council, save that by pretended obedience he may further his own ends and devise fresh plots? Depend upon it, that is what he is doing now, and he only wants an opportunity to let us hear from him."

"Again I say, my lord, as I have often said before, you judge Auchendrane wrongly. He is a sworn friend of mine, and I must stand by him and for him until he prove himself otherwise, and his oath a fraud."

"That is a point on which we are not likely to agree, uncle. Auchendrane is no angel—take my word for it; but if I do

him wrong, he is but one, and our foes are many. Were I to
take Auchendrane at your estimate, there still remain Dinmurchie and Bennan, and Cloncaird and Chapelton, and
Dalreoch and the Dalrymples of Stair, and a score besides.
Am I to disband my forces and let them harry and raid as
they will, and transform Carrick, from the Doon to Glenapp,
into a seething cauldron of devilry ? "

" Ah, nephew," was Sir Thomas' answer, as he laid his hand
on the Earl's shoulder, " you judge them all by yourself, as a
young man would naturally do.   This feudal warfare is the
curse of the country.   Many a good man has gone down in it,
and many a one will follow, if you refuse to take warning.
Why not let me go to Auchendrane and have peace arranged ? "

" You may, if you like, uncle, arrange peace for yourself,
but there shall be no peace for me.   Peace ! " and the Earl
laughed scornfully at the idea.   " Peace with John Mure of
Auchendrane, who is even now plotting to take away my life,
or yours, for all I know to the contrary !   Peace with Thomas
Kennedy, who tried to shoot me as I rode up the Vale of
Stinchar !   Peace with all my hereditary foes, the men who
hate me as I hate them !   It is impossible, uncle, so you may
desist from your pleadings and your arguments.   It is unreasonable, besides.   Has not Auchendrane, though warned
off my lands and forbidden to carry arms, ridden past this
very house above us, followed by a dozen of his men, every
one of them armed to the teeth ? "

" Once more, my lord," replied Sir Thomas Kennedy
proudly, " let me say that you do not know Auchendrane as
I do, and that you judge him on imperfect knowledge and on
interested hear-say."

" No more of this, Sir Thomas Kennedy," was the sharp
rejoinder of the Earl, " you have heard all I have to say on
the subject at present.   Go your way, if you like ; I go mine,
whether you like or not.   Hark ye, uncle, d'ye see that dule
tree up there ? "

" Yes."

" Well, if Auchendrane had me in his power he would hang me from the dule tree of Auchendrane; and if I had him in mine, by the skies above us and Him who dwells beyond them, I would hang him up there as I would a dog."

Sir Thomas was about to make indignant reply when the conversation was interrupted by the advance of two of the Earl's squires, Hew Kennedy of Pinwherry and George Fergusson of Threaves.

" Oh, Pinwherry," said the Earl, addressing Kennedy, " you look as if you had tidings to tell ? "

" So I have, my lord," he replied, " though they are not serious. To-day we have ridden by the Doon as far as the march of Auchendrane. Our spies have been watching the roads leading to the Tower, and they report the comings and goings of Mure's visitors. Auchendrane and his friends are in daily conclave, and to-day as we ourselves lay concealed we saw two of them enter the house."

" These were ? "

" Thomas Kennedy of Bargany, and Walter Mure of Cloncaird."

" Just as I expected," replied the Earl, " their visit bodes no good. Do you hear the tidings, Sir Thomas ? "

" I do, my lord, yet I fail to see why they bode ill."

" You seem to me to see no harm in anything that Auchendrane can do. And yet seriously, uncle," continued the Earl, " with all your love of Auchendrane, and your sworn friendship to boot, I do not believe you would put yourself at his mercy were there no such thing as consequences."

" Again you are wrong, my lord. Auchendrane and I have much in common, and we frequently meet in converse."

" That may be, uncle, but I am persuaded that at heart you trust him as little as I do myself."

" On the contrary, my lord, I trust him implicitly; and I am even now arranging that, when I go up to Edinburgh next week, I shall attend to business of his as well as my own."

"Well, I suppose I do you wrong, uncle, though not him. He will play you false yet, before you have done with him."

"I am not afraid of his doing so."

"There are none so blind as those who refuse to see," replied the Earl of Cassillis in tones which conveyed to Sir Thomas Kennedy that the conversation was at an end.

Mure of Auchendrane, as the Earl surmised, was not sleeping; never, on the contrary, had he been more active. Anxious to obey, in appearance, the injunctions of the Privy Council, he was determined to force Cassillis to take the initiative in a new departure; and it was to bring this about that he had called Bargany and Cloncaird to consultation, and instilled within them the necessity for watching warily, and at the same time taking a step so serious that the Earl would have no alternative but to resume active operations and re-open the feud in the field. The Earl was to be the aggressor—how was it to be brought about?

Auchendrane sat at the head of the table in the dining hall of his Tower by the Doon. On the one hand was Bargany, on the other Cloncaird; lower down two of Auchendrane's most trusted and unscrupulous retainers, Thomas M'Alexander and Thomas Wallace, soldiers of fortune, but as ready to do the bidding of their chief as if they had a vital interest in the upshot of the struggle. The dining hall was spacious, thick walled, gloomy, with oak roof and oaken panels; and from all sides looked down on the living company, the faces of a race of Mures, all called hence. These stern faces quivered and danced in the light of the log fire which, spring time as it was, burned in the spacious fireplace, and whose ruddy glow not even the steadier light of the candles in the silver candlesticks on the oaken table, could still into repose. At one end of the room was a well-appointed stand of arms, muskets, and arquebuses, lances, spears, battle-axes, and daggers. The house was still, for the hour was late, and the only sound which broke in upon the conversation, and that without interrupting it, was the ceaseless song of the river as it hurried on to the sands of the Carrick shore.

"I like not the enterprise," said Thomas Kennedy of Bargany, knitting his brows and frowning gloomily, "I like it not, Auchendrane; there is too much murder about it. To kill a man in the open field, when his sword is unsheathed and his right arm is free, is one thing; to jump upon him and hack him to death, another. Blithely would I ride forth to meet Culzean, were he backed by his followers; but to stop him as he rides along the highway, bound on a peaceful errand, and kill him as you would a dog—I tell you I like it not. It goes against the grain."

"So it does," replied Auchendrane; "so it does. I thought so too at first, until I came to reason it out with myself. But these things are not to be viewed as solitary acts, but as the links in the whole chain. The question for us to consider is not so much how we would like a certain thing to be done, but whether the doing of it is justified by necessity in itself, and, more important still, likely to be justified in the result. Sir Thomas is the uncle, and tutor, of Cassillis, and you may depend upon it that it was he who instigated the combat that led to your brother's death. Your brother's murder, I call it—and there can be no harm in opposing murder to murder— can there?"

"No, perhaps not, Auchendrane. But even if Culzean did bring the combat about, he fought it like a man, and took the open risks about it."

"He was on the field, if you like, but took care not to fight himself. He is the very man to plot for others to do what he dare not do himself. I'd lay my life against a groat that it was he who instigated the fight at the Brockloch Burn, and so was the direct cause of your brother's murder."

"If I were sure that it was so," replied Bargany, "I might

4

come to your way of thinking, and do the deed. But, I say, Auchendrane, if you are so anxious to have him killed, why set us on to do it? Why not do it yourself?"

"For two good and sufficient reasons, Bargany," was Mure's reply. "His daughter is married to my son, and it would be nothing short of unreasonable that I should be expected myself to lay violent hands upon him. And, as I have told you, he has sent me word of his going to Edinburgh; and it would be a direct breach of the confidence he has reposed in me. It would not become my honour to slay him. The business is yours, not mine. It is your house he has sworn to overthrow, your family tree he would tear up, root and branch. It is you, not I, who are the rival of Cassillis and the enemy of his might in the west country, and it is your death he would bring about if he could only manage it."

"There is something in all that," responded Bargany; "but still, I tell you again, I was never born for such an unholy enterprise."

"Unholy enterprise, sir! it is a duty you owe to yourself, to your position, to your murdered brother. How would your brother have acted had Culzean slaughtered you? Even as it was, he preferred to die rather than turn aside from the King's highway at the bidding of Sir Thomas Kennedy and his creature and nephew, the Earl of Cassillis; and, until he is avenged, his blood will continue to cry out from the ground against you. Besides, Bargany, you know you dare not ride abroad. What joy it would give to the Earl of Cassillis were he to see you dangling from his accursed dule-tree! Many a pretty fellow has hung suspended there, like Mahomet's coffin, between heaven and earth, and you would be the next if Cassillis had but the chance."

"I know that, Auchendrane; but Sir Thomas Kennedy is not the Earl of Cassillis," said Bargany.

"True, so far; but strike the cub through the old fox. And what a glorious revenge it would be to expiate your brother's death by the slaying of the very man who instigated his slaughter!"

"But why not lend a hand yourself, Auchendrane?" replied Bargany, coming back to his fence. "His daughter may be your daughter-in-law, but what of that? and you know you are as deeply sworn to this feud as any man among us. And, if it comes to relationship, both Cassillis and Culzean are not far removed from me and mine."

"How can I show you more clearly, Bargany, that this is your affair and not mine—yours primarily at any rate? Why are you so chary of this method of revenge? How long ago is it since you fired at the Earl from the hidden shelter of a ruined house? Is there any difference now?

"Not much, I grant you. But now that you recall it, wherein lies the difference between you joining with us now, and you shooting at him two years ago as he rode past the yard of Sir Thomas Nisbet at Maybole?"

"We were not related then, as we are now," retorted Mure, somewhat non-plussed by the question. "Ah, that was a mirk night and rainy, or there would have been no need for this now. But as I said before, Bargany, this is your business now, not mine, and if you let him escape when the Lord hath delivered him into your hands, yours be the wight, and you will live to regret it. Besides, you can easily do the business and escape—it is a long cry from Culzean to Edinburgh."

The Laird of Cloncaird, who was not much troubled with qualms of conscience, nor with delicacy in his perception of right and wrong, joined in the conversation.

"Yes, it can be done, easily enough too; but what about yourself, Auchendrane? The thing will be brought straight home to you in any case."

"How to me?" queried Mure.

"Because," rejoined Cloncaird, "you told us that the message regarding Sir Thomas' going to Edinburgh was brought to you direct, and that it was in writing."

" So it was, by a poor wretch of a scholar called Dalrymple, who chanced to be in Maybole at the time. I have thought of that. Dalrymple can be secured and kept out of the way. He need not be dangerous; and if we can secure his secrecy, I am safe, while you, being unseen and unknown, are safe too."

" As long as Dalrymple lives, your life is in his hands," observed Bargany.

" I shall see to that myself. The risk is nothing."

" But you must not kill him," spake out Bargany decidedly, " he has nothing to do with the quarrel."

" Do not trouble yourself on that score. I shall not kill him—only keep him out of the way. What say you then, Bargany, are you ready ?"

" I like it not," Bargany replied, striking the table with his clenched fist, " and yet it would be a stern revenge."

" Aye, and a glorious," added Auchendrane.

Thomas Kennedy rose from his chair, and restlessly paced the floor. His passions were strong within him, his mind working. The deed projected he liked not, least of all because Sir Thomas Kennedy had unsuspectingly taken Auchendrane into his confidence. The decision trembled in the balance; but when he thought of the traditionary feud, when he had remembered that he had already laid plans for an equally cold-blooded slaughter of the Earl of Cassillis and had been balked of his purpose, and when the memory of his slaughtered brother and his death-bed injunctions rushed across his mind, the goading on to revenge was too strong for him, and he yielded to the fiend.

Silently he resumed his seat by the table, around which sat his silent comrades waiting the result of the mental conflict.

" It shall be done," he said, clenching his teeth, " my brother's death demands it, and the honour of Bargany."

" Resolved like a man," Auchendrane cried, with gleeful

triumph in his voice, " your brother shall be avenged, and " he added to himself, " my sworn friend swept out of my path."

Cloncaird accepted the situation; so did M'Alexander and Wallace, to whom it was very much a matter of business; and nothing remained but to make the necessary arrangements. What concerned them all equally was to do the deed so that it should leave no trace behind it. Culzean must be swept out of the way, as the avalanche sweeps the wayfarer into the crevasse.

In Auchendrane they found a ready and a wary counsellor, and ere the party broke up, the plot was complete, and its details filled in to the last iota.

" Culzean," muttered Mure to himself, as the night wore on and his guests retired to rest, " Culzean once brought me before the Estates of the Realm of Scotland; within seven days' time I shall usher him into a higher realm. He once sought my overthrow—I shall accomplish his."

CHAPTER IV.

SLAIN IN THE WOOD OF ST. LEONARD'S.

It was on the morning of the eleventh May that Sir Thomas Kennedy set out from Culzean on his visit to Edinburgh. The old castle of Culzean stood—the old and modern combined, stands—on the summit of a rock overlooking the Firth of Clyde, about nine miles south of Ayr. It was a dwelling meet for the times. Its surroundings were wild and picturesque. In the dark days of winter, when storms rioted in the North Channel and the big billows chased one another as they tumbled across the narrow strip of sea separating the Scottish from the Irish coasts, the spray dashed up to the windows, and the seas rumbled in the caves and fretted themselves sullenly to pieces on the rocks underneath. The sea-mews

screamed around, and the fierce westerly gales howled and
shrieked as they struck the promontory and rushed past into
the stretching forests behind. The Castle looked out on the
riotous domain of Father Neptune and saw the fates ride on
the breakers; and many a gallant ship, bluff in stem and
square in stern, was ground in pieces on the jagged precipices
which caught the surge of the breakers.

In summer it was not so. The vista embraced a succession
of scenes, which for variety, beauty, and grandeur, could
hardly have been equalled. From conical Ailsa to the Cum-
braes, and on a specially clear day to Ben Lomond, nature
was represented mainly in its marine aspect; Arran looming
up as the centre of the picture, and the yellow sands and
brown cliffs of Ayrshire doing duty in the foreground. But
the age was not scenic. The barons and knights of the times
were practical, fighting men; scenery, or the cultivation of it
as an art, had not yet been invented; and summer suns shone
and winter storms beat unnoticed, save and except they were
uncomfortably warm or exceptionally boisterous, as the case
might · be. The blasts of Boreas, rude, blustering, and fitful,
were the true prototype of the age; and the seething Firth of
Clyde was not more restless than was the surface of Ayrshire
society and the ambitions and plots of the leading actors in
the historic drama.

The scene that enrolled itself to Sir Thomas Kennedy that
fine May morning as he rode away from the Castle, was all
well known to him. Everything had a familiar aspect.
Every rock and scaur and undulation on the tortuous coast
was an old acquaintance; he knew every indentation, every
round knoll, every copse and dell on Carrick Hill. Arran
pierced the summer sky and threw its jagged peaks into the
reflective glass of the estuary; and full well he knew it.
Even the sea birds, these restless, tireless creatures, which
never seem out of place, but which never seem to feel exactly
in it, looked like old friends. Mochrum Hill looked exactly

as he had known it ever since he was a boy; and the venerable trees of the field and of the forest were putting on the
very same hues they had always done at the season, ever
since he could remember. Maybole, too, was the same as ever.
In its college churchyard lay slumbering whole generations of
Kennedys; and the walls of the Castle loomed up against the
sky, the one prominent feature of the High Street.

Sir Thomas Kennedy was in high spirits, and as he rode
along he chatted familiarly to his servant, Lancelot Kennedy,
an humble member of the family—far-removed, but still a
Kennedy.

Leaving Maybole and its castle behind, he again turned towards the coast and rode towards Greenan, one of the strongholds of the Earl of Cassillis, standing on the verge of an eighty
or ninety feet high sheer precipice, about three miles to the
south of the town of Ayr. Greenan could not boast of its
architecture. A small square tower, and a " wing," to land-
ward, was all it possessed; but, if it had no pretensions to
magnitude, it occupied a site whose suitability for the times
could not be denied. The door opened on the very edge of
the cliff, which was only, at its extreme point, large enough to
hold the castle. On three sides it was impregnable, and only
required defence on the eastern, or land-ward approach.
Whether from the nature of its position, or from the fact that,
as compared with other fortalices of the Kennedys it was
relatively unimportant, Greenan was never subjected to
assault, and it stood looking over a fair vast stretch of country
untouched, but commanding in aspect.

If the Laird of Baltersan, who held the castle for the Earl
of Cassillis, could not boast of his plain, rugged peel, he might
at least, had he so minded, have boasted of the prospect
which it commanded. Not only, as at Culzean, was the
estuary of the Clyde with its attendant majesties within his
ken; in addition, he overlooked the lower stretches of the
Doon, and saw it winding its way mid sand and shingle to

its ocean bed; the broad lands of Kyle were full in view, from the misty heights of Wardlaw and Cairntable, right down to the mouth of the river Ayr; and the burgh town itself lay beneath him, three miles off as the crow flies.

Sir Thomas Kennedy was to do some business for Baltersan in the metropolis; and the two friends spent the afternoon and evening in talking it over. Culzean slumbered soundly the live long night; for nature gives no warnings, and concerns itself naught with the just more than the unjust. No kindly guardian spirit told him that the conspirators of Auchendrane had seen him as he rode quietly along to Greenan, and that, while he slept, they were awake and discussing how best and most surely they could kill him.

The date of Culzean's setting out was known to Auchendrane, but not the route which he intended to take; and, once resolved on the enterprise, they had taken care to observe his movements. Bargany and Cloncaird themselves undertook the duty of spies; and they saw their intended victim as he climbed the shoulder of Carrick. It was a moot point with them, indeed, whether they would not kill him then and there and have done with it; but they refrained for two reasons. He was well mounted and might escape unless caught in an ambush; and if they succeeded, the spot was too near Auchendrane Tower and therefore too incriminating. Thus it was that they let him go, and returned to the house of Mure to tell what they had seen, and to draw fresh inspiration at the fountain head.

"It is wonderful," observed Mure sententiously, after they had discussed the situation, "how Providence opens up a man's way if he has only faith in Him, and in himself."

"The devil rather," growled Bargany, "it seems to me that Carrick is under his thumb, and that we're all playing his game as hard and fast as we can."

"Not so, Bargany; not so. Everything must be looked at with an eye to the end that we hope to achieve. We must not, it is true, do evil that good may come; but is the killing of Sir Thomas Kennedy necessarily evil? I do not think it is. He is an agent and abettor of the Earl of Cassillis; the Earl of Cassillis is the author of the tyranny under which you and I live; it is the duty of every man to free himself from tyranny—is not that so?"

"Yes, I suppose it is," assented Bargany.

"Then it follows, of course," continued Auchendrane, "that Culzean being aider or abettor of Cassillis—his chief instigator, if I may use the term—it is our duty to slay him. He has merited death."

"I think he has," replied Bargany, "death of a kind. I wish I could think that he merited cold-blooded slaughter on the highway."

"The manner of his death is nothing, Bargany. If the death be justifiable, the manner of it is quite a secondary thing."

".What will the world say?" queried Bargany.

"The world is an ass," was the rejoinder of Auchendrane. "It is this way with the world. If we win this fight against Cassillis, it will call us patriots; if we lose, it will call us rebels and insurgents. So, if we want to stand well with the world, we must win at any cost."

"We must try to win, at any rate; and it will not be my fault if we lose."

"Then this deed must be effectually done, and no trace of it left behind. Servant and all, they must go."

"Servant and all. I confess I don't relish the slaughter of the youth, but that, I daresay, arises from a feeling, a false feeling, of humanity. I would fain spare him; but the motives which justify the slaying of Sir Thomas being in our own interest, it necessarily follows that we must despatch the servant too."

"Certainly, of course we must," assented Cloncaird, yawning as he spoke, "and if we are to be fresh in the morning, the sooner we are in bed the better."

Auchendrane assented, and the company retired to rest.

It was necessary that they should be early afoot. Mure roused them from their couches, and escorted his associates along the approach until they came within sight of the main road. Here he turned, and bade them God-speed.

"Make sure of your work," he said, by way of parting injunction, as he wrung Bargany by the hand "make sure of your work. Strike hard and deep, and see that you make no mistake."

"We have gone too far to make a mistake now," rejoined Bargany. "We have not undertaken this morning's work to fail; and the sun will not have risen above the tree tops ere the Knight of Culzean sleeps with his fathers."

And with these words, he followed his companions towards the main road. They were six in number. Bargany was leader; by his side rode Mure of Cloncaird; behind came the two soldiers of fortune, M'Alexander and Wallace, who, still regarding the affair as a matter of business, chatted pleasantly to one another to beguile the time; and bringing up the rear were a borderer, William Irvine by name, who could be doubly trusted, and Bargany's servant, a lad named William Ramsay.

Half-an-hour's easy riding brought them to the chapel of St. Leonards, about a mile southward from the town of Ayr. The chapel stood in the centre of a thick set plantation, through which ran the road which the Knight of Culzean would have to follow to reach the highway leading from Ayr to Edinburgh. Bargany knew that Culzean would not enter the town of Ayr, for the passions of the burghers were high, and they had not forgotten the fray in which their friends had been worsted, and in which so many of them had fallen. Not wishing to be seen, Bargany, with his associates, retired into the shelter of the wood, and waited with as much patience as they could command. At intervals he sent the lad Ramsay to scan the road from Greenan; and, on his every return without tidings, the waiters grew more impatient, and cursed the slowness of the victim's coming.

Bargany's promise to Auchendrane was unfulfilled, for the sun had risen above the tree tops ere Ramsay brought word that Sir Thomas Kennedy was approaching.

The Knight of Culzean was unsuspicious of evil. When he shook hands with Baltersan by the gateway of Greenan, he congratulated himself on the glorious summer day through whose long hours he intended to ride. Lanark was to be his halting place for the night; and he counted that, making easy progress, he could accomplish the distance ere the sun set in the sea behind him. The lark mounted and sang, and sang and mounted over his head as if life was an everlasting joy to both of them; and the linnet trilled in the hedge rows its melodious accompaniment. Nature was green and fair to look upon; and when he glanced at the Firth of Clyde gleaming in the sun, it, too, smiled with unboding loveliness.

Before him lay the wood of St. Leonards. It also was in summer garb, inviting as to its shade; the light forenoon breeze from the sea rustling in the tree tops, and making melody of its own. There are sermons in trees; but no warning voice reached him from the arboreal choir in the branches, or from the swaying wind that waved them. Yet there were voices in the wood, and this is what they said—

"Now comes the time for action"—it was Bargany who spoke—"Wallace and M'Alexander, you seize the horses, and see that you do not let them go. Gilbert Ramsay, remain you here, and shut both your eyes and your ears—you have nothing to do with this morning's work; Cloncaird, upon you and me falls the work of judgment, and we shall have the stout arm of Irvine here, who will not fail us in an emergency."

"That will I not," replied Irvine, smiling grimly, and passing his hand along the blade of his sword; which he had already unsheathed, and on which his grasp was set.

"Then get to your appointed places," said Bargany, as he himself retired behind the shelter of a sudden turn in the path which shut out the approach and rendered the watchers invisible to the coming travellers, "I hear the sound of their horses' hoofs."

Bargany's order was at once obeyed, and the associates concealed themselves as well as the thick foliage and the inequalities of the path permitted.

The lark carolled away in the sky, and the linnet trilled in the copse and in the hedge row as the Knight of Culzean passed within the drooping shadows of the trees. He had taken his last look of the sun as it smiled and shone on the scene; for as he rounded the bend in the path-way Wallace and M'Alexander sprang out of their concealment. The former grasped the bridle rein of Sir Thomas Kennedy's horse, the latter that of Lancelot Kennedy's, Culzean's attendant. In an instant both drove the rowels into the sides of their horses. The animal on which the servant rode plunged forward with spasmodic bound, driving M'Alexander heavily to the ground, stunning him momentarily, and bearing its rider out of the way of danger. The lad did not attempt to return to the scene. He knew how impotent any aid was that he could render; and getting clear of the plantation, waited at a safe distance the issue of the scene. Wallace's grip was surer, and the plunging efforts of the frightened horse failed to extricate his rider from his fateful plight. The animal reared on its hind legs, but Wallace never for a moment lost his hold.

The Knight of Culzean realised the situation. It flashed on him in an instant. He put his hand to his belt, where he carried a heavy pistol, and was in the very act of drawing it when Cloncaird sprang upon him, thrusting at him with his lance, and inflicting a wound which made him reel in his seat. Turning to face his assailant he was met, not by Cloncaird, but by Bargany, who, thrusting his associate aside, waved his naked sword on high, and, with eyes flashing fire, stood for a moment face to face with his victim. Bargany spake never a word; he was in too stern and grim a mood for that; but attacked Culzean so impetuously that with the first blow he fell from his saddle.

"Ah, traitors!" was all he muttered as he sank helpless upon the ground and fixed his eyes on Bargany, who, instead of at once following up his advantage, stood gazing on him with a mingled expression of hatred and of satisfied revenge.

"No time to lose," said Irvine, the borderer, as he drew his long dagger, "we must away," and, without further preface, he despatched Sir Thomas Kennedy by a savage blow in the chest, which all but pinned him to the ground.

"Come, Bargany," said Cloncaird, "it is all over with him. Your brother's spirit can rest now. We must be gone."

Bargany felt the necessity for instant flight, and, calling his associates, they mounted their horses and rode off southwards towards Carrick. Irvine remained behind and robbed the body of the murdered knight of his money, completing the infernal transaction by cutting the gold buttons off his coat. Then he made haste to flee, not towards Carrick as had done the others, but across country by the way which Sir Thomas Kennedy had intended to travel.

All that need be said of Irvine is that he was never heard of again. Retribution ought to have followed him, but it did not. Plunder and all, he made good his going, and if any search ever was made for him he succeeded in eluding it.

All the morning long, Mure of Auchendrane paced restlessly about. He tried to compose himself. He went hither and thither about the castle, and paced along by the river where he could be seen and recognised, so that all men might hear and know that the foul deed was none of his doing. His mind was a turmoil, and the higher rose the sun the more distraught he became.

"What can have happened to keep him?" he murmured to

himself. "Surely they have not miscarried. If I only thought they had—but no, it is impossible. Bargany cannot have flinched from the duty, though I liked not that hesitation of his. If his conscience—tush, no—he cannot have been so weak and faint-hearted as to give up the enterprise. But if he has—what then? And even if he has, Cloncaird would do it himself. He has no scruples when anything like this is in the wind. And the rest dare not give it up. By heaven, if they have, the dungeons of Auchendrane will give them rest. Why don't they come? The suspense is worse than the deed itself—curse them all."

Thus Auchendrane's thoughts and muttering kept pace with one another. Time and again he ascended to the summit of the tower and watched, and strained his eyes, and listened, and fancied he heard the rattle of hoofs; and every time he descended he was the more distracted. The sweat broke out on his forehead and became clammy. He wiped it off, and more followed it. He walked down the avenue and among the trees, and again by the Doon; but go where he might, there was neither rest for his mind nor for the sole of his foot.

He had all but begun to curse himself for having anything to do with such triflers as he conceived his associates to be, when, borne on the still air, came to his listening ears the sound of horse hoofs. It was a solitary rider; but that was as it should be, for he had instructed the party to separate from one another as soon as the deed was done, and not to be seen in company. The sound was from far off, but it was increasing with the cantering of the horse. It was coming nearer. A moment's pause and he heard it in the avenue of Auchendrane. Along the line of trees rode the horseman, never staying, never hurrying, leisurely cantering; and as he drew near Mure went in-doors and watched his approach from one of the windows.

The rider was Thomas Kennedy of Bargany, the same

Thomas Kennedy who had ridden away from the tower in the morning, unchanged, save that his brow was darker and more knitted, as if he meditated on something that troubled him. He was not excited, and he reined up in front of the house, and leisurely walked his horse to the court-yard behind.

Auchendrane's pulse beat high. What, again, if they had failed ? What if they had succeeded ? He hoped and feared, he feared and hoped ; and stern man and all as he was, he shook from head to foot as Bargany pushed the hall door open and entered the dining-hall.

" Is it done ?" he asked in quavering tones, which he did his utmost to steady into assumed indifference.

Bargany threw himself heavily upon a couch, stretched out his legs as if they were fatigued with the saddle, and laid aside his composure. He too was excited, and now that they were alone, he did not care to conceal the reaction.

" Tell me, man, is it done ?" repeated Auchendrane.

" Yes, it is done."

" And well done ?"

" Aye, well done."

" Thank God for that," ejaculated Auchendrane, as he grasped his associate by the hand.

" Aye, well done," repeated Bargany, " yet not well done."

" What do you mean ? You do not mean to say that you were interrupted ?"

" No, there was no interruption, and Sir Thomas Kennedy sleeps with his fathers ; but his servant escaped."

Auchendrane stamped his foot. " That is bad, very bad. How did it happen ?"

" Very simply. He escaped with a whole skin—that is all."

" All ! The deed is only half done. The servant knows you all."

" Every mother's son of us ; but that can't be helped now. We tried to do for the pair of them ; but whatever be the consequences, they are immaterial to Sir Thomas Kennedy."

"Dead men tell no tales. So far, so good," replied Auchendrane, "but living men do, and you and Cloncaird will have to seek safety in fight."

"I know that. Cassillis with all his men would level your tower to the ground in twenty-four hours did he but know that I was here ; so I must even seek the Borders and stay there till the bruit has ceased. I start to-night."

"As for Cassillis," observed Auchendrane, "he will not haste about this business if he only knows you have gone. Cloncaird goes with you ?"

Bargany nodded assent.

"Then I stay behind and court inquiry ; and in the meantime I must go and break the tidings as gently as I can to James's wife."

"Yes, poor girl," replied Bargany, "it will be sad news for her to hear that her father is no more."

"It will indeed, but I shall temper the wind to the shorn lamb as well as I can. A great deal depends on producing a good effect at the outset. I shall send a messenger to Culzean to convey assurance of my sympathy to Lady Kennedy, and after that I will lie on my oars to see what the upshot is to be."

Bargany rose and looked out of the window. He could not face the cool devilry of Mure, and he was afraid to trust himself to speak of it. The thought indeed crossed his mind that if Auchendrane could play so falsely and malignantly with the widow and daughter of the man whose murder he had planned, he might, to suit his own purpose, play fast and loose with him as well; but he strangled the idea with the conviction that if he was in Mure's grip, Mure was in his, and that animal instinct would prevent him breaking faith.

"Your brother is avenged at last," said Auchendrane, in order to withdraw Bargany from his meditations.

"Yes. Get me something to eat, for I am starving," was Bargany's response.

And Auchendrane, seeing he was not in a mood to be trifled with, at once gave orders to have the table covered.

The same day after the sun had set, Bargany set out from Auchendrane and took his way across country in a south-easterly direction. The Border counties were the home of men who cared nothing for a man's antecedents if he had only a strong arm and a stout heart; and he knew where he would be welcome.

About the same hour of the night as that which witnessed the departure of Bargany, a melancholy cortege passed along the road which led from Ayr to Maybole. Sir Thomas Kennedy's servant, as has been said, succeeded in effecting his escape, nor did he return to the wood of St. Leonards until he heard the assassins of his master make good their escape.

The scene which met his gaze was exactly that which he expected to witness. In a deep pool of blood lay the man by whose side he had ridden a short half-hour before. Nothing around had changed, save he. Still the lark, still the linnet, still the sun shining and smiling in his strength, still the wind playing on the harp-strings of the wood, still the leaves rejoicing in the light. Life and death—the blessing and the curse—Ebal and Gerizim.

It was too late to do any good to the Knight of Culzean. He was with his old foeman, Bargany; his slayer, Bargany still, was making arrangements for fleeing the scene and leaving the consequences behind. Lancelot Kennedy would fain have left St. Leonards wood and carried his direful tidings to Maybole; but he had a sadder burden to bear than the tidings, and beside it he watched until the sun began to creep down to the sea and he received assistance to replace what remained of his master on the back of the horse which was to have carried him to Edinburgh. This accomplished, he set out, and the sun darkened on him as he led the horse at slow walking pace up the ascent of Carrick. There was no need to hurry; and he felt that unconquerable aversion to haste

5

with evil tidings which comes over a man when he has a painful duty to do and is loath to do it.

Bargany was just about to leave the avenue which led up to Auchendrane, when he heard horsemen approaching on the main road. He drew within the shelter of the trees and watched, and waited, until they had passed. One of the two sat erect in his saddle—Lancelot Kennedy, the servant of Sir Thomas Kennedy; the other dangled on either side of the horse, limp, for ever helpless—the Knight of Culzean.

And when they had passed Bargany shook himself rid of the omen, and rode off.

CHAPTER V.

FORESHADOWING VENGEANCE UPON AUCHENDRANE.

CARRICK was in turmoil. A blow had been struck at the ascendancy of the Earl of Cassillis; and from Cassillis House to Ard-Stinchar Tower there was commotion. The names of the assassins passed from mouth to mouth; and according as they were syllabled by friend or foe, they were uttered with blessing or with curse. The adherents of the Earl deplored, and grieved, and swore to vengeance; the friends of Bargany applauded the exploit and extenuated the deed. By none was it regarded as a simple case of murder. It was an incident in the contest, a link in the chain, one of those things that had to be reckoned with. The same thing might happen to Bargany to-morrow, if he were rash enough to return when blood was hot.

The law would have risen up in its majesty and hanged a sheep-stealer, or a forger, or a coiner of base metal, and society would have approved the exceeding grinding power of its mills; but when, under God's bending heavens and in the light of day, one of the leading men of the shire, and who, as

times went, was a most estimable gentleman, was cruelly
hacked to death in a plantation, it practically stood aside, or
at least waited for somebody to set it in motion. The deed
was a matter of course, part of the blood feud; the feud was
recognised as a natural outgrowth, if not an actual necessity,
of the times; the men who were engaged in it were in some
respects as powerful as the law itself; and, therefore, inaction
was the order of the day. Had Bargany and Cloncaird, instead of retiring into hiding, remained in Carrick and flaunted
the exploit in their faces, the criminal authorities would, no
doubt, have either laid them by the heels, or had them bound
over to appear when called on; but, seeing they were away,
that was enough in the meantime, and the future would take
care of itself. The English border was a far off country, and
it was out of the question to look for them in that land of
freebooters and rovers and malcontents.

The Earl of Cassillis was in bed at home when the tidings
reached him. They were brought from Maybole by one of
the followers of the house, who clattered down the steep
High Street and out into the country ere yet the body of Sir
Thomas Kennedy had been decently laid out in the Castle.
The distance was not great, nor was the night far advanced
when the warder on duty heard the horseman ride up under
the tall plane trees and by the side of the winding river.
The news was soon told; and, admitting the messenger, the
warder roused the Earl from bed and summoned him to the
hall.

To say that the Earl was at once shocked and grieved is to
say all that is necessary to depict the feelings of regret with
which he heard the announcement. But whatever regrets he
felt or manifested, there were feelings deeper in his breast
than those of sorrow. He loved his uncle, and respected him
besides; but he postponed sorrow in view of the other emo-
tions which were uppermost in his mind.

A severe blow had been struck at his ascendency.

His enemies had hit him hard, and in a vulnerable spot;
and to-morrow the news would spread far and wide, and give
strength to the foe.   There was not a hamlet on the whole
wide acreage of Bargany where the news would not be welcome; there was not one of the "wee lairds," who formed the
coalition with which he had to contend, who would not be
nerved to fresh exertions.   More blood must be shed, and
that speedily.   To that Lord Cassillis had no objections.
Vengeance was his, and he would repay.

The assassins were Bargany and Cloncaird—where was
Auchendrane ?   Wallace and M'Alexander, and the Borderer
who had completed the work, were nothing.   Even if they
had done it alone, they were only worth powder and shot at
the best.   They were not in the Earl's thoughts; he would
as soon have given up the feud as trouble himself about
them.

Bargany and Cloncaird were on another footing.   They
were the killers, the slayers, not the murderers or assassins,
of his uncle.   They were working towards an end which the
Earl could appreciate as well as thwart.   He thought none
the less of them for the deed; it was quite consistent with
the chances of a fratricidal, guerilla conflict such as that they
were carrying on.   Vengeance, again, was his, and he would
mete out double measure.

Auchendrane—what of him ?   "I'd wager a hundred
crowns," said the Earl to himself as he conned the matter
over, " that the old fox is at the bottom of this.   He has hidden
his hand; but the deed is his none the less.   Too cunning to
do it himself, he has sent Bargany and the rest of them to do
it for him, while he remains at home to play the innocent.
But no, Auchendrane, no, no,—you can deceive yourself into
the belief that you can pose as a guiltless man; but the stain
is on your soul, the red stain of Culzean's blood, if it is not
on your hands.   Now I know the reason of the comings and
goings to and from the lair of the old fox; but we shall

unearth him, cunning as he is, and if he does not die the death, the fault will not be mine."

As thus he cogitated with himself, the door of the apartment in which he sat, opened, and in walked unheralded, his brother, the Master of Cassillis. Not for six months had he crossed the threshold of Cassillis House. Family jealousies, perhaps not quite unnatural, all things considered, had evoked a coldness between the brothers. The Earl was the head of the house; but his brother was still his brother, and not merely a scion or cadet to dance attendance on the first born. Lord Cassillis' wife was so old that issue was out of the question; and the Master, looking to the chances of war and of life and of the times, which were rather disjointed so far as longevity in active feudalists were concerned, speculated on the reversion of the title, and regarded himself as on an equality with his brother. With the Earl, equality was out of the question. The heir to the Kingship of Carrick, he must have no equals, certainly no rivals. Coolness and jealousy developed into open rupture, and the Master, not content with standing aloof, had associated himself with some of the plans of Auchendrane. This the more enraged the Earl; and it was little wonder if, as his brother entered the room, Lord Cassillis looked at him askance.

The Master advanced to the table with outstretched hand. His brother hardly deigned to look up.

For an instant it seemed as if reconciliation might finally bid the scene adieu, for the Master, stung to the quick, turned on his heel. But he had come to say a certain thing, and he would say it ere he left. So he turned again, set a chair in at the table, and sat down facing his brother.

"To what do I owe the honour of this visit, sir?" queried the Earl, looking coldly at him.

The Master bit his lip, but he stifled the angry expression that he felt inclined to use.

You have heard the news?" he asked his brother, evading both insult and question.

"What news? What news can there be of sufficient importance to account for your visit?

"The death of Sir Thomas Kennedy—nothing of less importance would have made me sacrifice myself so far as to return unasked to Cassillis House."

"I have heard, even now, within these few minutes, of the death of Sir Thomas Kennedy. But why should that have brought you within these walls, where you have been unseen these six months?"

"It is quite true I have not been here these six months, my lord," replied the Master coldly; "but no man knows better than you do why I have not been here. Had I not been driven hence by your own coldness and austerity, I would not have been such a stranger. But I did not come here to justify myself; I need no justification at your hands, I came to speak of the future, not of the past."

"Well?"

"Well, I am here to let byegones be byegones. I am here in the cause of the family honour, which is as dear a legacy to me as ever it can be to you. Blood is thicker than water."

"Not always, Hew, not always. It has not been so with you. You would not have said that a month ago, when you were foregathering with Auchendrane and with other foes of our house."

"That may be. I don't care to dispute whether it is so or not; but that I am here at this hour of night, and after six months' absence, proves that it is with me. I am come to take counsel with you, if you will allow me, and to consider how best the deed is to be avenged, and how most speedily. I am here to execute the vengeance that must follow."

"Vengeance on your friend, Auchendrane?" queried the Earl a trifle less coldly, but still coldly.

"I am not here to accuse Auchendrane of the murder, or

to say that the work is his, when I do not know whether it is or not. I do not know whether his hand was put to the plough or not; but if it was, if you can convince me that it was, I shall send him home by the same road that Culzean travelled this morning from the planting of St. Leonards."

"Spoken like a Kennedy," said the Earl, his demeanour changed, grasping his brother by the hand; "when you speak like that I know I can depend on you."

"Yes, you can depend on me; but, first, I must know something more. I am not going to kill Auchendrane on suspicion."

"There will be no need; we should kill him on the certainty, and to a certainty."

"Yes, but I must know that it is a certainty. I hate killing anybody on suspicion, as a general rule."

"So do I. But I suspect Auchendrane of a hand in this tragedy, for many reasons. He was, as you know, related to Culzean, and it seems cruel in me to insist on his being such a desperate villain. To my mind, that marriage of James Mure with Helen Kennedy, was, so far as Auchendrane was concerned, used more as a blind to cover his own purposes, and conceal his motives, than anything else. It was a wedding at the instigation of the King, forced on him without a doubt. Poor Helen! I'm afraid it's been a sad wedding for her. The old fox never ceased to associate with the enemies of Culzean. He has been the source of their inspiration, the fountain whence they drew their resources of thought. They have never been long out of his house. Day by day I have marked their comings and goings; they have left Auchendrane Tower at all hours of the night and the morning, and have crept into it and out of it as if they were afraid or ashamed of being seen. Last night Bargany and Cloncaird slept there, and Mure accompanied them a bit of the way, as they rode off for St. Leonards. It is quite true he stayed at home himself, but what else would you have expected?

Mure will only put his head in the noose when he can get no other body to do it for him."

" Strong presumption, truly, in what you say !"

" Strong presumption, indeed ; but that is not all. Culzean told me here the other day, that he had written to Auchen-draue, telling him when he intended to set out for Edinburgh, and offering to transact some business for him."

" That makes the chain tolerably complete—complete enough to warrant his death," assented the Master, who, after all, was not very difficult to convince.

" Not a doubt of it, Hew, it is as clear as daylight. Auch-eudrane has waited long for this."

" Legally, I am not quite sure that we can bring the murder home to him, but if we can only do it morally, that will be sufficient to justify us in seeing that he is properly disposed of."

" The impossibility of bringing it home to him—if, indeed, it be impossible—only adds to the depth of his guilt. And apart from that, you may depend on it that we shall have no peace so long as he lives, and I am determined to rid society of such a pest. He is worse than a score of Barganys."

" But we must work in more ways than one. To kill him is, I admit, the easiest and least perplexing way out of the difficulty—might we not, though, lay the matter before the Privy Council, and have him outlawed ? Or does that involve too much trouble ?"

" I am afraid it does, though it might, perhaps, be tried. There is time to think of that; we can do nothing till after Culzean's funeral, and revenge can wait till to-morrow, and grow in the waiting."

Next day the conversation was resumed. The Master had suggested an appeal to the Estates of the Realm, but he, as well as his brother, favoured a shorter, simpler, method of punishing Auchendrane. That they should be thwarted by a man whose acres were counted by the hundred, while theirs were counted by the thousand, who could stand on the summit of his tower and survey nearly the whole extent of his domains, while they could ride for days in theirs and never come to an end, was past enduring. Policy might lead them to have recourse to legal methods, and if it did, good and well; in the meantime, they must cap a great revenge with a greater, and re-establish the supremacy of the Earl beyond either doubt or question.

The tidings which reached the Earl of Cassillis late the preceding night, also reached Culzean Castle about the same period. Lady Kennedy had retired to rest, and was asleep, blissfully unconscious of the terrible awakening she was to receive. It was not an easy task to tell her that her husband's corpse lay silent in the Castle of Maybole; but, when such a task is undertaken, it must be discharged. Only the morning before she had seen her husband ride away, hale and hearty; and though she had long suspected the hollow character of the "truce of God" between Auchendrane and her husband, so far as the former was concerned, and was conversant with every turn and feature of the feud which had kept the district in unrest and disquiet, she never dreamed of the possibility of such a terrible tragedy as that which had robbed her of her husband, and cast a lengthened shadow over the remainder of her life. It is not necessary to tell how the tidings were spoken, or to raise the veil which shuts out the sacred sorrow which smote her so heavily.

As the wife of a Kennedy had need to be, the Lady of Culzean was a woman of courage and of energy; and while she lamented for her husband as a woman, she did not confine herself to useless lamentation. Like the Earl, she distrusted Auchendrane. Upon him she laid the guilt of the tragedy. She knew that Mure was conversant with her husband's intention to go to Edinburgh, and so little faith had she in her kinsman that she unhesitatingly reached the conclusion that he was the arch-plotter, and the actual perpetrators of the deed but the creatures whom he had sent forth to do his bidding. Proof she had none; but that sudden perceptive instinct which jumps to right conclusions without knowing how was hers in abundance. And with accuracy in this instinct she had courage to make it known.

The body of Sir Thomas Kennedy was buried in the College Kirk of Maybole. He was with his ancestors at last, with the lords of grey Dunure, who for more than a couple of centuries had directed their forays from the storm-mantled keep, once the home of the doughty Norseman; with men, every one of whom had a history, from the sire of old renown who delivered himself up captive to the Lord of Galloway, and demanded in chapel, by the very horns of the altar, at the point of the sword, the purchase-price that was upon his head—and received it, too—down to the fiery Earl Gilbert, who in the dark vault of the Yew Tree fort had roasted the Abbot of Crossraguel until he had signed, with charred fingers, the transfer of the Abbey Lands to Cassillis.

These old lords—they were quiet enough now as they lay and crumbled and mouldered and went back to the dust from which they were made. The raid and the fight were not for them; the hands that once had wielded the blade, and the feet that had rushed to the fray, were for ever at rest. The busy brain had ceased from its labours; and pride, ambition, courage, had all passed on. Yes, these men *had* passed them on. In all the vault there lay not one upon whom the finger of scorn could have been laid, of whom it could have been said that he lacked in the great essentials requisite for an Earl of Cassillis, indomitable determination and self-confidence.

It was in this company that they laid the Knight of Culzean to rest. From near and far the Kennedys gathered in to witness the bearers carry up the narrow aisle the remains of the murdered Knight. Men who had sheltered under the roof-tree of Culzean, and who had kept watch and

ward on the keep of Cassillis, who had ridden armed by the
Doon, the Girvan, and the Stinchar, and far across the hills
of Galloway, were gathered together in the little kirk-yard.
Again the banner of Revenge was unfurled—"Revenge my
cause, O Lord"; and many a hardy yoeman, as he saw its
folds catch the passing breeze, and the scroll straightened out
in the face of day, read it with an eye to the future, and felt
for the hilt of the sword which he bore even in the tabernacles
of peace.

But the mourning, such as it was—and it shaded away
very easily into a deeper feeling—was soon over. Lady
Kennedy returned to Culzean to weep, and to think, and to
act where she could, and to rear her sons to carry on the
family name and traditions; and the Earl of Cassillis, and
one or two of his friends, who had come to testify their
respect for Sir Thomas Kennedy, adjourned to the Castle of
Maybole and held an informal council. It was not a moot
point with them whether the murderers should be punished—
that was already settled—but how it should be done. The
Earl was for instant action; processes of law dragged
heavily and wearied him; and he urged immediate retaliation.
The Lairds of Craigie and Barnbarroch, on the other hand,
who were of the Cassillis faction, were rather inclined to set
the law in motion, and if not to allow it full scope, at least to
give it a fair start in the race for revenge. After it had
begun to act they might back it up, or forestall it as the Earl
might think fit.

What were they to do with Auchendrane? That was
rather a delicate question. The Laird of Barnbarroch advised
them to "wait a wee;" a piece of advice which seemed rather
to commend itself to the Laird of Craigie; but the Earl
insisted that they should leave Mure to him and not trouble
themselves about him. Whatever they did, in any case, he
would reserve the right to act for himself.

This settled, the Laird of Barnbarroch asked the Earl of

Cassillis whether he had any reason to conclude that Auchendrane was the instigator of the deed. In reply, the Earl told
what he knew and what he inferred, in language similar to
that which he had employed to communicate his conclusions
to his brother, the Master.

The letter written by Sir Thomas Kennedy to Mure of
Auchendrane, wherein he intimated his intention to proceed
to Edinburgh, had been sent from Maybole to Auchendrane,
by the hands of a poor scholar, named William Dalrymple,
who earned his living as a letter-writer and transcriber of
deeds, and, generally, in making up the educational defici-
encies of his betters. The letter was either written by him,
or by the schoolmaster of Maybole. The duty was delegated
by Sir Thomas to the dominie, and that worthy being deep in
the throes of learning, called in Dalrymple to help him. It
was with a quaking heart that the schoolmaster received the
summons of the Earl to repair at once to the Castle. He was
in great trepidation. Schoolmasters were little thought of
when the seventeenth century was young. They neither
carried pistol, nor wielded a truncheon, nor swung a battle-
axe, nor laid a lance in rest. They belonged, as far as
practice was concerned, to the peace-at-any-price party,
and were consequently subjected to open indignities at the
hands of those who could neither read nor write, but who
esteemed it a more manly thing to ride forth to the fray or
to lie in wait to kill.

When he reached the Castle, the schoolmaster was at once
ushered into the presence of the Earl and his friends. He was
resolved, if at all possible, to make the best impression he
could ; and accordingly when he was ushered into the Council
Chamber, he bowed to the ground in reverence to the as-
sembled company.

"Dominie," said the Earl, cutting his salutations short,
" tell us what you know about this."

" Alas, alas," replied the schoolmaster ; " this is indeed a woeful summons. Ah, me! that I should know aught of this foul and unnatural transaction!"

"Well, tell us what you do know," gruffly interrupted Lord Cassillis.

"My lord," was the schoolmaster's response, "it was but the other day that the valiant Sir Thomas—the Lord rest him!—came to my humble dwelling. He informed me, my lord, that he was going to Edinburgh upon a certain day, and desired me to communicate in writing the same unto John Mure of Auchendrane, whom he would have gone to see himself save for the danger of riding openly abroad which hath even characterised this district these years bygone, my lord. The lad, William Dalrymple, and I, concocted the letter, indited it, subscribed it and sealed it, and he, the lad Dalrymple, carried it hence to Auchendrane, where, he credibly informs me, he handed it to John Mure himself, who took it from him and bid him return even here unto Maybole. That, in brief, my lord, is all that I know of this woeful matter. As for me I am sore exercised that I should, wilfully or unwilfully, directly or indirectly, have had a hand, or been art and part in this lamentable occurrence. Far be it from me to wish ill unto any man, my lord, but it is my earnest wish and my constant prayer, that they who slew the most valiant and worthy Sir Thomas Kennedy, Knight of Culzean, and gave unto the earth his blood, may be visited with plagues many and judgments various and diverse, and may have no rest nor peace of mind, until they realise in their unhappy experience the truth of that ancient Scriptural declaration, which I humbly conceive to be applicable to modern as well as to primeval days, to those isles of the sea as well as to the oriental climes where it was first made— 'He that sheddeth man's blood by man shall his blood be shed.'"

"These are very creditable sentiments, indeed," said the Laird of Craigie, "they do you honour."

The Dominie evidently thought so himself. He bowed low, and effected his exit with scholastic dignity.

The lad Dalrymple, who was in even greater dread of the dignitaries than the schoolmaster, was next called. In trembling tones he told how he had carried the letter to Auchendrane, and had delivered it into the hands of Mure himself. Mure had read it in his presence, and had dismissed him without making any observation regarding the missive.

When Dalrymple withdrew, the Earl of Cassillis at once plunged into a hasty and acrid denunciation of Mure, and intimated his intention of taking instant and summary vengeance upon him.

"Far be it from me," said the Laird of Craigie in reply, "to desire in any manner to check the measure of your lordship's righteous and natural wrath and indignation; but it seems to me that it would be much better and in every way more laudable, desirable, and satisfactory, were we to endeavour to bring him to the dungeon and the scaffold."

"The dungeon and the scaffold!" replied the Earl fretting, "these mean time, chance, and disappointment. Auchendrane is not the deil; but you need just as long a spune to sup kail with him as with any imp of darkness that ever fell. The law! Auchendrane could buy and sell you all at that. No, no, the shortest way is the best. He is playing the innocent game, staying at home. Let us treat him as he treated Culzean."

"There is great wisdom in what you say, my lord," responded the Laird of Craigie, "great wisdom; but if you will not abandon your right to the authorities to execute vengeance, as I still think you might safely do, you will at least permit us to exercise what influence we have to have Auchendrane put on his trial."

"No, I will not interfere with you, so long as you don't interfere with me. You will find whose way is the best in

the end.   I shall have him stark and stiff before you get your
indictment framed."

The Laird of Craigie smiled at the grim remark.

"We shall see, we shall see," he remarked.   "The Law
versus the Sword, whether of the two is the sharper?"

"The sword," answered the Earl.

"I'm not so sure of that," observed the Laird of Barnbarroch, "it all depends.   The law is sharper than the sword,
especially to him that uses it.   It is a double-edged and very
effective weapon, and I think that, concurrent with his
lordship's plans, we should set it in motion and see if we
cannot among us bring Auchendrane's grey hairs in sorrow
to the grave."

"For he richly deserves it," appended the Laird of Craigie.

A conclusion on which all were agreed.

CHAPTER VI.

AUCHENDRANE AND HIS SON GROW SYMPATHETIC.

UPON Helen Kennedy, the wife of James Mure, only son of
John Mure of Auchendrane, the news of her father's death
fell with crushing weight.   It was not conveyed to her by
Auchendrane himself.   He changed his mind about tempering the wind to the shorn lamb, for it struck him on his way
to attend to the tempering process, that it would at least be
suspicious were he to be the first, and at such an early hour
after the transaction, to carry the tidings.   So he delegated
the duty to his son, with instructions to break the news as
gently as he could on the following morning.

"Leave me," said James, "to apply the balm of heavenly
consolation.   I am not your son for nothing."

Auchendrane frowned at the observation, but said nothing.
James was in some respects a different man from his father;

but wherever the difference, the comparison was to the advantage of the latter. He was the true creature of the seamy side of the times. He was a bull-dog for courage— physical courage. He did not know what danger was; and he fought and brawled on the streets of Ayr as blithely as he rode harrying across Carrick. His delights were of the sensual order. He drank; he gave way to sensuality; a cock-main was his glory; no terriers like his for drawing the badger. Conscience did not make him a coward, for no conscience had he. His manners were of the stable, and his companions were the grooms and lower servants of his father, who ministered to his vanities, and took his frequent recriminations with an eye to the future. In form he was square built, and of good proportions; and, when not weakened or besotted with liquor, a dangerous character either in melee or brawl. He had no scruples on the subject of killing; self-interest was his god, and he subordinated everything or anything to his selfish deity.

It was to this man that Helen Kennedy, the daughter of the Knight of Culzean, was married; it was this man that was despatched by his father to break to her the news of her father's death. James Mure did not understand his wife— he did not exhaust himself trying to understand her. He had married her because he was told to; because, in his judgment, one wife was as good as another; because there was a chance of some material advantages by the union; because his father urged him to it, and promised him as good an allowance whereon to live as the resources of Auchendrane could admit. She had accepted the situation, and the husband, with sad misgivings. But what could she do? Her parents gave her away; they were dominated in the matter by the Earl of Abercorn; he, in turn, was the representative of the King; and the King, to go to the root of the offending, had thought to still the feud in Carrick by a junction of the families of two of the leading feudalists. It

was a marriage of convenience, of policy—not of love.   Love
was never dreamt of in the transaction.   It was, in short, a
transaction.   But Helen Kennedy had tried to make the most
and the best of it, to temper her husband, to soothe his
father's asperities, to prove herself a veritable olive branch, ·
peace-shadowing, peace-bringing.

James Mure thought that a woman's tears were a necessity
of her being.   He could not comprehend the feminine heart·
Woman was born for the benefit of man ; why should she not
fit into the groove ?   And if she refused, why should she not
be forcibly fitted into it ?   He knew that his wife would cry,
and wring her hands—she was soft-hearted—but the sooner
her crying and the wringing of her hands were done the
better.   If consolation were needed, he could apply it in his
own way.   He had heard his father tell how best it could be
done ; and as his father was his only authority and guide in
these matters, he would follow his leading, and console as he
knew how.

So the following morning, after a good night's rest, and a
substantial breakfast—for James Mure did not allow anything to interfere with his rest or appetite—he set about
breaking the intelligence.

" Come here, Helen," he shouted over the staircase to his
wife, who was below. · " Come here, I've got something to
say to you."

" I shall be directly, James."

" Well, don't be long ; it's very particular."

When his wife joined him, he bid her sit down on the
couch.   She obeyed.

" Helen," he said, " your father was murdered yesterday."

Strange to Mure, his wife made no response.   She fixed
her eyes on him ; a half-set, half-vacant, wholly dazed expression, came into her face ; the colour left her cheeks and
lips, and she gasped for breath.

" Yes, murdered, Helen," he repeated, " murdered in the

planting of St. Leonards, near Ayr. Bargany, they say, did
it, and Cloncaird, and one or two more. They lay for him
among the trees, and when he came up they hacked him to
death."

Still the same strange look. James did not like it. What
did it betoken? What did Helen see that she looked so
queerly? Did a whole rush of thoughts pass into her mind?
Did she grasp the initiative of the tragedy?

"For God's sake, Helen, don't look like that."

Not a cry escaped her. She still looked far away, beyond
him. The terrible fact was only beginning to dawn on her
in its ghastly realisation. She tried to rise. He offered her
his hand, but she did not see it, or take any notice of him.
And then, to make matters worse, she fell headlong on the
floor and swooned away.

This was a contingency which Mure had not reckoned on.
He had counted on frantic grief, and he had a dim idea of
what he was to say to stifle her sobs, but that she should thus
faint away, and lie still and motionless on the floor, was what
he did not understand.

Auchendrane himself, however, who was hard bye, under-
stood it without any difficulty; and he rushed into the room.
James was standing helpless in the middle of the floor, his
wife prone on it.

"Curses on you, you stupid idiot," he said, "what have you
done?"

"Done, father? What have I done? Nothing, but tell
her about her father. I thought the shortest way was the
best."

"You have killed her with the shock."

"Killed her? Not a bit of it. Women don't die so easily.
She'll soon come to, if you only give her time."

James was right, for in a few seconds, the poor girl—for
she was little more—came to herself by degrees and sat up.
Her eyes sought those of her husband and father-in-law, but

neither of them cared to speak to her. As soon as she regained full consciousness, she rose to her feet, and casting a frightened, fearful, cowering glance upon them, hastened from the room to her own chamber, where, in holy solitude, she gave vent to her feelings in a flood of tearful anguish.

The same day Mure and his son talked the situation over.

"It is not twenty-four hours since it was done," said James, "and the whole country literally rings with it."

"That was to have been expected, James; such deeds are not easily kept secret. But now that it has been accomplished, that is the end of it, I think, so far as you and I are concerned, any way."

"I wish to God it were," replied James, "but it seems to me, on the contrary, that it is only the beginning and not the end. I hear that everybody blames you just as much as if you had gone out and killed Sir Thomas yourself."

"I suppose they do," rejoined Auchendrane with an air of indifference, though he winced all the same, "I suppose they do—it is the way of the world. That will soon cease, though. I am not the man to take guilt to myself, and so I intend to remain here quietly, and face it out. Besides, Bargany and Cloncaird have made it easy for me; they have taken guilt to themselves and have left the district, and that is one strong point in my favour, anyhow."

"In one way it is; but it is only a strong point in your favour, because it is a strong point against themselves. The Earl of Cassillis must know, so must Lady Kennedy, that you were the only man who knew that Culzean was going to Edinburgh; and they will infer from that, at least, that you set Bargany on to do it."

"That doesn't follow necessarily. How do I know that Sir Thomas Kennedy was not just as communicative to everybody else as he was to me—to Baltersan, at Greenan, for instance? Besides, were Bargany and Cloncaird not at feud with Cassillis and Culzean just as well as I? Were they not

on the outlook for a reprisal? Were they not watching their
chance just as Cassillis is watching for his against us? It
was no midnight murder this. Culzean fell in the light of
day, not the victim of any personal revenge, but the victim
of this everlasting squabble for supremacy in Carrick."

"All very true, father," replied James, "he deserved to
die, and I do not regret his death, though it was a terrible
bungle letting his servant off with a whole skin. But what
concerns me is this—that Dalrymple's story must be known
to the Earl of Cassillis, and if he can be produced as a
witness, it will go hard against you."

"So it might," said Auchendrane, feeling the force of the
reasoning, "but Dalrymple must be secured, and that at
once. You are ready in resource, James, as well as in
resolve—have you nothing to suggest?"

"Yes I have," was the blunt response; "I have this to
suggest, that Dalrymple be put out of the way without loss
of time."

"Put out of the way, James? What do you mean?"

"What do I mean? What I say. Dalrymple must be put
beyond the reach of the Earl of Cassillis at once and for
ever."

"Not murdered, James, not murdered: we cannot stain
our hands with the ignoble blood of an ignorant scholar."

"Why not, father? Is the life of an ignorant scholar, as
you call him, as valuable as that of Mure of Auchendrane?"

"By no means, James; but we must not kill him—at
least not yet."

"I would do it with my own hands—nobody would be a
bit the wiser. But if you don't like it, we must get him at
once into our power. If he can be kept secluded, or imprisoned, or sent abroad, or sent at least to the house of some of
our friends at a distance, the death of Culzean may go a
wool-gathering for evidence that will incriminate you. But
I don't like these methods, father, you are getting over scrupulous."

"James," Auchendrane replied, "there is killing, and killing. There is a killing that is murder, and there is a killing that is no murder. It is killing, but not murder, when Sir Thomas Kennedy is slain; it would be both killing and murder to slay Dalrymple if we can secure ourselves otherwise. Whether for good or ill, this country side is the prey of contending houses. It is a laudable ambition to struggle for the mastery and to rule. If that be so, the houses which dispute the claims of each other to predominance are lawfully and morally entitled to use every means in their power so long as those are directed against one another, but it may come to be a very different thing when the strife involves those who are only indirectly, and innocently, concerned."

"Well, father, there may be something in what you say, though I can't see it. It seems to me that, if all our ambitions are so laudable, we would be quite right to secure our own safety by the death of this fellow Dalrymple. What is he? Nothing, nobody. He would never be missed. But if you are so scrupulous, we must, at the very least, set about securing him at once. He is dangerous out of our hands, and you may live to regret the day that you prevented me putting him out of the road."

"Perhaps so, James. Were his death a necessity, it would be otherwise. It will be time to think of it when it is a necessity. In the meantime, though, we must lose no time."

"Leave me to see to that. If he can be had at all, I shall have him in Auchendrane before he is much older."

"Whatever you do, James, don't be rash. That might undo us altogether. What does Helen say to her father's death now? Have you seen her since the morning?"

"Yes, two or three times. She says very little, cries away to herself, moans, and wrings her hands. She has nearly used up all my patience."

"Don't speak like that, James. She is your wife."

"Yes, I know; but I have only enough patience for one,

not for two, and, when I see her going on as she is doing, it is all I can do to keep up my look of grief for the death of her father." And James smiled at the recollection of his grief assuming.

"She suspects nothing?" queried Auchendrane.

"Not a groat," laughed his son, "what could a woman suspect? Besides, she dare not suspect."

"You'll see to that?"

"I will."

"Do not overdo your grief, whatever you do. There is a medium in all things. Remember that Helen knows you thoroughly, and if she sees you so changed all at once, she will think that, if you aren't all at once become a saint, you're degenerating into a devil."

"She couldn't think as deep as that, father. Besides, I don't overdo it, I just assume the necessary amount of grief to suit the circumstances. I've said very little to her about her father's death. Every time I get on to talk of him, she goes off into a fresh burst of hand-wringing and blubbering, and then I forget all the good things I was going to say. D'ye know, father, I came very near remembering a verse out of the Bible."

"For heaven's sake, don't play that game on her. But what verse was it?"

"I don't exactly know, but it was something about 'Well done, good and faithful servant.'"

"A good thing you did forget it, though it was well done of Bargany and Cloncaird all the same. But, James, eschew the Bible. If you begin to quote it, she'll suspect us at once."

James thought his attempts at condolence were good subject for merriment, and he was beginning to enlarge a little more at length upon his efforts to apply consolation, when the door of the room in which they sat was suddenly opened, and his wife, calm but pale, entered and stood at the foot of the table where her husband and father-in-law sat. James at once assumed what he considered an expression of heartfelt sympathy, burying his head in his hands and watching his wife through his fingers. Auchendrane, who had more regard for the proprieties than his son, rose, and in silence offered Mrs. Mure a chair. With an apparent effort, which amused himself mightily, to overcome his sorrow, James raised his head and addressed his wife.

"Father and I, Helen," he observed, "have just been talking over this melancholy tragedy."

"Yes, indeed," she replied, "it is a melancholy tragedy."

"And we have been discussing how best and most effectually the deed can be avenged, and the assassins secured."

"That should not be very difficult," was his wife's response, as she looked him full in the face. The words were spoken with the most perfect self-possession.

Quietly as the reply was made, James gave a perceptible start, while Auchendrane himself was sufficiently disconcerted to stroke his beard, and then to rise from the table and look out of the window.

What did the words mean? Could it be that this woman knew more than they suspected? Why should she not? She knew all the comings and goings of the associates of her father-in-law. She knew of their midnight visits, and of the low-voiced conversations around the oaken tables. She knew that Bargany and Cloncaird were with Auchendrane the previous night. Why should her words not have a meaning? But what if they had, even? Was she not a Mure as well as a Kennedy? And was it not consistent with the duty of a wife that she should espouse the cause of her husband, even. to the detriment, if need be, of that of her father? Still, the observation was disquieting.

While Auchendrane looked out of the window and meditated, James recovered himself and his affectation of grief.

"How very sad it all is, to be sure," he said, "to think of your worthy father, the soul of honour and rectitude, a man without suspicion, and who never did anything to provoke suspicion—how sad to think of him going forth in the prime of manhood to meet his death at the hands of a party of "— he paused a moment for a word, and then added—" assassins!"

"The will of the Lord be done!" piously ejaculated Auchendrane, resuming his place at the table. "Man that is born of a woman is of few days and full of trouble."

"Born to trouble as the sparks fly upward," interjected James, with a determination to say something applicable to the circumstances.

Auchendrane shot a lightning glance at his son, which checked any further attempt on his part to quote scripture. Then, turning to Helen, he asked,

"What brings the fair Helen here? Does she come for advice or sympathy?"

"For neither, sir. I come to crave permission of my husband to go and visit my mother."

This was a request that had not entered into the calculations of the Mures. Father looked at son—son at father. James was wise enough to leave the decision with his father, and the latter, desiring a moment or two's consideration, rose again and resumed his place at the window. James tided over the emergency.

"You want to go home and see your mother, Helen? Am I to understand that such is your desire?"

"Yes."

"At once?"

"Yes, at once."

"Ah! at once. Have you made any preparations for going?"

"No; I have none to make. I mean—with your permission—to start as soon as I can, and ride across."

"You mean to ride across, Helen? That's rather dangerous, 'isn't it? You are a Mure, you know, and there is no saying what might happen were the Kennedys of Cassillis to get hold of you."

" I am not afraid of the Kennedys. I did not cease to be a Kennedy when I became a Mure. I am still my father's daughter as much as ever I was."

" Well," there's something in that, Helen, I daresay. What do you think of it, father ? "

While this conversation was going on, Auchendrane was thinking. Should he let her go, or prevent her going ? It was dangerous to do either. If she had no suspicions, she ought to go, by all means; if she had suspicions, would it not be as well to try and disarm her of them by apparently willing compliance with her request ? Something told him—his own fears and his sense of the nature of things, and the chain of circumstances evolved under her very eyes—that she knew more than she pretended to. If that were so, would she tell ? She certainly would if they persisted in keeping her at home, for they could not shut her up a close prisoner ; she might not if they sent her to Culzean with evident willingness and with expressions of sympathy with her mother in her trial.

" I think," was Auchendrane's reply, "that you ought not only to sanction Helen's visit to her mother, but to send her across to Culzean as befits her position. Her request is most natural ; her desire to be with her mother in her bereavement most praiseworthy."

" I want no escort," said Mrs. Mure. " I very much prefer to ride across alone. The distance is not great."

" Just as you desire in that respect. James, you will see to Helen's going ? "

" I will."

Mrs. Mure was about to leave the room, when Auchendrane resumed. " You will convey to your mother, Helen, our heartfelt sympathy with her. Assure her how deeply we feel the loss she has sustained, and that we shall leave no stone unturned to bring the perpetrators of this horrible and atrocious outrage to justice."

Helen bowed her head, and, without attempting reply, left

the room. No sooner had the door closed than the Mures looked at one another.

"Do you still think she suspects nothing?" asked the father.

"Nothing whatever," replied the son.

"I'm not quite so sure of that," observed Auchendrane.

"Women don't suspect, father. They take things as they come. But if she does suspect, why let her go?"

"Why? Because it would be more dangerous to prevent her going than to let her. I suppose," added Auchendrane, drily, "you don't intend to ride as far as Culzean with her, yourself?"

"No, not exactly. It is a long ride to Culzean, and the air of that part of Carrick does not always agree with my constitution. But you might go yourself?" rejoined James in the same tone.

"Yes, I might do many a thing, but not that. I am not a lady's man."

The same afternoon Helen Mure rode forth alone to Culzean. James attended her as far as the door, and saw her mount. He even went the length of pressing his company upon her, and volunteered his escort; and the more resolutely she declined, and the more firmly she announced her intention of going alone, the more apparently anxious he became to accompany her. It is just possible that, in the end, James, if not anxious to go, was at least hurt in his own way at being practically compelled to remain where he was; but if he was, he did not allow such a feeling to weigh him down. So long as he could find congenial society, neither care nor the future sat upon him; and as this sort of society was seldom absent from the stable-yard, his opportunities of indulging in care-scattering recreations and amusements were never few nor far between. So to the stable he went to carouse, while his wife rode solitarily over the shoulder of the hill.

It was a sad ride. Before her lay the house of mourning,

behind her the house of strife and treachery. In the one was her widowed mother, in the other her husband—the one bent in anguish by the untimely death of her husband, the other unable to hide the satisfaction which nothing but her presence made him endeavour in a sort of way to conceal. She was not so easily deceived as her husband thought. No woman in her senses would have been, let alone a woman whose youth had been spent amid turmoil and contention, and who knew the depth of the Carrick undercurrents as she did. It had not been a matter of doubt with her for a moment that Auchendrane and her husband both knew more than they cared to reveal. What, then, of their sympathy with her mother and with herself in their sorrow—what but a lamentable attempt to disarm suspicion and so get rid of responsibility ?

Full eight miles lay between Auchendrane and Culzean, but Mrs. Mure was well mounted, she had travelled the same way oft and knew every inch of it, and the miles sped away quickly. She crossed the Brockloch Burn hard by the spot where the late chief of Bargany received his death-blow, and skirting Maybole to westward of the town, she turned towards the coast. It was twilight when she reined up in front of Culzean—the sun had dipped behind Goatfell, and only the last jagged peak of the mountain retained a farewell glimpse of the orb otherwise below the horizon. The castle was under strict surveillance, and the guard, as he paced his weary round, challenged her as she was about to alight.

" Who goes there ? " he said.

" Helen Kennedy," was the answer.

" Mrs. Mure ! " said the guard, as he recognised to whom he was speaking.

" Alas, yes—Helen Mure."

And with these words she handed the reins to an attendant, who was speedily on the scene, and entered the house.

CHAPTER VII.

AUCHENDRANE RESPONDS TO THE SUMMONS OF THE PRIVY COUNCIL.

WEEKS passed over; they grew into months. All the time Carrick was waiting on a new development, and the retainers and friends of the Earl of Cassillis were in constant expectation of a summons to arms. Auchendrane, though apparently determined to play the innocent game, was by no means so unapprehensive as a consciously innocent man would have been. It was rarely that he stepped beyond the bounds of his house; and, though no open demonstration of the fact was made, his tower by the Doon was strongly, if not numerously garrisoned. Full fifty men in arms were behind its rude ramparts; regular communication was maintained with friends in Ayr; and had the Kennedys of Cassillis come down upon him in force, they would have received a welcome which might have taken them by surprise. For Mure was an old campaigner, and Auchendrane Tower was strong by nature, and well fortified. It boasted one or two cannon, and Mure had men trained to work them. Nothing was left to chance. He staked his hopes of being left alone on his apparent innocence, but he staked his immunity not less on his followers, and the knowledge he had of his ability to hold his enemies at bay.

The Earl of Cassillis and his brother, the Master, fretted and chafed over the delay. Though indisposed to such a course, they had agreed to wait the issue of criminal proceedings against Mure at the instance of the Privy Council. If Mure could be condemned in Edinburgh, and executed, as he would be, if condemned, so much the better; if difficulties interposed, the alternative was still open to them. Law first, then freedom of action. If the former struck, good and well; if not, there still remained the wild justice of revenge.

Once set in motion, the authorities, after innumerable

delays, summoned Auchendrane to appear in the Parliament House of Edinburgh, early in the following month of November. The actual murderers of Sir Thomas Kennedy were similarly summoned, but they remained safe where they were, and submitted rather to the sentence of outlawry, than risk paying any heed to the legal steps being taken to bring them to justice. Bargany and Cloncaird despised " horning," as the process of outlawry was called, knowing that, as times went, their misdemeanour would very soon be condoned if they only walked warily, and feeling strong enough in arms, and in influence, to bid the law a fair measure of defiance. What they counted upon was lying concealed for a few months, and then returning quietly to Carrick when the din of strife and the remembrance of the crime enacted in the wood of St. Leonards had died away.

Curiously, and unaccountably enough, the Earl of Cassillis did not keep hold upon Dalrymple, the one important witness in the charge against Auchendrane, when he had him. Nothing would have been more easy, nothing more natural. Taking it for granted, however, that Mure's feigned innocence would prevent anything like strategic reprisal, he permitted him to return to his home in Ayr on condition that he should appear when called on to accompany his lordship to Edinburgh, to tell in the witness-box what he knew of the tragedy. This remissness on the part of the Earl was speedily known to Mure, who had at once commissioned his son James to secure him, and bring him to Auchendrane Tower.

" That will I," said James, " dead or alive."

" No, not dead, James," replied Auchendrane, " we want no dead men here."

" You want to prevent him telling tales, don't you ? "

" Yes."

" Then dead men tell no tales. However, if you don't like it, I'll bring him here."

" How will you manage it ? "

"Easily enough. Dalrymple does not know me; he has never seen me. I'll get him without trouble. I'll tell him I want some old deeds transcribed, or sermons, or something of that kind; and by the time he knows where he is being taken, it will be too late for him to return."

"Be careful what you do; don't frighten him."

"No fear of that, father. I'll play the saint on him better than I can do with Helen. But I say, father, there is one thing I never can fathom at all, and that is your repugnance to let me have my own way with this fellow, and despatch him out of hand."

"Conscientious scruples, James—nothing else."

"There is too much at stake, it seems to me, to let conscientious scruples prevent us stilling this man's tongue for ever. For if ever he escape you, he will be your death."

"No fear of that. We will keep him as long as our safety demands it. After that, he can go his way, and he will never go his way until he can do us no harm."

"What are you going to do with him when you have him?" asked James.

"Keep him till I get a chance to send him across to Arran. Montgomery of Skelmorlie will see that he is safe enough there. In the meantime, however, we must get hold of him—it will be time enough to send him away when we get him. So lose no time, James."

In due course James resorted to Ayr to look for Dalrymple among his kinsfolk and acquaintances. Dalrymple was still little more than a lad. He had received his education at the expense of one of those guilds or endowments with which the royal burgh then abounded. It was but a sorry education he had at the best; but, compared with the usual run of the towns-folk, he was a paragon of lore. He could study first hand the ponderous tomes of theology in which the seventeenth century ecclesiastic delighted. He could transfer his thoughts, and the thoughts of other people, to writing, and

eked out a humble living by acting as amanuensis to the
worthy burghers whose souls were above education, and who
set the art of buying and selling and getting gain far beyond
the wisdom of the fathers.

James Mure lost no time in cultivating the acquaintance
of the young scholar. He succeeded in keeping his own
identity secret, and, under an assumed name, led Dalrymple
to the belief that he was of rather pious tendencies than
otherwise.

"My father," he said to the youth, "has great store of
manuscripts of the holy fathers; but, unfortunately for me, I
am unable to read them."

"You have not been trained in the Latin tongue, sir?"
interrogated Dalrymple.

"Alas, no, I have not. Would that I had! But if I had
some one who could translate the manuscripts into the Scottish tongue—and do so for a fair, and not an extravagant,
remuneration—methinks I might even profit by the wisdom
that lies hidden in their pages."

"I am glad, sir," replied Dalrymple, "to meet with one so
minded; and were you to bring these manuscripts here to
me, not only might I be able to translate them, but also to
teach you how you might even read them and understand
their beauties in the original."

"No doubt," was Mure's answer, "but I cannot bring them
to you. My father, who lives in Carrick, sets great store of
wealth by his precious possessions, and would not readily part
with them. But were you to accompany me into Carrick you
should be well done by, and fairly remunerated."

"I am afraid to enter Carrick, sir," said Dalrymple, "it is
a country that I do not like. Its sons are turbulent, and for
ever striving with one another; and who knows whether I
might not innocently fall a prey to their brawling and fighting?"

"It is true—ah, too true!—that Carrick is as you describe

it, but there are quiet spots there still where religion is respected and where its sons have not followed their fellows in their evil courses; and such a place is the house of my father."

"Yet I am loath to go thither," responded Dalrymple, " I have had enough of Carrick. Would I had never heard of it !"

" Would that you never had," said James thoughtlessly, " by which I mean," he continued, seeing the strange, distrustful look that passed over the scholar's face, " that you would not have formed so poor an impression of the district to which I belong."

The reply satisfied Dalrymple. James was by no means ungenerous in his offers of remuneration, it being an easy thing for him to promise when he had no intention to perform. Two or three interviews were enough to stifle the scruples of the poor scholar and to satisfy him that he was going to congenial duty. Mure pledged himself that he should be well taken care of ; and when Dalrymple innocently informed him that he might be suddenly called away to Edinburgh to give evidence against Auchendrane in the matter of Sir Thomas Kennedy's murder, Auchendrane's son expressed virtuous indignation of the deed and his readiness to give the young man every facility for going to Edinburgh. There was nothing, in short, that Mure did not promise him to allay his suspicions.

Dalrymple thoroughly assured, the two set out on their journey to Carrick, and they passed along the road in improving converse. It was not until they reached the gateway leading to the Tower of Auchendrane that Dalrymple manifested, or indeed entertained, the remotest suspicion; but when James turned in thither, he halted.

"I cannot go with you there," he said.
" No ? Why not ? "
" Because that is the gateway to Auchendrane."

"That is where you are going," said James Mure decidedly, taking hold of Dalrymple by the arm, "that is where you must go, so come on."

Dalrymple grew pale. "That is where I dare not go," he said.

"Dare not go—why?"

"Because Mure would murder me. Why should you wish to take me there when, as I told you, I may be cited as a witness any day against Mure himself?"

James saw no good in further prevarication or reasoning.

"Listen, Dalrymple, and don't be unreasonable. I am the son of Auchendrane, and I guarantee you that if you come quietly and willingly with me you shall be taken care of, and not a hair of your head shall be harmed."

"And if I refuse?"

James shrugged his shoulders. "If you refuse you will have to come all the same, and your treatment will be very different."

"Why did you not tell me who you were, in Ayr?"

"Why did I not tell you?" laughed Mure. "Ask no further questions, or ask sensible ones. I have said all I need say to you just now. You can choose either to come as a guest or as a prisoner. Take my advice and make your stay as pleasant as you can. We bear you no malice, and will do well by you, if you will only let us."

Dalrymple was completely taken aback; he thought for a moment to resist; but when he looked at the determined countenance of James Mure, and contrasted his own weakness with the robust and sinewy frame of his companion, he bowed to the inevitable, and accompanied Mure to the tower of Auchendrane.

Dalrymple secured, Auchendrane felt less uneasy in the prospect of appearing at the bar of the Privy Council than he otherwise would have done; but he was none the less determined to use all the influence he had in the west country to make his acquittal the more certain.

7

Strange as it may appear to-day, the courts of justice were the playgrounds of contending factions, which regarded friendship and influence of only secondary importance, and not always secondary, to justice. They held the scales, but they held the beam as well. Auchendrane knew this; and ere, as the autumn stole on, he made preparations to answer to his summons in Edinburgh, he secured a large and powerful muster of his friends and associates to accompany him to the capital.

The party met in Ayr a week before the date fixed for the trial. Here Auchendrane joined them, and laid before them such a statement of the charge trumped up against him, as he most solemnly assured them it was, that without any hesitation they one and all agreed to escort him, and to see justice done without partiality. It was quite a calvacade that rode up the old High Street of Ayr behind Auchendrane, as he set out for Edinburgh. Nine lairds of greater or less importance were in his train; and each of the nine were accompanied by a number of their followers, all well armed and ready for the perils of the road. For who knew whether the Earl of Cassillis, knowing, as Auchendrane knew, that the principal witness for the prosecution had disappeared without leaving a trace behind, might not attempt to anticipate the action of the Civil Tribunal, and render the trial of Mure for the murder of Sir Thomas Kennedy, unnecessary?

History has left us the names of the nine lairds. These, to call them as they are designated in the narrative which scrupulous care has handed down to us, were the Lairds of Lainshaw, Rowallan, Auchinleck, Blair, Caldwell, Bombie, Blair younger, Hazlehead, and Mure of Rowallan. Their journey to Edinburgh occupied four days; and the gay cavalcade as it passed from village to town, and from town to village, excited the admiration of burgess and peasant alike. It was more like a triumphal procession than the journey of a man to Edinburgh to be tried for being accessory to a cruel

and brutal murder. The Carrick feud was familiar in Scotland, though news travelled slowly; the names of the leading
actors were household words in the dwellings of the west;
and even in Clydesdale, the natives, when they heard that
Auchendrane and his friends were on the march, turned out
to see and to admire.

In Edinburgh the sight of a hundred armed men on horseback was no unusual one. The citizens were familiar with
strife. The metropolis was the town residence of all the
Scottish gentry of importance; and as the lords and squires
of high degree were valued largely in proportion to their
fighting strength, the city and its dwellers were but too
familiar with the emblems of strife as well as with strife
itself. Still, the Ayrshire lords made a gay show; and they
walked their horses up the historic High Street with an
amount of dignity of which they were fully more conscious
than those who stood for a moment as they passed and
wondered what the cavalcade meant.

The two days that elapsed ere the Privy Council was to
meet were fully taken advantage of. Mure himself saw as
many of its members as he could influence; and his friends
made loud complaint, in the same quarter, of the indignity to
which their innocent friend was being subjected, in order to
gratify the whim, or satisfy the vindictive ambition, of the
Earl of Cassillis.

The Privy Council met in the Parliament House of the
realm, that historic chamber whose walls know more of
Scottish history than either muniment or archive. The
Lord High Chancellor presided, and, in addition to the Lord
Advocate and the other crown officials of court, there were
seated on the tribunal, at whose bar Auchendrane was ar-
raigned, the Earls of Argyll and Angus; of Fyvie and
Loudon and Roxburgh; of Blantyre and Kilsyth; Sir Patrick
Murray, and a score of others, noblemen and gentlemen, of
lineage and name, of fame and might.

The Court constituted with the accustomed formalities, the macer, or crier of court, called the diet against Mure of Auchendrane, Kennedy of Bargany, and Mure of Cloncaird, as well as against M'Alexander and Wallace, and Irvine the borderer—in short, against all who were alleged to have been privy to the murder of Sir Thomas Kennedy. James Mure was not included in the list.

Of course there was no response by any of the accused save Mure. The others were far enough removed from the scene, and Bargany and Cloncaird no doubt felt safer in their Border stronghold than they would have done in the Parliament House of Edinburgh. Mure alone responded to the calling of his name. He was sitting at the back of the hall, surrounded by his friends, watching the preliminaries with interested gaze, and searching in the deep oak ceiling for fresh courage to face the ordeal. He was to protest his innocence; his friends were to do the rest; and when the crier in sharp tones called out his name, the whole party arose and advanced. They were armed, every one of them; booted and spurred; and as they had rallied a few more supporters in Edinburgh, they presented a formidable appearance as they trod the floor with heavy footsteps. It was no new sight this, to the members of the Privy Council. Many such had they seen. But none the less it impressed them. Its members, the greater part of them at least, were themselves feudalists; some were friends of the Earl of Cassillis, others of Bargany and Auchendrane. More than one were at that moment, in other parts of the country, in active feud, and did not know how soon, in the turn of affairs, they might have to stand where Mure was standing. Hardly one man of all the throng saw in Mure even a possible murderer. He might have directed the killing of Sir Thomas Kennedy. But what of that? Unless there were circumstances of an exceptionally aggravating character, it was nothing so very bad after all. Besides, was it likely that a common murderer should

be surrounded by so many friends, all conscious, all convinced
at least of his innocence ?

When no response was made on behalf of Bargany and his
absent associates, the crier proclaimed their names at the door.
Still no answer; so sentence of outlawry was at once passed
against them. They were adjudged to be put to the horn, and
denounced as rebels.

Charged at the instance of the Lord Advocate with being
actor, or art in part, in the murder of Sir Thomas Kennedy,
Mure haughtily denied complicity, and demanded at once to
be heard in his own defence. What followed would have
seemed strange to the decorous jurists of these latter days.
Instead of waiting to hear what evidence could be brought
against him, Auchendrane took the initiative, and at once, in
stern and bold accents, rebutted the accusation under which
he lay.

" I am here, my lords," he said, " at your lordships' summons,
charged with being an actor in the melancholy tragedy by
which Sir Thomas Kennedy, Knight of Culzean, lost his life.
I am not charged with being on the scene of the tragedy, because the Lord Advocate very well knows that I was not
there; but I am accused of having instigated to the crime
these men against whom you have but now pronounced sentence of horning. Consider, my lords, the character of the
relations which existed between me and Sir Thomas Kennedy.
Years ago, indeed, I was at feud with him ; but years ago that
feud was terminated at the instance of his most gracious
Majesty the King. Since then we have, as I shall show your
lordships, been on terms both intimate and friendly. Many
a time he has tarried at Auchendrane ; many a time have I
resided in Culzean. His daughter is my daughter-in-law.
Her union to my son cemented the truce arranged by his
Majesty, and I put it to you, my lords, whether it is consistent with the nature of things, with our all but blood relationship, and with our plighted friendship, that I should seek

revenge against Sir Thomas Kennedy for deeds or actions
which both of us have forgotten, or remembered only to
forgive. It is incredible. I am here, my lords, in response
to your summons, but at whose instance? Not at that of the
Lord Advocate, whose name the complaint bears, but at the
instance of the Earl of Cassillis, a sworn enemy of me and of
mine, and of every man in the west country who dares to raise
any standard or own any allegiance save his own. It is to
gratify his hate that this indignity has been heaped upon me;
and I demand now, either that the charge be made good or
that I be permitted to depart to my home in peace, my fair
name untarnished, my honour undimmed."

The Lord Advocate, who took no notice of Auchendrane's
words, explained the causes which had led to the connection
of Mure with the crime. He had intended, he said, to place
in the box as witness the lad Dalrymple, who had conveyed a
letter to Mure informing him of Sir Thomas Kennedy's projected visit to Edinburgh; but since proceedings had been
taken, this lad had gone amissing and could not be found;
and he had reason to suspect that his disappearance had been
caused by Auchendrane, who had him in confinement either
in his own house or in some other locality or shelter belonging
to some of his numerous friends.

Auchendrane laughed scornfully. "You hear, my lords,"
he said, "to what straits my enemies are put. They seek to
identify me with the disappearance of this wretched scholar;
and for no other reason than that they fail to produce him,
they affirm that I have spirited him away, or have him in
hiding."

The Chancellor interposed, and asked Mure pointedly
whether he knew nothing in reality of Dalrymple's disappearance. Mure, calling God to witness that he spoke the
truth, replied in the direct negative. He knew nothing of
Dalrymple's disappearance, he said, and cared nothing; and
he demanded afresh that, if nothing was to be laid to his

charge, further than could be substantiated by the testimony of the missing witness, the charge against him should be unconditionally and absolutely withdrawn.

His friends clamoured loudly for his release. The Lairds of Auchinleck and of Blair were specially urgent, and demanded, with a vehemence which in these later days would infallibly have led to their apprehension and imprisonment for contempt of court, that Mure should at once be exonerated and set at liberty. Their demand was as loudly emphasised by the other friends of Auchendrane, and an angry altercation ensued between them and the Lord Advocate in the first place, and afterwards between them and various members of the Council who sat as judges on the assize. The Lord Advocate refused point blank to do more than adjourn the diet *sine die*, and asked the court to compel the accused to find caution in a thousand pounds Scots for his reappearance when called upon.

This evoked a fresh storm of disapproval, and of threats—deep and loud—on the part of Mure and his friends; nor was it allayed until the Lord Advocate refused to proceed further in the case on account of the turmoil and the illicit influence which it was attempted to bring to bear upon the Council.

My lords took the proceedings with great equanimity. It was no strange scene to them, that of which they were witnesses, but neither were they for a moment shaken by the disorderly conduct of the west country squires; and they complied with the prayer of the Lord Advocate and refused to liberate Mure unless caution to the amount of one thousand pounds Scots was found for his reappearance when cited.

Mure was, at heart, well enough pleased with the result, though he made indignant show of demurring to the finding; but, as the alternative was imprisonment in the Heart of Midlothian, he finally submitted with what grace, and with what protestations of injured innocence he could command.

His friends at once expressed their readiness to find the demanded caution, and a few minutes thereafter the Ayrshire
lairds, with Auchendrane at their head, were walking the
High Street of Edinburgh with an enhanced consciousness of
their own importance.

CHAPTER VIII.

MURE SEEKS SAFETY IN THE HOUSE OF NEWARK.

AUCHENDRANE was safe within the walls of his Tower ere the
Earl of Cassillis heard the result of his trial in Edinburgh.

Mure had lost no time. He knew to a certainty that if the
Earl only had time to intercept him, he ran an unusually
small chance of ever seeing the Doon again; and accordingly,
late on the evening of the day on which he had stood at the
bar of the Privy Council, he, accompanied by one or two of
his most trusted friends, left Edinburgh, and rode westward.
All night they journeyed, for they knew not the issues which
might hang on an hour's delay. The night was long, and the
moon shone on autumn advanced in the fields, in the hedge
rows, in the trees, and lighted up the country through which
they urged their horses, with weird and beautiful sheen.
Town and village and cot were all asleep as, ere the first grey
streaks of the November sun shot into the dark blue sky the
premonitions of coming day, they lighted in the High Street
of Lanark. Here they spent the greater part of the day, resuming their march late in the afternoon, and hastening with
all the speed they could maintain, into Ayrshire.

Midnight found them skirting the town of Ayr; and Mure
shuddered as the moon-beams struggled and glimmered weird
and ghastly through the trees of the wood of St. Leonard's.
He was not a wholly unimaginative man; he partook fully of
the superstitions of the day, in feeling, if not in judgment;
and his mind was ill at ease until he emerged from the droop-

ing shadows and silent voices of the plantation. Who knew, he unconsciously asked himself, whether, after all, it was not possible that departed spirits might not be permitted to re-visit the glimpses of the moon; and if so, what more likely than that the shade of the murdered Knight of Culzean might not at that moment be haunting the spot whence it had been despatched on its last long journey? And if not, were these not the very trees, was that not the very spot that had witnessed the fateful struggle? The spirit of the scene was there, if naught else; and as Auchendrane felt its indescribable in-fluence, he involuntarily quickened his pace.

Relieved of the malign influences of St. Leonards, the party hurried on towards Carrick. The Tower of Auchendrane was gleaming under the soft light of the queen of the night as she sailed silently athwart the blue; but the warders heard the horsemen approach, and gave them challenge. A word from Auchendrane changed the challenge into a welcome; and once more, as the heavy door, iron studded, iron bound, closed behind him, he felt comparatively safe, even though the square house of Cassillis was but over yonder amid the trees, and the Earl was conning over the future.

The tidings were not long in reaching Carrick. Those who were in league with Mure rejoiced; the party of Cassillis were enraged. Both at once prepared for the future. It was clear enough to them all. The law had failed of its intent; and Mure knew that the Earl would take up the sword, and try to cut the Gordian knot which criminal juris-prudence had miserably failed to unravel.

The Tower of Auchendrane was a strong tower, as befitted the day; but it was too near Cassillis, and too liable to be taken at a disadvantage by the vastly superior force which the Earl could bring into the field. Mure resolved, therefore, to transport the whole of his available force to the house of Newark, leaving behind him only a sufficient number of his followers to prevent Auchendrane being burned to the ground.

He judged that the mere sacking, even the burning or the razing of the house itself, was not worth the Earl's while, if it was at all stubbornly defended by a few good men and true. What Lord Cassillis would try to accomplish was something more than the destruction of the house; the destruction of Auchendrane himself. And that was to be avoided.

Once resolved, Mure made instant preparations for a change of quarters. The house of Newark was hardly more than a mile distant; it was in the possession of Mure. It occupied, and still as of yore occupies, a commanding position on the eastern slope of Carrick; and there it may be seen standing to this very hour a witness to the stormy times which called its thick walls and its heavy battlements into existence. Behind it rises the hill, slope above slope, here wooded, there the bare rock jutting out from' the sparse vegetation, here flecked with gorse and heather, there with fern and bracken. Beneath, the hill runs down to the very banks of the Doon, bespanned, even as early as the period of which I tell, by the auld brig, destined to be of pious memory, and to live in history as the scene of the witch's unearthly cantrips as she plucked the tail from the grey mare of Tam o' Shanter.

A varied vista opens beyond—Ayr and the valley of its river, the Firth of Clyde, and the steep crags on the other side, yellow sands fringing the main, and far off peaks melting into the blue, a richly wooded country blending into upland and moss-hag—all lay, all lie, within ken. It is worth a day's journey to see it all. And a strong house was the house of Newark. It was here that Mure fortified himself for the issue; it was hither that he transported his wife, who is hardly more than a vision in this history, and his son, and his son's wife. James Mure rode in close company with Dalrymple, the poor captive scholar, and behind came a full hundred men armed to the teeth. And once within the thick walls, and with the sentries set, and with everything in readiness for the fray, which he knew soon must come, Mure waited with calmness and determination the movement which would ere long be taken to compass his destruction by the Earl and the Master of Cassillis.

The Earl of Cassillis was furious when he heard that Mure of Auchendrane had been discharged from the bar of the Privy Council for want of evidence. From the first he had favoured more instant remedies than legal ones; and he reproached himself bitterly that he had deferred to the advice of his friends. Auchendrane had been liberated because of the absence of the lad Dalrymple. The Earl had no idea where Dalrymple was to be found, but he entertained a belief, amounting to conviction, that Auchendrane had him safe and meant to hold him. More furious than he was his brother the Master. All his old friendship for Auchendrane had passed away like a tale that was old. He forgot their old association in common; he forgot that ever he and his brother had been at warfare; he remembered only the family honour; and his former friendship for Mure became gall and wormwood. There was to be no halting now between two opinions. The law had been tried and found wanting, and a sterner arbitrament must follow.

The Countess of Cassillis was a woman of peace. More than fifty years of age, she was full of experience and of wisdom. She had not been the wife of the late Lord Chancellor, Lord Thirlstane, for nothing. She knew all the workings of Scottish society, its ups and its downs, and the best methods of transforming the "downs" into the "ups;" and though she felt aggrieved that the Privy Council had acted as it had done, she was not a whit less anxious to prevent hasty developments which might work their own ruin. She was proud of her lord, not yet seven-and-twenty years of age; but, while she appreciated his ambition and his power, and was as anxious as even he could be for the maintenance of his position, she did not allow her zeal to eat up her discretion, or her husband to go unwarned and unadvised.

Lord and Lady Cassillis were seated in their oaken-panelled dining-room. The Master paced the floor, restive and angry.

"Aye, aye," he broke in, repeating what he was about to say for the sixth or seventh time, "the old fox has outwitted us after all, has he?"

"He has," assented the Earl, whose mind was in hurricane sympathy with that of his brother. "The day is his."

"So it is," responded the Master, "but not the morrow. That is ours."

"Wheesht, wheesht," interposed the Countess, "do you not know what the Book says, 'Vengeance is mine, I will repay,' saith the Lord."

"True, Jean," replied the Earl, familiarly addressing his elderly spouse, as she placidly looked up from the embroidery work on which her fingers nimbly plied, "it is His in the next world; it is ours here."

"It is His here too, John," was the response, "and it is only yours if He uses you as His instrument to effect His purpose."

"We shape our own courses, and leave the result to Him; but so far as we are concerned, we must do our duty," was the Earl's reply.

"But, John," replied his wife deprecatingly, "you would not forestall the judgment of the Almighty? If Auchendrane has, indeed, been concerned in this foul and unnatural tragedy, as I fear me he must have been, you may depend on it that the judgment will overtake him either here or hereafter. Punishment follows guilt just as naturally as one day follows another."

"Not necessarily," said the Earl. "It is some consolation to think that Auchendrane will have his deserts in the next world in any case; but my business is with this world, for I cannot pursue him beyond the grave. I want to see him hung as high as Haman, Jean—as high as Haman. It is not as if the murder of Sir Thomas Kennedy, or the avenging of it, were all that is at issue. He has tried, and he will try, to thwart

me by every means in his power. He would take my life to-
morrow if he had but the chance; and it is for my own
safety, and for yours, that I mean to settle accounts with
him. I'll fire the tower of Auchendrane, but I'll have him
out of his nest."

"Will you, John?" replied the Countess, a faint smile
lighting up her features. "Auchendrane Tower would be
hard to burn, I'm thinking. Besides, do you think you have
nothing more to do than go down there and bring Mure back
with you? Remember, you will need all your caution if you
are to be even with Mure."

"All *your* caution, you mean, I think," responded the Earl
smiling.

"Well, well, all my caution if you like. You remember
the proverb that says, 'Ye need a lang spune to sup kail with
the deil.'"

"So you do, too. That's what I've heard before about
Mure; but cunning and all as he is, I don't think he's the
deil. Even if he were, though, we have a lot of long spoons
hanging on the wall there, and in the armoury," and the Earl
pointed to a score of lances suspended against the panelling.

"If all you say be true," rejoined Lady Cassillis, "if not
the deil, he has a lot of the deil in him. He is as wary as an
old fox, and you will have to be wary too if you circumvent
a man of his experience, who was fighting before you were born,
and who has been defending his own interests ever since. So
don't be rash. Mure is laying his plans as well as you; and
it would be a woeful thing were he to despatch you on the
same long dark journey as that on which he has despatched
Sir Thomas Kennedy.

"There's little fear of that, Jean, but whatever the risk it
must be taken. We know with whom we have to deal, and
we are not going to walk into the lion's den without knowing
how we are to walk out of it again."

"It seems to me," interposed the Master, "that we are

wasting time.   The question is not whether Mure is to be
attacked, but how is he to be attacked, and how soon are we
to do it ? "

" Rash as usual, Hew," remarked the Countess.

" No, not rash, but ready, sister.   It is on me that this
enterprise must fall, and not upon your husband.   I have
undertaken it, and I think I can bring it to a satisfactory conclusion without any very serious risk, or without any unnecessary loss of time."

" Don't underestimate the risk, Hew," replied the Earl.
" Auchendrane has a ready pair of hands, and a cool head, and
he knows how to use both.

" Yes," assented the Countess, " Mure will know how to
take care of himself, and you will need all your wit and all
your wisdom if you are to circumvent him.   But seeing you
are to be the avenger, Hew," she added, making no secret of
her gratification that her husband was to be spared the
dangerous enterprise, " I wish you all success."

Early the following forenoon the Master of Cassillis set
about the execution of his project.   In and around Cassillis
House were fifty retainers of the Earl ; and those he summoned to his assistance.   His object was to reconnoitre, in
the first place, the Tower of Auchendrane, to attack it if he
found it undefended, and to take Mure prisoner.   Neither his
brother nor he wished to kill Mure in combat ; they had a
greater indignity in store for him than to fall under the
sword of the avenger.   The dule tree was suggestive of the
means by which the laird of Auchendrane was to effect an
unwilling exit from the scene of his plots and his subterfuges.

The country wore a dreary aspect as they rode away from
the front of the Castle.   The Earl had spoken a few words of
encouragement to his retainers ; and when they left Cassillis,
it was with a firm determination, if not to achieve their end
that day, at least to gain such information as would enable
them to storm the Tower in force ere many days had passed.

The cold, bitter blasts of November had stripped the trees in the Dalrymple forest of their foliage, and the Doon, swollen by heavy rains among the moors and mosses, and the cloud-capped hills beyond the natal loch of the rushing river, ran turbid and yellow to the main. The fields had been stripped of their harvests, and the inhospitable country presented a depressing contrast to the byegone days of summer and of the early autumn. It was a gloomy day, the sky overcast; but the gloom did not affect the cheerfulness and ardour of the Master, who, now that action had taken the place of waiting, was in the highest spirits, and eager for revenge. They went warily, not knowing what might be in store for them. Crossing the boundary of Cassillis, they were in the enemy's territory—and a wily enemy was the laird of Auchendrane. So they rode slowly along the narrow path by the river, past Dalrymple village; but foe, they saw none; nor did they encounter mortal, until, advancing steadily, they called a halt in full view of the rugged Tower whither they were bound.

All was silent about and around the grey old house. It was placidly sleeping amid the trees, its approaches secure and neither man nor woman was seen amid the silence and solitude in which it sat. The Tower had a look of conscious strength about it; and the Master of Cassillis realised as he looked at it, and scanned its frowning battlements and its loopholed walls, how impossible it would be, with the force at his disposal, to storm it in teeth of anything like formidable opposition. If inmates there were, they gave no sign. The silence was worse than hostile demonstration; for it implied security and strength. The Tower looked like some giant asleep, conscious of safety in his own inherent might. That it was not untenanted, was evident from the smoke which curled lazily up into the cloudy sky; but what the force which held it, was a question which outward tokens could not demonstrate. The Master halted in full view of the Tower for more than an hour; but the Tower looked as if it was all the same whether the halt should be continued for an hour or a century. Whoever was in it, sign there was none.

To stand there all day idle was out of the question; so by way of ascertaining exactly how matters were, the Master of Cassillis and his men sought the house of one of Mure's retainers who lived in proximity to the Tower. Riding rapidly towards this house, they surrounded it ere the inmates had any suspicion that danger was nigh. A loud shout brought to the door a peasant woman, to the skirts of whose dress clung two curly-headed children, who trembled and cried when they saw the formidable gathering around their humble home. The woman was not slow to speak; and in reply to the Master of Cassillis, she willingly vouchsafed such information as she possessed. That was simply this, that the Tower was in the hands of a small body of Auchendrane's followers, but that Mure himself and a strong force of his friends and retainers were ensconced in Newark, whither they had betaken themselves to await contingencies.

Satisfied that the information was correct, the Master and his men rode round Auchendrane and examined it at their leisure. Some of the men were anxious to fire the Tower; but as that necessitated the forcing of it, and as any attempt might not only result in unprofitable bloodshed, but perhaps lead Mure to garrison Newark even more strongly, they satisfied themselves with a careful inspection which they treasured up with an eye to the possible future. That inspection was not by any means assuring; for the approaches were all under fire of the guns which sullenly projected from the battlements, and which looked glum and threatening enough even in repose.

The house of Newark became the destination of the party. They could not attack it; but they could, at least, reconnoitre, and, mayhap, they might accomplish something by surprise or by peradventure. And they were, as events happened, within measurable distance of effecting their main purpose, and securing Auchendrane himself. Mure calculated on being attacked; but he was quite conscious of the strength of the position, and three or four days at least must necessarily elapse ere the Earl of Cassillis could muster a force sufficient to attempt assault with the faintest hope or prospect of success.

The country all around was quiet; no whispering rumours were abroad of coming, or at least of early, judgment, and Mure resolved to revisit the Tower, with the object of transferring thither two or three of the lighter pieces of artillery, in order to add to the defensive strength of Newark. Accordingly, accompanied by his wife, and ten or twelve of his followers, he prepared to ride across to his house on the Doon. Just as they were about to set forth, Mure received a message from one of his friends in Ayr, with whom he was in communication, which required immediate attention. It was a lucky fate that kept him back, though the master of Newark would have called the Providence by another name.

"You ride on," he said to his wife, "I will follow you instantly."

She obeyed, accompanied by four or five of the men who were to compose the escort. She suspected nothing; but so constant was the sense of impending danger, and so restless the influences amid which she lived, that almost instinctively the Lady of Auchendrane kept a sharp look-out on either hand. She passed one small clump of trees after another; everything was still, and sign of enemy there was none. At length she reached a grassy hillock by the foot of Carrick, around which swept the road she had to traverse. The sound of her approach, the noise of the horse hoofs, reached the party of the Master as she was approaching this spot. They concealed themselves as well as they could, and waited to see who was coming. Nor were they long kept in suspense.

Her ladyship, a woman past middle life, a hard-featured determined woman, who seemed to have assimilated a portion of the inherent capacity for riding on the crest of the social storm that distinguished her husband, was talking familiarly with one of her attendants, openly discussing the purpose of their visit to Auchendrane. Her words were overheard; had they not been, the Master of Cassillis would have captured her on the spot. He gathered, however, from what he did hear, that Mure himself was behind; and, checking the excitement that was among his followers with a look and a gesture, they kept well out of sight behind the knoll.

But quietly as they lay, the Lady of Auchendrane did not pass them without observing their place of concealment. She gave not a sign; she neither slackened nor quickened the speed of her horse; nor did she even cease from the conversation with the attendant until they had left the knoll behind and were out of hearing.

"Did you see nothing behind that hillock as we passed?" she enquired of the attendant.

He replied that he had seen nothing.

"There is a large party of men hidden behind it," she continued. "Ride back to Newark as fast as you can, and tell Auchendrane to beware, for if I mistake not the hidden watchers are the Kennedys. Quick, quick," she added, "ride for your life—and his."

"But I will be seen."

"No, you must not ride by the way that we have come; you must take the way across the hill."

"I know it," he replied, as he cut off at a right angle from the party of Lady Auchendrane and took to the fields.

"Then make haste," were the words the attendant heard follow him as he put spurs to his horse.

He did make haste; but ride as he might, he was too late to prevent Mure leaving Newark. For he had already left it, and, with his followers—a mere handful—was cantering his horse in the direction of the knoll, where the Kennedys were waiting for him.   This the attendant perceived; and riding back at an angle towards the road, he hurried with all available speed to execute his errand in time. Auchendrane was not more than a couple of hundred yards from the hillock; the attendant was more than double that distance from Mure himself.

Anxious not to raise any alarm, the attendant pressed on in silence, until he saw that if he contented himself with signalling—and so far, thanks to the nature of the country, Mure had not perceived him—he must fail in his attempt to warn his leader.   There was no help for it but to shout; and shout he did with might and main.

"Ho!" he yelled, at the pitch of his voice, "the hillock, the hillock!   The Kennedys!"

Mure caught the words; so did the Master of Cassillis. The former reined up on the instant; but when he saw a troop of horsemen dash out from behind the knoll, he turned his horse's head for Newark, and stayed not a instant on the order of his going.   He had a good start; he was fairly mounted; but he took nothing for granted.   With heel and whip he encouraged his horse; and the horse, partaking of the excitement so suddenly sprung upon them, laid himself down into a long striding gallop.

There was racing and chasing; the road was uneven; a distance of a hundred yards was all that intervened between the pursuers and their prey; and the strong shelter of Newark was half-a-mile away.   An excellent horseman, Mure took all the speed that was available out of the steed which he bestrode.   If the Kennedys lessened the distance, it was imperceptible.   The Master encouraged them to the utmost; and they dashed pell-mell along the slope of the hill without regard to the ruggedness of the way.   Pistol shots were fired at the pursued, but the distance was too great; and the only result of the shots was that the warder on duty on Newark heard them, and called out to the walls a strong party of the garrison who were ready at hand. They saw Mure as he strained up the approach, and the Kennedys in hot pursuit; and they stood by the outer gate till he passed within the portal. No sooner was he within than they closed it. It went to with a loud clang, and the chase was fruitless.

Once inside, Mure hastened to attempt reprisal. The guard, which had turned out in reply to the summons of the sentry, opened fire on the Kennedys, but without effect; and the Kennedys, on their part, fruitlessly fired their pieces at the strong battlements, and rode round the walls, yelling out taunts begotten of anger and disappointment.

Ordering his men to cease firing, the Master of Cassillis and his followers rode near the gateway which had been closed upon them. Mure surveyed them calmly from one of the loopholes in the wall hard by. Brandishing his sword, the Master fiercely called on Mure to come forth and defend his honour. Mure laughed scornfully.

"Come out, bloody souled villain," shouted the Master, taunted beyond description by the reception of his challenge; "come out. The blood of Sir Thomas Kennedy is on your soul."

"You lie!" retorted Auchendrane, discharging a pistol at the Master. The shot failed of its mark, but took effect on one of the Cassillis followers who was standing by the side of his leader. The man reeled in his saddle and dropped upon the ground.

"I do not lie," cried the Master defiantly; "and you know that I do not lie. You are afraid to face me, coward! Come out, I tell you, and I will establish in single combat the cause of justice and of right."

Auchendrane laughed again, and ordered his men to discharge a volley at the Kennedys. This they did with fatal effect. Three of the followers of the Master of Cassillis fell, never to rise again; several were wounded, and the horse which the Master bestrode was hard hit, plunged violently, and fell forward. The Master swung himself clear of the wounded animal as it came heavily to the ground, and stood facing Newark. Mure looked at him, and laughed again.

"Monster," shouted the Master, wrought up to fury, "you have the advantage now; but your time is at hand. Look well to Newark, for its time is short."

"You will find us here when you return," replied Mure, calmly.

"You will not have long to wait," was the answer.

"Go, rash young man," was Auchendrane's answer; "it would serve you right were I to lay you dead where you stand; but go this time. And beware the day of your return."

The Master was about to reply; but, checking himself, he mounted the horse of one of his men who had fallen, and ordered his followers to retreat. This they did, bearing with them their dead and wounded comrades.

On their return to Cassillis, wrathful, but neither dispirited nor shaken in resolution, the Master was accosted by his brother.

"What cheer, Hew?"

"Scant cheer for us," replied the Master. "Auchendrane has foiled us again, and driven us defeated from Newark."

The Earl bit his lip. "The devil is good to his own," he observed, "but we can afford to wait, and to strike, too."

"We can afford to strike, at all events," replied the Master, "and we shall strike hard, and home, when we do."

CHAPTER IX.

THE TIDE OF BATTLE SURGES AGAINST THE WALLS OF NEWARK.

MID-WINTER drove on with bitter wind and rain, with sleet

and snow and frost, ere the House of Newark sat in its strength, face to face with the Kennedys.

For weeks Carrick had been in turmoil. Its kingship was in the balance. In Cassillis the Earl fretted and fumed, and directed operations; and from Craigneil, in the south, to the river Doon, there was the sound of coming conflict. Mure sat still where he was, ready, waiting, determined. His store of arms was good, his courage high, his confidence unshaken. His son, James, was in his element. The fray was not far off; and if ever James Mure was competent to shake off the lower man and rise to something better, it was when the ardour of the conflict took possession of him. The valour may have been bull-dog courage; probably it was; but there is something to admire even in that, when dissociated from other qualities less admirable.

But while Mure waited on the assault, he was careful to make assurance doubly sure. He must trust nothing to chance. The poor scholar, Dalrymple, was still an unwilling guest at his table. The theologic tomes which he had ostensibly come out to translate were non-existent; the wisdom of the fathers found no resting place either in the Tower of Auchendrane or in the House of Newark. He lived in a chronic state of fear and anxiety. Many a time he conned over his chances of escape, and wasted his time devising futile plans with that intent; but the consciousness that he was strictly watched kept him from ever attempting to carry his plans into effect. From Newark he could see the town of Ayr, almost the very house in which his parents lived; and as his eye glanced over the short stretch of country which separated him from his home, his heart abridged the miles, and he longed to be away. Dalrymple lacked experience; he lacked courage of the kind necessary to dare an enterprise; and he was forced to content himself with unavailing longings doomed to be unrealised.

For one night, after dark, he was rudely bidden to follow

James Mure. · He obeyed without questioning. James, who carried a heavy pistol by way of intimidation, conducted him along the side of Carrick, towards the shore. It was a dark, cold, unsympathetic night, calm but unimpassioned. A light wind blew off the shore. Reaching the mouth of the river Doon, James directed his steps towards a small craft with whose whereabouts he was well acquainted. It was manned by two men, and lay in the channel of the river with main-sail hoisted and flapping idly in the breeze.

"What do you mean to do with me?" enquired Dalrymple, as the idea flashed across him that his destruction was pre-meditated.

"Nothing much," replied James, laughing. "We are going to give you a short cruise."

"You do not mean to drown me, surely!" pleaded the youth in pitiful accents.

"No, no," was the answer, "we do not mean to drown you. Only, if you make any attempt to escape, depend on it your cruise will be a longer one than you would like. You are going across to Arran—that is all—to stay there till you are sent for. Get on board."

Dalrymple tremblingly obeyed. The boatmen were versed in what they were to do. They seated him in the stern of the little craft, and, pulling the sheet home, the land breeze filled the sail, and the Ayrshire coast dipped in the darkness. James Mure stood until the craft and her occupants were out of sight, and then returned to the House of Newark.

By day and night a fleet horse stood harnessed in the stables of Newark. Mure and the burghers of Ayr under-stood one another; and no sooner should the Kennedys be on the march than one of Auchendrane's followers would mount the charger and ride across the intervening miles which lay between the scene of conflict and the neighbouring town. The garrison were trained both in the house and out of it.

Mure gave them confidence in his generalship; they gave him confidence in return, in their fidelity and courage.

The winter days came and went, till the year was all but gone. The delay was advantageous to Auchendrane, for it gave him time to perfect his defences, just as it gave the Kennedys time to muster their men to the fray. This was to be no child's play; but a combat to be fought out to the bitter end.

"They come, do they?" said Mure to a horseman who galloped up to Newark early on the forenoon of the twenty-eighth day of December, "they come, do they? How many of them?"

"Not less than three hundred horse and foot."·

"The gates are closed?"

"Yes."

"The messenger has ridden off to Ayr?"

"He is across the Doon by this time."

"Then I think we can hold our own," said Mure, as he rose to superintend operations, "they will drive us hard if they reduce Newark this day."

The Kennedys had come at last, three hundred strong and more. They were visible from the house as they rounded the shoulder of the hill, the horses walking leisurely, no trace of hurry in the march. Determination sat upon their deliberation. They were not approaching to fire a few random shots, but to remain until their purpose was done. Many a gallant fellow would bite the dust ere the sun sank behind Carwinshoch; but what of that, when such issues were at stake? The Master of Cassillis rode at the head of his men, composed but firm; and Mure, as he scanned the cavalcade, felt the fighting blood mount in his veins, and his hand tighten its grip on the hilt of his sword.

"Who are these," asked James of his father, "who are these in rear of the horsemen?"

"The only dangerous men we have to fear," replied Auchendrane, "these men are dragging behind them a battering ram. They mean business."

"Apparently they do," was James' answer, "but we have provided for that too."

"Yes—still, I tell you there is danger there."

The battering ram had been cut down in the Dalrymple forest, a straight heavy fir tree pointed at the lower end, and bound strongly together with clamps of iron.

As the Kennedys neared Newark, the followers of Auchendrane raised a defiant shout, half cheer, half yell, which ran along the hill, and which was taken up and sent back with increased volume by the men of Cassillis. It was the opening of the conflict; for hardly had its echoes died away than the garrison made rampart and loop-hole musical with the discharge of musket and pistol. Still the Kennedys came on, until they were within range of the house, when, scattering themselves over the uneven ground, they replied briskly to the fusillade, and the fight began in earnest. It was still a preliminary however; but the firing was maintained on both sides with a vigour, and a constancy, which looked as if the fray were to be confined to one of small arms.

The Kennedys were at first rash in exposing themselves; but the defenders firing from behind shelters, against which the bullets of the enemy flattened themselves harmlessly out, they sought such cover as they could, and watched embrasure and loop-hole with the object of picking off the defenders as they took aim from within. Auchendrane himself was everywhere, encouraging his men to the defence, while his son, excited with the ardour of battle and with the expectation of coming relief, emulated the example of his father and cheered on the garrison.

But the combat was not to be settled by such means. The Kennedys might have kept up the fusillade till doomsday, and Newark would have kept them at bay without any defenders at all. And this the Master of Cassillis knew full well. Several of his men had already fallen, others were wounded; and if an entrance was to be effected at all, it must be by the rough and ready battering ram. He accordingly concentrated his men in front of the outer gate, which, with its heavy oaken planks and iron bolts, barred ingress, and ordered them to keep up a steady fire at every point where the defenders showed themselves. Auchendrane saw what was intended; he met the intention as best he could; and every loop-hole and embrasure on that side blazed out into fire. The withering rain of lead pattered against the walls, and among the trees where the Kennedys sheltered themselves; and yell and answering shout combined to turn the ordinarily placid slope of Carrick into a pandemonium of contending demons.

"Now comes the critical moment," observed Auchendrane to his son, as he saw a score of the Kennedys pick up the battering ram.

"Will the gate stand?" asked James.

"Not if they hit hard enough, and long enough," was the answer.

Advancing under cover of the fire, the Kennedys came on with a rush and a yell; and the excitement blazed out more furiously than before. Banded in common impulse, the Kennedys wrought with the concentration and the spirit of trained soldiers, while the men behind the ramparts stood the more bravely to their posts, and took aim with a stronger determination to do fatal mischief. A loud shout from the roof of the building announced that they were not unprepared for the assault about to be delivered. For days they had been engaged robbing the hill-side of its rocks and boulders; and, having transported these to the summit of the house, Mure's retainers were ready to meet a rude weapon of attack with ruder and more dangerous weapons of defence.

On came the Kennedys with a rush. Staggered by the infernal hail of bullets which rattled everywhere, and before which more than one of the Cassillis' retainers went down never to rise again, they paused, but only to rally. They must drive in the gate or perish in the attempt. So long as it barred progress their efforts were wasted; and oaken beams, iron hinges and iron bolts, down it must come.

There could be no retreat now. Passions were at fever heat; the blood coursed rapidly through the veins of the contending warriors, surging up into fury and recklessness of life. Down from above came stones and rocks, crushing out of existence for ever a third of the men who bore the battering-ram. As they fell, their places were filled up; and amid fire and fury, and the rain of boulders, crash upon crash, they reached the gate and drove the stout tree against it. It was a tough gate, made for tough times. There it stood up as if sympathetic for Mure, dour, grim in its very strength; and against it, more dour and more grim than itself, came the Kennedys and their ram, surge upon surge. Amid the din rose yell upon yell from defenders and besiegers; and in the lulls there struggled up into the winter air the groans of the wounded and the dying, and the ping of the whistling bullets on their errand of destruction.

Shock upon shock. No faltering. Living men in the place of the dead. Still the same long, swinging blows—blow upon blow. Still the yell of combatants and the red blood running down upon the ground and over the stones of grey Newark. Stark and stiff the dead were lying among the grass; and the wounded were crawling and creeping, gashed and gory, into the shelter of the trees.

But no cessation. Loud rang the blows of the ram. The gate shakes and trembles. "Hurrah, my men," shouts the Master of Cassillis gleefully; "it moves, it moves; drive it home. The gate shakes again; and oaken timbers splinter and crack and open up. Nothing can prevent the collapse; nothing will prevent it. Another blow and away it will go. The other blow is given, the gate tumbles, shattered, broken, in fifty pieces; the hinges are torn out of their sockets. And there—there is now nothing between the hall door and the charging, angry, determined Kennedys.

Mure sees the situation. He feels it is desperate. What is to be done? In a few minutes the Kennedys will be in the hall. Surrender? Never—no surrender. He grasps his sword the tighter and sees to his pistols. He calls his men together and tells them what to do. The besiegers will rush the door; that infernal tree will splinter it at the first blow. As the final rush is made rock and bullet must have their victims, and then, ere the door is driven in, the defenders must meet in the hall. There their final stand must be made. There they must look in the Kennedys' faces; and there they must kill, or, if need be, die in the Kennedys' grip.

Again the Kennedys come on. Again the battering ram. Again, down from the roof come the stones and the rocks. Again the yell and groan of the wounded. The bullets find their billets. Still, the Kennedys are in force. Killed and wounded, they have not lost fifty men yet, and there are plenty remaining to carry the place by storm. Auchendrane is cool; his blood is careering through his veins, but his demeanour is calm, his voice steady. His sword is unsheathed. Bullets have been whizzing past him; he is unharmed. So is the Master of Cassillis. He never has flinched. Where danger was, there was he; and around him has passed the deadly hail, leaving him unhurt. He is as full of metal as he was when the fray opened; and where the battle is deadliest, there he is to be found.

Crash, crash, and the door is in. Another moment for a final rally, and then the rush.

The scene in that hall—how can it be depicted? Men everywhere, from the head of the stairs, where the Mures are gathered close behind one another, to the door into which the Kennedys are pouring. Hell broken loose in the House of Newark. Men gripping one another by the throat and driving

daggers into one another's hearts. Pistols discharged at ten—
at five—at one pace. The floor bloody, slippery, covered with
shrieking, groaning, dying men, their lives being trampled out
in the infernal rush and stamping and struggle. Backward
and forward surge the struggling, straining crew, now the
Kennedys gaining a foot, now the Mures—every foot disputed
with a grim obstinacy that never calls for quarter. Auchendrane fighting like a fiend, and his son cleaving his way with
fiery fury, and arm nerved to anything. The Master of
Cassillis straining and encouraging, his face covered with
blood,—a stern picture of war. Confused noise, and garments
rolled in blood. And so, now ebbing, now flowing, the tide
of battle rolled.

Hark! The blast of a bugle. What does it mean? It is
without. Is it friend or foe? Have the men of Ayr come
upon the scene, or have the Kennedys mustered a new force
to the battle? Mure catches the note with an inspiration.
Cheer upon cheer rise from the besieged, and heavier fall their
strokes, and more fiercely they drive back the impetuous
Kennedys. The rush of horses, the riders throwing themselves
from the saddles to the ground. Fire behind the Kennedys—
axes and daggers and swords in front. What does it all
mean?

The relief has come. Another host rushes into the battle.
A mighty arm is there, wielding a weapon that kills where it
strikes. As the tornado sweeps upon the homestead, so
dashes the leader upon the Kennedys; and above the din and
the charging and the contending, the clash of swords and the
crack of the pistols, rises his battle cry—

"Remember Bargany!"

"Good God," exclaimed the Master of Cassillis, as he
turned to confront his new foe, "it is Bargany himself."

It was, indeed, Bargany; and behind his tall, lithe form
drove on the men of Ayr who followed him. The Master of
Cassillis was between two fires—Mure in front, Bargany be-

hind. The allied forces were not so numerous as his; but the presence of Bargany was an inspiration; and the Kennedys knew that the assault had failed. They might have held their own; they could not take the House of Newark.

So round they turned them to seek the way by which they had come; and grimly contesting every inch, they retired to the plantation from which they had rushed to the assault, baffled, defeated, everything but broken.

Not quarter of an hour elapsed from the moment Bargany winded his bugle until the Kennedys were on the defensive in their woodland shelter. Here they were safe, for the defensive was theirs.

Bargany would have fought them where they stood, but Auchendrane was content.

"They will come to Newark no more, Bargany," he said, as he grasped Thomas Kennedy by the hand. "We have driven them hence for the last time."

"No time like this," was Bargany's answer.

But Mure held him back, and the fray was over. It was terminated by common consent; and the combatants, stiffening as they rested, had time to count the slain and the wounded.

Never in its previous history, as never from that hour to this, had Newark House been the centre of such a scene. It sits to-day smiling over the same scene, the main features in the landscape unchanged since then. It is Nature's panorama that it opens up, not man's. And if you choose you can go at this very hour and behold the spot where once the tide of conflict ebbed and flowed, where the fiery Mure held his enemies at bay, where the impetuous Master of Cassillis grimly contested his footing, and saw victory snatched out of his hands at the moment when he had won it, and where Bargany fell like an avenging angel on the Kennedys of Cassillis and turned conquest into rout. It is hard to realise it all; for never a mansion sits more placid than Newark; nor is there a house in all the westland that looks out and away over a more peaceful and soul-stilling scene. Yet happen it did, to the very letter.

The short day was darkening into night; the red, winter sun had set behind Carrick; and the broad firth of Clyde was shaded with the coming gloom of the December evening ere the Kennedys collected their dead and wounded, and returned to Cassillis by the way over which they had come. Anticipation, growing into realisation, had been shorn of its fruits. There were great gaps in the army of the living, who that morning had gathered high in hope and prowess in front of Cassillis. Not a man, indeed, was awanting. The Kennedys told their full tale of retainers; but nearly a fifth of them were laid out in silence beneath the sombre shade of the dule tree, and as many more were borne on rude litters, the blood dripping from their wounds and leaving a red track to mark the way by which they had been carried.

Auchendrane had suffered less severely. Fighting behind breastworks his followers had not been exposed as the Kennedys had been, to the fury of the fusillade. In all he lost ten men, though a score besides had received wounds which remained to tell the story until the day they died.

What a gloomy night it was that darkened down upon Carrick! Like a great pall, the dule tree waved its branches in the moaning wind, tribute to the gallant fellows who lay stretched all night on the green sward beneath it. From house to house, from clachan to clachan, from village to village, the news spread with the proverbial rapidity of evil tidings; and there was weeping and wailing by the Doon and the Girvan, to be taken up on the morrow by the clear Stinchar and the dark flowing Duisk. Never since the feud had begun had the men of Cassillis suffered more severely— not even in that stubborn struggle by the Brockloch Burn.

The retainers of the Earl were drawn from a vast extent of country. The majority resided at Cassillis and in and

around Maybole; but the remainder had come, some from the
Carrick shore, some from the shores of Loch Ryan; some had
seen the sun sink for the last time from beneath the shadow
of Knockdolian; others had taken their last glimpse of home
in the far-stretching woodlands of Carrick; others had come
from the hills and from the sides of the lochs on the steep
borderland of the shire; and others still had hailed from far
away, from Galloway and from "laigh doon by the cruives of
Cree." Over all the country of the Kennedys the news
travelled; and there was hardly a homestead on their
domains in which the angel of death did not leave his evil
tidings. To some he told that never more would the husband
or son return; to others, that some dear one had met his fate
hard by the gate of Newark; and to others still, that the
horrid scaurs of war had defaced their friends in the deadly
grips of the castle hall.

It is a long time since these things happened; and one is
tempted to ask whether the country was satisfied to accept the
strife as a necessity, and whether those who suffered loss felt it
as keenly as would their descendants of to-day. The first
question is easily answered. The feud was a birthright. It
was the doing of the will of the gentry. The tenants and vassals
of feudalism were born to do the behest of their master; and if
it was the master's will that they should fight and suffer and
die, why, that was the end of it. The people did not
question; they did what they were told, because it was their
destiny, and they held no responsibility in the matter. The
feud itself was nothing to them; but they were clannish to the
last drop of blood in their veins; the laird was their Providence, his will their predestination.

Were sympathies as keen as they are now? The answer
is not far away; human nature is human nature all the world
over; and without a doubt, "there was sighing and moaning
in ilka green loaning," when the staunch fellows who had
ridden so blithely, and fought so desperately, and who had

fallen before the leaden hail of Newark, on the sterile slopes of Carrick, were borne home, cold and lifeless, from the spot whence their souls had ascended, amid the din of battle, through the mirky air of the chill December.

The Earl of Cassillis had not himself joined in the fray. He saw his followers depart from underneath the shadow of his keep; and then retired to the house to wait, and to weary, and to reproach himself. "Why had he not gone himself ?" he asked twenty times as the day wore on. Why were his men assaulting the House of Newark; struggling, perhaps dying, while he remained in the tents of peace ?"

He had never doubted the result. Had he entertained one qualm of distrust as to the upshot of the attack, he had not stayed behind; for the Earl was bold and skilful in fray. Sharp the contest might be, and bloody; but what were the defences of Newark to the sustained onslaught of so powerful a band of Kennedys? Naturally, however, as the day wore on, he became more restless. He could do nothing but repair to the summit of the castle and look out over the Doon, and over the trees and the fields, towards Newark on the side of Carrick. The house itself he could not see; but occasionally he fancied he heard the noise of the combat, and pictured to himself his gallant retainers driving in the iron-studded gate and measuring their prowess in combat, resulting in victory, with the followers of Auchendrane. As he thought of the stern old feudalist by whom he was opposed his brow darkened; and a more revengeful set of feelings crept into his heart than those inspired by honest combat.

Thus he moved about, now in the house, now out of it, and now on top of it; and thus still he was engaged when the sun set behind Carrick and left the winter darkness to brood o'er the scene. What was it to evolve? What could it evolve save victory? We know what it did evolve—that it brought back the Kennedys broken and discomfited; dead men slung across wounded horses; warriors wounded, begrimmed and bloody; and disheartened and weary combatants who had struggled the live-long day for nothing.

The Earl knew what it meant. He did not require to look upon his brother, the Master, to know that the assault had failed; and that if ever there had been a moment when the kingship of Carrick hung in the balance, that moment was now. The tale needed no words. It told itself more plainly than words could have done. Yet in presence of his followers he maintained his outward composure with a stoicism that not even the long row of the dead could move to display; and it was not until he and the Master of Cassillis had entered the house that he broke silence.

"Tell me, Hew," he said, as he stood by the table at which the weary Master had seated himself, "tell me how it happened. I do not need to ask what has happened."

"No, you do not; and the story is simply told. We attacked Newark as we arranged to do. Everything was going on well; we had driven in the hall door, and were fighting within the very house itself, when we were attacked from behind by Thomas Kennedy of Bargany."

"Bargany!" echoed the Earl.

"Yes, Bargany himself, and a strong force of men whom he had collected in Ayr. Bargany came upon us like a whirlwind, and the day was lost. We could have held our own; but hope of carrying Newark was gone."

"A very serious result for us," said the Earl, still standing by the table, "we shall have a host of hornets about our ears. Every petty laird who has stood aloof to see how the wind would blow, will from this day forth side with Bargany, and ride with him too, when occasion requires it. Every man who has been afraid of us, and too frightened to take arms against us, will flock to the standard of Bargany and Auchendrane."

"And if they do, what then?" asked the Master, rousing himself and speaking with animation. "Cassillis has been harder beset in its day, many a time. Not even Bargany and all his friends would venture to attack us in this house ; and if all we want is to be let alone, nothing is easier."

"Nothing, I grant you," replied the Earl, " if all we want is to be let alone ; but there is no standing still for us. We must prosecute this warfare to the bitter end, and attack on all sides in turn. Stand still ! Never was there a time when we could less afford to stand still than this."

" I did not mean that we should think of such a thing. It would be to our everlasting shame to halt in this warfare for one single hour ; and it would better befit us to prepare for what must come, than to calculate even on the possibility of failure."

" I do not calculate on any such thing," said the Earl, " nothing is further distant from my mind ; but I wish to look the opposition straight in the face, and then I shall know the better how to meet it.   We can talk of this anon ; in the meantime, tell me all who are killed and wounded. But first, was Cloncaird there with Bargany ?"

" Yes ; so was the Master of Stair."

" I thought as much," was the Earl's reply, " they are never far away when Bargany is about."

Leaving the Master of Cassillis to tell his brother who they were that had fallen, and who that had been wounded in the fray, let us return to Newark. At Cassillis there was lamentation over the slain ; at Newark, Mure and Kennedy of Bargany were shaping the future.

CHAPTER X.

AUCHENDRANE PLOTS, AND BARGANY EXECUTES.

A WATCH was set round the House of Newark that night. The Kennedys had disappeared ; but stranger things had happened than that they should return when the night was at its darkest, and endeavour to complete the work of the day. The demolished gate, crashed into splinters by the battering ram, was removed out of the way; and a temporary barricade was erected to prevent surprise. The dead were reverently laid out in one of the rooms of the house; the wounded were cared for; and all the garrison who could be spared from duty lay down to rest. They had had a hard day's work; and the excitement wearing off, lassitude and reaction took its place. They had recounted their feats as they partook of the evening meal; but even remembrance and reminiscence were not sufficient to stand up against exhausted nature.

Mure and Thomas Kennedy of Bargany sat together by the roaring fire which flashed in the spacious fire-place of the dining-room. The former was too old a warrior to have much reaction; and Bargany's share in the contest, though sharp, had been short. They talked the earlier part of the night away, Bargany detailing the story of his life on the Borders, Mure recounting the events which had happened in Carrick since Bargany and his associate, Mure of Cloncaird, had sought safety in the south.

"You are not afraid to return, Bargany?" observed Mure after they had brought the story of their on-goings up to date.

"Afraid? Why should I be afraid?"

"You do not know, then?"

"Oh, yes, I know well enough," replied Bargany, "that I have been put to the horn and denounced as a rebel, and that everybody who harbours me is guilty of contempt of the laws of the land and liable to be called to account for it. But these things don't last long, and the cold of winter has killed the finding of the Privy Council. Besides, I haven't come home to foment strife, but to retire to Bargany and live as quietly and as peaceably as they will allow me. That, at least, was my intention until I came to Ayr. Events past and future, I admit, are rather strong for me."

" Yes, not a doubt of that. Your coming on the scene this afternoon was an event that the Earl of Cassillis is not likely to forget."

" No; but he is not likely, all the same, to seek the protection of the law, seeing he himself has reopened the quarrel. And so long as he leaves me and minds his own business, things may go on as they like for all I care."

Mure laughed incredulously. He fancied he knew the man to whom he was speaking better than he knew himself.

" And if they don't leave you alone, what then ? "

" I have five hundred men on whom I can depend, and with their aid I shall do the best I can. And if that fails, the sea is open, Holland is open, and there are fields and to spare, on the Continent, for a strong arm and a stout heart. You see I am not so hard bestead after all."

" I never thought you were so very hard bestead," rejoined Mure. " But, Bargany," he continued, " this feud might be brought to a close in a month—do you understand that ? "

" You speak in riddles, Auchendrane. The feud brought to a close within a month ? "

" Yes, within a month."

" Explain yourself."

" The Countess of Cassillis," said Auchendrane, " is in Galloway. She went there a short time ago ; and in ten days she returns."

" I do not grasp your meaning. What has the Countess of Cassillis to do with bringing the feud to a close ? "

" This. In ten days, I tell you, she returns to Cassillis House. I have it on information that cannot be questioned. The Master sets out in three days to bring her home. Now, do you see what I mean ? "

" No, not yet."

" John Dick is one of her escort—Dick, who struck the

fatal blow that killed your brother at the Brockloch Burn."

"Well?"

"Well, what I propose is this. They cannot expect any attempt at capture. The whole escort will not exceed twenty at the most. Why not lie in wait for them, capture the Countess and the Master, kill John Dick, and hold her lady-ship in captivity until we dictate our own terms?"

"A noble suggestion," said Bargany, rising to the enterprise. "It can be done."

"Can be done?" queried Mure.

"Shall be done, Auchendrane. This game is worth the candle."

"I thought as much," observed Mure, with no attempt to conceal the gratification which he felt, "I thought you would not hesitate. There is no other man in Carrick to whom I would have entrusted such an enterprise."

"You will join us, of course?" observed Bargany.

"Join you?" replied Auchendrane, "no, I cannot join you."

Bargany flashed out in anger and in contempt in an instant, "No," he said, "you will not join us. You devise the enter-prise, and leave others to carry it out. Yet you owe me, I think, some recompense. It is not six hours yet since the Kennedys of Cassillis had their hand upon your throat. But for me, the House of Newark would have been in ashes by this time, and you yourself would have been dangling from the Earl's dule tree. And yet you will not join us in this enterprise!"

Bargany rose to his feet, and walked angrily backward and forward in the room. Not giving Mure time to interject a word in his outburst, he continued—

"Yes, I tell you, you owe your life to me, and all the re-compense you offer, is to devise a desperate scheme which may involve me in ruin. You stand aside—I ride over the hills, and lie in wait and make the capture. I risk my life to bring the Earl to reason; and if I succeed, you get the benefit as well as I.   No, Auchendrane, you must share the risk, or there shall be no risk for me.   Many a time, I tell you, as I have lain hiding in the Scottish border, I have thought of the killing of Sir Thomas Kennedy of Culzean.   You devised that—I carried it out.   You stayed at home—I fled the scene.   You were comfortable under your own rooftree— I spent many a night in the cold and the wet.   You pleaded innocence and cast the blame on me; you went up to Edinburgh and threw dust in the eyes of the Privy Council; you secured the only witness that there was to bring against you; and you rode off triumphant after hearing me put to the horn, and declared a rebel and a traitor."

"Bethink you, Bargany," responded Auchendrane after a pause, "Have I not suffered as well as you ?   Who was it that was shut up as a prisoner in his own house for months, unable to move abroad without risking certain death ?   Who was it that had to stand the indignity of trial in Edinburgh, while you were free and safe in the border country ?   Who was it, but the other day, that had to flee like a hunted deer for his life ?   And who was it that had to face the brunt of that desperate attack this very day, on this house in which we are sitting ?   Besides, Sir, whose is this quarrel— yours or mine ?   What gain I, if you do carry off the Countess of Cassillis ?   You will be lord of Carrick, not I—remember that."

"I tell you, Auchendrane, I am sick of it all.   When my blood is up and when danger calls, I am ready to fight to the death ; but when I am alone, a weariness creeps into my soul, and a longing to have done with it."

"You cannot have done with it, Thomas Kennedy, if you would.   You must fight or be conquered.   You must be strong, or for ever be weak.   You must keep up this conflict, or lay down your position in Carrick for ever.   The Earl of Cassillis will never yield.   He has a long score to wipe off;

and were you to go down to Bargany to-morrow and to live in peace, he would hunt you down. Then, what of your friends? Are you ready in the face of so many who are willing to follow you, and who are only waiting on you to unfurl your banner—are you ready to disappoint all their hopes and leave them to be broken in turn on the wheel by your hereditary foe? You cannot stand still, Bargany, who-ever may."

"I am ready to do my share of the work, but no more. I want peace, though I am prepared for war. But, Auchen-drane, why not join us in the capture of Lady Kennedy?"

"For sufficient reasons. This is your business, not mine. The fewer hands that are engaged in it the better. You must take the Countess to your own house at Bargany, and keep her hidden there. The success will be yours, and yours alone. Think of that, Bargany—think of what you will gain. You want peace? Well, here it is to your hand. Once capture the Countess, and you can trade with her as you like; for the Earl is bound hand and foot while you have her in your possession. Besides, I cannot stand against him as you can. My resources in men, in money, in arms, cannot cope with his; yours can. I am ready to serve under you; you know that you will never be asked to serve under me. The risk is worth running. If you want to humble the Earl, yours will be the glory; if you want peace, you have it in your hand."

Thus Mure urged on Bargany to the enterprise. Bargany was distrustful of his ally, and he made no secret of it. How could he be otherwise than distrustful of a man who planned dangerous and risky deeds and refused to execute them? He could not argue with Mure, for Auchendrane was plausible and persuasive to a degree; and though he ultimately yielded and agreed to undertake the capture of the Countess of Cassillis, it was not without grave misgivings. He began to doubt Auchendrane; he kept himself too clear from danger. He had been the means of driving him into seclusion already;

and, although in return, he had come upon the scene at Newark at a critical moment, and saved the life and the fortunes of the instigator, the blood had not ceased to flow from the wounds which had been inflicted in the fray ere he was again urging to danger, and, at the same time, placing himself carefully beyond legal suspicion. Bargany could not openly quarrel with his ally; but into his mind crept a doubt as to his fidelity, which remained there until the close of the chapter.

In the solitude of his chamber Bargany thought the situation out. A generous impulse had brought him from Ayr that day to strike a blow for the common cause. For whom had he struck it? He was still under sentence of outlawry; he had been proclaimed as a rebel; and he knew that the sentence had not been revoked. Auchendrane, on the contrary, had escaped trial; he had so managed matters, that though he had dictated and directed the murder of the Knight of Culzean, he had still been able to maintain a show of innocence; yet here he was urging to another exploit as dangerous in its way as that which had culminated in the plantation of St. Leonards. For himself, he would take no part in it; it was his to think, and to plot; but he was to remain safe in the House of Newark, while Bargany and his men were to ride across the rough country in the dead of winter, encounter a hostile force, and, if successful, stir the enmity of the Earl of Cassillis to its deepest depths.

On the other hand, if Auchendrane remained silent—and his own safety dictated silence as a necessity—would not the exploit be worth undertaking in his own cause alone, and leaving Auchendrane out of the question? He was, as he had told Mure, getting sick of a feud which involved so many dangers and hardships; his long residence in the Borders had soured his relations with Auchendrane more than he cared to acknowledge. But here was a chance of striking a blow for himself. Could he but secure the person of Lady Kennedy, the Earl's hands would be tied. He dared not endeavour to retake her by force of arms; he would not invoke the law, which he had broken in assaulting Newark; and he would, perforce, have to sue for peace. Bargany could then dictate terms, and the feud would be done.

Once resolved, he lost no time in setting about preparations for the enterprise. He left Newark the following night, accompanied by a small body of his own retainers, and rode southward in the darkness towards Bargany. He was not afraid of observation or of capture; and he skirted the very Castle of Maybole, and saw it loom up in the darkness as he passed it. The roads were bad. Like most thoroughfares of the time they had been originally constructed to lead from town to town, taking in their course the various farm-houses by the way. These, in turn, were, as a rule, built on rising ground; for drainage was yet in the future, and a command-ing site, free from the rush or the overflow of water, was a desideratum. Consequently, the king's highways ran over many a hill and down into many a hollow; and in winter, when the rains were loose and the floods were out, travelling, especially by night, was no easy matter.

But such trivialities as narrow, rough, dark roads were nothing to Bargany. He had ridden by the same way times without number; and the various farm-houses and villages and hamlets which he passed were all familiar to him. They were old friends, and his heart warmed within him as they loomed up against the night and told him how quickly the intervening miles were slipping away beneath his horse's hoofs.

Bargany was reached in the short still hours of the morn-ing. Thomas Kennedy's reception was all the more welcome that his coming was unexpected. Roused from her slumbers, his mother gave him a cordial greeting. Many a night she had lain awake since he had fled the west country, and let her thoughts wander to her son as he lay in concealment in the borderland; and ever as she thought, the memories of husband and of son, both of whom had fallen in the same feud in which Thomas was now engaged, filled her mind. Happiness had long since ceased to be her daily companion. Anxiety for her son oppressed her, and a sense of impending trouble, the fear of evil tidings, kept her on the rack. Thomas's home-coming was, therefore, all the more welcome. For the moment she forgot, in her present happiness, all the misery of the past.

Bargany had great faith in his mother. As a rule, he took counsel with her; but now, when he meant to embark on the capture of the Countess of Cassillis, he kept his intention to himself, and made his preparations in secret. He knew that Lady Bargany would not approve of his doings; and he did not mean to court disapproval beforehand.

Between thirty and forty followers he rallied to his assistance; and ordered them to meet him at a distance from Bargany. He, naturally, did not intend to raise suspicion; and the party, on the day appointed, left the district without exciting any more than the curiosity of those from whose families he chose his escort.

The road by which the Countess of Cassillis and her escort travelled, entered Ayrshire by a wild, mountainous district, beyond the little clachan of Barr. A purely pastoral country, craggy and uncultivated; here the high hills towering up to the drooping sky and the rain-laden clouds; there the river Stinchar, young, but carrying in winter a heavy body of water, rushing between steep banks or overflowing the level haughs through which in summer it meandered placidly. There was comparatively little woodland; a pine wood here and there, the hardy mountain beech, spare oaks stretching up their rugged arms to meet the elements which break with no uncertain force in these rocky solitudes; but no long stretch of treeland worthy to be denominated forest. The path—for only path it could be called—lay along the valley of the Stinchar. It crept round its circuitous turns; it touched the lips of its rushing waters; it swept past rocks and crags and across moss and muirland. Bad enough at all seasons,'but most of all when the clouds sat low on the hills, and when all along the valley the floods lay deep.

This was the way by which the Countess was coming; and towards this path, as it crossed the parish of Barr, beyond the clachan, Bargany and his associates directed their course. Mure of Cloncaird and the Master of Stair accompanied their friend. They were always ready for enterprise; and the quest on which they were engaged was just of such a nature as suited their adventurous spirits. The Laird of Dinmurchie was likewise in Bargany's train, a stout old follower of the House, who was never far away when there was war with the Kennedys of Cassillis. They knew—Mure of Auchendrane had told Bargany—the exact date at which the Countess was to leave Galloway, and they timed themselves accordingly.

The distance from Bargany to the spot selected for the capture was ten or eleven miles; and that they traversed by night. By daylight the traveller of to-day anathematises the road; what it must have been on a winter's night so long ago passes comprehension. But men are made for the age and the country in which they live; so are horses; and in this case the ride was overtaken not only as a strict necessity for the immediate future, but with that stern strange satisfaction which buoys up the actor in a dangerous drama. Bargany was playing for high stakes; and no torrents from the hills above the Barr, and no mosses in which the horses struggled for a footing, and no ford whose crossing threatened destruction, and no steep winding path by rock and boulder, were sufficient to abate by one single jot the courage which animated him.

Ere daylight broke on the hills beyond them, the party of Bargany were in the centre of the wild country whither they were bound. Solitude reigned around, above, beneath them.

They startled the wild fowl from the gorse, and the fox and the hare in their coverts, but save a stray cottage here and there on the slopes of the hills, human habitation there was none. There was no difficulty in seclusion. Hiding places that would have gladdened the heart of a wandering Covenanter, abounded without number; and they chose a stunted plantation wherein to spend the hours in waiting, not because it was exceptionally secluded, but because it commanded the path by which the Countess of Cassillis must approach. A watch was kept on a neighbouring summit; the retainers picketed their horses, and availed themselves of the shelter of the plantation as a protection against the elements, which, if not riotous, were at least sufficiently trying to make the trees a welcome shelter against the cold wind which played across the highlands of southern Ayrshire.

Noon had hardly passed ere the watcher announced the approach of the Cassillis party. In an instant Bargany's followers began to make their preparations. These were simple. The road was barred by a collection of rude boulders, which they rolled from the hillside on to the narrow pathway. One half of the force, under Mure of Cloncaird, was stationed so as to command the rear and prevent retreat; the remainder, under Bargany, were placed so as to face the advancing party and intercept their progress in the direction of home. On the one hand the hills were steep; on the other, the country was open; but Bargany conceived that escape was impossible in that direction, and even, if escape were attempted, that there would be no difficulty in overtaking the fugitives.

The Master of Cassillis rode beside the Countess at the head of the small body of followers who accompanied them. They were jogging along easily. In another hour they would emerge from the rocky scenery of Barr, and, from the heights to the northward and eastward, catch their first glimpse of the comparatively level country where Cassillis nestled among the trees. Thought of danger there was none. A traitor in the camp was never dreamt of; and yet Mure of Auchendrane knew exactly when the Countess was to leave Galloway and undertake her return journey to her home by the banks of the Doon.

Unfortunately, want of suspicion does not imply that there is no danger. Every step homewards was a step into hazard, as the Master of Cassillis and his party were about to realise ; for, as they rode on, they suddenly found the road blocked. Hardly had they discovered the barrier than there was a sudden rush of men ; behind them and before, they emerged from the solitude of the plantation above; and in less time than it takes to tell it, Bargany himself came to the front of his men and ordered the travellers to halt.

To say that they were surprised is to state a necessity of the situation. The Countess was more than surprised—she was alarmed to a degree, and she shrank back as she observed Bargany, sword in hand, backed by a strong force of his retainers; heard him command a halt; and realised that behind her, as well as in front, there were angry fellows in the way. The Master of Cassillis was surprised, but not daunted nor dismayed, and he indignantly demanded—

" What means this, Bargany ?"

" It means that you are my prisoners," was the reply.

" Beware, Bargany, what you are going to do. We are travelling on the King's highway ; here we must pass without let or hindrance ; and if you interfere with us, on your head be the consequences.

" I am willing to take the consequences," replied Bargany ; " it is not the first time that the Earl of Cassillis has stopped a Kennedy of Bargany on the King's highway. I am doing nothing more than your brother did to my brother a year ago on the way from Ayr to Maybole."

" The Earl of Cassillis," responded the Master, " never made war upon women. We are here as the escort to ladyship, the Countess of Cassillis, and I demand that she be allowed to go upon her journey unharmed."

"That she cannot do. The safety, the life of the Countess of Cassillis is assured. She shall go home, but it shall be with me and not with you, save that both of you shall go to Bargany together."

The Master surveyed the situation, and as rapidly acted on the results of his survey. He formed his men into a square, with the Countess in the centre, and, turning his horse's head towards the road by which they had come, gave the order to charge. The retainers whom he led, were trained to implicit obedience. They laid their long lances in rest, and, like a hurricane, drove down upon Mure of Cloncaird and the party whom he commanded. The shock was a sudden one. Bargany's followers were at a disadvantage in not being ready to receive the charge; besides, not being armed with lances, they were unable to reach the Cassillis men as they rode in compact body through their midst.

Bargany was furious. Had his prey escaped him ?

"After them, men," he shouted, as he leaped his horse over the barrier, "after them. Remember Bargany."

Ere the pursuers got well under weigh, the Cassillis men had obtained the advantage of a start of nearly two hundred yards. Such a start was not to be despised. The nature of the country prevented rapid travelling; but pursued and pursuers alike urged on their horses to their utmost speed.

A mile away was the farm-house of Auchensoul, and thither the Master of Cassillis directed the course. Bargany led the chase and cheered on his men. Over moor and moss, over the rough hill-side, whence the horse hoofs sent the loose stones rolling down the steep, through the courses of the burns which sought the valley below, and across the holm lands under tribute to the overflow of the Stinchar, dashed the human chase. Neither stop nor stay. The pur-ued had every conceivable motive to press forward, and the pursuers were not less interested or determined in the accomplishment of their purpose. Bargany outrode his men and all but succeeded in overtaking the flying escort from Cassillis.

Almost, but not quite; for ere he attained his purpose Auchensoul was reached; the Master and his followers dashed into the courtyard of the farm; the heavy, ponderous gate shut to, with a clang; and the irate Bargany reined up his horse in sight of his prey.

CHAPTER XI.

AUCHENSOUL FIRED—THE COUNTESS AND MASTER OF CASSILLIS IN THE TOILS.

THE farm-house of Auchensoul, out in the secluded country far away from the busy haunts of men, was the last place that anybody would have chosen willingly to defend. It had never been built for defence, but for agriculture; and the labourers, as they gathered in the stones from the hillside and fashioned the farm steading, house in front, outhouses, completing a square, behind, had no thought of doing more than constructing a tenement sufficient for the needs of the occupants. The dwelling house was thatched; the front door looked down the hillside on which it opened; the windows were small and barely sufficient for their purpose. The byre, stable, and sheds, formed the other three sides of the little square; and at the mouth of the "close," as the passage into the square was called, was a heavy gate, which was shut at night, not so much for purposes of protection as to keep the young cattle, which strayed about the yard, from wandering. It was this gate which had been closed in the face of Bargany and his followers; it was in front of it that he reined up his horse.

The Master of Cassillis was in a trap. He knew from the first that he could not escape without serious risk of life; and while blood-letting was never repugnant to him, he was anxious rather to get her ladyship, the Countess, off, than to shine in arms. The first thing to be done, however, was to make the best of the circumstances. The Countess was assisted from her horse and conveyed into the dwelling-house; the horses of the escort were put under cover; and the men were kept in readiness to be moved to the spot where the attack was likely to be made.

Bargany rode round the steading and took in all its details. He thought, first of all, of driving in the gate, which would have been no difficult matter; but he conceived rightly that after this was accomplished, he would be no further on than before. The house itself would be closed against him; his men would be confined in a small compass where they would be exposed to the fire of the enemy; and, equally important, it was quite as easy to assault the house in front as in rear. Previous to beginning operations, he summoned the Master of Cassillis to one of the windows of the dwelling-house.

"Well," asked the Master, as he looked out, "what is it you want? Is it not enough that you have shut us in here, that you must also summon me to your presence?"

"Would it not be better," replied Bargany, "that you should wait to hear what I have to say ere you proceed to revile me? You know you are in my power."

"I know nothing of the kind," was the answer. "I know that you have caught us in a trap from which we cannot escape; but to be shut up is one thing, and to be captured, another. You must take us if you want us, for we are not going to give ourselves up.

"We shall see to that bye-and-bye," replied Bargany, "I am anxious to save life, not to take it. But I am not going to waste time in talking, unless you are prepared to hear what I have to propose."

10

" I am waiting to hear what you have to say," said the Master defiantly.

" Well then, listen. We are not here, I tell you, to take life if we can avoid it, save the life of one man ; and the fault will be yours, not ours, if blood be spilled. We shall protect your life and the life of the Countess of Cassillis, and let your men go free and unharmed, save John Dick, who must die the death for the treacherous wrong he did at the Brockloch Burn, when he foully struck my brother to his undoing. As for you, and the Countess of Cassillis, you must return with me to Bargany, where I shall keep you prisoners until a treaty of peace is concluded, between the Earl of Cassillis and myself. Once that treaty is concluded you shall both be permitted to return to Cassillis, and not a hair of your head shall be injured."

" Is that all you have to propose ? " asked the Master defiantly, " you wish to slay one of my men in cold blood, and to take the Countess of Cassillis and myself prisoners ! And do you expect that we shall be so false to our duty and to our honour as to yield up our charge at your bidding ? "

" I care not," was Bargany's reply, " whether you do or not. But the blood that shall be spilled will lie at your door, not at mine."

" I care not at whose door it lies," retorted the Master, " you have had your answer, and you can come and take us if you dare."

Bargany turned on his heel, and the Master withdrew from the window. To the former, it seemed quite a feasible thing—as no doubt it was—to carry the place by assault. But that mode of attack was open to grave objection. He was really solicitous to save life ; he was anxious that not a hair of the head of the Countess should be harmed ; and he had no wish to risk the lives of his own men when it could be avoided. So he leisurely surveyed the house a second time, had the heavy gate blocked with rude implements which lay around, so that sudden escape would be an impossibility, and noted that in one of the outhouses was a large door opening on the outer wall, which it was necessary to watch, in order to prevent any sudden rush for freedom. The defenders were clustered together in the dwelling house, which was best adapted for defence; and here they were prepared, as he knew, to give him and his a hot reception.

The Laird of Dinmurchie, who waited upon Bargany, discovered the means by which the house was to be reduced without danger to the assailants. The roof was heavily thatched; and though winter rains had soaked the straw, and years had coated it with rude lichens and grasses, he suggested to Bargany the ·possibility, if not of burning out the Master and his party, at least of smoking them out. A stack of hay stood outside the steading, supplying ready means for effecting the purpose.

No sooner suggested, than orders were given to pile the hay close up to the wall of the house. A score of willing hands were instantly at work; the stack was dismantled and steadily piled up against the wall. The party within could do nothing to ward off the danger, for no sooner did they shew themselves at the windows than a strong force of the men of Bargany covered them with their muskets, and a few well-directed shots drove them into shelter to await further developments.

At length the hay was piled high by the wall; a handful of powder and a flint and steel were brought into operation; and a loud shout informed the Master of Cassillis that the flame had caught, and that the danger was increasing. Bargany stood quietly and watched the progress of the fire. Slowly it made its way into the heart of the hay; a dense volume of smoke betokened that the material, while not sufficiently wet to resist the attack of the flames, was still damp enough to prevent them leaping up at a bound and exhausting their fury in fruitless attempts to attain the end for

which they had been kindled; and in a few minutes the house
was wreathed in dense white smoke, which found every chink
in the window frames, and permeated every apartment within.
Pile upon pile of fresh material was added to the heap. The
forked tongues of fire licked the thatch on the roof and
played upon the walls; and within twenty minutes from the
time the light was applied, the roof was in flames.

Out from the dense smoke the defenders fired frequent
volleys, which were returned by the men without, who kept
up a constant fire from their guns, riddling the windows and
blowing away the wet thatch in order to let the conflagration
have better play.

The Master of Cassillis, realising the danger of his followers
being either suffocated or roasted to death, took hurried consultation with the tenant of Auchensoul, who saw with dismay
the flames destroy the roof which had so long sheltered him
and his family, and learned from him that the only possible
defence was the courtyard behind, where a stand might be
made, and whence there was some faint hope of escape. They
accordingly evacuated the dwelling and retreated to the yard.
The entrance was blocked; but there was still the large gateway in the outer wall of the barn, which must be utilised in
an emergency. Fortunately the wind blew from the rear of
the steading, and the volume of smoke rolled away down the
hill.

At best the shelter could only be temporary. Escape must
be made at once if it was to be made at all. The horses were
brought from the barn and mounted; the tenant of the farm
stood ready to throw open the large door which was to let the
besieged out into the open country; and all was ready for the
rush by which alone anything like safety was possible. But
this was not to be. Bargany was growing steadily more and
more impatient; and ere the Master of Cassillis, with the
Countess and their escort, could escape, he had the barriers
removed from the gate which hung across the entrance, and

the gate itself driven in. Then there was a furious rush by the besiegers; and the Master, instead of gaining the open country, found himself face to face with the irate chief of Bargany and his men.

Bargany attacked the Master with characteristic impetuosity; his followers rushed in pellmell behind him; and pouring upon the men of Cassillis in much superior force, they made their assault with a fury which could take no denial. The Master of Cassillis was knocked from his horse and fell to the ground bleeding freely from a nasty gash on his forehead; and though the tenant of Auchensoul threw open the door by which exit had been planned, it was too late to enable the Countess, who stood bye watching the encounter and unable to help herself, to effect her escape. Two or three of the Cassillis retainers, however, dashed out into the open country. One of these was John Dick, who, knowing the fate that was intended for him, galloped his horse into the smoke, which still rolled away, dense and impervious, from the burning house, and disappeared down the hill. Nor was his disappearance noted until it was too late to effect his capture.

The combat over, Bargany turned to the Countess, who apparently calm, but inwardly perturbed, sat on her horse an unwilling spectator of the scene. Gladly would she have made her escape, but she knew not what to do, or whither to turn. Her brother-in-law lay senseless on the ground, the blood streaming from the gash in his forehead; and of the men who composed her escort, some were already out of reach, and the remainder powerless for good. What could she do? The Fates had been against her; and recognising her helplessness, she welcomed Bargany's approach. He raised his cap from his head in salute; then reaching out his hand, he grasped the bridle rein of her horse and led her forth from the courtyard. Mure of Cloncaird and the Master of Stair he instructed to see to her safe conduct; and, leaving her in their keeping, he re-entered the square. By his directions the Master of Cassillis was laid under cover on a heap of straw; and this done, he turned to the tenant.

"Auchensoul," he said, addressing the farmer, who looked on his homestead in flames with lachrymose visage, "this has been a bad day's work for you."

"It has, indeed," replied the farmer, "bad enough, in truth."

"Things might always be worse," observed Bargany sententiously.

"They might," was the tenant's reply, "but not much in this case. Who is to repay me for my goods and gear consumed in a fight that never concerned me, and that I do not understand?"

"Providence," responded Bargany, a smile lighting up his features.

"Providence will not put a roof on my house, nor thack it again. I'll have to do it myself."

"Then do it yourself, and come across to Bargany when you have time. Who knows where your providence resides? But, don't you think, Auchensoul, that we might be getting the fire put out, instead of standing talking here—fiddling, like Nero, when Rome was burning."

"'Deed, and I think we might," replied the farmer.

"Now then, men," directed Bargany, addressing both his own men and the followers of the Master of Cassillis, who still remained on the spot, "give your assistance here, and get the fire put out before it catches the steading."

It was not a difficult task, and willing hands were there in plenty. Ladders were placed to the walls of the outhouses, the thatch in the vicinity of the flames was torn off, water was passed up in buckets and dashed upon the fire, which crept slowly up in teeth of the wind; and in half-an-hour more the danger of its spreading further was past.

"So far, so good," observed Bargany, when he saw that there was no danger of the flames regaining their hold; "now, let us see to our prisoners, and then for the banks of the Girvan!"

While the retainers of Cassillis and Bargany were engaged in their conflict with the fire, Mure of Cloncaird and the Master of Dalrymple were doing their best to console the Countess of Cassillis and to make themselves generally agreeable to her. The Master of Stair opened the conversation.

"Be under no apprehension, Lady Cassillis," he said, "your ladyship is in safe hands; for we do not war upon women."

"Though it looks very like it," added Mure of Cloncaird facetiously.

The Countess shrank from the unseasonable pleasantry.

"Do not misunderstand me, madam," continued Cloncaird, "you are indeed in safe hands; and although you may be subjected to some inconvenience, and possibly to a temporary separation from your husband, you will certainly be restored to him ere long."

"That you certainly shall," assented the Master of Stair, "it is only one of the necessities of the situation that we should keep you out of harm's way. There are angry men inside there, in the court-yard, uncultivated and rude, who might not understand the courtesies of life as applied to a lady, were she in their hands. So compose yourself, madam, for you are quite safe."

The Countess made no response to those well-meant but somewhat weak and meaningless generalities; and the two young men, unable to find anything further applicable to the unwonted situation, relapsed into silence, which was maintained until the return of Bargany, who led out his followers, and those of the Master of Cassillis, from the square so lately the scene of conflict. The Master of Cassillis was laid across the back of his own horse, which was led by Dinmurchie, who showed as much attention to the wounded man as was consistent with the circumstances.

Bargany's first act was to bid the retainers of Cassillis go about their business. These needed no second bidding, riding off all the more quickly, perhaps, that they had been deprived of their weapons for reprisal. When they had disappeared, the march to the house of Bargany was at once entered upon. The way was long, the afternoon waning, and these long miles had to be crossed ere the tired men and horses, and the more than tired Countess of Cassillis, could hope for rest. The Master of Cassillis continued unconscious. It was a long ride, a rough ride; but stop or stay was there none. Night met them as they descended towards the valley of the Girvan. By that time the worst of the journey had been accomplished; what remained was comparatively good, though, save relatively, it was bad enough.

The laird of Bargany rode by the side of the Countess. He was busy with his own thoughts; he knew that she was busy with hers, and he did not want to take the initiative in breaking in upon her meditations which, he knew, could not well be otherwise than unpleasant. For a time after leaving Barr, and while the horses toiled up the steep ascents, she retained silence; but when night came down, its companionship made her the more lonely, and she broke the ice.

"What is the meaning of all this, Bargany?" she asked.

Bargany bade his companions and followers ride on a little in front, and turned to the Countess to reply.

"What do you mean by this?" again she asked.

"I think the meaning is very clear, Lady Cassillis. Do you think that I am likely to undertake such a risk as this without a meaning, and a very clear meaning too? I am only sorry that it should have been necessary to incommode and to frighten your ladyship as we have been compelled to do."

"Compelled! What compulsion, pray, was it that bade you way-lay a harmless woman and carry her off captive?"

"The compulsion of stern necessity."

"You will excuse me if I do not comprehend you, or your

meaning, Sir. But are you not aware of what the consequences of this ride may be to you?"

"Quite, Madame. I am quite aware of what the consequences may be. I reckoned with them beforehand. I know perfectly well that the Earl of Cassillis may never forgive me for what I have done; it would be contrary to reason to expect that he should. I know that he may try to involve me in ruin by every means within his power. He has tried it already, partly succeeded and partly failed. He has had me put to the horn—outlawed; but here I am in spite of horning, and here I intend to remain. Until now, I admit, he has had the advantage; but, from this on, the game is mine."

"The game yours? How so?"

"Yes, the game is mine. You are in my possession; you are henceforth the key to the situation, and with you I shall unlock it, or it will be hard to unlock. The Earl dare not attempt to rescue you by force, because Bargany House is strong when it is strongly held, and because he will be afraid of what the consequences might be to you; therefore, he will have to recover you by treaty, and so long as you are in my hands, I can dictate the terms."

"You think so, perhaps; but you do not know the Earl of Cassillis when you so speak. He will muster the whole of his followers and pull down Bargany House about your ears, ere he consent to trade or traffic for his wife."

"Pardon my differing from your ladyship. There will be no reprisal, and no attempt at armed reprisal, so long as you are in my hands. It is unreasonable to think otherwise."

"Perhaps it is; but what do you expect to gain by thus stealing an innocent lady, who has never done you any harm?"

"What do I hope to gain? Much, madam. I anticipate that through your influence and your husband's, the sentence of outlawry will be cancelled, and that is worth a bold attempt. The Estates will not care how peace in Carrick is brought about, so long as it is brought about. They will leave us to arrange matters for ourselves, if only we arrange them. Then, I anticipate that your husband will come under honourable obligations to cease from his eternal efforts to traduce me in high quarters, and that we shall be able to put a lasting check on his efforts to obtain supreme power in Carrick by putting his foot on the neck of every laird and squire in it. I hope, too, as good may come out of evil, that this fratricidal strife which keeps Carrick in a chronic condition of unrest may be brought to a close, and that hereafter we may be able to live in peace and let one another alone."

"Well, if you succeed in bringing about peace, I will never regret it. But," continued the Countess, "tell me this, Bargany—Is not the hand of Auchendrane with you in this?"

"In what?" asked Bargany. "In the longing for a cessation of the feud?"

"No, in this enterprise which has ended so disastrously for me."

"I assume the responsibility, Lady Cassillis, for all that I do. Auchendrane can answer for himself."

"And what is to be done with me, meanwhile?"

"Meanwhile you will be the guest of my mother—and that ought to be sufficient assurance that you will be well done by, and your person duly respected. I am sorry to have to take you, contrary to your will, to Bargany; but the duration of your captivity depends entirely upon your husband. Meanwhile you will be well provided for, and everything will be done to make your sojourn as pleasant as the untoward circumstances will allow."

The conversation was maintained at intervals during the remainder of the journey. Night was sitting upon the hills when the party reached Bargany House. Lady Bargany heard the horse-hoofs. Her son's absence had reawakened the uneasiness which his return from the Borders had temporarily dissipated; and she hurried into the hall to welcome him home. Great was her surprise to see him assist a lady from her horse. What could this mean? A passing suspicion shot into her mind that her son had been playing the part of a Lochinvar and had brought home a bride; but as the struggling light fell on the face of a lady past mid-life, whose countenance betokened weariness and anxiety, the suspicion fled.

"Mother," said Bargany, after he had responded to the maternal greeting, "this is the Countess of Cassillis."

Lady Bargany could do nothing but stare. If there was mystery before, here was double mystery indeed. The Countess of Cassillis—the wife of the sworn enemy of her house—what fate had blown her hither? Bargany dismissed her perplexity.

"She is our guest, mother—an unwilling guest, so far as she is concerned. She has fallen captive," he added, laughing, "to my sword and to my bow."

"Oh, Thomas!" was all Lady Bargany could say. But she led the Countess within, and did her duty as a hostess, though still sorely wondering at it all.

The Master of Cassillis was all but spent and lifeless when they lifted him from his horse; but he was borne to a chamber in one of the upper storeys, carefully and tenderly. Not till this was done, nor until the Countess' immediate wants had been seen to, had Lady Bargany an opportunity of exchanging confidences with her son.

"How could you do it, Thomas?" she asked, anxiously.

"Don't ask me, mother, how. I have done it, you see. I shall tell you all my motives bye-and-bye; in the meantime, I have the Master of Cassillis here, sorely wounded, and all but dead. You will see to him—you are an adept in wounds. See to him then, mother, without loss of time."

Lady Bargany needed no further adjuration. She was, as her son had said, an adept in wounds. Wonder it would have been had she not, for she was a daughter of the feud, and many a cut and hack she had treated since her girlhood. She lost no time in seeing to the wounded Master's immediate requirements.

The following morning saw the Master of Cassillis out of danger. He was so weak he could not raise his head from his pillow. The wound was deep, but not in any way vital; and it was only a question of time and of nursing when he should be himself again. He was a born soldier, and took the bitter with the sweet with the greatest equanimity. Withal, however, he was unmistakably thankful, though he would never have confessed it to his host, that Bargany had spared his life; but he wondered why a man against whom he had fought, and who held in his hand the keys of life and death, so far as he was concerned, should not have left him to his fate, or settled it at once and for ever when he had the chance. Escape, even if he were well, he knew to be impossible; so he lay thinking what Bargany's object could be in treating him so tenderly. Had the situations been reversed, he said to himself that he would not so have acted—though, not improbably, he was doing himself wrong in such a self-confession; but, wonder as he might, he could make nothing out of it. But he steeled his heart to kindness, and fortified himself with the assurance that the feud was a necessity of his being, and that this was only a break in its active continuance.

For two or three days Bargany left him to his meditations, and it was not until he was sufficiently recovered from his wounds to take gentle exercise in the chamber in which he was confined, that he received a visit from his host.

Bargany, with all his rough, impetuous demeanour, and fearlessness in combat, was yet in his own way thoughtful and politic. He had none of the low cunning of Mure of Auchendrane; he preferred to go straight to his ends, and was impatient of double-dealing. But when he had a distinct advantage, as he had now, he recognised his advantage, and tried to make the most of it. It would be too much to say that he was as yet quite tired of feuds and of alarms—he had been born to them—but he had an undefined longing for some kind of rest.

Rest! He had never known since he came to the years of manhood what it was to rest. The Bargany side of the Carrick feud had been instilled into him since ever he was a child. His nurse had told him of the glories of his race, and recounted to him the brave deeds of his ancestors. As a boy he had heard how his forbears had ridden across the moat by which he played, to fight and to foray, and he had resolved to fight and to foray, too, when he grew up to be a man. He had kept his word. Young he still was, but he had fought and bled. He had been beaten, and he had been victorious; he had fled, travel-stained and weary, on jaded steed, before his foes; and he had pursued them with shout and yell and fury. He had done desperate deeds; he had suffered for them. So while he was hardened to the life, he was weary of it. It had its charms for him, and no man could say that he did not rush to the combat as to the banquet; but the perpetual, depressing knowledge that his life was unsafe, that he was an outlaw, that at any moment dire revenge might claim him as its own, was beginning to have its effect.

And when he entered the chamber from whose window the Master of Cassillis looked out upon the setting sun as it dipped behind the hills and the woods which shut out the coast-line and the sea beyond, it was with a genuine longing, though unconfessed at the time, that he might, by the aid of his prisoners, bring about the dawn of an era of peace between the rival houses of Carrick, and restore the stretching country-side to something like quiet and repose.

It was not a hopeful enterprise that suggested itself to him; but he must pursue his scheme now; else the capture of the Countess and the Master of Cassillis was worse than useless.

———

CHAPTER XII.

BARGANY ENLISTS A NEW ALLY.

"You are my guest, you know," observed Bargany as he entered the room where the Master of Cassillis was busy pondering over the why and wherefore of his position, " you are my guest, you know, though, I dare swear, you are not a willing guest."

"That you may safely swear," was the Master's reply, "and not risk your soul over it either. But I am not your guest, but your prisoner."

"That depends exactly upon how you are inclined to look at it. You are my guest thus far, that I am taking good care of you."

"Yes, fattening me up, like the savages, before eating me," snapped the Master with a harsh laugh over the unnatural pleasantry.

"You are my guest, I say," resumed Bargany, not noting the interruption save by the mantling blood which sought out his forehead, "and I am, at least, entertaining you hospitably. You are my prisoner, too, so far as I do not mean to let you go free until I have gained the purpose which impelled me to bring you and the Countess of Cassillis hither."

"Or until you are compelled to let me go, Bargany. You do not think the Earl of Cassillis is asleep all this time?"

"I do not trouble myself wondering whether he is asleep or awake. He may be awake to your undoing; he may be asleep to his own, and your, benefit."

"I do not understand you ; you speak in riddles. But do

you think he will leave me cooped up here like a bird in a cage, and his wife imprisoned in your house in addition, without trying to set us free ?"

" I should not wonder if he were taking things a vast deal more easily than you imagine.   He knows that both you and the Countess are in my power, and he knows, too, what I could do, and what I might do, were I so inclined, both to his wife and you.   He knows that the Kennedys of Cassillis, with all their power, could not harm one standing stone in this house of Bargany.   Your brother reasons like the rest of us—at least, I give him the credit of reasoning like his fellows—and I have sent him word that, so long as he holds his hand, both Lady Cassillis and yourself are safe and sound."

" And if he does not hold his hand ?" queried the Master.

Bargany shrugged his shoulders.

" It will be time enough to answer," he said with à laugh, " when we see him in front of the house."

" You reason naturally," rejoined the Master of Cassillis, looking out of the window, " but you do not know my brother."

" Oh yes, I know him.   Earl and all as he is, he is mortal like the rest of us.   I know him of old.   I have tilted with him more than once.   I have crossed swords with him, and he with me.   I have felt his vengeance, and he has felt the weight of mine.   The spirit is in him to do all you would like done; but he may undo the very thing he is most anxious for unless he is cautious.   In the meantime, you are safe enough, though out of this you cannot go, save as it suits me."

" Why then, if that be so, do you come here to taunt me ?" asked the Master, the warm blood rising to his forehead.

" I did not come here to taunt you, Sir.   I came here to talk with you.   I came to reason with you, and if you are amenable to reason, as I hope you are—as I think you are

—why, you may go away home again as soon as you can mount your horse."

"That would I gladly do, Bargany. Imprisonment is not to my liking, and I prefer the Doon to the Girvan any day. But the terms?'"

Bargany, who had seated himself during the conversation, rose from his chair and walked to and fro in the chamber. Pride was .struggling with the flashes of his better nature. Across his mind swept the memories of all he had suffered from the day when first he rode out to battle a stripling, down to the weary months when he had lain in enforced seclusion in the south country; and but for the whispering of a better angel, he would have closed the converse for ever.

But as he walked, his soul calmed. He had come to say a certain thing. He knew exactly how he was to say it; though, truth to tell, his train of thought was getting knocked off the line by the confusion of ideas and fears and aspirations which pressed upon it. He rallied, however, with an effort, and resumed his seat.

"Be seated, pray," he remarked, addressing the Master, who still stood by the window. The Master assented to the invitation, and sat down.

There was a minute's silence. Bargany hardly dared prosecute his mission.

"Hew," at last he said, with an effort, addressing the Master familiarly, "I am weary of this."

"Weary of this! Weary of what?" asked the Master, surprised at the tone of voice so unfamiliar in Bargany, "you are weary of what?"

"Weary of this perpetual disquiet and unrest. I am weary of fighting and fleeing, and endless plotting, and I want to put an end to it."

There was another pause—a pause that both felt to be awkward. The words had been uttered half-ashamedly.

Bargany had never been good at confession; and the father-confessor whom he had chosen—his kinsman, his enemy, sworn to feud against him, fiery-souled, ready-handed Hew Kennedy of Cassillis, who would have cleft his head sooner than willingly eaten of his bread—was not the man, had there been any choice in the matter, whom he would willingly have selected as his father-confessor. A man thinks quickly, and all the time that Bargany had been speaking he had been wondering what the Master would think of his weakness. Had he a heart to understand that weakness and strength went often together ?

The Master was equally confounded with his host. He could not comprehend the situation; he could not help Bargany out of it, even if he were so inclined. He was as bad a father-confessor as the other was a penitent, and he sat and stared at Bargany, hardly comprehending what he was saying.

"I want to stop it, I say," at length resumed Bargany. "Ever since I was a little boy it has been nothing but fight or flee. Twice have I had to seek shelter beyond Carrick, and twice have I returned to find the country as torn and distracted, as much broken up into factions, as when I left it. You think that I am impelled to this life by my own passions and ambitions! It is not that. I cannot get rid of it; it haunts me, dogs me, drives me on, I come back to Girvan side, and I find things as I left them. My friends are in arms, plotting and counter-plotting, as when I left; and they come to me to fight and to plot with them. I have not the courage to refuse them. I cannot be a recluse when they are working in my cause: and so I take my place at their head, where I ought to be, and fight with the lave. You hear what I say ?"

"Yes, I have heard what you say, Bargany; but your repentance comes late."

"Repentance never comes too late, if it comes in time.

11

But I am not repenting of the past—do not misunderstand me. Let the past alone—it will speak for itself—I only do with the future."

"And wherein does this concern me?" replied the Master. "Do you think the best way to sow the seeds of peace is to make war? Do you think to sow the wind and reap aught save the whirlwind? Do you expect to bring in a reign of peace in Carrick by stealing the wife of your rival, by firing the house of an innocent man, and by flaunting your rivalry to the Earl of Cassillis in the face of day and in sight of all men?"

"That is past, I say. Let it alone, if you can, and listen to what I say," rejoined Bargany hotly, and very unlike the half-penitent, reflective Bargany of a moment before.

"Let it alone if I can! How can I let it alone," demanded the Master of Cassillis, "when I am a prisoner in your house, unable to step beyond these four walls? Let it alone! when the Countess of Cassillis is similarly imprisoned? Go to Cassillis House if you dare, Sir, and make your appeal to the Earl, and see how it will fare with you."

Temper was rising. Bargany smote his hands together.

"A curse on Cassillis House," was his reply, "and on everything about it. No, Sir. The Earl must come to me—not I to him. I would not venture my life within cannon shot of the Doon, without my men behind me, for all the broad lands between this and that."

"Then you had better close your confession, Bargany, or make it to some other body. I'll have no more of it. What do you expect? Am I to forget and forgive the murder of my uncle, Sir Thomas Kennedy of Culzean, in the wood of St. Leonards, or those who smote him so basely? Am I to forget how, but the other day, you drove me from the walls of Newark, and snatched the prey out of my very teeth? Can I forget, Sir, that arch-traitor of hell who has prompted you in all your doing? No, Bargany, I would rather lie on

that bed till the day I died, or hang from your gateway, than
forget or forgive Mure of Auchendrane. I.have sworn his
death—by my Maker, I have sworn it—and, if the executioner does not lead him up the Grassmarket of Edinburgh,
he shall die by this hand, or," added the Master gloomily, "I
shall die by his—or here."

Bargany's mercurial temper underwent another change—a
series of changes, indeed. The peremptory manner in which
his advances had been cut short, nettled him; to have been
so received by a prisoner, and so spoken to, offended his sense
of their relative positions; and his outburst against Auchendrane kindled a feeling which Bargany could not explain,
even to himself. He distrusted Auchendrane; but for him to
distrust him was one thing, for the Master of Cassillis to revile him and to doom him to death, was quite another. He
was still feudal friend to Mure, and he could not bear to hear
the man with whom his destinies had been allied, so
spoken of.

He repented having unburdened himself. Why should he
prolong the interview any further? Why should he not con-
summate his capture of the Master of Cassillis, and hang him
out of hand?   It was a sore conflict that surged in his soul,
and hard to fight it down.   But fight it down he did right
manfully.   He drove the evil spirits out of his mind, and bid
his better angel re-enter.

"Hew," he said, speaking rapidly, and as if afraid that, if
he paused, he would rue again and not be able to command
himself, "I am going to try it at any rate."

"Try what?" was the curt interrogatory.

"Try to have done with this eternal, this infernal warring.
That is what brought me in here to speak with you. Do you
think that I have humbled myself thus without a motive?
God forbid! Bargany has not sacrificed his pride without
knowing why. I mean," he added abruptly, "to let you go."

"How to let me go?"

" To give you your freedom."

" When ? " asked the Master, not affecting to conceal his surprise, " when, and on what terms ? "

" Whenever you are able to ride hence.   I shall send an escort with you as far as the Castle of Maybole—two days hence, if you are able to go so soon.   And what I want you to do is this—tell your brother, the Earl of Cassillis, what I have said to you ; tell him I am willing to bury the past, and let byegones be byegones, if he will but do the same.   If not, tell him I am here to fight him out to the bitter end, to take no quarter to give no quarter.   Tell him that I hold the Countess a hostage, that she is regarded here, and treated, as befits her position, and that, as soon as a treaty of peace for the future is agreed upon, she shall be sent home to him in safety."

The Master of Cassillis was too weak and too excited to pace the room, as he felt inclined to do, but he rose to his feet and looked out of the window for a few moments, as if to catch an inspiration from the nodding trees beyond. His face was pale and bloodless. He cast the matter over in his mind, cogitated over it and looked at it in all its bearings ; but though something whispered a faint echo of peace and good will far down in the depths of his perturbed spirit, he preferred the surface rockings of disappointment and revenge to dictate his reply.   It came slowly, but it came resolutely.

" I cannot take my freedom on · these terms," he said, " and I shall carry no such message hence."

Bargany looked him full in the face.   The Master, undaunted, returned the stare.

" You refuse then to bear my message ? " said the former, constraint ringing in every tone of his voice.

" I do."

" Then, a curse upon your stubbornness," broke out Bargany, driving his constraint to the four winds of heaven.

"What is there to prevent me hanging you up from the gateway to-morrow?"

"Nothing to prevent you doing it now. You have done worse things than that."

"Beware how you tempt me further, sir. Remember that you are my prisoner, and that I can launch you out into eternity whenever it suits my purpose."

"I know you can; but I prefer death now, and here, to interfering with the course of justice."

Bargany bit his lip, and resumed his walk to and fro, in silence. Again the contending hosts of good and evil marched hither and thither in his soul. They gained the ascendancy alternately, first the bad and then the good. He was strung up to a high pitch of excitement, and, had the Master not kept silence, the consummation of his destiny would in all probability have been reached then and there. But the silence was soothing, and reflection and hope dawned anew.

"Yes, I might hang you," were Bargany's words, "and have done with you for ever; but I am no assassin. God never formed me to do work of that kind. I can't kill in cold blood now, and never shall again. Had I killed you at Auchensoul, as I might easily have done, I had not regretted it; but to hang you up like a common felon—that will I never. Yet, why shouldn't I?" he added meditatively, "your brother would do as much for me."

"Aye, that would he, and so would I, were this Cassillis and not Bargany, and you my prisoner and not me yours."

Bargany took time ere he replied decisively.

"No, Hew, you would not."

The words were simply spoken, almost pathetically, and as Bargany uttered them the Master's eyes fell before his straight, unquivering gaze. He waited on his host to resume the conversation.

"We shall speak again of this to-morrow," was all that

Bargany said, as he withdrew from the chamber, and closed the door behind him.

Naturally enough the two young men retired to rest that night with mingled feelings. Bargany was half-ashamed of his weakness, half-angry at having committed himself to the Master of Cassillis, who had so slightingly treated him and his better nature. Had he not been in earnest, deeply, grimly in earnest, he would have closed negotiations with the interview: but he was so resolved to bring about his purpose, that he set-to to devise means by which he could influence the Master to do his bidding.

The Master of Cassillis, on the other hand, was ashamed of his precipitation and temper; and half-fevered he lay tossing on his couch the better part of the night, wondering how far he was in the right, how far he was wrong—to what extent the Earl, his brother, would forgive him for what he had done. He was in temperament not much foreign to that of Bargany. The same blood was in their veins—the same hot, impetuous stream; but there was this difference between them, that while Bargany was honest enough to confess his readiness to have a truce—a perpetual peace, even—the Master was still so dominated by the twin spirits of injury and of revenge that he could not brook to humble himself by purchasing his freedom on any terms whatever. He knew he had done wrong; but he did not, and would not admit it.

What was Bargany to do? The initiative lay still with him. Was he to accept the inevitable and act on it? Was he to prepare for fresh enterprise? If not, was he to return to the argument? Was he to plead with his captive?

It was easy to settle that. He was not to plead.

Bargany was strong-willed and determined, and he resolved to try again, but by other means. If he failed this time, let the blood rest where it ought to rest.

Early the following day the laird of Bargany went out to commune with nature. He wanted solitude. There is no

solitude like the company of nature. It is a real companionship, unobtrusive, yet felt; voiceless, yet responsive. There
is a sympathy in the glades, dark in shadow, with the wind
whispering in the tree tops and rustling through the pine
boughs, monotonous, yet never wearisome. The stretching
uplands are sympathetic as they rise away in the distance
and present their familiar panorama of beauties; and the
river, as it runs or ripples or dashes seawards, sings its song
of sympathy to the ear of him who has a heart open to response.

Bargany took his way to the winding banks of Girvan. On
his one hand ran the river, brown and drumlie from the
rains which had fallen amid the hilly solitudes of Barr; on
the other rose a thick pine wood in whose depths he had
often wandered, and every notable tree in which he knew by
head mark. They were old friends of his, those trees. He
had played among them as a boy; he had nested in their
branches; and now, as he walked under their shadow, they
stretched out to him their long drooping arms, and waved
gently in the breeze to him, as if in recognition of the sympathy which he had come out to find. The estate which he
owned lay all around him, though beyond its confines to the
south and east he could descry the uplands of the Earl of
Cassillis. He went slowly, and he went pensively. He was
not thinking of the landscape. The song of the birds fell unheeded on his ears; the startled rabbit scurried and scamp-
ered into his burrow unseen; and the royal salmon leaped in
the river's pools without evoking any trace of longing in the
mind of the sportsman.

Bargany was still on his errand of the future, still determined, notwithstanding his interview with the Master of
Cassillis, to accomplish his purpose.

He spent the greater part of the forenoon roaming at
large; and mid-day had passed ere he received the inspiration
he was in search of. Why not negotiate through the

Countess of Cassillis? Strange—he had never thought of that before. What more natural than that she would sympathise with his longing for repose? The times must be out of joint to her as well as to him; she must be anxious to return home; and it would be unnatural were she so bent on seeing the issue fought out to its conclusion as not to lend her offices to inaugurate a peace that could not do otherwise than add to her future happiness.

No sooner had he resolved on invoking the aid of Lady Cassillis than he retraced his steps to the House of Bargany and obtained an interview with the captive Countess.

"Good morrow, Lady Cassillis," he observed with a brusque cheery air, which sat naturally on him, though for the moment it was assumed, "I hope your ladyship is enjoying your sojourn among the bonnie woods of Bargany."

"I must even endure it," was the Countess's reply, "if I cannot cure it; though, in faith, I would rather dwell in the Dalrymple forest than here by the banks of the Girvan. But to what chance do I owe the honour of this visit?"

"To no chance, madam. I have come hither on set purpose; and if you will but grant me permission I will e'en tell you my errand."

The Countess inclined her head in consent that Bargany should proceed, and he repeated in substance what he had said to the Master of Cassillis the previous evening. His words this time did not fall on deaf ears, or hardened heart. They fell upon good ground, and at once took root.

The Countess of Cassillis was not a young woman. Before her husband was born she had been wife to the Chancellor of Scotland. Quarter of a century ago she had held carnival in the halls of Edinburgh, and had trodden in state the oaken floors of Holyrood. Knights and earls of high degree had bowed low to her; and she had possessed the graces and enjoyed the charms of society. She knew what it was to intrigue. She had seen many a plot hatched, and many a plot unravelled. The rudeness of west country life was strange to her; and distasteful as it was unfamiliar.   It was not that strife and broil were total strangers to her; but she had now reached that age when a longing for rest came natural, and when the ceaseless call to arms and to reprisal had done more than pall upon her.   She had resolved in her own mind how to effect a reunion of the rival houses of Kennedy; and as Bargany pleaded his cause, not for his sake, but for hers, and for the country devastated by the long feud, she reciprocated his advances and encouraged his hopes.

Her brow clouded when he told her how he had been received by the Master of Cassillis.

"Hew is a fiery-headed youth," she said; "but Hew," she added proudly, "is not the Earl of Cassillis."

"True," replied Bargany; "but he is not a retainer of Cassillis either; and it is not a year ago since he was plotting with Auchendrane against his own brother."

"True also, but he can be reasoned with.   He is hot-headed and intemperate in language; but, I think, could I but see him, that I should be able to gain him to our side."

"You gratify me, indeed, Lady Cassillis, when you speak of our side.   It is many a day since such words have been used by a Kennedy of Cassillis to a Kennedy of Bargany.

"Still it is not too late to use them; and could I but see the Master I think I could bring him to see as we do."

"You may see him now, if you like," replied Bargany, "though, I warn you, you may not find him quite as tractable as you wish."

"Very likely not," was the Countess' answer; "intractable men are not always the worst to deal with.   You have not been so very tractable, I think, yourself, Bargany, if all stories be true."

Bargany laughed.   "No," he replied, "perhaps not; but you know that I have not been surrounded by very tractable neighbours, and a man is very much what circumstances make him."

"That is quite true, as a rule; but the Master of Cassillis has all along tried to rule circumstances to his own advantage; and therein lies the difficulty in dealing with him."

Once the Countess of Cassillis had deferred to the request of Bargany, and promised to lend her aid to the undertaking which was to ensure a happier future in Carrick, Bargany felt quite relieved. He had noted—and it had given him secret satisfaction—that his mother and she, thrown together by untoward circumstances, were rapidly entering into one another's good graces.

A door of hope was opening up to Lady Bargany, and she was greedy to enter in. It had not been ever thus with the rival houses of Carrick. When, thirty years before, Lady Bargany had come to Girvan side, a sprightly, beautiful bride, the feud had not arisen. Earl Gilbert's authority was undisputed. He was the head of the house of Kennedy, and then acknowledged as such by the progenitor of the present laird of Bargany; and often she had walked by the Doon in company with the mother of the present Earl and enjoyed the hospitality which Cassillis was so rich in affording. For ten years times had been altered. The feud had grown in its dimensions until it had swept in all the smaller lairds and barons between the town of Ayr and the confines of Galloway. The first born son of Lady Bargany had fought with the husband of Lady Cassillis, had way-laid him, had conspired against him, and had been outlawed for the conspiracy; and, finally, had ridden out from Ayr one stormy winter day to meet his fate at the hands of the Earl by the Brockloch Burn.

Lady Bargany remembered all this. There dangled, too, before her mental vision, the banner of revenge, which had been borne before the bier of her ill-starred son. What wonder if, amid all the dignity with which she entertained the captive Countess, there nestled deep the sad memories of the decade which had gone, and if even she felt a trace of triumph that the wife of the greatest enemy of her race was a prisoner within the walls of her home? If, however, there lurked the shadow of such a satisfaction, the Countess of Cassillis was none the wiser of it.

The memories of the Countess were of a different kind; they were neither so far-reaching nor so inwrought, but they were imbedded in a softer nature. The kinsmen and the followers of her husband had indeed fallen victims to the men of Bargany, but her own roof-tree had been left untouched. The angel of death had not fanned the peel by the banks of the Doon with his shadowy pinions. None the less, however, was she weary of the troubled state of Ayrshire society and of the storms which rolled from the Doon to the Girvan, and from the Girvan far beyond Glenluce and Glenassel, into the very heart of Galloway. It did not consort with her ideas; and she undertook her mission to the Master of Cassillis not only full of the importance of her office, but fired with the determination to carry out her mission to a peaceful conclusion.

It was in this spirit that she entered the chamber where the Master of Cassillis sat, half-reproachful, half-revengeful, wholly susceptible to judicious light and leading.

CHAPTER XIII.

HUNG FROM THE YETT OF CRAIGNEIL.

WHEN the Countess of Cassillis entered the room tenanted by her brother-in-law, Bargany went out into the evening to soothe his mind in solitude. He strode restlessly up and down, in front of the house, deep in his thoughts, seeking by active exertion to relieve the strain which oppressed him within doors. He was fearful lest his plans should prick like a bubble and vanish in thin air; and in this fear what troubled him most was his self-humiliation in the presence of the Master of Cassillis. How the Master himself would laugh at his scruples, and pursue his ends all the more daringly and desperately on the faith of his weakening in the contest! How Carrick side would stand amazed when tidings ran along it, that the bold Bargany was weary of the fight!

He had his solace. The natural man was not dead yet, and it was he who supplied the consolation. The Master of Cassillis was not a free man. These strong walls held him captive, and would hold him captive till the day he died, unless he consented to do his bidding. There were human bones in the dungeon keep—what was there to prevent their multiplication? In any case, out of this he would never go save on an errand of peace. As for the Countess, he had more hope in her. He believed she was as much in earnest as he was himself. Still, she must either go hence a hostage of peace, or remain where she was until it suited his purpose to let her go free. So long as he held her he held the Earl safe—for, fret as the lord of Cassillis might, he was helpless for revenge when the very consummation of his revenge might involve the death of his wife.

Seriously, Bargany never thought of wreaking vengeance on the life of the Countess; but he hardly knew, as his thoughts chased one another in rapid succession, what he might have to do ere the clouds were cleared away, or broke in hurricane.

The shadows of the castle and trees made sombre the secluded spot. The moon glanced out occasionally at the scene, and lighted up the strong battlements and the little barred windows, and deepened the shadows until they became suggestive. The wind rustled in the trees, and the music of the whispering pines found echo in the rapid flow of the river which ran seawards past the walls of the Castle. The spot was one for thought, because history brooded over it; Nature's accessories deepened the thought itself.

Bargany sometimes varied his sentry-like tread to and fro in front of the Castle, by gazing out into the night. His gaze was all but an unconscious one. He heard the wind, he heard the river's flow, he heard the murmuring trees, but he heard them not. They were mournful in their plaintiveness, and, unknown to himself, they sent their influence into his presently impressible mind.

As thus he walked, or paused to wrestle mentally with some new phase of his thoughts, his quick ear detected at a distance the sound of horse hoofs. These were far away, but the air was still and resonant, and neither moaning wind, nor flowing river, nor whispering pines made the sound less distinct. Nature's sounds were pervading,—the horse hoofs penetrated through them and came up on the night with gathering clearness.

Bargany was accustomed to night alarms, and was not easily driven from his propriety; but as the nearing sounds grew more distinct he forbore to speculate on the chances of the interview going on within, and turned his attention to the horseman who, familiar with the approach to the castle, cantered rapidly up the avenue. He wondered who and whence he was—what he portended. Was it a call to arms, or did the rider bear good tidings? Were the men of Cassillis on the march?

A cloud flitted across his brow as he thought that the Earl had summoned his retainers and was, perhaps even now, on his way to attempt the rescue of his captives. If they were —but no, he dismissed the thought. The walls were thick, and he could speculate afterwards.

Something told him that the horseman was the bearer of tidings. He was not simply some benighted groom hastening homewards,

As Bargany turned over his hopes and fears the rider drew near and laid his speculations to rest. He was not one of his own retainers. He was servant to the Master of Stair, and had followed his leader in the affair at the Brockloch Burn. He had been present at Auchensonl farmhouse when Bargany had fired its timbers, and when the Countess and the Master of Cassillis were taken prisoners.

Bargany walked forward to greet him as he drew rein in front of the house and saluted him with brief remark.

"You have ridden hard, Walter!"

"I had need to ride hard," was the reply. "Murder hastens our goings."

"Murder hastens our goings! What do you mean? You come from home?"

"Yes—the Master of Stair is murdered!"

Bargany was not unaccustomed to tidings of murder and rapine, and had he been in a more bellicose frame of mind than he was he would have accepted the intelligence with that equanimity that spelt Revenge; but in his present distracted condition he was dazed, and could only re-echo the servant's words.

"The Master of Stair murdered! Tell me, is that so?"

"It is too true, sir."

"Tell me how?" Bargany said, bracing himself into composure.

The horseman jumped from off his horse, which stood panting and flecked with foam, his heaving sides telling how hard he had been ridden.

"Walter," remarked Bargany, as he glanced at the jaded animal, "take the horse round to the stables, see that it is cared for, and return here as soon as you can. I will wait your return."

The servant obeyed. He led his horse round to the stables and delivered him in charge to one of the grooms, who undertook to see to his comfort.

On the return of Walter to the front of the Castle he found Bargany, as he had left him, peering out into the night. He had regained his composure, and, though deeply interested and as deeply affected, he betrayed his feelings neither by word nor look. The Bargany of a few minutes before had disappeared; the old Bargany, grim and resolute, hardened to hard times, had taken his place.

"Let us sit here, Walter," he said, as he motioned the servant of his late friend to a rude oaken seat close by the doorway, "the night is fine."

Walter obeyed. He seated himself on the rough but not uncomfortable bench, and without waiting permission from Bargany told his story.

"It took place only this morning," he said, "just as the day broke. Last evening the Master bade me harness his old black charger. You know the horse. Many a time I have told him he ought not to ride that horse. Six years ago when he was in his prime he was a good, sound, speedy animal; but his best days were past, and in these times and in this country a man, when he is mounted, ought to be well mounted. Else, he should go on foot. I put the harness on the horse as he bade me, and he rode away. By his order I went with him, though I took care what horse it was that I bestrode. It was that chestnut I rode to-night. He was at Auchensoul the other day. You know the horse?"

Bargany nodded assent.

"Well, we rode as far as the Yett of Craigneil, and had all but completed our distance from home when, as we rounded the sharp turn of the road below Craigneil, we were all at once face to face with the Earl of Cassillis, and at least two score of his men."

"Ah," said Bargany, warming in interest, "say you so?"

"As soon as the Master saw them," continued the servant, "he called to me to fly, and turned his horse's head as quickly as he could. We had hardly got our horses well away ere the

Earl himself discovered who we were, and gave instant orders to have us caught and taken back to him. We were determined not to be caught. The Master had his pistols; and as we rode off he drew one of them out of the holster and held it in his hand ready for use. I had no weapons, save a short sword, which was useless; but I knew that unless I was shot, I could not be taken, because the chestnut has not his marrow in horse-flesh in all the country side. The Earl's men at once gave chase. The old charger seemed to know he carried life or death on his back and he struggled on gamely, but we had not ridden a quarter of a mile before I saw that we must be overtaken. "Fly, Walter, fly for your life," said the Master, "never mind me." I told him I could not leave him, but at his request I kept a little ahead of him so that I could make my escape if worst came to the worst. As the Cassillis men came on, riding and shouting like demons, the Master looked behind, and saw that the first man in the chase was John Dick."

Bargany muttered an oath between his clenched teeth. It was John Dick who had given the fatal stroke to his brother that winter day by the Brockloch Burn.

"He waited until Dick was less than a dozen of yards from him, when, turning round, he fired full in his face. The shot was true. Dick reeled in his saddle and fell, never to rise again."

"Thank God for that at least!" said Bargany as he breathed a sigh of relief. "What then?"

"Why, then we rode on as hard as we could, till the old charger could go no further. The Master pressed him to the top of his speed, but as he struggled gamely he plunged forward and fell, throwing the Master half a dozen yards ahead of him. Before he could rise he was surrounded. I could do nothing. To have waited meant two men caught instead of one. So I gave the chestnut the rein and hurried home as fast as he could gallop. The Cassillis men followed me hard, but I soon left them out of sight and escaped."

"You escaped? Why did you not stay and die with him?"

"A living man," replied Walter, doggedly, "is worth ten dead men. If I had stayed, I would not have been here now to tell you."

"True, Walter, you are quite correct—what then?"

"I do not know exactly how it all happened; but they threw the Master of Stair, wounded and bruised, across the back of his own horse and led him back to Craigneil, where the Earl of Cassillis was waiting his coming. They kept him all night in the vault of Craigneil Castle. This morning the Earl gave him an assize and hanged him to the yett. He died, I hear, as he lived, true to the last. The Earl tried to make him swear fealty to him and to his, and to persuade him to turn traitor on you, but he scouted his requests with indignation, and declared that he would rather die ten times than turn against Bargany."

"Poor Dalrymple!" ejaculated Bargany, a feeling of sorrow stealing into his heart and softening his voice.

"That is all I have to tell," observed the servant, rising, "and, if it please you, I shall ride home again."

"Who sent you here?"

"The Laird of Stair; and he bade me warn you to be on your guard."

"You must not go home to-night. Rest here till to-morrow—if I want you I shall send for you—if not, you can go at daylight."

Walter did not think of questioning Bargany's instructions. He returned to the stables to see his favourite chestnut and to spend the remainder of the evening, previous to snatching a brief repose, in the society of the grooms, to whom he related his story with magnified detail, and with unstinted praise of the horse which was now resting from his hard run.

Left alone, dark thoughts crept into the mind of the young Laird of Bargany. His better angel fled the scene.

It was hardly to be wondered at. At no great distance

12

from his own door his mortal enemy had slain his most trusty
associate, his most intimate friend. With two score of horsemen at his back he had ridden along the very march of Bargany. His purpose had not been, the Laird of Bargany knew,
to slay the Master of Stair—it had been deeper than that;
and he felt that he himself had nothing to hope for, save from
his own bold heart, his strong arm, his staunch and fearless
retainers.

Revenge breeds revenge. To sue the Earl of Cassillis for
peace and friendship was no longer to be thought of. Bargany felt that he had demeaned himself in even soliciting the
kind offices of his prisoners. So far as the Master of Cassillis
was concerned, the secret of his heart-opening, his confession,
must die; and with the death of the secret, another death
must eventuate.

Once started on a train of thought such as this, Bargany
fell to plotting his revenge. He would retain the Countess
captive in his own house where help she could have none;
and scour the country of the Cassillis Kennedys to wreak
vengeance. He would strike at the Earl himself, and by one
grand stroke rid himself of his most dangerous foe, and rival.

"Truce! there must be no truce now," said Bargany to
himself, his revengeful animation manifesting itself in his
hurried stride and clenched hands. "What would be said of
the laird of Bargany were he to sue for peace now? Dalrymple's blood cries from the ground and its cry is not
unheard."

Yet, withal, a feeling of sorrow, deep and oppressive,
welled up in his breast. His hopes had suddenly been dashed
to the ground, and he saw stretching away before him a
succession of alarms, of fights, of forays. Still for the moment he had the key to the position. His captives were more
valuable than five score of mounted warriors; and so long as
he held them he held the powerful Earl of Cassillis in a
leash.

As he turned to the entrance hall and strode over its oaken floor, it was with a heart hardened for whatever was to happen. The world might buffet him and his; he would buffet the world as best he could. And as his world was confined to Carrick, his determination boded no good to the bailiary.

Bad news spreads with proverbial rapidity. The servant of the Master of Stair told the grooms and the men-at-arms, who, as was the custom of the times, resided in the baronial keep of Bargany, of the fate that had befallen his master; and ere the Laird himself strode angrily into the house, every man and woman, from Lady Bargany down to the humblest menial in the dwelling, were talking or pondering over the event, and speculating as to the course likely to be taken by the fiery young chieftain.

His mother's heart failed her as she thought—and natually thought, and from experience—how he would estimate his duty in relation to the cruel tragedy. She trembled for her captives; for dutiful and loving son as she had, she knew the code of honour of the times, by which he was all but certain to regulate his conduct. As for the men-at-arms, they callously counted on action, and their spirits rose with the anticipated excitement.

Lady Bargany sat by the fireside of the old dining-hall. She laid her embroidery down on her knees, and, gazing into the warm light of the ruddy flames which roared up the wide chimney, was lost in thought. An hour ago she was hopeful and expectant—now she was expectant and fearful.

Again, as if it had happened but yesterday, she saw, in imagination, her eldest son ride out through the snow-drift from the town of Ayr, high in heart and indomitable in resolution; she heard the sounds of the conflict on the hillside, the clash of arms, the shouts of the combatants; she saw her son ride dourly up the ascent from the Brockloch Burn; and then the assault, the hand-to-hand encounter, the cruel stroke

of the lance, the reeling chieftain.   She stood by his bedside
in Ayr, and watched, in imagination, his spirit as it winged
its flight from the scene of his conflicts and his battles; she
saw his remains brought home to the house and to the very
room in which she sat, and she remembered how silence came
down over the dwelling, how dimly the tapers burned, how
poignant her grief.   Again she followed in the long cortege
which wended its way down the bleak valley of the Stinchar
in the dead of winter, and again she stood in the vault where
the dead chiefs of Bargany lay waiting resurrection.   And
now that Thomas had taken the place of the young warrior
who slept all so soundly—what if this fresh tragedy should
fire him to re-enter the lists of combat, and to pursue anew the
course which had wrought so disastrously to the House of
Bargany ?

It was with anxiety depicted on every feature, an anxiety
that sprang from the deepest recesses of her soul, that she
raised her eyes to the gloom-darkened face of her son as he
threw open the door and entered the room.   He seated himself by the fire opposite the chair in which Lady Bargany sat,
and, as she had done a minute before, fixed his eyes upon the
flames as they danced upwards, and resumed his cogitations.
His mother was wise, as such a mother had need to be, and,
instead of interrupting him, she resumed her embroidery, and
worked away in silence as if all unconscious of his presence.

Some natures are best left to vent themselves at home,
upon themselves.   Bargany's was one of these.   His mind
was a veritable tempest, torn, distracted by fast-flying thoughts
and by hasty but determined resolutions.   It was terribly
active.   What should he do, and do first ?

Bye and bye he emerged from his mental exclusiveness.

"Mother," he said, "you had better tell the Countess of
Cassillis never to mind prolonging her interview with the
Master.   It will come to nought."

"Why so, Thomas?" was the reply.

"Because there is no need for it. I have changed my mind. I want no conciliation. The Master of Stair has been murdered."

"I have heard the news," replied Lady Bargany quietly.

"I thought you had," said Bargany after a brief pause.

Lady Bargany kept silence until he spoke again.

"You know all that this means, mother?"

"No, Thomas, I do not. But tell me," she added, "what you mean?"

"What ought I to mean? What can I mean but the one thing? I mean to hang the Master of Cassillis and to keep the Countess a close prisoner until I have had my revenge. I mean to do by Cassillis himself as he has done by the Master of Stair; and I mean to lose no time over it either."

"Thomas," said his mother quietly, and without any outward emotion, "why should the death of the Master of Stair, sad as it is, stimulate you to such revengeful feelings?"

"Because he would do to me what he has done to Dalrymple, if he had the chance. Because it is no use now crying peace, or hoping peace. Because I am not willing that he should ride rough-shod over me and treat me as a vassal instead of a kinsman; and because I have sworn revenge."

"Sworn revenge? To whom?"

"To myself. I was a fool when I allowed myself to hope for a change for the better. I am a fool no more."

"Oh, Thomas," said Lady Bargany, "why do you allow your worse nature to overcome you? An hour or two ago you cast a bright light over my pathway. God knows it has been dark enough these years—why becloud it anew?"

"Not I, mother. I do not becloud it. But the very ashes of my father and my brother would rise up in the judgment and condemn me if I broke faith with my own honour and their memory. I have allowed myself to forget the banner of revenge. You know the motto it bore that day my brother was carried to his grave—'Revenge my cause, O Lord.' "

" I do not forget it. But why not leave the revenge to God ? Vengeance is His, and He will repay," said Lady Bargany, unconsciously repeating almost word for word, the language of the Countess of Cassillis to her husband, months before.

" Yes, and vengeance is mine, and I, too, will repay," replied Bargany, rising from his seat and pacing the floor. " Yes, mother, vengeance is mine, too; and if the Earl of Cassillis come to his grave in peace, it will not be because Thomas Kennedy has forgotten his duty."

Lady Bargany braced herself for an effort. She knew well the fiery, impetuous temper of her boy; but she knew, besides, the better side of his nature, and to that she appealed.

" Thomas," she said, " try for a little to forget the death of the Master of Stair. Remember that the Earl of Cassillis is ignorant of your desire for peace and friendship. He has no reason to think that you do not harbour your old feelings of revenge against him. You and your friends took captive his wife and his brother. You took them prisoners on his own land; you fired the house of one of his tenants; you all but killed the Master of Cassillis. Can you wonder, then, that he has come hither under cover of the evening, or when his spies told him the coast was clear, to ascertain what he might ? Did you expect him to sit quietly in Cassillis House and lament the loss of his wife, until she was sent back to him? What else could you imagine but that he would bestir himself ? The Master of Stair was with you when you took the Countess prisoner—he followed your brother on the day that he was slain near Maybole ; and he filled up the measure by shooting John Dick, by whose hand your brother died. ' Dick deserved his death, Thomas, for he was a traitor. But do you expect the Earl of Cassillis, as I say, to mope at home when he ought to be astir? That is not the way of these Earls of Cassillis, is it?"

"No, mother, by my soul it is not!"

"He has done nothing that you yourself would not have done had you been situated as he is. Has he?"

"No, nothing."

"And is it not more likely that, having had his revenge against the Master of Stair, he would be the readier to come to terms with you?"

"That may be, mother, but Carrick expects me not to fail in my duty; and, besides, I have sworn revenge."

"The Master of Stair has fallen as many a good man has done before him, but to what purpose? And what good can you do even if you succeed in your projects? Do not be rash, Thomas," continued Lady Bargany as she rose from her seat and clasped her son's right hand in both of hers. "Think of what a happy future there might be for you, for me, for the country-side. Why keep two thousand men in continual alarm of fire and sword?"

"Mother, I am not rash. I will not be rash, but neither must I fail in my duty."

"Nor must you break faith. You have promised me that you would make for peace. You have unburdened your mind to the Master of Cassillis, and you have brought the Countess to reason him into acceptance of your proposals. You are trebly pledged."

"Yes, but that was before Dalrymple was murdered. When I have atoned for his death then I will make for peace again."

"It will be too late, Thomas. You must do it now or never."

"Then never be it," replied Bargany, growing firmer in tone as his resolution was being shaken.

Lady Bargany burst into tears, and continued long in the melting mood. Her dream idol was shattered; and now, through her blinding tears, she saw troop away once more the bright visions of happiness with which she had been dallying her hopes. It was well for her that she could cry, and well for the cause which she had at heart that she did; for while she wept her son softened. He was ashamed to see his mother weep; he reproached himself bitterly with having wrecked the happiness which she was trying to conjure up; and, after a series of passionate, pathetic appeals; after he had exhausted himself in attempts to console her; after he had wrecked his reasoning powers to convince her that his was the true and honourable path, and that he must follow it; after he had adjured her by the memories of all she held dear to permit him to tread the path of stern glory; and after he had endeavoured to influence her by the repetition of suffering and trial, and had found his successive efforts in vain to allay the storm which he evoked, he agreed to do nothing further until he should hear the result of the Countess' interview with the Master of Cassillis, and until he had slept over it.

Bargany had not conceded anything—at least, he said so to himself; in reality, he had conceded everything. If not, why did he whisper, " What will Auchendrane say ? "

CHAPTER XIV.

CASSILLIS AND BARGANY RESOLVE TO BURY THE HATCHET.

THE Countess of Cassillis had no easy task before her. The Master was bold, rash, revengeful. His pride was wounded. He bore on his forehead, and would carry to the grave with him, the marks of the prowess of the Laird of Bargany. He was, besides, a prisoner in the house of his enemy. His pride revolted lest it should be thought that he was about to purchase his freedom by becoming in any way an emissary of Bargany.

He fancied that by some means or other he would achieve
his freedom. Not that he was blind to the chances of a short
shrift. Bargany had treated his prisoners summarily before
now—there was no reason why he might not rid himself of
him in similar fashion. Still he thought that, somehow or
other, it was not his lot either to perish in the dungeons of
his foe or hang from the stretching limbs of one of the noble
plane-trees which adorned the park. The Master of Cassillis
was a fatalist, and his destiny, he told himself, was not yet
accomplished. He felt that it was yet to be his to ride in the
van of the men of Cassillis and to wipe out the indignity of
imprisonment, upon his captor.

The Countess plied him with argument. First of all she
dangled before his eyes a very vivid picture of his own execution. That had no effect. Then she tried him with his
duty to his fellow-men and the grand opening afforded him
of being the saviour of Carrick, ridding it of the strifes and
alarms indigenous to the blood-feud of the Kennedys; but
the Master was not to be won by reasoning which interfered
with his destiny. Next she reminded him of the unnatural
and unchristian character of the warfare which he and Bargany were waging against one another, kinsmen according to
the flesh; but that was, in his opinion, no earthly reason why
he should be the go-between. It was not he that had stimulated the feud—why should he allay it? Finally, she
enlarged on his duty towards herself, as the wife of his
brother and as his own sister-in-law, and argued so closely on
the lines of her own freedom, that the Master gave way con-
ditionally, and with the worst possible grace. He took care
to shew the Countess that he was averse altogether to bearing
the white flag, though whether he felt quite as much averse
as he tried to look, may well be left an open question.

To this he agreed, that he would bear to the Earl of
Cassillis the messages of the Countess and of Bargany. He
would tell the story of his captivity from first to last, truth-

fully and without exaggeration. He would use no influence
of his own to swerve his brother either in one direction or the
other; and if he failed in his mission, he would return to
Bargany and resume his captivity. He would not take a free
departure; he was to be on parole.

Bargany, having "slept over it," arose the following morning in a most uncomfortable frame of mind. It would be
more correct to say that he had tossed all night in bed, over
it than that he had slept. The memories which hung about
the Castle haunted him; Mrs. Gamp, who existed even in
these early days of Carrick story, haunted him; and had he
not gone so far that to retrace his steps would have been as
difficult as to go forward, he would, without a doubt, have relegated his repentant frame of mind to the byegone, attributed
it to a passing—and for ever past—spasm of weakness, and
braced himself up for future and sterner contingencies. But
he had gone too far to go back—at least, unless something
very serious crossed him.

Nevertheless, comparatively little would have done it. A
taunt from the Master of Cassillis would have been enough
to drive the last forty-eight hours yielding into the impenetrable shade, and to restore Bargany to his old self—Bargany
the bold, the revengeful, the unforgetful.

Fortunately, when he descended into the dining-room,
where breakfast awaited him, he found everything as favourable to inducing a continuance of his good offices as could
have been desired. His mother and the Countess of Cassillis
were seated beside one another; and, like elderly ladies of
similar temperaments generally, were warming to one another
over the recital of events which had happened in their youth—
for it must be remembered that, though the Earl of Cassillis
and Bargany were both of about equal age, and each still in
the early dawn of his manhood, the mother of the latter was
not a whit older than the wife of the former.

They had met a score of years before, though, as a matter

of fact, it took a good deal of reminiscence and of connecting
one incident with another to recall their meetings.   At that
time the Countess of Cassillis was, as wife of the Scottish
Chancellor, one of the queens of Scottish society in the Metropolis.   It was there that she had met Lady Bargany, in the
stately halls of Holyrood, and in the quaint old houses which
flanked the High Street—high and venerable mansions, many
storeyed and wondrously gabled—but neither more high nor
venerable than the families which dwelt in them.   One remembrance begat another; that evoked a third; and so the
Countess and Lady Bargany rambled on among the list of
their kinsfolk and acquaintances, until they talked themselves
into the very comfortable and satisfactory conclusion that
twenty years ago they had been the most intimate cronies.
We need not find fault with them; if their resurrected
friendship was not quite as genuine, or as securely founded
as they tried to believe it was, at least it was well meant, and
not a whit more out of place than the every-day reminiscences
of byegone men and times which are dished up quite palatably
for public consumption.

Bargany bid them good morning and sat down to breakfast.
Neither of them required to be told that his humour was an
uncertain commodity.   The scowl was as often on his face as
off it; and though he did not permit his feelings to interfere
with his appetite, it needed no penetration to discover that he
had better be left alone until he thawed out, of his own
accord.

And so the ladies resumed their theme and chatted away.
Bargany at first heard them as though he heard them not;
then he listened at intervals; then he listened until he became interested; then he joined in the conversation and supplied details of his own; then he forgot all about the Master
of Cassillis upstairs and the dead Dalrymple hung from the
Yett of Craigneil; like a true Scot, he began to expatiate on
the glories of Edinburgh, and the greatness of the kingdom;

and finally, and absolutely of his own accord, he took up the theme so nearly broken off for ever, and expressed himself in language not to be mistaken and not to be discounted, as determined on his side to let the dead past bury its dead.

So far well; but the difficulties were not yet out of the way. What might eventuate?

The Earl had yet to be consulted. He would do much to get back his wife, and Bargany had little reason to doubt in his own mind that he would give truce for so excellent a bargain. He thought, moreover, that, with the Countess on his side, the Earl might even extend the truce into a perpetual peace to him and to his.

But there were others to be considered. What of Auchendrane? Was he to be included in the truce? If not, was he to give him up to his fate? Bargany stood in a peculiar relation to Mure. They had secrets in common, they had deeds in common; they had the same enemies. Besides, as yet, there was nothing more than hope of peace concluded. The whole thing might eventuate in a return to strife; and if it did, how could he go back to Mure and solicit his aid, were he now coolly to throw him overboard to drift on, or be driven on, to his fate? Left to himself, Auchendrane must fall—would he be justified in leaving him to himself? On the other hand, had not Auchendrane been the direct cause of all his recent troubles, and did he owe him any gratitude for these? There were two sides to the question, and two very distinct sides.

And besides Auchendrane, there were other lairds and squires whom he could not desert. He must carry them into the peace, if peace it was to be. They were his friends and allies, were ready to fight for him, were willing to suffer for him; they had fought for him and with him. These could not be left to be broken on the wheel by the King of Carrick, as assuredly they would be if deserted by the potent chief of Bargany.

Bargany himself hardly knew what to think in the flocking contingencies which troubled his mind; and, like a sensible man, he forebore to create difficulties. If, he felt, he could steer his own bark through the rapids, the steering of the barks of others would not be so difficult; if his negotiations suffered shipwreck, there was no need to trouble himself about the concerns of others. And so he let the future take care of itself. He had launched his plan—that was enough in the meantime. It would not be his fault should it miscarry.

As soon as the Master of Cassillis was sufficiently recovered he took his departure under solemn promise that he would return if his mission failed. It was nevertheless with a glad heart that he emerged from the dark shadow of the grey keep of Bargany and turned his horse's head towards Maybole. The Master was not what is generally called a thinking man. He took things as he found them. He had been fighting more or less all the days of his manhood. It was natural, therefore, to him, that he should accept the condition of feud as quite normal; and he could not understand how a mind like that of Bargany could exist in the breast of a man whom he knew to be, when occasion required it, bloody, bold, and resolute.

What could possess Bargany? He was the hero of more than one tragedy already. Had he not lain hidden in the dark trees of St. Leonards until Sir Thomas Kennedy of Culzean rode within their fatal shelter? Had he not been one of the conspirators who plotted mischief against Cassillis, in the tower of Auchendrane? Had he not hidden among the sand dunes of Prestwick in order to take the life of the Earl as he was riding past on his journey to London? Had he not reached the House of Newark in the very nick of time for Auchendrane—just as the Kennedys of Cassillis had driven in the oaken door and met the besieged hand-to-hand in the very hall of the castle—fallen on the invaders like a blast from heaven, and driven them from Newark, routed, and leaving many of their followers lying red among the brown heather of Carrick? And had he not intercepted himself and the body-guard of the Countess of Cassillis, fired Auchensoul farm-house, captured the Countess, unhorsed and captured himself in addition, and kept them in durance until now? What should tempt such a man into softness of heart and into a longing for peace? It was a mystery. Why had he stayed his vengeance, and bid him, the Master of Cassillis, his bitterest foe, begone? Wonders would never cease—that was all the conclusion he could reach, and he reached it, when he could do no better, without much difficulty.

The men of Maybole were surprised when the Master rode slowly down the steep High Street. Could the grave give up its dead? Or, what was equivalent, could Bargany House give back its captives freely—without money and without price? The garrison who held the castle plied the Master with questions; but the Master knew how to be taciturn and uncommunicative. He checked their eager questionings sharply; and, finding that his brother was not in Maybole, but in his thick-walled peel by the banks of the Doon, he continued his journey without stay, leaving garrison and burghers holding up their hands and observing that wonders would never cease. They could not understand the situation— hence they satisfied themselves with a repetition of the aphorism which had brought comfort to the mind of the Master himself.

The surprise of the warders of Cassillis, as he rode up beneath the extending branches of the dule tree and dismounted by the Castle door, was equal to that of the men of Maybole. He was alone, unattended, all but unarmed. He rode leisurely, as a man not bestead, not driven either by active pursuit or by impulse. He dismounted with as much *sang froid* as if he had never been absent a day.

Here was a mystery indeed for the gossips; and as all the men of Cassillis had to talk about was this Kennedy feud, they were all gossips for the nonce. Some of them reached the conclusion that the Master had effected his escape—the remainder, like their neighbours elsewhere, concluded that wonders would never cease, and awaited elucidation.

He entered the dining-hall, where sat the Earl, wrapped in thought. Ever since Bargany had made captive of his spouse, Lord Cassillis had been in a quandary. He was at a loss what to do. Conscious that any rash step might defeat the very end he had in view, he had confined himself to one single ride as far as Craigneil, and had enjoyed the temporary satisfaction of seeing the Master of Stair dangling from the Yett of that strong fortalice by the river Stinchar. He was seriously thinking of laying his grievances before the Privy Council and invoking its aid; but there were two good reasons why he should not. It was he who had reopened the feud; and, more important still, he would rather, if at all possible, work out his own salvation without the assistance of the powers that were. To summon extraneous aid would be to show the white feather; and that the Earl was loath to do.

Lord Cassillis could hardly believe his eyes when he saw his brother enter the room. But if, for a moment, he thought himself in presence of wraith or familiar, his brother's cheery voice soon dispelled the illusion.

"Why, Hew," exclaimed the Earl, as he grasped the proffered hand firmly, "you are the last man I ever expected to see again."

"Well," replied the Master, "a week ago I hardly thought to see either you or the walls of Cassillis again; but here I am. And when I tell you why I am here, you will be as surprised at what I have to tell you as I am to tell it, or as you are to see me."

"Tell me then to what good luck do you owe your freedom?"

"Guess."

"Escaped?"

" No.   Try again."

" Rescued ? "

" No.   Try again."

" Try again !   Not I; I give it up.   Tell me—but first, what of the Countess ? "

" Oh, the Countess was well and happy the last time I saw her, sitting by the fireside with Lady Bargany, embroidering, and listening to Lady Bargany telling of her old days, and of her visits to this house."

" You surprise me more and more.   What can have happened ? "

" Well," replied the Master, " sit down—it's not a short story.   Short enough in telling, I dare say; but perhaps not so short in consideration of it.   I hardly know what to make of it myself."

" To make of what ? "

" Of Bargany sending me here to conclude a peace with you."

" To conclude a what ? " gasped the Earl, hardly believing his own ears.

" A treaty of peace."

" Explain yourself, Hew," said the Earl in a tone of command.

Thus directly appealed to, the Master of Cassillis told the story.   Beginning with the hour when he found himself a captive within the hostile walls of Bargany, he told how the Lady Bargany, with her own hands, treated his wounds, and ministered to his wants, and how carefully he had been nursed into convalescence.   To do him justice, he laid stress on Bargany's kindness, and succeeded in awakening in the storm-tossed mind of his brother, something like an approach to reciprocal gratitude to his sworn foe by the Girvan water. Then he narrated how Bargany had come to him one evening and broached the subject of conciliation ; how he had scorn-fully refused to be the bearer of any such message of mercy

as that which he was asked to convey; how Bargany had
brought to his bed-side the Countess herself, and how she had
argued the matter in every phase, and with every weapon of
reason and of entreaty that she could muster; how nearly the
unfortunate execution of the Master of Stair had hardened
the growing softness of Bargany's heart into something like
its old adamant; how Lady Bargany and the Countess of
Cassillis had persuaded him to resume the all but broken-off
negotiations; how, subsequently, Bargany had yielded; and
finally, how, after much cogitation and self-reproach, he himself, the Master of Cassillis, had consented to bear his
message to the Earl, and had promised, if he failed to arrange
at least a truce, to return to Bargany House as a prisoner.

The narrative filled the Earl with astonishment. He could
no more understand the mainsprings of Bargany's action than
could the Master. They were beyond their grasp. They had
heard of such things, but had never known them from experience. And what made the task of comprehension still more hard
was that they knew that there was not one atom of cowardice
in Bargany, that from his scalp to his heels he was as true a
soldier and as bold a man as ever raided between the
Stinchar and the Doon. They discussed his motives, it is
true; but as their discussion was on a wrong basis, and left
them rather mystified than anything else, it may very well
be relegated to excision.

But the Earl was quick of mental grasp when his own
interests were concerned; and he saw Bargany's strength of
position at a glance. If he refused his overtures, what then?

Clearly this—that Bargany would see his proffers scornfully rejected—that he would in all probability treat the
Master of Cassillis, on his return, exactly as he himself had
treated the Master of Stair, and that, in addition, he might
even, in the first heat of angry passion, give the Countess
herself short shrift, or at least immure her in some secluded
spot and keep her captive so long as it suited himself. And,

13

besides, he would at once resume the feudal warfare, and plunge the country-side into all the horrors of a fresh fratricidal strife.

It was a hard fight with the Earl. His pride was at stake. He, the King of Carrick, the head of the house of Kennedy— was he to be sued on equal terms by one whom he regarded as an inferior member of the house? Powerful and bold Bargany was—but still, in the eyes of the Earl, he was but a scion of the sept of which Cassillis had long been the recognised head.

He would have refused the proffer of Bargany at first blush, if he could. But he could not. Circumstances were against him; and strong as he was, these circumstances were still stronger. He could not control his destiny; and, what troubled him still more than that, he could not get back his wife unless he reciprocated the friendship expressed in the message brought by the Master. Then there was the Master himself—would he be justified in sending him back to die? He was his only brother, and the prospective heir to the Earldom.

The Earl was not much of a courtier, but he knew his position too well not to know that he could not give way without protest. At all events he reasoned so with himself that, if he at once accepted Bargany's terms, Bargany would claim the moral victory, and would boast that he had brought him to his knees. Personally he had no great antipathy to Bargany, but he hated Mure of Auchendrane, who was Bargany's councillor and associate; and, come what might, he was not to be deprived of his legitimate revenge on the scheming old Baron, who had done so much to shake his supremacy in Carrick.

Had the Earl of Cassillis not been open to the advances of Bargany, the negotiations would without a doubt have been more protracted than they were; for, as he and the Master were discussing what they ought to do—and the discussion

was continued at intervals over three days—tidings were
brought from Galloway that Mure of Cloncaird had, in
revenge for the killing of the Master of Stair, ridden into
Galloway and wreaked his vengeance upon the master of
works of a new house which the Earl was erecting there.

Probably no incident in the whole narration is more
strikingly illustrative of these feudal times than this. The
deed was simply done. The Master of Stair had been suspended between earth and sky from the cruel Yett of Craigneil. The news reached Mure, in Cloncaird. This was a
vantage which must be discounted. How was that to be
brought about? Only one method suggested itself to
Cloncaird—he must kill somebody in return—somebody
closely associated with the Earl of Cassillis. Why he did
not remain in Ayrshire and do it, is open to surmise; at all
events he did not remain in the county, but rode over the
hills to Galloway right into the heart of the Earl's domains
by the Cruives of Cree. Here a new castle was being
erected; and, necessary then as now, the building operations
were being carried on under the supervision of a master of
works. This official had no connection whatever with the
feud; he was simply a superior workman, paid to watch the
builders in their operations. But it was enough for Cloncaird
that he was in the Earl's pay and at work upon the Earl's
house. The Earl would feel his death after a fashion. For
the death itself he would care but little; for the slight to
himself he would, Cloncaird concluded, care much. Therefore,
he struck at the great Carrick chief through his humble
servitor, waylaid him as he was going home from his work,
and cruelly murdered him by the wayside. This done,
Cloncaird felt that he had transferred the vantage to the
other side, and retraced his steps.

The Earl was angry when the word was brought; but he
did not let the last tragedy, which he felt was small in comparison to that which he himself had ordered at Craigneil but

the other morning, stand in the way. Such a trifle must not block the channel of communication; so he gave it the go-bye, and resumed consideration of what was the path of interest. He called it to himself the path of duty.

Within a week of the Master of Cassillis riding Cassillis-wards from Bargany he was mounted anew and on his way south again towards the Girvan water, bent on one of the most peaceful errands which he had ever undertaken. His departure filled the men-at-arms at Cassillis with astonishment —for they conceived nothing else than fresh excitements and new adventures, and had nightly been furbishing their arms, and sharpening their cutlasses, and scraping the flints of their fire-locks, in order to the reprisal which their experience had taught them to expect. Astonished, however, as they were, they were denied enlightenment, and could nought but wonder. What their providence in the House of Cassillis might do, was none of their business. It was theirs to obey rather than comprehend; for they were relieved the trouble of thinking in these good old times.

And as the Master rode through Maybole and looked in, as he passed, on the armed dwellers in the square tower which represented the strength of Cassillis in the capital of Carrick and told them curtly, and without one word of explanation, that he was bound for Bargany, their amazement knew no bounds. Conciliation on this side of heaven, at all events, between the rival chieftains by the Doon and the Girvan, was not one of the things dreamt of in their contracted philosophy.

The peace which ensued was not the work of one single interview, but of several, between the Master of Cassillis and his brother on the one hand and Bargany on the other. It was not a written treaty, that which was ratified. Pen was never put to paper on it. But the Earl pledged his word to its fulfilment, and so did Bargany; and that was as good as an bond so far as they two were concerned.

The feud between the two rival families of the Kennedys was, in the meantime, declared to be at an end. The future must guard itself; but, so far as the past was concerned, there was to be no reprisal. The Earl was to be free to ride from Cassillis, southward, through the lands of Bargany without let or hindrance, and the Laird of Bargany was no longer bound to pay the once customary salutation call as he rode past Cassillis. All Bargany's associates, with the exception of Mure of Auchendrane, were to enjoy the fruits of the peace, and to be unmolested. Even Mure of Cloncaird was exonerated for having slain the master of works in Galloway. As for Mure of Auchendrane, the Earl bound himself not to employ other than legal methods to identify him with the crimes with which he stood charged. Bargany had hard work getting even such good terms as these for Mure, but he stuck to his point and carried it.

These conditions were to be regarded as ratified when the Countess of Cassillis was restored to her liege-lord, together with the Master of Cassillis.

Each successive ride of the Master to and from Bargany set the militant groups a-wondering. There was something in the wind, to begin with; but what on earth could be the meaning of a Kennedy of Cassillis riding, apparently of his own free will, out and in to the jaws of Bargany House? They could not comprehend it at all, though they discussed it to the top of their bent.

The wonder culminated in amazement when one day the Countess of Cassillis, with Bargany on the one hand and the Master of Cassillis on the other, rode into Maybole right up to the very walls of the Castle. Here the Laird left them, exchanging greetings of the most friendly character, and retraced his steps southward. The Countess and her brother-in-law rode on to Cassillis. It was with a glad heart that the former saw the Doon and not the Girvan; the tall plane trees by the sinuous river, and not the pines of Bargany; and was finally welcomed by the lord of Cassillis himself to her own home.

And now we turn to Auchendrane and to more serious on-goings.

CHAPTER XV.

AUCHENDRANE TRIES TO RID HIMSELF OF DANGER.

WROTH was Mure of Auchendrane when word was brought to him by his son James that his friend, the Laird of Bargany, had concluded a treaty of peace with their sworn foe, the Earl of Cassillis.

James heard the tidings in Ayr, and satisfied himself they were genuine. They evoked no small sensation in the county town. The feud of the Kennedys had lasted so long that it had come to be recognised as a necessary chapter in current Ayrshire history. Now, to all appearance, it was at an end. Carrick was henceforth to slumber at ease; the call to arms was no more to be heard; midnight rides by the Doon, the Girvan, and the Stinchar, on errands of destruction or of revenge, were passed away; and forays across the hills to Galloway were ended. The burghers of Ayr discussed the situation in all its phases; and the douce townsmen rubbed their hands, and predicted that Bargany and the Earl of Cassillis would not long be able to keep their hands off one another. How could they be expected to? reasoned these worthies. The feud was chronic. It had been going on for years; blood had been shed like water—how, then, could the Earl and Bargany, by a compact betwixt themselves, at once bring order out of confusion, and still the long-raging storm into a calm? The burghers could not answer their own question; so they very naturally concluded that it was unanswerable.

When James Mure heard all he could hear, and learned all he could learn, he at once hastened home to Auchendrane. He could not keep his father in the dark; for James, though at times he bearded his sire, was at bottom afraid of him. The son lacked mind; the sire did not—hence the ascendancy of the latter over the former.

"It cannot be true," was Auchendrane's reply to James, when he had unburdened himself of his story.   "Bargany could not have done it."

"It's as true as God's truth is true," replied James seriously.

"What?   That the Countess has gone home to Cassillis, that Bargany accompanied her as far as Maybole, and that the Master of Cassillis and Bargany shook hands on parting—do you tell me that is true?"

"Yes, it is quite true.   I had it from one who saw them ride into Maybole together."

"Repeat what you said about me, James."

"That the feud is at an end with you too, unless you begin it afresh, but that Cassillis is going to have the law of you if he can manage it."

"Is that true, too?"

"Gospel," was James' answer.   "Every word I have told you is as sure as death."

"Bargany must be mad," said Auchendrane firmly, "with the game in his own hands, and with Cassillis at his foot, to give up the fight.   Do you tell me that he has voluntarily given up the Countess?"

"I do."

"What has possessed him?   How has he lost heart?"

"They say in Ayr," rejoined James, "that he never had much heart in the work; and, if ever he had, he is sick of it."

"By my soul I can hardly credit it.   And yet, I remember now how he rated me for not joining personally in his capture of the Countess.   I thought that it was nothing but a display of temper on Bargany's part. Little did I dream that I was despatching him on an errand that would result in his undoing."

"If it was his undoing, alone," observed James, "it would matter very little; but it may be ours as well."

"May it? We shall see to that, James. A curse on Bargany and his stupidity! But we shall see to ourselves, and make assurance doubly sure. You say the Earl cannot attack us?"

"So he has pledged his word."

"And that he has reserved, and received the right to prosecute me before the Privy Council?"

"So I am informed."

Auchendrane muttered a series of curses between his teeth, and fell to cogitating over the affair. He saw, at a glance, the full meaning and importance of the treaty, so far as concerned himself; but he was less disturbed over probable consequences than he was incensed at the action of Bargany. That he could not comprehend. He rated Bargany at a lower level than he deserved to be rated.

It is worth recalling, at this point, that the only witness directly connecting Mure of Auchendrane with the events preliminary to, and directly associated with, the murder of Sir Thomas Kennedy of Culzean in the wood of St. Leonards, was the poor scholar Dalrymple, whom Auchendrane had sent across the Firth of Clyde to the safe keeping of Montgomery of Skelmorlie, who owned, at the time, a large tract of the rugged, sparsely inhabited, and half-civilized island of Arran. It was Dalrymple who had conveyed to Mure the letter from Sir Thomas Kennedy, announcing the intention of the Knight of Culzean to pay a visit to the Scottish capital. It was through the contents of this letter that Auchendrane became cognisant of his movements, and of the way by which Sir Thomas was to proceed to Edinburgh; and acting on the knowledge so conveyed, Bargany and his confederates, at the direct instigation of Auchendrane, had lain in wait for the unfortunate Knight, and despatched him cruelly and relentlessly.

Bargany had been one of the chief actors in the tragedy, and the Earl knew that he had. He had confessed guilt by fleeing into the border land; he had allowed himself to be outlawed rather than appear in answer to the summons of the Privy Council.

Yet the Earl had forgiven him his share in the tragedy of St. Leonards in the full knowledge of his participation in it. Lord Cassillis, however, discriminated between the direct actors in the tragic scene and the man who had devised the scene itself, and who had betrayed the friendship of the victim. Mure had wrought in the dark, the others in daylight. Mure had thrown the open risk upon his confederates, and in security in his strong tower by the Doon had awaited the tidings that the work was done. The difference in the degrees of guilt is not easily discriminated; but feudal times were ruled by feudal ideas; and it is easier to accept this explanation than to seek for another more consistent with the eternal principles of justice.

The Earl of Cassillis was quite aware that unless he could secure the person of Dalrymple, he could not bring home to Auchendrane the complicity which he was so anxious to prove; and he had pledged his word to Bargany that he would not seek revenge by any shorter and simpler method. Auchendrane was equally conscious, on the other hand, that his life depended on keeping Dalrymple out of the way.

Why had Mure not finally disposed of Dalrymple when he had him in his power? That was a question that frequently troubled his son. James would soon have got rid of the encumbrance—why then should his father, with much more reason for doing it, hesitate? The truth is, as already stated, Auchendrane and his son had not been cast by nature in exactly the same mould. The former had a conscience code of

his own, and had still some sense of honour left him; the code
of the latter was pure selfishness. Mure, however, was not un-
aware of the risk which he had voluntarily contracted; and it
must be recorded as a remarkable fact that, notwithstanding
that, he preferred the risk to the assassination of the poor
scholar, and the securing of his own safety through Dalrymple's
death.

The dungeons of Auchendrane told no tales. Many a
better man than Dalrymple, many a more consequential, had
entered their dark solitudes, never again to see the light of
day, never again to hear the sweet voices of nature, save the
ceaseless ripple and run of the river Doon, which swept past
the walls of Auchendrane as it swept past the walls of
Cassillis above. Dalrymple would, in all probability, never
have been missed; and if he had, who was there to trouble
himself over the disappearance of so miserable a unit?

In Dalrymple's poverty and personal innocence of any
connection with the Carrick feud lay the secret of his
salvation. He was beneath the vengeance of the Baron of
Auchendrane; and Mure's mind, torn and distracted as it was
and ever on the alert in his own interest, had not yet con-
descended to common, cold-blooded, plebeian murder. Had
the poor scholar been a scion of the house of Cassillis, ever so
remote, there would have been no hesitation in dealing with
him. His death would have seemed no murder, to Auchendrane; and the honour of Mure would have been safe!

Six months had passed from the time when James Mure
had escorted Dalrymple to the Carrick coast and seen him
sail for Arran. They were weary months for the poor lad.
The Ayrshire shore was in sight every day, with its long
yellow sands and the bluff Heads of Ayr, and with the gentle
slope of Carrick in the back-ground. At times a stray fisher,
storm-bound, or driven across the Firth by contrary winds,
entertained him with stories of home and kin; and with every
such conversation his longing to return increased. Smugglers,

too, were not by any means rare; and these he made his con-
fidants. As the days lengthened out, and as he saw the
sinking sun, ere it set behind Goatfell, strike on the coast
line of his own native shire, his weariness of Arran became
intensified, until he resolved, come what might, to return
home.

Dalrymple had begun to realise that he had a strong hold
on the Mures of Auchendrane. If that were so, why should
he continue a fugitive and a vagabond in Arran? Would he
not be justified in receiving a price for his silence?

Had he known Mure of Auchendrane, and the danger of
running counter to him, he would have thought more of
safety than of profit, and would have given Ayr and Carrick
a wide berth until the closing chapters had been reached in
the history of the stern old baron in his tower by the Doon.
But Dalrymple estimated Mure at another than his true
value, and thought to make terms with him advantageous to
himself.

Longing, home sickness, and self-interest grew into resolution, resolution developed into action; and one summer
night, as darkness was creeping over the sea and shutting out
the mainland, and when a strong fresh breeze blew in from
the Atlantic, Dalrymple was conveyed on board of a small
sloop, which, carrying a contraband cargo of whisky, distilled
amid the silence and the slopes of Arran, at once set sail for
the opposite shore. It was a choice night, though risky for a
smuggler—for the coast was well watched, and the revenue
officers were sharp of vision.

The skipper of the sloop had made tryst to be at the Doon
foot before the streak of grey, which never left the western
horizon, had broadened into daylight. He kept his appoint-
ment; for at the darkest hour before the dawn the keel of his
little boat grated on the pebbles at the mouth of the river.
Dalrymple at once leaped ashore, and made for the town, two
miles away, leaving the smugglers to dispose of their illicit

cargo as they saw fit. In half-an-hour he passed within the Sand gate.

Once in Ayr, Dalrymple made no secret of his return; and consequently it was not long until the news travelled as far as Auchendrane. Mure had many friends in Ayr. Some of these knew that he had sent the scholar across to Arran, though they did not know exactly why. They presumed, however, that he must have acted with reason, and so they lost no time in letting him know that Dalrymple had come home again.

The news alarmed Auchendrane, and gave rise to a stormy recrimination between him and his son James. The latter wanted the resourceful mind of his father; when he saw danger, he had no other ambition than to get rid of it by the speediest and most summary means in his power; and he had bitterly reproached his father when Dalrymple was sent to Arran, that he had not despatched him on a longer journey— on a journey, indeed, to that land from which return is impossible.

" Had you hearkened to me six months ago," he said to his father, as they discussed the lad's return, " there would have been no need for action now. Dalrymple should have been killed. That's what I said then, that's what I say now. Who would have known anything about it? But, if we get him into our power now, and he is never seen again, everybody will miss him."

"Not so fast, James; not so fast. I might have killed him when I had him, or left you to do it, which would have amounted to the same thing; but to what purpose, if we could rid ourselves of him without taking his life?"

"You are growing sentimental, father. You would have killed the Earl of Cassillis if you could, and thought it a glorious victory over the Kennedys; and you did kill Sir Thomas Kennedy of Culzean—and yet, when it comes to taking the life of this miserable go-between, whom nobody would ever miss, you grow mawkish and sentimental."

"Don't say that again, James," said Auchendrane, who did not relish being so spoken to, "I never killed Sir Thomas Kennedy. It was not my hand that did the deed."

"No, indeed," replied James, sarcastically, "it was not your hand that did the deed, but it was your head that planned it, which is very nearly the same thing."

"How often must I tell you, James, that there can be no parallel between Culzean and this lad Dalrymple? Culzean was the foe of our house; at least, he was a Kennedy, and Cassillis has sworn by every stone in his house, that he will root out Auchendrane, and lay both us and the old tower in ruins. But as for Dalrymple, what is he? A miserable scholar, a poor clerk, who has nothing more on what he would call his conscience, than the carrying of a letter from Culzean to me."

"That's not the way I look at it," replied James, bluntly. "Sir Thomas Kennedy was my father-in-law—though I can forgive him that; but if I had schemed away his life, I would not have stickled to lay this accursed Dalrymple by the heels at the same time, so that he would never have troubled us again."

"You don't discriminate, James, as I tell you. Do you think I am going to dirty my fingers by cutting the throat of Dalrymple? It would be against all the rules of fair war."

"Would it?" was James' answer, "I tell you again that I would have swept him out of the way as I would a serpent. What a pretty mess we're in now—at least, you are in now—with your code of honour! You've brought it on yourself—you can't deny that—and by God," he added, angrily, "it serves you right for your squeamishness."

"Silence, James," Mure replied, "I tell you again the thing was impossible. The whole country-side, if the thing got noised, would have hooted us. I can risk a deed of honour with any man, but I am not a common assassin. No, thank God, I am not come to that yet."

"Well, well," said James, somewhat more softly, seeing that he was rousing a dangerous side of his father's character, "we'll say no more about it just now. The past is past, as the parson says, and we can't recall it.' Besides, we have enough to do with the present, as far as I see."

"Yes, yes, let us talk of the present. What do you propose to do now, James?"

"Well, that requires some consideration. You see, Dalrymple is at home with his friends in Ayr; if he is afraid of us, and determined to avoid us, then it seems to me we shall have some trouble to get hold of him. If he is not afraid of us, and thinks the old story is forgotten, and that we shall not trouble our heads over him, he can easily be decoyed. If he has come home to brazen it out with us, and under any suspicion that he can levy blackmail, he will walk into our hands. In any case, we must get hold of him without loss of time, and get rid of him for ever."

"Not for ever, James, not for ever, unless it cannot in any other way be avoided. We can easily get rid of him without killing him."

"So we can, father; there's many a way. There are half a dozen men within call who will kill him accidentally, if you but give them the hint, and take their chance of the consequences."

"Yes, yes, James, I know that; but that is not what I mean. We can get him sent away out of the country—sent to the wars in Holland, for instance. Men don't come back from the Low Countries as a rule; and if they are killed in the trenches, or in the assault, they are never missed. And besides, James, they die a natural death."

"So they do, father," replied James, "a very natural death. But is this wretch worth the risk, worth the candle? Why not despatch him out of hand, and have done with him?"

"My conscience," responded Auchendrane, "is tender on that point; I don't mind confessing it. I've seen many a

prettier man than he is, kiss the maiden, or lay his head on
the block, or suspended to a tree, but I like to draw the line
somewhere, and Dalrymple is about the mark. But, first of
all, we must get hold of him. It will be time enough to see
how we are to get quit of him after he is here. If he is given
to reason and will go away, he may save himself and us too;
if he is stubborn and insists on staying, we can "—

"Kill him," interposed James, savagely. "Mark my words,
father," he added, "you'll live to regret the day when you
allowed that conscience of yours to awake from its long slumber. You may send him away; he will come back on your
hands. You will have to kill him some day, or I will; but I
don't like such a business to be delayed an hour longer than
there is any occasion for. Why not leave him to me?"

"Because I don't choose to leave him to you or to any other
body, and you can take that for a final answer. I will not
kill him unless I can't avoid it. When once I see him
seriously in my path I shall sweep him out of it as if he were
vermin; but if he is reasonable, he will find me reasonable too."

"Very well, father, so be it," replied the callous young
man; "if you say so, we shall let him live a little longer.
But don't say you were not warned—we shall have to kill
him some day."

"Then let the day declare it when it comes; meantime let
us see how we are to get him into our possession."

The result of the long conversation that ensued was that,
on the following day, James Mure took horse for Ayr, where
he consulted with one or two of his tried associates. Even to
these he did not tell the overwhelming necessity for getting
Dalrymple into his hands. Nor were they over-curious to
know. The state of society was such that a man in the position
of Mure had always friends who were ready to do his bidding
without either let or question. They were on his side;
Dalrymple, they were assured, was on the side of the Earl of

Cassillis, and a potent instrument in his hands; his security in the keeping of Auchendrane, was a necessity of the situation—and so they consented to secure the person of the helpless youth and to hand him over to the tender mercies of the Mures, to be dealt with by them as suited their emergency.

James Mure had none of the qualms of conscience, or delicacy of finesse which characterised his father. The latter was crafty, cruel, generally unscrupulous; the former, hotheaded, hot-blooded, and instant in action, in addition. He could not afford to waste time endeavouring to persuade Dalrymple to yield himself up voluntarily; all that he wanted was to get him into his possession with as little risk and trouble as he possibly could. Naturally he was anxious to avoid danger; but, on the other hand, he was still more fearful least the Earl of Cassillis should forestall him and obtain possession of the person of the coveted youth. If this were to happen, the consequences might be serious. He was the missing link of salvation for Auchendrane; to Cassillis he was the one witness by whose aid the Earl hoped to bring Mure to the scaffold.

So that the stakes for which James Mure was playing were desperate. He could not afford to lose. His father's life was the forfeit.

Dalrymple knew the Mures, but he under-estimated their character. He regarded them as part and parcel of the country life with which his limited experience had made him acquainted. Many a country squire who owned broad acres and dwelt in the halls of his ancestors was at this period unable to do more than write his own name—in many cases not so much. They were familiar with the sword! their literature was the stirring scenes of the fray and the banquet; and the book of nature their complete library. Book lore was good enough for the monk in his cell or the minister in his pulpit, or for the poor scholar like Dalrymple who earned a miserable sustenance as an amanuensis and was permitted to pick up the crumbs which fell from the rich man's table. It was not fit for men who lived up to the rude standard of the times.

With all this Dalrymple was familiar. He did not read character. He did not discriminate between the Mures or the Cathcarts or the Kennedys or the Boyds or the Dalrymples of Stair. All were alike to him. He despised them all alike in his heart—for he had access where they were denied—rather, which they denied themselves—to the tree of knowledge; and he did not try to gauge the possibilities or extremities of their character. They were but rude Barons, the product of the times, and he assessed them all on a level.

And perhaps, in the main, he was right. Hardly one of their number would have hesitated to have offered him a sacrifice on the altar of his own needs; hardly one but would have swept him ruthlessly, remorselessly from his path, had he crossed it with as dark a shadow as that which he threw upon the way by which Auchendrane had to travel. But as it was— as Fate or chance had it—it was Mure with whom he had to deal—a man who invariably endeavoured to make circumstances subservient, but who, pushed to the wall, was an extremely dangerous character.

Had Dalrymple been gifted with second sight, it had been well for him. He would not then have so readily walked into the trap which Auchendrane laid for him. Mure knew it was no use inviting him to return under pretence of engaging his literary gifts, or remunerating him for translating theological tomes of the fathers. That had served its purpose once already. He was afraid to take him by force, lest the partisans of the Kennedys of Cassillis should come to know of it. So he employed a wily lawyer, who did duty for him in Ayr, to send for him and to treat him according to his instructions. These were of a character to indicate that

14

Auchendrane was not an inapt student of mind and of character. Ensconsed with the lawyer, Dalrymple learned that Auchendrane feared him and was anxious to purchase his silence. That he would do handsomely; and the limb of the law so wrought upon the tender susceptibilities and self-interest of the raw youth that he not only agreed to put himself into his hands, and to meet with Mure and arrange terms; not only consented to have no dealings meanwhile with the Earl of Cassillis, in any shape whatever, but actually walked on his own feet, and alone, to Auchendrane to receive the first instalment of the purchase money for his silence.

Auchendrane was delighted beyond measure. "The Lord hath delivered him into our hands," he exclaimed to his son, who was quite as much delighted as his father. "What a pity it would have been to have slain so innocent a youth!"

James thought otherwise, but said nothing. Dalrymple's coming was so sudden, so unexpected, that they hardly knew what to do with him. They calculated on more scheming, more plotting, more wire-pulling—perhaps man-stealing; but here he was in their possession, without ado or trouble.

"I tell you, James," said Auchendrane, who could not conceal his gratification, "it is a wonderful thing predestination. Events are so wisely ordered. Who would have thought it possible that this lad should have walked into the snare of the fowler before the net was rightly stretched?"

"Not quite so much predestination about it as foolishness, I think," was James' answer. "So stupid a fool would have been very dangerous in the hands of the Earl of Cassillis. But what are you going to do with him, now you have him?"

"Leave me to manage him," replied Auchendrane. "I'll warrant I'll make sure work of getting him out of the way this time. It will take a day or two to arrange matters, and all that time we must treat him hospitably and give him something to engage his attention. Such innocence, James— such innocence! I thought it was dead this side of heaven."

"I've heard you say, father," said James, "that you had some old monkish literature that once belonged to the friars of St. John's, and which you got from the red-nosed priest who used to eat your dinners and give you his benediction cheap. Give him that, and let him decipher it. It will improve his time and divert his thoughts."

Auchendrane laughed. "James," he said, "the very thing. I'll set him to translate that into a Christian tongue. It will do no harm anyway. So send him up, and—mind, James—be civil to him. We must keep the cub sweet."

Dalrymple entered the room without any misgivings; or if a latent suspicion haunted him, it was immediately dissipated by the cordiality with which Mure received him. As the young man entered he extended his hand, which Dalrymple respectfully touched without clasping, and bid him be seated. Dalrymple obeyed.

"Well," began Auchendrane in friendly tones, "you felt Arran lonely, did you?"

"Yes, sir, I did."

"Got homesick, I suppose? Wandered about on the beach and watched the heights of Carrick across the Firth, and so on? Quite natural, too. Arran is a melancholy hole at best.

"Yes, sir," said Dalrymple, "it is not cheerful; besides I could make nothing of the Gaelic tongue in which everybody spoke; and they eschewed me because I was not one of themselves."

"Very clannish these islanders," assented Mure. "I don't blame you for making off. But why did you go without informing Skelmorlie that you were going to leave? It was lucky for you that he did not get hold of you—for Arran is a quiet place, and the outside world has no ears for these savage solitudes."

"I did not tell him," Dalrymple replied, "because I was afraid that even if I hinted at leaving he would take steps to prevent me. These vassals of his would slay the king himself, if only they were bidden."

"I believe they would slay even the Lord's anointed, and they would never stickle at anything or at anybody short of His Most Gracious Majesty. They are useful people at a pinch, though not after your scholarly tastes."

"No, sir, they are certainly not suited to my tastes."

"I thought not. Well, Dalrymple," said Auchendrane, still continuing to speak in friendly tones, "you know that I have been anxious to see you. I mean to do something for you; for it is a pity to see so goodly a youth wasting his time in wandering over the country. We shall talk of the future anon; meantime you will remain here for a day or two, and translate for me some old documents that I got from one of the friars of Ayr, a very godly man, one of the few that be chosen. He was a dear friend of mine; but," he added, glancing upwards, "He has called him to Himself. They are in the Latin tongue, these documents, which I do not profess to understand, and it is my desire that you should transcribe them into the Scottish language. You are versed in Latin, I believe?"

"Yes, sir, I am acquainted with the Latin tongue."

"You shall lack for nothing while you are here, and you shall have a safe conduct hence. But you know that the roads leading hither are dangerous to travel on. The Kennedys of Cassillis are not a law-abiding people. They neither fear God nor regard man, and if you go without you may incur some risk. Therefore you will not think that I am treating you harshly if I ask—nay, if I insist—that, while you are engaged on this work, which will occupy your hours for a few days, excluding Sabbaths, when I desire that you should take bodily and soul rest and enjoyment, you will not leave the house."

Dalrymple bowed assent. He knew what the times were, and left Mure to do the thinking for him. Besides, why should he quarrel with so friendly a patron? Auchendrane offered him liberal terms, and these were a consideration to the poor lad, whose long days in Arran had been the reverse of remunerative from a financial point of view.

Dalrymple set to work in earnest on the old manuscripts, and day by day witnessed progress. Mure and his son James were, on the whole, rather agreeable companions than otherwise; the student was beginning to feel that Auchendrane's reputation had been sadly sinned against, and that he was one of the most godly old men in Carrick, when he was suddenly confronted with a new train of circumstances, which caused a speedy change in his mind, and led him seriously to doubt the piety of the baron.

For while Dalrymple was poring over the black letter of the friar, Auchendrane was making arrangements with Buccleuch, whose regiment was engaged in active service in the Low Countries, to provide him with a recruit. Buccleuch was in nowise averse, for the ravages of war were playing sad havoc with his gallant borderers; and the result of the communications was that, without his consent, without even his knowledge, Dalrymple was entered for a military career. No term of servitude was appointed—the fixing of that was left with the Flanders musketeers, and the fevers of the swamps and morasses of the Low Countries.

And so, one evening when the scholar was poring over the friar's manuscripts, and dreaming of his remuneration, he was ordered in harsh tones, by James Mure, to quit his drudgery, for they were going to make a man of him. In answer to all his enquiries, James told him to exercise his patience, and to hold his tongue, and he would see, if he lived long enough, where he was going and what he was to do. And when night dropped on Carrick, Dalrymple was mounted on a stout horse, and, accompanied by three of Auchendrane's retainers, escorted on his way to Leith, where, three days afterwards, he embarked on board a transport sloop, which was to convey him and other sixty or seventy recruits to the battle-field of Europe.

It was not until the Berwick Law went down on the horizon to leeward that Dalrymple fully realised his simple folly in placing himself for the second time in the hands of Auchendrane. His one experience should have been enough, he communed; he had had a second, "and may the foul fiend flee away with me," he added, "if ever I have a third."

CHAPTER XVI.

MURE IS REAWAKENED TO A SENSE OF DANGER.

SIX long years passed away, slowly for Auchendrane, slowly for Dalrymple. Carrick enjoyed comparative repose. Men began to feel that the saints had not all fallen asleep. They were permitted to cultivate their fields and reap their crops in peace and in security; and the sentries and retainers at the houses of the lairds and barons became fewer in number. There was no sleeping at arms, no fear of the call to battle in the silence of midnight, no hard-ridden raids or forays by the pale light of the moon. So quiet was society, lately so disturbed, that the older men began to talk of the degeneracy of the times, and to lament the good old days when Carrick *was* Carrick, and when " boot and saddle " was heard in the land. The memories of the feud were a fireside talk, to which the rising generation listened open-mouthed. All this in six years!

Kennedy of Bargany had taken to himself a spouse; and two or three little Kennedys were already prattling on the hearth. His fighting days were over. For him the feud was no more; and he exhausted his superfluous energies in other ways less exciting to himself and less harmful to the bailiary.

The quarrel between Mure of Auchendrane and the Earl

of Cassillis was still in suspense. The latter had foresworn summary vengeance. Many a time he regretted it, and as often he felt inclined to break his word, but he still hoped that the slow justice of events would work out a far more effective revenge than he could hope to bring about. So he hunted the great forest of Dalrymple when at home, and repaired, as was the custom among the Scottish gentry, to Edinburgh, when the season came round.

Mure never slacked off any of his furtive watchfulness, or abated one jot of the suspicion which he entertained towards his powerful neighbour. As he grew older he grew more watchful and more suspicious, until he became all but a recluse. Shut up in his strong tower, he seldom went abroad by day; but at nightfall it was his custom to ride within his own grounds and breathe the free air of heaven when the frost or the dew descended on the grass. He permitted his hair and his beard, which was now snow-white, to grow long; and, as he galloped hither and thither, the peasant who caught a passing glimpse of him thought of the unseen world and hurried on.

Strange, weird stories began to float around the countryside of uncanny doings in the old Tower of Auchendrane; and the frightened peasant whispered to his cronie that the rushing river carried many a queer muttering to the sea. As the tale passed on, it grew in the passing, until the grim form of Satan himself appeared in the back-ground as the friend and familiar of the haggard, gaunt baron; and with him wizards and witches and the whole array of the infernal army. In Mure's youth, and on through his life, Auchendrane Tower had witnessed many a wild scene; many a last faint cry had fallen on the irresponsive walls of its dungeons, and many a captive had passed beneath its gloomy portals never to emerge again or breathe heaven's free air. Even the spirits of these unfortunates were dragged back from another world by the peasants, and made to minister to the infernal torments which drove the old man out into the darkest night and forced him to seek solace from the kindly contact of nature. The mothers on the slopes of Carrick and in the valley of the Doon hushed their children with threats of handing them over to Auchendrane for final disposal; and the belated rustic wayfarers hastened past the environs of the Tower, fearful lest some "Thing" of evil omen might flash out of the forest and bear them bodily away.

Making every allowance for exaggeration, the life led by Mure was certainly not joyous. The misdeeds of his earlier days rose up in an impenetrable, unrelieved phalanx before him. In all likelihood, but for the palpable fear which assailed him, and the uncertainty of the future amid which his days were spent, he would have been able to forget the past—at all events to regard it as atoned for, or, at best, as an uncomfortable, occasional nightmare. He might, for all practical purposes, have outlived the memories altogether; but as suspicion haunted him and unceasingly dogged his dragging footsteps, and as no tidings ever reached him of the lad whom he had sent abroad to die, so conscience wakened up proportionately, and refused to be lulled to sleep again, until he cursed the day of weakness which had prompted him to let Dalrymple for the second time beyond his reach. And in addition to his other miseries, he knew that the Earl of Cassillis was neither a forgetful nor a forgiving man, and that the blood which had soaked into the horse track which led through the wood of St. Leonards was yet unavenged. Weary of life, he yet clung to it tenaciously, and he trembled at times to think that there were angry fellows not far away who might one day fall on him and crush him.

He was practically shut up to the society of his son James, still, as six years ago, a man of ungovernable lusts and passions, and to that of James' wife, the daughter of the murdered Knight of Culzean, a quiet, broken-hearted lady, who sought as much seclusion as she could secure, whose sole happiness and comfort and hope lay in the possession of two little children, and who, but for these, would gladly have lain down to rest for ever in the green kirk-yard of quiet Alloway, or in the still, dark, funereal vaults of grey Culzean.

James drank and hunted and swore and feasted; he yielded himself up a prey to the cravings of a lustful nature; gambled recklessly as long as he had money, and laid his hands on all the money he could get; and as he felt occasional twinges of that poverty amid which the family of Auchendrane finally became extinct, stooped to every means that suggested themselves, and without regard to their morality, that seemed to open up the path to the recouping of his shattered fortunes.

The long bloody wars in the Low Countries had drawn to a peaceful close, and the Truce of Venice was signed; and the shattered remnant of the regiment of the bold Buccleuch embarked for home.

In his six years campaigning, William Dalrymple had exchanged the outward aspect of the beardless, over-grown, raw-boned youth for that of the veteran weather-tanned soldier. His mental had kept pace with his physical growth. He came to learn something of men, and manners, in a rough school, but still practical, and to reason out cause and effect; and many a night as he lay in camp or in the trenches, his thoughts had reverted to the strange chain of events which had so far guided his destiny, and which had driven him into scenes so different from those which he had anticipated. By dint of reasoning, he came to realise more clearly than ever why Auchendrane was so solicitous for his absence from Scotland, and how much he had to fear for his return; and growing more reliant as he grew older, and became familiar with battle and with danger, he had resolved to return to his native land and to demand whatever advantages were due to the supremacy which he now knew he exercised over Auchendrane. He had paid a dear price for his innocent complicity— why should he not have an ample reward?

It was in the autumn of 1610 that Dalrymple disembarked
in company with his discharged comrades, rich in honours,
but poor in resources, on Scottish soil.   Better for him that
he had remained where he was, than that he should tempt
the fates which lurked in the breast of Mure.   For, to face
or thwart Auchendrane was the one step betwixt him and
death.

On his arrival at Leith, Dalrymple naturally turned his
face and his footsteps westwards to the land of his home.   It
was a weary journey, by rough roads and devious highways;
but to a soldier like him, not by any means an uncongenial
experience.   Three days after bidding adieu to his comrades,
and leaving behind him the high peaked dwellings of the
Scottish metropolis, he sighted the town of Ayr and the once
familiar Firth of Clyde.   Many a night he had seen them in
his dreams as he lay beneath the drooping skies of the Low
Countries, and his heart warmed with a kindly feeling to each
well-remembered spot.   Everything in the landscape was as
he had left it ; there was hardly any change even in the old
burgh town ; the burghers themselves were unchanged, save
that those with whom the world had gone well were more
portly and dignified and self-important than when he had
left them.

His intention was to remain at home with his friends, to
ascertain the changed phases of the affair of Auchendrane,
and to regulate his precise line of action by the course of
events; but circumstances were not long in eventuating,
which forced him to change his plans, and to seek a safer and
a more retired shelter.   What these circumstance were it is
necessary to explain.

It was during one of his drinking bouts in Ayr that James
Mure learned from experience that the man of whom, of all
others, he was most suspicious, and from whom he had most
to fear, had returned to his native country.   James was
carousing, as was his wont, in a low ale-house, of which he

was the presiding deity, in the High Street, with a few choice
spirits whose minds and habits were somewhat akin to his
own. They were not men who, socially, had any right to
associate on terms of close intimacy or familiarity with the
heir to the barony of Auchendrane, but loose characters,
toadies, loafers—men who were quite content, for such
patronage in friendship and in liquor as they received, to regard him in the light of a patron. They always knew when
a badger was to be drawn, a cock main fought, or a bull to be
baited—pastimes which synchronised perfectly with the
brutalised tastes of James Mure.

The cup had been circulating freely; oath, ribald song,
coarse jest, obscene merriment, had been flowing in unabated
stream. The night wearing away towards midnight, the
half-inebriated, riotous company had started, either to seek a
lower depth, or to make the best of their way home. Arm-in-
arm they swept the centre of the street, and the hurrying
wayfarer gave them a wide berth as they noisily and un-
steadily strode along, making the night hideous with their
songs and execrations.

As thus they made the crown of the causeway disorderly,
they met three or four young men approaching quietly from
the opposite direction. These gave neither occasion for insult
nor for quarrel, and would have passed the roysterers without
notice; but the opportunity was too good a one for Mure and
his boon companions to miss, and, spreading themselves out,
they checked their progress, and hustled them rudely as they
attempted to pass. One of the strangers promptly resented
the insult, giving his special insulter a lusty push, which
sent him sprawling into the gutter. James Mure at once
took up the quarrel, and rushing to the spot where the
stranger stood awaiting further developments, sprang towards
him with a wild threat of vengeance. The young man stood
on one side, and as the half-intoxicated Mure lounged blindly
at him in passing, struck him a blow which for the moment

settled both the dignity and the standing of the scion of Auchendrane. But the blow had a sobering effect on Mure. He collected his senses with wonderful speed, and set about the task of overcoming his antagonist with determination and with comparative coolness.

The light was uncertain, for the darkness of midnight was hardly relieved by the ghostly flickering of an oil lamp hard-bye—a species of illuminant which tended to do little more than render the darkness visible. Still it was good enough for the purpose of the fight, for it afforded advantage to neither of the combatants.

Mure's friends would willingly have lent him assistance, but he ordered them back.

"Leave him to me," he said, with an oath; "if I am not good enough to manage him, let the devil take us both."

So adjured, his boon companions stood aside, and encouraged him to the combat. The friends of his antagonist in similar fashion gathered close round the struggling figures, after the time-honoured custom, "to see fair play."

Mure was the stronger man of the two, and had he been in anything like the physical condition of his opponent, who was lithe and supple, and sound in wind, he would no doubt have succeeded in getting the better of the fight. But he had been carousing too freely; his tissues were too soft for a sustained struggle, and he himself felt the necessity of forcing the combat before debauched nature should give in. So he rushed again to the conflict with an ardour worthy of a better cause, and gripped his antagonist by the waist, trying with all the energy he could command to throw him heavily. But in this he failed. The training of the stranger stood him in good stead; and though he was less powerful, he was still a skilful wrestler, and kept his feet in spite of the herculean exertion of brute force which was brought to bear on his overthrow. The longer the struggle lasted the more Mure felt his chances diminishing, so, collecting his energies, he concentrated them in one final effort, which resulted in both him and his antagonist coming heavily to the ground, where they rolled over one another with arms interlocked and each endeavouring by every means in his power to overcome the other.

Unfortunately for the settlement of the issue, at this moment the three officials of the burgh, whose duty it was to keep the peace for the lieges, came up unobserved in the darkness and called on the combatants to cease. To the invitation neither paid the slightest heed. They lay as closely on the causeway as if they had been pinioned together, Mure breathing out imprecations, the stranger silent and with teeth compressed, and both panting heavily from the severity of the physical strain.

"Pass your lantern round this way," said one of the officers to another, "and let us have a look at their faces."

The officer did as he was told, and swung his lantern full in the face of the prone antagonists; and for the first time they obtained a glimpse of one another. The effect on Mure was remarkable. For an instant his fingers relaxed their grasp, his breath came in spasmodic respirations, and his eyes seemed to be all but starting out of their sockets.

But he was unnerved only for an instant. Rallying with wonderful speed, he sprang afresh, like a wild cat, upon the stranger, grasped him by the throat, and with one superhuman exertion, rolled on top of him and fixed him with choking grip to the ground.

"Villain," he hissed into his ear, "you have come back again to curse us with your infernal presence, but by all the furies beneath us, you shall not escape me now."

And, but for the presence of the officers, he would have made good his words. These, however, seeing the danger, closed in upon him, and by the exercise of all the force they could command, succeeded in releasing the nervous fingers from the throat of the half-strangled man.

"Shame on you, Mr. Mure," said one of them, "brawling and fighting in this style! Is this the way you maintain the credit of the house of Auchendrane?"

James Mure spoke no more that night. He was not without wisdom of a kind, and such as he had speedily impressed him with the danger of either putting his adversary on his guard or committing himself in the presence of other people.

Dalrymple—for the stranger was none other than he—was not long in recovering himself. Until the officer had spoken he had not the faintest suspicion of the individuality of his antagonist; but, scanning his features, he had no difficulty in recognising them.

"You have given me a hard tussle," he said, gazing steadily into Mure's eyes, "but see if I do not make the tussle all the harder for you. You have had your time; see that I do not have mine."

The burgh officers were not by any means eager to land so liberal a patron of theirs as Mure in the Tolbooth; so, after rating him severely and with some measure of dignity, they let the antagonists go; and these disappeared in different directions.

Half-an-hour later James Mure was riding homewards. Ayr was asleep as he left it behind him, and his horse's hoofs awakened the echoes of the forsaken High Street. As he cantered through the plantation by the Chapel of St. Leonards his strained imagination brought vividly before him the scene which the quiet trees once had witnessed. He saw the conspirators lying hidden; he heard the approach of Sir Thomas Kennedy. The rush of the assassins; the attempted escape; the murder; the dead body of the slaughtered knight with face upturned, on the crimson-dyed sod—these rushed before him, and he quickened his pace until clear of the haunting, pervading presences of the woodland. Through the dark shadows of Rozelle he passed, and past the solitary, slumbering hamlets which, here and there, relieved the painful

lonesomeness of the way. He caught a glimpse of the Auld
Kirk of Alloway, all unconscious of the unhallowed orgies
yet to be evolved within its sacred walls; ignorant as yet of
the time to come when, "in winnock bunker in the east,"
Satan himself would

> Screw his pipes and gar them skirl
> Till roof and rafters a' did dirl ;

blameless of the witches' dance, or of the hellish procession
which was to pass through the windows, when sudden darkness ensued on the thoughtless observation of the belated
farmer. He clattered across the narrow bridge of Doon,
innocent as the kirk itself of the infernal chase yet to be arrested by its magical keystone; and, crossing the Doon,
entered Carrick.

The tower of Auchendrane was buried in woodland and in
darkness, only one faint light glimmering from one of the
windows. It was a distant glimpse of this light that made
the gossips hurry past, for it twinkled in presence of Satanic
mysteries and winked at scenes which no mortal tongue could
tell.

James Mure knew that the light was nothing more than
that of the lamp in his father's chamber, and that the old
man had not yet gone to bed; so he led his heated horse to
the stables, unharnessed him, tied him up, and left him. This
done he wended his way through the familiar darkness to the
house itself, and a few minutes thereafter surprised his father
as he sat ruminating and brooding over his life's mischances.

Reckless, callous man as he was, Auchendrane was deeply
incensed at the riotous conduct of his son. He was proud
and haughty as became a baron of the times; and displeasure
filled him when he thought of James' ongoings, of the company he kept, of the baseness of his pleasures, of the lascivi-
ousness of his desires, and of the future to which his conduct
necessarily tended. He foresaw troubles ahead to the house
of Auchendrane, and though he could not live to see them

realised, they rankled in his breast and led to many a stormy
interview with the brutalised man upon whom must, in the
ordinary course of nature, descend ere long the rights, privi-
leges, and responsibilities of an old and once honourable race.
Consequently, when James, with blood-encrusted face—for he
bore upon his countenance the marks of Dalrymple's valour—
with breath painfully suggestive of the pot-house, entered
unbidden on his presence, he at once turned savagely upon
him with the remark,

" What has brought you here at this time of night ? "

" I have come to talk with you," was James' curt reply,
curtly given.

" You can talk with me to-morrow, I am in no mood for
talking with a half-drunken fool who has been brawling over
some slut or other, and who seems to have got the worst of
it."

" No, I don't think I did get the worst of it," responded
James, stung by the reproach, and reflecting on what was due
to his prowess, " If I had been left alone I would have made
short work of him anyhow."

" You are dead to all remonstrances, James.   I have tried
all I can to waken you to a sense of your duty and of your
position.   You play the game of the enemy in the best way
possible for him, lowering the credit of Auchendrane, making
the name of the House a bye-word on the streets and in the
brothels of Ayr, and making yourself the laughing-stock of
the country side."

James was not in a mood to be trifled with.   His nerves
were unstrung, his passionate blood ran quick, and he
retorted savagely—

" I know that I am not a saint, but neither are you.   Besides, when I have an enemy in my hands I do not let him
go, to turn up like some infernal spectre of ill-omen when it
least suits my purpose.   But for you I never would have
borne these scars.   They are not very deep," he continued

with a forced laugh, "but they are deep enough for my purpose."

"What is your purpose?" queried Auchendrane sharply.

"My purpose is to kill the man who inflicted them. Come wet, come dry, I'll kill him, too, as sure as my name is James Mure," was the fiercely uttered response.

"I dare be bound you brought the fight on yourself?"

"Perhaps I did; but whether or not, he must die."

"Who must die?"

"The man who drew blood from me."

"Who is he? Why do you not tell me?"

"Because you have never asked me. Who is he? He is William Dalrymple."

Auchendrane, sitting as he was, reeled in his chair, and gasped for breath. His eyes grew filmy as he fixed them on his son; a cold perspiration broke over his body, and bead-drops sprang on his forehead; he grasped his chair convulsively with nervous fingers; and in a husky voice, in which fear and passion were strangely blended, repeated the words—

"William Dalrymple!"

"Yes, William Dalrymple."

There was a pause for a few seconds, as father and son gazed into one another's eyes, and read death in their light.

"Go to bed, James," said Auchendrane huskily. "We shall speak of this to-morrow."

James obeyed. He was glad enough to get away from his father's presence. He had never seen him look so before; for his eyes were, in James' distorted imagination, fixed on something he himself could not see. What if, as the rustics declared, his father was in league with the Prince of the Powers of the air? What if fiends, or evil spirits, stood attendant on him, to the commission of acts which ordinary mortals could not dare? It was the current belief of the country-side that witches still rode on nocturnal excursions through the midnight sky, and that there were men who had sold themselves to the devil in consideration of benefit on

15

earth, bartering their long future for their short present. Why should not something of this kind be mixed up with his father's experience? His blood-shot eyes, sunk deep in hollow sockets; his parchment-like skin, tanned by the suns and the winds of eighty summers and winters; his long grey hair hanging down over his shoulders; his nervous bony fingers still firm in clutch; his determined, inflexible demeanour— all these bespoke possibilities that James Mure could not reckon with. And, therefore, they troubled him, and made him thankful to escape from the room.

But what was it in reality that Mure did see?

Before him stretched the pall of an unknown future; and through it there struggled rays from the far beyond. He steadied his gaze upon them.

One fell athwart the Tolbooth of Ayr. Another struck the walls of the Heart of Midlothian. Beneath the sparkle of a third he saw a thronging crowd press into the halls of Justice. A fourth shone on the interior of the Court of Justiciary, and lighted up the Judge on the bench and—— and the prisoner at the bar. As he withdrew his gaze lest he should see the prisoner, and directed it to the deepest gloom of the pall, still another shot into the intensity of the black- ness and revealed beneath it——a scaffold. Hence, horrible shadows!

But still he gazed. And through the gloom he espied a tortuous path that lit up the way to salvation. It lay through crime and bloodshed, but it swept past the base of the scaffold, and it left the headsman behind; and by this winding way Auchendrane elected to walk.

CHAPTER XVII.

THE MURES PREPARE A HORROR.

LEFT to his own meditations, Auchendrane, with tempest- tossed mind, spent what remained of the night in thought.

Daylight was breaking over the tree-tops, and the birds were beginning their morning song ere he flung himself on his couch in search of repose. It was in vain that he courted the drowsy god; for as he closed his eyes, visions of the past trooped up in close unhallowed sequence through the darkness, and deeds darker even than the night through which he had passed—deeds that had long slumbered—awoke into fresh vigour and into painfully striking relief.

All brought him to the one regret and to the one conclusion, that he had permitted Dalrymple to escape him in an hour of weakness, but that now he must sternly atone for the mistake he had made. He cursed the chances of war which had taken others and let Dalrymple escape. Dalrymple had been sent to the Continent to die, as others better than he were dying; but the war was over, the fray and the bullet and the cannon shot were all in the past, and the one witness who could bring him to account for a deed over which watched an unslumbering Nemesis, had returned to his native country, no longer a half-souled stripling, but a man in his early prime, inured to trial and more dangerous than ever.

The danger was imminent. No time was to be lost. There was only one way by which to get rid of the peril, and that was to get rid of Dalrymple quietly, effectively, and for ever.

How was it to be done? Whether by hired assassin on the streets of Ayr, or in some secluded spot in the country where no mortal eye could witness the deed, or in the dark cold dungeons of Auchendrane?

Auchendrane's mind was still pursuing its distraught but desperate career when his son, who had the benefit of a few hours' slumber, joined him. James's was a different nature from that of his father, and the unexpected return of Dalrymple neither affected him in the same fashion nor to the same extent. He was not troubled by premonitory remorse when he contemplated the murder of the man who, the previous evening, had revealed his presence so forcibly to him

on the streets of Ayr. His death was an absolute essential,
so it awakened neither qualms nor scruples of conscience.
Necessity knew no law; here was the necessity; and the effect
must follow the cause as naturally as day night. No more
half measures for James Mure. Had his advice been followed
five years ago there would have been no need either for fearing or for scheming; and he rather prided himself than
otherwise on the murderous advice he had tendered, and
which his father, in his weakness, had seen cause to reject.

It is not easy to discriminate between the *morale* or motives
of two intended murderers, or to place the animating principles
of the one on a higher level than those of the other. With
James, however, it was a simple matter of common necessity,
which demanded a short effective remedy, and which did not
trouble his mind, or stir his callousness. The deed itself
barely cost him a thought. All he desiderated was that it
should be done after such a fashion as would keep him free
from the consequences. But with his father, the necessity,
was justified by more complex and less brutal impulses. He
had still a faint touch of the humanitarian left in him, and,
even to secure immunity, did not regard bloodshed, cold and
calculating, as anything short of a horrible necessity. Nothing, indeed, but absolute necessity convinced him that
Dalrymple must be removed; and in the still hours of the
morning he had had to fight down impulses which might have
led him to the adoption of other courses. But he had convinced himself of the necessity, fought down the impulses,
and was ready to act. And when James entered the room he
saw the determination livid on his father's face.

"Well, father," was James' opening, as he threw himself
upon a chair, "are you convinced at last that you made a
mistake six years ago when you permitted Dalrymple to
escape us?"

"No need to talk of that, James, we have enough to do
with the future."

"True," replied James, with the air of a man who was anxious to justify his earlier wisdom, "but if you had taken my advice then, there would have been no need to solve the riddle now. Carrick would have forgotten by this time that such a man ever existed, you would have been saved six years of bother and anxiety, and Dalrymple would have been six years sooner in heaven, and had six years less of soldiering in Flanders."

"I did it for the best," responded Mure, somewhat abashed by the knowledge that for once James had shown superior wisdom.

"Yes," laughed James, "you thought to get rid of him the way David got rid of Uriah, but you failed, which was more than David did. But David played with loaded dice."

"Yes, and didn't make very much of it after all. Let us leave David alone, though, and talk business."

"Yes, that suits better. First and foremost, we must—I have been thinking the business over—get to know where Dalrymple is to be found; then, how we can get hold of him without anyone being a bit the wiser; and, after that, how we can dispose of him most easily and speedily."

"Whatever is to be done must be done at once. Were Cassillis to get hold of him before we do, it would be a bad lookout."

"Yes—for you, not for me. You know I had nothing to do with Sir Thomas Kennedy. You did not even consult me about it, so that I fancy I am rather generous than otherwise in coming to your assistance. I was willing to help you when you had hold of Dalrymple the last time; and I am willing yet—more so, indeed, than ever, because, by my soul, he gave me an infernally tight grip last night. I have my score to pay off as well now, and if you don't pay off yours, I'll pay off mine, which will be pretty much the same thing in the long run."

"There must be no rashness, James; we must proceed

cautiously as well as quickly. If we are to be identified with the disappearance of such a common fellow as Dalrymple, it would be far better, for our credit, to leave him alone and take our chance for the death of Culzean."

"Yes, I think it would; but don't forget what I tell you, that I am free from that, and have nothing to fear from the death of a dozen Culzeans, so long as I had no finger in the pie. But tell me," continued James, "have you quite got over the weakness that tempted you to let this fellow off scot-free?"

"Quite," replied Auchendrane, in a determined tone. "I am one with you now. There is only one lane of escape, and that is through the death or life-long imprisonment of Dalrymple."

"Look here," said James, angrily, "if you talk of imprisonment I'll have nothing more to do do with the matter, or, if I have, I'll act for myself, and on my own responsibility. I'll have no imprisonment in the matter, except the imprisonment of six feet of mould."

"Well, death then, if there be no alternative. I do not want you to take Dalrymple into your own hands," replied Auchendrane, who had no very high opinion of his son's discretion. "We must act together. It will double assurance, and leave less doubt of success. Besides, I should never be satisfied unless I saw him disposed of."

"Your desire can easily be gratified," laughed James. "But there must be no mistake this time; so I am going to see you through with it."

This little preliminary settled, Auchendrane and his son proceeded to discuss how the "taking off" of Dalrymple was to be gone about. Clearly, nothing could be done until his precise whereabouts was known; so it was resolved that James should return that same day to Ayr, and should discover his residence; and, if possible, take steps to secure the person of Dalrymple. Mure enjoined the utmost caution on his son, not so much, he endeavoured to argue, because they were doing, or about to do, an illegal act, or even because there might be some resultant danger in the consequences, as because it was absolutely essential to the accomplishment of the deed itself.

" You know, James," he observed, addressing his son, " that we are about to do what the world calls murder. It is not murder, though. It is a justifiable act we are going to perform. It is essential to my well-being that Dalrymple should die; because, if he is permitted to live, the end of his living might be my dying. Now, pitting life against life, whether is the more valuable—his or mine? Whether is it more important that the Laird of Auchendrane should live, or this nameless scoundrel, whom nobody would miss? And you have a direct interest, too, in his death. You say you have nothing to lose—have you not? Attaint me, and you attaint the family name. You lower the honour of the house of Mure, and you run the risk—a risk that would fall on you, James—of having the estates forfeited to the Crown—which means, in other words, forfeited to the Earl of Cassillis. Thus, you and yours become disinherited, and the name of Mure of Auchendrane passes away."

" What's the use of talking like that ? " interrupted James. " We have agreed to kill Dalrymple. Is that not enough, without all that rigmarole ? "

" What I want to show you," resumed Auchendrane, with a highly virtuous tinge in his accents, " is that the removal of Dalrymple is a solemn duty that devolves upon us, and not a common assassination. Even the servants of the Lord, in his own land of Judea, did not hesitate to remove those who stood in their way. Elijah brought down fire from heaven and consumed the captains of two fifties, with their fifties, for no other offence than commanding him, in the king's name, to come down from a mountain ; and Elisha did not hesitate to curse the children when they mocked at him, the result being

that two bears destroyed forty and two of them.   In neither
of these cases was there the same necessity that exists here—
and we only propose to destroy the life of one man who has
my life and our property, so to speak, in his hands."

"Yes, and we have no she bears," James laughed, "to order
out to tear him in pieces, so we must do it ourselves."

"Yes, or perish ourselves.   Indeed, we are only entering on
the fulfilment of a duty."

"Of course we are," assented James, who was not troubled
either with the need for precedents or analogies.

The same afternoon James Mure took horse for Ayr with
the object of discovering Dalrymple's whereabouts.   He
sought out his boon companions of the previous evening, and
heard from them tidings which stimulated his energies.   They
had learned that after the fight the night before, Dalrymple
had threatened to make the house of Mure suffer for the
insult which he had sustained at the hands of James.   Dalrymple, indeed, in the first flush of anger and excitement, had
let fall words which boded no good for those against whom he
had directed his threats.   He knew as much, he had said, as
would bring Auchendrane to the gallows.   Pressed to explain,
he had refused; but he had indicated that it would be no
easy matter to purchase his silence.

What made matters worse was, that early that morning
Dalrymple had set out on foot for Carrick.   Whither had he
gone ?   Was he by this time in actual conspiracy with the
Earl of Cassillis ?   Had he already entered on his revenge for
his enforced six months' stay in Arran, for his enforced six
years' soldiering in the Low Countries, and for the attack
which James Mure had made on him the night before ?

Remembering his father's advice, and inspired with a good
deal of personal caution on his own account, James succeeded,
by the aid of his friends and by judiciously conducted inquiries, in learning that Dalrymple had not as yet sold
himself to the enemy.   Fearing that the Mures would

endeavour to exact instant vengeance, he had gone into hiding with the object of throwing a cloak over his movements and taking time to consider how best he could advance his own ends. These were the securing from Auchendrane of a large ransom for silence. In other words, what he wanted was hush-money. James endeavoured by every means in his power to find out where Dalrymple had secreted himself. On this point no one could give him the least information. He had gone to Carrick—that was all he could ascertain, and had left Ayr by the road running parallel to the coast.

In the route he had taken there was exceptional danger. The strongholds of the Kennedys were on the Carrick shore, saving Cassillis, which was inland. He must in his journey pass the rock on which Greenan stood; he must skirt the very walls of the black vault of Dunure, and if he still kept on by the sea line he must pass under Culzean Castle. What if he should be recognised and taken captive? Once in the hands of the Kennedys, it remained for them to dictate to Dalrymple, not for Dalrymple to dictate to Auchendrane.

For the next few days the Mures, still proceeding with caution, made inquiries in all directions. It was clearly impossible that they could themselves ride hither and thither asking the natives if they had seen a man answering to the description of William Dalrymple; but fortunately for their intents, there were other means of finding out his whereabouts than this. They had numerous friends all over Carrick, men who were bound to them rather by antipathy to Cassillis than by friendship for his rivals. The Mures were feared, not liked ; but this fear was quite sufficient, coupled with feudal sympathies or hatreds, to enlist in their cause those who otherwise would have scorned them assistance. Accordingly they confided their secret to one or two of the most tried, and most dyed, of their associates. They explained neither the object which they had in discovering Dalrymple's whereabouts, nor their intent on discovering him. Detailed explanation was

unnecessary.   All that was necessary was the assurance that
they wanted to find Dalrymple.   That was enough, especially
when accompanied by a hint that his discovery would be a
blow at the house of Cassillis.

The search went on for ten or twelve days, and it resulted
in the finding of Dalrymple resident in the farm house of
Chapeldonan, on the Girvan shore.   A more unfortunate
residence he could not have chosen.   The tenant, James
Bannatyne, whose protection the young man had craved, was
a vassal of Auchendrane.   Distantly related to Dalrymple,
and ignorant of the fatal bond of connexion between him and
the inflexible baron, he had unhesitatingly afforded the former an asylum on his arrival at his farm.   Dalrymple had so
far kept his counsels from Bannatyne.   Knowing something
of the influence which Auchendrane exercised over him, and
fearful on the one hand of the possibility of betrayal, and, on
the other, of implicating his kinsman in any consequences
that might ensue as the result of harbouring one whom the
Mures had every reason to fear, he had kept a discreet silence.
His days he spent wandering by the shores of the sea and in
assisting in the work of the farm; and it was while thus engaged in manual occupation that he was seen and his presence
reported to the Mures.

"The Lord hath, indeed, again delivered him into our
hands," said Auchendrane when he heard the news. "Things
couldn't have better befallen us."

"Yes, we can get him now, for sure," replied James, "and
take him when it suits ourselves."

Another consultation followed, the result of which was that
Mure himself, late the following afternoon, despatched a
messenger to Chapeldonan farm to request Bannatyne to
come to Auchendrane with all convenient speed, and to keep
secret from all the fact of his coming. He rightly argued that
Bannatyne would interpret the request as a command not to be
disobeyed, and that he would lose no time in acting upon it.

Nor was he disappointed. The tenant of Chapeldonan had no idea of any incriminating connexion between his kinsman Dalrymple and the Laird of Auchendrane. Had he imagined for a moment the danger which lurked beneath the command, he would have obeyed it all the same, but he would have taken care that Dalrymple should be beyond his influence ere evil results could follow from his residence at the farm. As it was, he smothered any recollection which still floated in his mind, of the rumours which filled Carrick when Dalrymple was sent off to the Continent, and next day mounted his horse and took his way across the country for the Tower of Auchendrane.

Mure was in waiting. The burly farmer saw James as he entered, but the heir to the estate by the Doon hardly deigned to notice him. Not so with Mure himself. He was exceptionally complaisant to his visitor, and personally conducting him to the dining-hall, saw that his creature comforts were well attended to ere broaching the business which lay to his hand. Auchendrane had thought the matter over, and had decided that he must to some extent take Bannatyne into his confidence; though not, however, in the meantime, to the extent of unduly informing him of what it was resolved should follow, or frightening him with the dread of self-incrimination.

"You know, Bannatyne," he said, after the farmer's heart had become enlarged by the good cheer bounteously bestowed, "that I have not brought you here simply to feast you, or to talk over old times. There is a time and a place for everything, so I will not keep you any longer in suspense. I want your assistance."

"Yes, sir," replied Bannatyne, "to tell you the truth, I have been wondering all the time why you sent for me. No danger in the wind, over there?" indicating with his finger the direction in which the house of Cassillis stood.

"Well, no; no danger—at least, not in the meantime. But

there might be danger bye and bye, unless I prevent it by some means, and I have sent for you to help me to prevent it."

"That will I do with all my heart. Times are quiet in Carrick in these days, sir, and there is a sad want of excitement to an old trooper like myself; though, to tell you the truth, I am beginning to enjoy the long peace."

"So am I, Chapeldonan," responded Mure, "yet the peace is not quite assured yet. But you and I between us can assure it, if we like. And it is because I place unbounded faith in you that I have asked you to assist me. You have William Dalrymple living with you at present, I hear?"

Bannatyne was not prepared for the sudden change in the conversation; but there was something in the tones of Mure's voice which awakened at once a strong suspicion—a suspicion he could not explain even to himself.

Mure saw the effect on the mind of the farmer—it had betrayed itself on his face—and proceeded with unruffled expression—

"Do not be afraid, Chapeldonan, of your kinsman. I am not finding any fault whatever with your kindness to an old friend. On the contrary, I highly appreciate it. All I want to ask you is, to bring him here to see me, or to give me an opportunity of an hour's conversation with him in some spot where we will not be liable to interruption."

"I cannot bring him here, sir," replied, Bannatyne. "Dalrymple is not easily persuaded against his will; and were he to see me anxious to bring him here, I am very much afraid he would scent terror in the air, and leave as suddenly as he came."

"Terror in the air, Chapeldonan! I do not comprehend you. Why should he be afraid to come to Auchendrane? The past is past. It is quite true, it was I who had him sent to Flanders to do a turn at soldiering; but that has made a man of him, I hear. Besides, I must see him, if the peace is to be preserved."

"Well, sir, I am not unwilling that you should meet him, so long as no harm can come of it."

"Harm come of it!" replied Auchendrane in virtuous accents. "What harm can possibly come of it? Yet, as I say, I must see him, and that at once; and, Chapeldonan, I look to you to help me. And I'll tell you why, because I know I can trust you. You remember the death of Sir Thomas Kennedy of Culzean?"

"Yes—he was murdered near Ayr, wasn't he?"

"Precisely, and a number of gentlemen in Carrick fled the district at the time of the offence—Kennedy of Bargany, Mure of Cloncaird, and one or two more. Well, at that time, the Earl of Cassillis swore to revenge. You remember how he prosecuted me—citing me to the bar of the Privy Council? You remember also, that the Privy Council found no fault in me, and dismissed the charge? Since that period, the Earl of Cassillis has never slumbered in the pursuit of revenge. Just now Dalrymple is the witness, the only witness, to whom the Earl of Cassillis can look to substantiate the charge. It is not I who have aught to fear. I have already tholed an assize, and, as I say, no offence was found against me. But there are others who are not so situated, and against whom Dalrymple's evidence might tell with other effect. So now that the deed is forgotten, and Carrick happy in peace, you will, I think, agree with me, that if we can preserve that peace by any legitimate means, it is our duty to do so. Sir Thomas Kennedy's death was one of the misfortunes of a family fight—why should it not be allowed to die away into silence for ever?"

"I see, I see," replied Bannatyne, "Dalrymple holds the key to the position; and you want him to give it up?"

"Precisely; that is exactly what I do want. We intend no harm to him, but rather that he should be rewarded for his silence. We wish him to leave the district and not return to it again, and are willing to treat him handsomely if he will agree to do so."

"You will do him no harm, sir?" the farmer asked, eyeing Auchendrane half-suspiciously.

"None," replied Auchendrane, steadily returning the gaze; "on the contrary, we will reward him for his silence."

"Pay him, that is, for holding his tongue! Just so."

Auchendrane repeated his assurances with a vehemence which left no doubt in the mind of the simple farmer of his sincerity. Once convinced of this, the remainder was comparatively easy; and ere Bannatyne started for home it was resolved that the next night he should bring Dalrymple at midnight to a given spot on the Girvan shore, without informing him of the wherefore of the untimely interview.

"Is it all arranged?" asked James of his father when Bannatyne was fairly on his road for home.

"Yes, it is all arranged; Dalrymple is to be on the Girvan shore, north of Chapeldonan Farm, to-morrow at midnight."

"That is well; there must be no mistake this time."

"No, James, though I must confess that I did not like assuring Bannatyne that we intended no harm. He will know soon enough that we do."

"Yes, that is true; but the whip is in our hands. Bannatyne hangs by the same cord as we do after that. All we have to do is to threaten him into silence by telling him that unless he is mute as the grave we will inform against him, and have him executed for murder. And if he is specially obdurate, we can serve him as we serve Dalrymple, and leave them so that when they are found the people will come to the conclusion that they have died together in combat. I say, father," as the light seemed to dawn on James, "isn't that a good idea?"

"James, James, don't suggest such a thing. Bannatyne will see it to his own interest to be quiet. Nobody knows of Dalrymple's whereabouts, and he never will be missed. Bannatyne himself was not wont to be so chary of letting out a drop of blood."

" No, but not in this style."

" True; though after all, what is the difference between splitting a · man's head open on the field or doing the same thing by him on the sea shore ?   It comes to the same in the end."

" Society doesn't think so, father; and there lies the difference."

" Yes, but the estimate of society is not the true gauge of action."

" And even if it were, we have gone too far to draw back now.   Besides, society is an ass, to begin with, and an ass to finish with, when all is done."

" So it is, James, so it is.   But to business !   How are we to go about it ?   How are we to dispose of him ?"

" The quicker the better.   Shoot him, and have done with it."

" No, James," replied Auchendrane ; " we must not shoot him.   It can't be done without a noise, and it might ruin us. Who knows who might be about ?   A revenue officer, or a fisherman, or a smuggler, or some traveller ?   A pistol shot sounds clear on a fine night."

" So it does, father," said James.

" Besides," resumed Auchendrane, " think of the bloodshed, trickling out of him and oozing through your fingers.   No noise, James, and no blood if we can help it.   Noise, as much as you like, and blood too, if we must have them.   Not otherwise.   I have been thinking it all over, and we must take more primitive weapons for the business."

" What kind of weapons ?"

" Of course we will carry firearms.   There's nothing like them in an emergency ; but for secrecy there's nothing like the hands."

" The hands !   Explain yourself, father."

"Well, what I mean is this. We must knock him down first, either with the butt-end of a heavy pistol, or of a whip, or with a club; and then, when we have got him down, tackle into him like two furies and hold him till he's dead—grip him by the throat and stop his powers of breathing."

"We must be sure he's insensible before we begin," observed James; "for a man struggles hard when he fights for his life."

"Oh yes, we'll make sure enough he's insensible," remarked Auchendrane, with the utmost coolness and deliberation, yet inwardly terribly conscious of the gruesome character of the work which he projected.

"Strangle him!" observed James musingly. "Then I'll tell you what it is. We must take a rope with us. I know this fellow too well to trust his throat in anybody's fingers. It's a clumsy way, though, at best, and I don't like it."

"It is a safe way for ourselves, and that's all that concerns us now. Besides, what matters it? It will be all the same to Dalrymple a week hence," was Auchendrane's rejoinder.

"Less than a week, I hope," remarked James.

"All the same thirty hours hence."

"Then I take it that we quite understand how this is to be gone about, subject to accidents or emergencies?"

"I suppose so; and as the conversation is not lively, I think I'll take myself off elsewhere."

"Very well, James. But stay," added Auchendrane, as his son rose to leave the room, "Don't forget the spades."

"The spades!" repeated James in surprise: "What spades?"

"We must hide it."

"Hide it—the body, you mean?"

"Yes."

"Well, you are deliberate, father! I would never have thought of such a thing. I'll see to getting the spades."

And James, darting a look of admiration at his father—

admiration begotten of the old man's forethought—left the room.

What a melancholy spectacle the Mures presented! Fortunately, an exceptionally uncommon one. But they were braced up for a deed which, in its cold calculating conception, in its ghastly realisation, and in its consequences, has few parallels in western story. The curtain was about to rise on the cruel tragedy of Auchendrane.

CHAPTER XVIII.

THE TRAGEDY OF AUCHENDRANE.

THE sun had gone down behind the peaks of Arran, and night was already casting its sable mantle over sea and hill and plain and woodland, when the Mures, mounting their horses, rode out from the courtyard of Auchendrane and set forth on their murderous errand. Their plans were all carefully laid. Both were armed to the teeth; James carried at his saddle bow a strong hempen rope, and across the back of each was slung a spade. The firearms were only for an extremity; the deed was to be done, if at all possible, by strangulation; and, with the help of the spades, they hoped to hide the record of their premeditated crime beneath the sands of the Girvan shore. Neither experienced a single pang of remorse or compunction. Even Auchendrane had steeled his heart against the faintest regrets; to him the necessity was a necessity not to be compounded.

The night grew dark as they struck the coast and kept on their way parallel to the sea. Not a sound was heard save the solemn requiem of the ocean, now rippling over a sandy beach, now breaking on the brown rocks guarding the coast, now rattling the shingle as the waves rose and fell. Twinkling stars shone kindly on them, and the night wind from the

16

westward fanned their foreheads; but they were out of con-
sonance with nature and paid no heed to her friendly greetings.

They had plenty of time on hand. Their intention was to
reach the trysting place an hour before Bannatyne and Dalrymple would arrive, to hide their horses in one of those
caves which are not infrequent on the rocky shores of Carrick,
and to dispose the weapons with which they intended to con-
summate the tragedy, so as to have them at hand when they
should be required.

They accomplished their purpose. It wanted an hour
and more from the noon of night when the black cliff which
had been chosen as a meeting place loomed up to view. Dismounting, they secreted their horses as pre-determined; and
having similarly disposed of their spades, sat down in silence
to await the coming of the farmer of Chapeldonan and his
guest.

The minutes passed slowly, painfully, to the watchers.
Neither spoke, save in occasional short spasmodic sentences.
Each had enough to think of as he peered out over the sea,
and moralised after his own fashion on the probabilities of
the event which they had predestined. Mure was anxious to
have the deed done. His son was anxious to do it. The
latter looked to the execution of the deed itself, the former to
the benefits which it was to bring about. James Mure was
going to kill a man ; his father was going to secure the future
by the death.

The road from Chapeldonan led down by a winding path
terminating on a long stretch of level sandy beach. The tide
was at low water, and the sand was bare and brown, and
gloomy as it stretched out into the darkness.

As midnight crept on the Mures became anxious lest anything should miscarry. What if Dalrymple had scented
danger? What if, acting on intuition of danger, he had
taken his departure from Chapeldonan? What if all their

preparations had been made in vain, and their whole scheming should result in their own destruction?

" It must surely be the hour," said James to his father in a
low voice.

" Hardly yet I think; but it cannot be far off."

" I wish it was all over, anyway."

Auchendrane grunted acquiescence.

" I've an idea," resumed James.

" What?"

" You see that long stretch of sand there?"

" Yes."

" Well, that's the very spot. The tide will remove all
traces, and we can bury him there besides."

" So we can, James; and so, when we hear them coming,
we'll walk out there and wait for them. Have you got the
spades handy?"

" Yes," replied James.

" And if Bannatyne should side with him and try to prevent the deed—what then?"

" Kill him too."

Auchendrane gave no response. He had none to give,
because he saw the force of the rough conclusion. Besides, it
was the answer he desiderated. Presently James ejaculated—

" Here they come. I hear their footsteps on the path."

" Well, let us lose no time; get out on to the sands."

Jumping to their feet, the Mures, availing themselves as
far as possible of the shelter of the dark beach, moved rapidly
on to the stretching sand bank; and when Bannatyne and
Dalrymple stepped upon the beach, and looked around, they
saw the forms of the laird of Auchendrane and his son
outlined against the night. As they approached, the Mures
kept their faces steadily seawards, and it was not until Bannatyne accosted them that they pretended to recognise the
presence of their tryst-keepers.

Dalrymple was in ignorance of their personality. The tenant of Chapeldonan had not found him hard to persuade with a representation that left him under the belief that he was to witness the running ashore of a contraband cargo of spirits. As they came forward, Auchendrane laid his hand on the butt of a pistol stuck in his belt, and accosted them—

"You have kept tryst, Chapeldonan?" he observed.

"Yes, we are here," replied the tenant.

"The night is dark," continued Auchendrane, "but quite light enough to see to talk by."

"Yes," assented James, "quite light enough for all we have to say—and do."

The last words struck Bannatyne as hardly in keeping with the interview which he had undertaken to bring about, and, addressing Mure, he said—

"You did not tell me, sir, that your son would be here?"

"I did not think it necessary, Chapeldonan," replied Auchdrane, "but come apart for a moment, I have something to say to you."

Bannatyne obeyed. Dalrymple, who did not yet seem to realise the danger of his situation, stood still where he was, at a distance of about a dozen paces from James Mure, who, apparently looking out to sea, was in reality keeping a set watch on him, and ready to act at a moment's notice in the event of any attempt at escape. Neither spoke to one another as Auchendrane, leading Bannatyne inland a distance of twenty or thirty yards, opened the conversation.

"Chapeldonan," he said, in a low voice, which he steadied with wonderful self-command, "I am not going to keep you in doubt any longer as to the nature of this meeting."

"I confess I do not understand it," was the reply, "and I confess equally I do not like it. But tell me, why have you brought us here, if not for the purpose you mentioned last night?"

"It is for that very purpose I have brought you here. It

is to make myself safe from this man for all time to come. And we have come hither to do it in the only possible, effective way.

"You do not mean to do him any harm?" asked Bannatyne.

"Dead men tell no tales, Bannatyne—do you understand that?"

The full meaning burst on Bannatyne like a shot. He saw now, what he had not imagined hitherto, that he had been used as a tool for the accomplishment of a tragedy. A cold sweat burst over the farmer's brow, as, grasping Auchendrane with both hands, he ejaculated—

"Oh, sir, you do not mean to kill him!"

Auchendrane gave no verbal reply; but he indicated by a gesture that Bannatyne guessed rightly.

"My God!" groaned Bannatyne, "you cannot mean it. Did you not swear to me that you would not harm a hair of his head?"

"Of course I did," was the cold reply, "but I had to swear it for my own salvation."

"But cannot you spare him?" pleaded Bannatyne in earnest tones. "He is my guest, my kinsman. It is I who have brought him here, and if you harm a hair of his head I carry my share of the guilt to the grave with me. Oh, sir, spare him—do spare him. Do anything with him you like, but spare his life."

"It is too late, Bannatyne, and appealing to me is wasted time. Do you not know that my life is in that man's hands, and that by his death I am free for ever? We have come here to kill him, and there is no need for further delay."

"I will not permit it," replied Bannatyne firmly.

"You will not permit it!" hissed Mure, suddenly covering the farmer with a pistol. "You will not permit it! Listen to me, sir. One word, one act of interference, and you are a dead man. What good would that be to you? What good would it be to Dalrymple? My son is watching him as th eagle watches its prey, and one step towards escape is the one step towards eternity. You are in my power. What would the world say of the deed ? That you had enticed Dalrymple here, on to these lonely sands at midnight, and murdered him, and that, ere you succeeded, he had wrought out his own revenge. One death is enough for me—it will be your own fault if there be two. Do you hear ? "

Bannatyne looked into Auchendrane's eyes and read murder in them.

" I can do nothing," he moaned.

" Then, to business."

As Auchendrane and Bannatyne drew near to the spot where Dalrymple still stood, James walked rapidly across towards the same point, and stepping in front of Dalrymple, hissed into his ear :

" Do you remember the man you outraged on the streets of Ayr the other night ?"

" I outraged no man," replied Dalrymple, firmly.

" You did, damn you," was the answer. " I swore then by all that is sacred, that I would have my revenge if I follow- ed you to the ends of the earth. The time has come sooner than I expected, I swear to have it now."

So saying, he rushed upon Dalrymple with an oath. Dalrymple sprang aside, and realising in an instant the full force of his situation, uttered a piercing cry and turned to flee. But as he turned, he encountered the stern features of Auchendrane himself, who, with his pistol upraised, covered his line of retreat.

" Stand still, villain," said Auchendrane, sternly, " or I will shoot you in your tracks."

Instinctively, Dalrymple obeyed. He turned towards Auchendrane and raised his arms as if to appeal for mercy, but ere he could utter a word James struck him from behind with the butt of his heavy pistol, and he fell upon the sand.

James sprung upon him and pinioned him down. The

unfortunate man struggled hard. He fought with all the energy of despair, but the unrelaxing grasp of James Mure was on his throat, and Auchendrane himself stilled his cries and his consciousness by a brutal kick on the head.

"He's quiet enough, now," James gasped, hoarsely, "but he'll soon come to again. No more blood than we can help. Where's the rope?"

Without a word, Auchendrane unwound the hempen coil from his waist and handed it to his son. The unfeeling wretch, giving the inanimate form of Dalrymple another kick, hastily took a turn of the rope around his neck, and without a word handed one of the ends to his father. Auchendrane understood the meaning of the action. It had all been rehearsed before. In an instant the compression was complete.

A few spasmodic struggles, and the soul of the unconscious man went out into the light; and the first act of the tragedy was complete.

All the while the deed was being done, Bannatyne paced to and fro, wringing his hands in despair. He could do nothing. Rivetted to the spot by terror, his face to the incoming tide, he strode backwards and forwards, the helpless witness of the horrible deed.

"That will do," at length said James, with an assumption of calmness, and rising from the sand on which he and his father had been seated as they tightened the fatal coils on the neck of the victim. "He is quiet enough now."

"Are you sure?" gasped Auchendrane, who was wrought up to a higher pitch of excitement.

"Sure? Feel him, he's getting cold already. Now to bury him."

"Quick, then," replied Auchendrane, "bring the spades. You run for them, James, and we'll not be long in hiding the proof."

James obeyed, and in less than a minute returned with

the spades. "Here, Bannatyne," sternly commanded Auchendrane, "you are younger than I, and more accustomed to
handle a spade. Here, dig for the love of God; dig for your
life."

Bannatyne approached. James thrust one of the spades
into his hand and himself at once set about the task of grave-
digging.

Nature and her forces never rest; and all the while that
the deed was being done the incoming tide was advancing
slowly, but steadily. Up it came, washing out the furrows
left by the last receding tide, and rippling towards them like
a Nemesis.

Bannatyne stood like a man in a dream, the spade in his
hand, his eyes resting on the inanimate form of the man who,
half-an-hour before, had been alive, walking with him, talking
to him. He felt as he had never felt before. But James
Mure speedily recalled him from dreamland.

"Dig, curse you, dig," he said, in hoarse sullen accents.

Still Bannatyne made no response. He turned his eyes on
the Mures, and read his chances in the deed already done.

"Be quick, Chapeldonan," said Auchendrane. "Dig, as
you are told; dig, if you do not want to be handed over to
justice as the murderer of your kinsman."

Thus incited, Bannatyne needed no further invitation.
He joined the Mures in their horrible, useless task; for,
ever as they dug, the water oozed through the soft, yielding
sand and filled up the hole. The longer, naturally, the task
became the harder; for the advancing tide crept up slowly
and unconcernedly, but as relentlessly as if Nature was
determined that the murder should not be hid.

Throwing down his spade on the sand, James Mure grasped
the body by one of the feet and drew it towards the hole;
but ere he could accomplish his purpose, the waves rippled
over a slight sandbank which had hitherto acted as a sort of
natural barrier, and filled up the excavation. In less than a

minute the work was undone. The shore would not cover the dead.

To leave the body lying where it was, was impossible. At high water, it would hardly have been covered, and at the recession of the tide in the morning, the deed would be the property of the whole district.

"Take him up," said Auchendrane, in accents which indicated how strongly he was wrought. "Take him up, and carry him up to the beach. We must hide him somehow. Quick, quick !"

James grasped the collar of Dalrymple's coat; his father one of the feet, Bannatyne the other; and carrying their spades with them, they bore the ghastly burden inland until above high water-mark, when they laid it down again upon the sand. They had hardly left the spot ere the sea completely covered it, washing out every trace of the struggle, and of the open grave, which, a few minutes before, had been prepared for the victim.

What was to be done ? The situation was a terrible one; and so dangerous that even Bannatyne became as anxious as his associates to get rid of the silent witness. Dead men, they say, tell no tales; but even in the darkness of the night, he fancied that not even the silence of death was sufficient for the extremity.

Mure himself was the most self-possessed of the three. James's callousness, indeed, stood the strain better than did his father's restless, nervous frame and quick-working mind; but he lacked the power of coping with the difficulty, and was ready, at a suggestion, to leave the spot and to trust the future to itself. At the worst, he reckoned, they could blame the tenant of Chapeldonan, if accused of the murder! Not so Auchendrane.

"How do the tides run ?" he suddenly asked Bannatyne. "Is there any current that sets along the shore."

"Yes," replied the farmer, "with the wind off the shore as

it is to-night, anything in deep water would go right out to sea, and be carried up the Firth."

"Then to the sea he must go," said Mure. "We must carry him out into deep water."

"I don't see any need for that," James rejoined. "Why not leave him where he is? or, if that won't suit you, why not carry him into that field over there and bury him below the sod."

"No, no, James," said his father, who was getting anxious to be gone, "we have no time for that, we must give him a sail."

The rude witticism evoked a gruff laugh from James; but, at once stifling it, he responded—

"I am not inclined to wade into the Firth up to the neck on a cold night like this, for the best man that ever stepped, let alone a thing like that"—and he touched the body of Dalrymple with his foot. "There is nothing like the earth to cover a secret. Besides, when the hue and cry is over at his disappearance—if anybody ever hears of it at all—Chapeldonan here can plough him down."

Bannatyne shivered at the suggestion. Auchendrane was strangely averse to the course suggested.

"I will have no land burial," he said firmly. "The earth has refused to hide him already, and God knows what we would do if it refused a second time."

"Tush, father," was James's impatient response; "the earth has never had a fair chance. It was only the sand that refused, and that was because the sea ran into the hole and filled it up."

"I say again, James, and it is no use your talking, to the sea we must give him up."

"More likely," was James's response, "the sea will give him up than the earth. He must come ashore one of these days, and that before long. If the current sets up the Firth, as Chapeldonan says it does, what more likely than that a week or ten days after this he may turn up on the sands of Ayr. That would be a pretty pickle for us to be in. But if you must put him in the sea, why not give him something to stay quiet at the bottom. A big stone would do."

"No need for stones," replied Auchendrane, who became more and more determined to have his own way. "We will carry him out into five feet of water and leave him. A week's immersion and the fishes will make him so that his own mother wouldn't know him."

As the father thus grew in resolution, so did the son.

"Well, you and Chapeldonan can do what you like with him. I'll help you to dig a grave if you like, but I'll not carry him out to sea."

Auchendrane flamed into instant passion.

"You refuse to do what you are told?"

"I refuse to do this, anyway."

"Remember, James, who struck Dalrymple down. You did it, sir."

"I know—what then?"

"Bannatyne and I saw you."

"Well, what then?"

"This, that if you refuse to do what you are told, and to take your share in this night's work, and if there is any hue-and-cry, Chapeldonan and I can ride off scot free by handing you over to justice."

This view of the situation was convincing logic to James's practical mind. In all probability Auchendrane had nothing more serious at heart than the threat itself; but the threat was quite enough. Stooping down over the body of Dalrymple, he grasped it a second time by the collar of the coat.

"Take hold, then," he muttered with an oath, "and let us get rid of the infernal thing at once."

Auchendrane motioned to Bannatyne, who, in desperate hands, saw himself in desperate straits. He was **afraid** to

remonstrate; hardly dared to speak. He could not look upon
the body, but blindly taking hold of one of the legs of his
murdered guest, while Auchendrane took hold of the other,
he proceeded to assist the Mures in the last scene of the
night's tragedy.

"Hold on a moment," said Auchendrane, as his feet touched
the rippling water, "when is the tide?"

"It will be high water in twenty minutes," replied Bannatyne.

"Then we must wait; the ebb tide will do the work better
than the flow."

There was no opposition offered to the delay. The night
was still comparatively young, and half-an-hour would make
little or no difference in jeopardising the unseen return to
Auchendrane of the Mures. Half-an-hour ago, Dalrymple
was alive and walking over the sands; so that, though the
deed and its accompaniments seemed to have occupied a much
longer period of time, the murderers had indeed gone about
their work expeditiously.

Still, all three inwardly fretted as they waited. The chill
air cooled them; the delay gave them time to think; the
silence which they kept was irksome; the corpse which lay
at their feet was real. Auchendrane had never murdered in
this fashion before, and while he felt that what he had done
was but stern necessity, his nature rebelled at the character
of the tragedy. James Mure was angry at the threat in which
his father had indulged, and began to dislike the presence of
the silent witness; and Bannatyne, still horror-stricken, was
anxious to flee the scene.

The twenty minutes crept slowly away, the tide rose to
the boundary line and lapped its highest margin of the shore.
Far out in the ocean the restless forces were still. But only
for a moment. As relentlessly as they had swayed themselves eastwards, so remorselessly they swung to the westward.

Auchendrane, who had seated himself on a sandy knoll,

rose as he observed the tide cease to flow and resumed his
hold of the corpse. His son and Bannatyne followed his
example, and without exchanging words they stepped into
the sea. The beach did not shelve rapidly, and it was not
until they had walked fully a hundred yards that Auchendrane gave the signal to let go. By this time they were up
to their armpits in the water, and it had not been without
difficulty that they had even reached so far. More than once
they had stumbled; and on one of these occasions, gruesome
to tell, the hand of the dead man had swung round and
struck James on the face. It was an evil omen; and James
was superstitious.

When Auchendrane gave the signal, he and Bannatyne at
once let go their hold. James, collecting his strength, raised
the corpse in his arms clear of the water and flung it three or
four feet from him, cursing at large as he did so.

"There now," he said, "there now, damn you. Surely
that's the last of you."

The body fell with a splash which sent up its watery
tribute in the faces of the murderers, and sank out of sight.
As the waves closed over it Auchendrane and his associates,
shivering with cold and shuddering with horror, turned their
faces homewards and hurried thither.

The deed was done now. William Dalrymple had kept his
last tryst. All that remained of him was the sport of the
waters of the Firth of Clyde. It might go out with the tide,
and in with the tide, now rising to the surface, now rubbing
along the sands at the bottom, to-day disfigured in its contact
with jagged rocks, to-morrow wrapped in sea-weed; tumbling
in the billows, gently floating in the smooth waters. It might
strand on the shores, disfigured, bloated—a mere record of
the fair semblance of humanity; or it might go out into the
deep caves of father Neptune, and never again be seen by
mortal eye. The fishes might devour it, or the sea-birds
scream around it.

But what of that? It was William Dalrymple no more; only the shell that once had held him. His spirit had left its tenement; and never more would he rise up in the judgment upon earth and tell his incriminating story. Not more silent were the deepest recesses of the sea than he.

The deed was done—why should the Mures and Bannatyne fly the scene? The Mures had done a deed that was to ensure their happiness and content, that was to allow the father to go down to his grave in peace, and the son to take up the inheritance. Why, then, should they start with every wave-roll on the shore, and haste to be gone? Were they conscious that there was One watching them who knows no slumber, and who looked through the darkness and saw the murderers at their work; or were they trembling lest the unfriendly ocean should give up its dead under their very eyes?

They hastened ashore, splashing one another in their eagerness to get to land. They dared not separate from one another so long as they were in the element which held their victim. He was safe enough, poor fellow; but the murderers would hardly have wondered in the excited condition into which they had brought themselves, had he risen out of his watery toils and pursued them, dripping, and with lack-lustre eyes, to the land. They were afraid to look behind them.

But once ashore, James was not long in recovering, or in affecting the recovery of, his courage.

"Well, that's done, anyway," he said, as he shook the dripping water from his garments, "Thank God, jobs like that come only once in a lifetime."

"Let us go away, James, let us go away," was Auchendrane's reply, as he strode across the beach.

"There's no great hurry now," replied James, "Dalrymple is quiet enough, I'll warrant. What say you, Chapeldonan?"

Bannatyne shuddered. "Would to God," he said, "I had been spared this night's work!"

"Tush, man," said James, "don't take on so."

"How can I be anything else than moved by such a deed?" replied the tenant of Chapeldonan. "It may seem a light thing to you to do a fellow mortal to death; but to me!—never did I expect to live to brand myself as a murderer."

"Hold your tongue, Chapeldonan," broke in Auchendrane; "this is no murder. It is death—death by violence, if you like—death by our hands, but not murder. We have saved the peace of Carrick; accomplished a great good to the country side at the expense of a little wrong done by ourselves."

"God forgive me!" exclaimed Bannatyne, wringing his hands. "How could we do it!"

"He will forgive you, Chapeldonan, but not if you take guilt upon yourself," was Mure's answer. "But haste," he continued, as they marched up the beach, "Bannatyne, I need not bespeak your silence. You will be silent as the grave for your own sake if not for ours. But, if not—take warning," and he pointed over his shoulder out to sea in the direction where the body had been cast, "a worse fate may befal you than even that. James and I are two, you are but one. Two witnesses are better than one any day."

Bannatyne read Auchendrane's meaning. He gave no reply. Nor was any required. He hastened homewards with all the speed he could muster, trembling at every noise, trying to shut out the sound of the incessant wail of the waters, starting at the scream of the night-bird as it flew overhead, scared at being followed by his own shadow.

Once in the house he threw himself upon his couch; but he dared not sleep. He would not have slept if he could; for, whenever he shut his eyes, he saw the pale face of his kinsman, his eyes set in everlasting reproach. So he lay tossing to and fro until the morning, when, collecting his senses and knowing that his only hope lay in pursuing the tenor of his daily way, he went out to toil in the fields, his

back to the sea, and fearful lest the remorseless waves should
lay bare their terrible secret.

Mure and his son collected their spades and their other
implements of tragedy, and, mounting their horses, rode off.
Their steeds were jaded, as, the grey dawn of day struggling
through the pall of night, they urged them through the
sombre woods of Auchendrane and dismounted by the Old
Tower.

CHAPTER XIX.

THE SEA GIVES UP ITS DEAD.

The few following days were a continual misery to the unhappy
tenant of Chapeldonan. Yet he steeled himself to the emergency to the utmost of his power. Collecting all his energy and
resolution he tried to' throw off the unhallowed influences by
which he was surrounded; and he rode hither and thither in
the district in which his house was situated, asking his
friends and neighbours if they had seen William Dalrymple.
Dalrymple had, he informed them, suddenly taken his departure from Chapeldonan. He had gone off under cover of
night; and he professed anxiety to know where he had gone,
and why he had left so suddenly.

There was no suspicion in the mind of anybody that
Bannatyne was playing false; for, bold man though he had
proved himself in the field, he was the last person who would
willingly have instigated or enacted a tragedy had he been
a free agent. Still, his mind was wrought incessantly; and
he could neither lay the apparition of his murdered friend,
nor allay the agony and unrest which oppressed him as he
had never been oppressed before.

By day he hardly cared to look out on the sea, lest, riding
on the billows, he should behold that which most he feared;
he dared scarce let his gaze rest on the sand or by the base

of the rocks, or amid the pebbles on the beach, lest he should
see, lying stark and stiff and swollen, the corpse of his
murdered friend.   To himself, he always in his thoughts—
and the dead body was never out of them—alluded to it as
"it."   "It" was always with him.   It walked with him by
day; it came into his bed-room by night.   He saw it at the
foot of his couch; if he looked out of his window, it came
between him and the starlight, now reproachful in visage,
now threatening him with the dread of consequences, now
mute and motionless as last he had seen it stretched on the
yellow sand when the tide came in.   He could not throw it
off, try as he might.   The unseen world with its relaxless
grip could not hold "it" from his visage.   He heard Dalrymple's voice in the breeze, in the rippling of the tide, in
the moaning of the night wind.   The sea bird scared him as
it screamed.

The Mures had laid their plans so astutely that they hoped
rather than feared.   It was true, as James said to himself,
that their lives were in the hands of Bannatyne; but was
not this squared by Bannatyne's life being in their hands?
He was but one—they were two.   Two witnesses agreeing
upon anything were better than one—and therefore they
were safe.   So James went on in his old mode of life, drinking and brawling as before.   He was careful, indeed, not to
drink too deeply; but other than this, and as the result to
some extent of premeditation, he departed not from his
customary methods of killing time and the losing of whatever shreds of reputation, dissipation and cruelty and callousness, a frightful trinity, had left him.

Auchendrane himself did not in his heart take quite such
a roseate view of the situation.   He knew the workings and
the possibilites of events better than did his son.   He knew
the influences that were at work, and he felt that were suspicion aroused Bannatyne might save himself by becoming
King's evidence.   He would have no difficulty in getting

17

himself accepted in this capacity. Stern as law was, it must yield to circumstances; and the Earl of Cassillis was quite potent enough with the Crown to secure the condemnation of two through the pardon of one, especially when the two were his sworn enemies, and the other but the miserable and unwilling accomplice of their guilt. Still, he regarded his position as tolerably assured, and himself as quite fitted to cope with any circumstances that were likely to arise.

A week elapsed and no tidings of the recovery of the body of Dalrymple had reached Auchendrane. Every day James was in Ayr, ears open for intelligence, anxious to glean the earliest information. But it was not from Ayr that the tidings were to come.

The night was advanced as Auchendrane, as was his wont, sat in his chamber, thoughtful and 'lone. It was dark without, and all nature was hushed save the rushing river which swept past to the sea.

It is only in the country that such complete silence as that which brooded over the old tower can be found. It is only in the country that stillness ever becomes irksome or painful. The ripple of the burn or the rush of the river, always present, does not interrupt the solemnity of the rural night. The peep of the half-sleeping bird is heard above the noise of the waters, and the hooting of the owl sounds loud and eerie from the copse. Every little sound that breaks upon the sleeping world is magnified by the stillness into individuality. And when these sounds are mute, one can feel, indeed all but hear, the silence itself, so susceptible is the atmosphere and so oppressive.

So, when Auchendrane heard rapid footsteps approach the Tower he listened as intently as if they were treading on his fate; and he heard in their tread audible prognostications of what he expected, and, expecting, feared. Proceeding downstairs, he opened the hall door as the night visitant reached the porch; and peering out, dark as it was, recognised in the dim light which glimmered in the hall the person of Bannatyne.

"Come in, Chapeldonan," he said.

Without another word, Mure led the way to his chamber. It was not without a somewhat curious, uneasy, undefined, " eerie " feeling, that the tenant of Chapeldonan trod the long passages of Auchendrane. In common with his neighbours, he had heard of the mysterious ongoings of Mure, and though in broad daylight he would have scorned to credit all that he heard, still, as the gaunt, long-haired, silent old man strode on before, he all but fancied that he heard uncanny sounds, and that the atmosphere he breathed was not wholly untenanted by the malign powers of darkness.

" Why, Bannatyne," exclaimed Mure, as he closed the door of the chamber, and motioned the farmer to a seat, " you look as if you had seen a ghost ! "

" Ghost enough," replied Bannatyne, " it has turned up."

" What has turned up ? " queried Mure, who was painfully alive, at the same time, to the meaning of the words.

" He has been found—Dalrymple."

" I thought as much. Tell me all about it. But stay," he added, as he opened the door of a cupboard and took out a decanter, " take a glass of that; you look as if you needed it."

Bannatyne complied, and at once proceeded—

" It was yesterday afternoon, just before the gloaming. They tell me "——

" Who tell you ? " interrupted Mure.

" Everybody tells me—it is the talk of the country side— that the Knight of Culzean, the son of Sir Thomas Kennedy, dreamed that as he was walking on the sands of the Girvan shore, he saw something coming into land; and coming in, too, against the tide. He watched it as it came on, slowly, never halting. The wind blew off the shore, but this thing kept on its way until it stranded on the beach right at his feet. So astonished was he, and so impressed with his vision, that he resolved to have the shore searched; and collecting a number of his friends and vassals, they walked along the shore until, right opposite the farm of Chapeldonan they found the body."

"You do not mean to tell me," Mure said, shewing visible traces of agitation, "that Dalrymple's body came ashore at the very place that we put him into the sea?"

"I do, indeed, as I have to answer to my Maker for what I say. I did not see it as it came to land, thank God; but it was not long after its discovery that I was sent for. I went at once, trembling with excitement, and fearful to look at it. There was a great crowd round it; for the neighbours all round had by that time reached the shore, and were congregated in groups about the corpse. I tell you, sir, it was the sorest trial that ever I was forced to encounter. It was a terrible experience for me. The body was fearfully disfigured, but the neck still bore traces of the rope with which Dalrymple was strangled. There was a livid mark round it, and the flesh all stood up except where the mark was, in such a way that nobody could fail to see it at a glance."

"I can understand how that was," observed Auchendrane, "the water would do that."

"There was no mistake about it," resumed Bannatyne, "and there could be none. Everybody saw it and spoke of it. They talked of foul play."

"Foul play, did they?" responded Mure, "and what did they say?"

"Wait a moment, sir. I went away to the house for something to roll the body in, so that I might carry it away as quickly as possible; and when I came back, they were all horror-stricken, because, when a little girl, who was with the Laird of Culzean, came forward to look at the corpse, the blood began to flow from it."

"Superstition," interrupted Mure hastily, "nothing but superstition. Such a thing was an impossibility."

" That may be, sir.   I know nothing of that.   But what was worse, the child was a grand-daughter of your own."

Mure started, and grasped the arms of his chair for support. He knew that the flowing of blood from a corpse so long dead was an impossibility ; but wrought up to such a height of excitement as he was, he could not clear from his mind the superstition that was prevalent at the time throughout Scotland, that if a murderer or a relative of a murderer was brought forward to the body of the victim, and made to lay his hand upon it, the corpse would emit blood—Heaven thus revealing guilt which otherwise must remain hidden. Auchendrane soon recovered himself.

" The child is James's," he remarked, " her mother and she are at Culzean just now.   Anything else to tell ? "

" I took the body up to Chapeldonan.   It is lying there now, in the barn.   Everybody in the neighbourhood has been to see it."

" Tell me, Chapeldonan," said Mure, " you do not need to be afraid to speak out.   Was my name mentioned at all ? "

" Yes, sir," replied Bannatyne after a moment's hesitation, " it was.   Your name was mentioned, and to-day it is on everybody's tongue."

Auchendrane was not slow to grasp the danger implied in the current rumour.   While he felt comparatively safe in the knowledge that the evidence of the deed was confined to those who took part in it, and while he realised that both superstition and rumour were at work, he could not burk the knowledge of having twice expatriated Dalrymple, and of that fact being public property.   As for the bleeding of the corpse, he set the greatest store by the rumour—not that he believed that blood had really flowed from the dead body on the approach of his grandchild, but that any statement to that effect could not fail to tell materially against him—for, so dark were the times, and so rife and reliable was superstition, that even in the Courts of Justice learned judges of the day still listened gravely to such narrations, and accepted them as credible evidence.

Dismissing Chapeldonan with a caution to carry himself bravely in the ordeal, and to be foremost in his open sorrow for the loss of his kinsman, and in his expressed determination to hunt down his slayers to the death, Auchendrane sat himself down quietly to think over what had best be done. That he was in danger admitted of no doubt; and danger, too, of a kind that brooked no delay. The idea of flight never occurred to him. He might go into hiding; but with what result? That the rumours would be accepted as incontrovertible, and that realising his situation, he had taken the only means possible to avoid the consequences. Things, he thought, had not yet come to that pass with him.

But they were sufficiently near it. The rumours were bad enough in themselves—what would they turn to when backed up by the powerful influence of the Earl of Cassillis, who, he knew very well, would exert himself to the utmost to have him brought to justice?

Driven on so far in crime, the same malign spirit that had dictated the death of Dalrymple once more took possession of Auchendrane. One crime must be wiped out by another, but of a different character. He must resume the feudal struggle, and distract attention from the murder of Dalrymple by a fresh outrage on a Kennedy. His feudal friends, who would have deserted him in a body because he had strangled a poor nameless, fameless soldier on the sands of Girvan, would rally afresh to his cause if he could but rekindle the old animosities and bring down the vengeance of the Earl of Cassillis on his head.

Hugh Kennedy of Garriehorne was an old enemy of his, and a staunch adherent of his powerful kinsman, the Earl of Cassillis—why should he not make him the scape-goat? His death would not be a crime. It would be nothing worse than a spirit-stirring episode in the closing chapters of the great

Ayrshire feud. This idea took possession of Auchendrane, and he spent the greater part of the night canvassing his intended methods and chances until in his waking dreams he saw the fratricidal struggle recommenced, and himself, as before, the moving spirit of the fight.

Mure did not allow the grass to grow beneath his feet when there was danger abroad; and the day following he took James into his confidence, and told him his resolve.

James listened carefully, but without betraying the faintest emotion. Another murder was neither here nor there to him, if thereby another danger was to be removed.

"I confess," he said, when his father had finished, "I do not see how this can avail you. What good end can it possibly accomplish?"

"No, James, I see you do not understand what I mean. But what I mean to accomplish is this—If we succeed in killing Garrichorne, I shall go into hiding; and, at the same time, I can make known my willingness to stand my trial for that, which will be far more easily proved than the affair of Dalrymple can be. I am not afraid of anything being done to me for the death of Garrichorne. He is a feudal enemy of ours, and we are quite influential enough yet to get the offence condoned."

"But if you fail to kill Garrichorne—what then?"

"No matter. I can take my trial for carrying fire-arms, which I am forbidden to carry, and the end will be the same."

"Father, this irresolution of yours will be the death of us yet. Why not kill Bannatyne at once? He is the only dangerous man we have to fear."

"Bannatyne is not dangerous, James. His tongue is tied; for though he laid no hands on Dalrymple, yet he was there when the deed was done, and was, as the law says, actor or art in part in it."

"I'm not sure of that," replied James. "Bannatyne's

evidence, backed by our having twice sent Dalrymple out of the way, would finish us. He must die."

"He must not die, James," was Auchendrane's reply; "but, to make assurance sure, he must be got out of the way for a time. I have thought of that. You will go and persuade him to cross over into Ireland."

"I would rather persuade him to cross the Jordan of death," was James's callous reply. "He will come back as Dalrymple did."

"Chapeldonan must not be slain, James. You understand that? God knows, we have enough on our consciences already."

"And what more Bannatyne than Garriehorne?"

"There you fail to discriminate, as usual. Garriehorne is a relative of the Earl of Cassillis, a feudal foe of ours. To kill him is to do no murder; to kill Bannatyne is to do murder, unless his death is absolutely necessary."

"Which it is," interposed James.

"Which it is not," responded Auchendrane. "You will see to Bannatyne's being sent to Ireland for a time. I will attend to Garriehorne myself."

"But you are not able to slay Garriehorne alone. He is too stout a man for you to attack alone."

"I shall not attack him alone. I shall see to there being no mistake."

The interview closed. James was by no means satisfied with the turn affairs were taking; but, as he had done before, he yielded to his father's judgment.

To assist him in his new crime, Auchendrane determined to enlist the sympathies and services of one of his staunchest followers, with whom his influence was predominant, and whom, he knew, he could trust to stand by him without either fear or compunction. While reckoning on re-awaking the feudal struggle, Mure little knew the change that had come over the scene, and how helpless at best he was to deal with the powerful race of Cassillis. For Bargany was not to be tempted to the fray any more; and the smaller lairds and barons who clung to Bargany were not followers of Mure personally. Besides, they were ugly rumours that were afloat; the best of Auchendrane's old comrades were shrugging their shoulders and shaking their heads when they fell a-talking of him.

Time passed. Spies were sent out to find where Garrichorne was to be found; and in less than forty-eight hours, Auchendrane learned that he was in the town of Ayr, and that his return home was projected for the night following that on which he received his information. His arrangements were not long in being completed. The follower whom he enlisted to aid in the perpetration of the atrocity was an old retainer, who, ever since he had followed Mure in their early days to continental battle-fields, had remained staunch to the banner of Auchendrane. William Morrison he was called.

"Come here, Morrison," said Auchendrane to him; "I want your assistance."

"That you shall have, sir," was the reply of the unquestioning servitor."

"I like that ready acquiescence, Morrison," responded Auchendrane, "it saves a deal of trouble. But before you do acquiesce, let me tell you what I expect of you."

"It matters very little, sir, but say on."

"Well I am going to re-open the fight with the Kennedys."

"I am glad to hear it, sir. My pistols are rusty from having nothing to do, and my bones are beginning to stiffen from the same reason. Ah, sir, these were grand times when we lived on the eve of constant battle, though, by my soul, I have almost forgotten what it is like—it is so long since."

"So it is, Morrison; but battle, at least action, is nearer than you imagine. You know Kennedy of Garrichorne?"

"Yes, of course I do, sir, a right strong man too."

"Well, he is the man that must go," said Auchendrane, emphasising the word "go," so as to bring out the full meaning which he intended that it should convey. "This must be done quietly, and in the dark. It will leak out soon enough who did it; at all events, when so stout a Kennedy as he is found dead, his death will be laid at our door, and the feud will be re-opened. I do not need to caution you to silence, Morrison?"

Morrison disdained answer.

"I understand," continued Auchendrane, "I did not mean to question your ability to hold your tongue. You would know why this quiet and secrecy are necessary were I to explain everything to you. I have no time now, but I will tell you all bye and bye.

"That will be as it pleases you, sir. Meantime you want him killed?"

"Yes, I do."

"And you want me to do it?"

"Yes, you are to do it, in company with myself."

"You go too, sir?"

"Yes, I want to see it well done. There must be no mistake."

"When is it to be done?"

"To-morrow night Garriehorne leaves Ayr, and will ride homeward. He intends to remain at Cassillis all night."

"If he ever gets so far," interrupted Morrison.

"Exactly, if he ever gets so far. My intention is that he should not."

"Where, sir, do you propose to kill him?" queried Morrison, with a nonchalance that would have done credit to James Mure himself.

"In the plantation hard by St. Leonard's Chapel at Ayr."

"Where Sir Thomas Kennedy was slain—a very excellent and well-adapted spot. And what are to be the weapons?"

"Pistols first, Morrison. Swords afterwards, if necessary."

" And when shall we start ?"

" Have horses here at the darkening. We shall have to wait his convenience."

" That is all right, sir. I shall attend your instructions," and so saying, Morrison withdrew.

Fortune favours the bold; frequently it seems to favour the wicked as well, though it generally deserts them when their need is the sorest. So it was here.

The following night the sun set in cloud and in gloom. It was essentially a dark night; and when Morrison brought round the horses to the tower of Auchendrane, the outline of the tree tops was already getting indistinct on the skyline. So much the better. Auchendrane's deed was not meant for the light. It had been calmly conceived in the hope that it might cover a multitude of sins; and if carried out to advantage, the more darkly it was done the more securely for him.

To say that Auchendrane felt a sort of exultation as he rode along with his faithful henchman at his heels, would not be saying to much. This was no mere murderous quest. It was no caitiff that he was going to condemn to a vulgar death, but a scion of the great house of Cassillis, a retainer of the Earl, who had ridden behind his chief when the bold Bargany went down for ever by Brockloch Burn, who had followed the fortunes of the more powerful branch of the Kennedys throughout, and who openly mourned the piping times of peace, and the deterioration of the men of Carrick. Auchendrane knew all this; he knew that Garriehorne had threatened his destruction if it could be lawfully—feudally—undertaken; and he felt, therefore, that he had some sort of reasonable excuse for the act which he intended to perform. So he rode along with something of the old warrior feeling in his heart, and in full expectancy of success. Morrison's business was to kill Garriehorne on the instructions of Auchendrane. These were enough justification for him.

By the time St. Leonard's wood was reached—strange scene wherein to repeat tragedy—the last lingering glimmer of daylight had died out of the western heavens. The night was calm and still. Occasionally an echo from the town of Ayr reached Auchendrane and his servitor, but other than this no sound broke in upon the silence of the night. Mure spent the time in conversation with Morrison. The horses were picketed at hand, ready for service, when the moment for action should arrive.

A couple of hours had passed ere they heard the approach of a horseman, who was leisurely riding along from the direction of the town. Horsemen were, by no means, so rare as to lead them to the unquestioning conclusion that this was the man on whose coming they waited; but, as they had their plan of operation all ready, they remounted, and remained in the centre of the narrow roadway.

It was, indeed, their intended victim who came jogging along the highway. Hugh Kennedy of Garriehorne was not a man to be trifled with. Of splendid physique and recognised fighting qualities, strong armed, and stout of heart, he was a dangerous opponent in a tussle—so dangerous that Mure and his retainer would have thought many times before embarking on their murderous mission had they not been well provided with fire-arms. He was careless of the dark, and void of superstition, and did not fear attack, so he whistled as he approached and entered the darker shadows of the trees.

Auchendrane and Morrison advanced to meet him. The ground was their own selection, and their horses all but brushed one another in the narrow passage where they encountered.

"Is that you, Garriehorne?" Mure queried in one of those impulsive fits which overcame at times his better judgment.

"Who wants to know that?" came back in ready tones

from Kennedy, who laid his hand on the hilt of his sword as he spoke.

"You shall know that soon enough," was Auchendrane's reply. "Now then, Morrison."

Garriehorne's danger flashed across him in an instant, but ere he could either speak or act, Mure and Morrison discharged their pistols at him simultaneously. The shots rang out together.

But the fates which deserted Sir Thomas Kennedy in the same plantation of St. Leonard's and Dalrymple on the Girvan strand, were more propitious to Hugh Kennedy. One of the bullets grazed his cheek, bringing the warm blood spurting over his face; the other, though fired at such close range, missed its mark entirely.

Garriehorne was nothing if not a man of instant action. Ere the intended assassins could draw a second pistol, he attacked them with his sword, spurring his horse in between them and striking to right and left as he passed. He might have escaped by riding, but Garriehorne had no such intention. His fighting instincts, never very soundly slumbering, were wide awake in an instant, and turning back, the assailed became the assailant and forced his foes to close quarters. Auchendrane was an expert swordsman; so too was Morrison, but both men were already far past the prime of life, while Kennedy was in the full flush of his manly strength and vigour. Still the combat was uneven. Two against one are at any time heavy odds, when savage determination backs out the strength of numbers. Auchendrane had no intention of leaving his work undone, and Morrison fought away because Kennedy was Auchendrane's enemy and had to be killed if he could manage it.

Auchendrane was the first to suffer. In one of the fell sweeps of Garriehorne's broad-bladed sword Mure received, on his sword arm, the full weight of the blow. The stroke was given with effect. The weapon fell from his arm, which was broken and dropped helpless by his side; and after an ineffectual struggle to retain his seat in the saddle, Mure succumbed to the inevitable and came to the ground. Having only Morrison to deal with, Kennedy had no great difficulty in beating him off.

But the danger was not yet quite over—for Mure as he lay in the roadway, drew a second pistol from his belt and discharged it at Garriehorne. Whether from Mure's weakness, or from the darkness of the night, the bullet whistled harmlessly past; and satisfied with the result of the encounter, and not wishing to run the risk of another leaden messenger in the dark, Kennedy turned his horse's head in the direction of Carrick and rode rapidly off.

Dismounting, Morrison raised Auchendrane from the ground; and being of old skilled in the treatment of wounds, succeeded in improvising a rude bandage with which he bound up the broken arm. Mure submitted without a word; and, supported by his henchman, the foiled assassins returned home.

"I might have known as much," was James' comment when he heard the news, "why did I let you go without me?"

"James," replied Auchendrane in faint tones, for he was weak from loss of blood, "what is to be, will be. It was all predestined, and no man can fight against predestination."

"Can't he?" was the sneering answer. "It is just as you take it. Predestination to-night would have meant death had I been with you. It never can resist determination."

CHAPTER XX.

IN THE TOILS.

ONCE more Carrick was in turmoil. Kennedy of Garrichorne had recognised Mure in the wood of St. Leonard's; and the name of Auchendrane was on everybody's lips. It was accepted as a fact that, directly or indirectly, he had been the means of doing Dalrymple to death, and from all quarters rose a cry for his immediate apprehension.

Mure was frightened at the intensity and volume of the execration. The walls of Auchendrane were thick, but not thick enough to keep out the noise of the tumult and the voice of the people. He read vengeance all round him. He had broken the peace, and set the Earl of Cassillis free to act against him.

Was it not known to the country-side that in a dream of the night the murder of Dalrymple had been revealed to a son of the man who, by Mure's instigation, was slain on the spot on which he had doomed that Kennedy of Garriehorne should die; and was it not common property that the blood of the man who had been slain had spurted forth in the presence of the grandchild of the murderer? Heaven had interposed to stop the career of Auchendrane and to bring him to justice. Why should the authorities hesitate to lay him by the heels and have him put on trial at once?

Mure all his life had been a man of action; and though eighty long years had chilled his blood, they had not tempered the quickness of his resolve nor his capacity for instant action. He could not hide his danger—he did not try to hide it; but he did try to gauge the chances of conviction, and analysed the character of the evidence with which he would be brought face to face. He had no time to waste or to lose. He was an old man now. Time was no longer on his side, and if he were to be saved disgrace and punishment, mayhap execution, he must not allow the grass to grow below his feet. Into hiding he must go, and that at once. Auchendrane Tower he must leave behind him, perhaps for ever. He was willing to thole an assize for his attack on Garriehorne, and from his seclusion he would, if at all possible, deliver himself up to justice to stand his trial for that offence. The other, he told himself, could not be proven.

"James," he said to his son, as they discussed the situation ruefully, "I confess to you that I do not like the turn that things are taking. I know that superstition is at work, and that nothing but superstition is at the bottom of it. People will believe anything; and it is, unfortunately, with people who will believe anything that we have at present to deal. Their cry against us is ascending into the air. The authorities will not, they cannot, close their ears against it. The Earl of Cassillis will be on the alert, using all the influence he has to have us at once apprehended and conveyed to Edinburgh. What are we to do?"

"What you are going to do," replied James, "is none of my business. What I am going to do is to remain in Auchendrane and face it out. It is not the first time that Carrick foes have tried to overcome us and we have foiled them; and I do not see why we should take guilt to ourselves and flee the scene. It shall never be said of me that I did so. A bold heart and a ready bearing will carry us through. But why were you so soft-hearted over Bannatyne? Dreams and superstitions will never put the cord about our necks, and if you had only permitted me to do to Chapeldonan as we did by Dalrymple, we should have been able to laugh the enemy to scorn. But no! You let that conscience of yours play you false; and I, stupid fool that I was, let you have your own way. Chapeldonan should have been beside Dalrymple on the Girvan shore."

"Perhaps he should, James; and it may be necessary yet. You say that he will leave the country, that he will go to Ireland?"

"He has so promised."

"Then all is well, so far as he is concerned. But if he return, James, from Ireland, you will know how to act?"

"Yes, sir, I will. As sure as Chapeldonan returns from Ireland, so surely will I kill him."

Auchendrane made no objection.

"It is this dilly-dallying," continued James, "that has been the death of us. If we had killed Dalrymple six years ago or more, when we had him in our hands, there would have been no need for any further trouble. But it has been irresolution all through."

"I know it, James, I know it. I was weak, I confess, and tender-hearted."

"You were, indeed," replied James, with a sneer. "Six years ago it would have been no murder to have slain Dalrymple. He would have fallen a victim, a necessary victim, to the feud. It is not that I care how he has died; he brought his fate upon himself; but now we have had as much trouble with him as if he had been an enemy worth reckoning with, and he is likely to be more."

"It was all meant for the best, James," was Auchendrane's apologetic reply. "It has always been a cardinal point of my conduct to avoid unnecessary slaughter."

"Yes," was James' answer, "so it has been of mine; but I see necessity where you see none. You see no necessity now for killing Chapeldonan—I do. It is a pronounced necessity. If he lives, you die, and I die, too. I was an idiot, a cursed fool, to let him go."

"If he buries himself in Ireland"—began Auchendrane—

"Buries himself in Ireland!" interrupted James. "Ireland will never bury him. He will come back. There is no b u :i like six feet of turf."

"That is quite true, in a general way," replied Auchendrane. "But what's done now can't be helped. For the present, what are we to do?"

"I have told you what I am going to do. I am going to stay where I am and brazen it out. And as for you, you can please yourself."

Auchendrane saw it was no use taking further advice from his son. The last shred of respect between them had departed.

18

Community in crime had not begotten community of feeling, save in selfishness. Each was now resolved to save himself—James, by remaining at home; his father, by retiring into seclusion and trusting to the success of his scheming capacities to get himself indicted for his onslaught on Kennedy of Garriehorne.

The last few days had told severely on Mure. The wound he had received had occasioned great loss of blood. His cheeks, ever wan and sallow, were more tightly drawn than ever. His sharp eyes shone with an additional lustre from out their deep-set sockets; and his long, straggling hair, falling over his shoulders, completed a picture on which there is no need to dwell. He began to be nervous. The sounds of nature without, made him start. He hated the sigh and the moan of the night wind; he hated the solitude by which he was surrounded; his distraught conscience poured terrors into his soul; and the deep darkness and gloom of night appalled him. He moved about like the ghost of his former self; and the ghosts of those whom he had sent to their last account waited upon him, and would not be exorcised. He was a veritable Magor Massabib, a terror to himself, and to those about him.

For six years the Earl of Cassillis had led a quiet and an uneventful life. It was something new to the hoary peel by the Doon to know the piping times of peace. For long years the tide of passion had flowed and ebbed around it, hardly less constant in its presence than the ceaseless river that wandered past its walls to the ocean. The Earl never, to do him justice, regretted the truce with his kinsman, Kennedy of Bargany, save in one single particular. He reproached himself with having included in the treaty Mure of Auchendrane, because he had a feeling of personal vindictiveness towards Mure, and because he felt that he could not trust him. He was conscious that his veteran opponent was ever on the outlook, nursing his wrath, and only waiting a safe opportunity to have his revenge. It mattered not a whit that Mure had no immediate cause for vengeance; it was implanted in his breast; and have it he would, if he could. That, at least, was the opinion of the Earl.

The Master of Cassillis, out of his element with Carrick at rest and in quiet, had hard work spending his time. He was poor, and he was proud. All that he had of his own was a little estate called Brownston, whose revenues were not sufficient for his exaggerated wants; and as, before the murder of Sir Thomas Kennedy, he had been on friendly terms with Mure, and had plotted for the Earl's overthrow, so now he began afresh to scheme towards the same direction. He committed no overt act of hostility; but he was none the less on the outlook for aught that might advantage himself. His one great consolation was that his brother had married a wife so much older than himself, that the birth of an heir was an impossibility. In course of time, if he outlived the Earl, he must succeed both to the titles and to the estates; and he did not care how soon the day of succession should dawn. His one fear was that the Countess might die, and that the Earl should marry a second time. And, between his fear and his consolation, he had an uneasy time of it. His brother read him better than he suspected. He divined the workings of his mind, and while he kept on openly friendly terms with him, he watched his ongoings without intermission.

As for the Countess, she was still hale and hearty; and like a sensible woman, she kept her lord in check when his ire was kindled against Auchendrane, or when his wrath broke forth in contemplation of his brother's ill-concealed aspirations.

Tidings of the murder of Dalrymple were not long in reaching Cassillis House; and close upon their heels travelled the news of the assault, by Auchendrane and his cut-throat servitor, upon Kennedy of Garriehorne. Garriehorne was his own messenger; and when he entered the halls of Cassillis with his face covered with blood, and told how Mure had endeavoured to slay him in the fateful plantation of St. Leonard's, all the Earl's long-treasured animosity and vindictiveness burst out afresh.

Here was his chance at last. A double revenge, indeed! Mure had outraged the terms of the treaty in attacking Garriehorne, and, by the outrage, had placed himself beyond the terms of the agreement with Bargany; rumour said he had murdered Dalrymple, and placed himself within the pale of the common law. No further delay or hesitation now. He would attack on both charges, take the Garriehorne incident into his own hands, and stimulate the criminal authorities to lay Auchendrane by the heels for the tragedy which he had enacted by the sea-side.

As the Earl pondered the matter, he saw the opportunity to bring about another result. Why should he not possess, as well as assume, the mastery over his own brother? Why not instigate him to do by Auchendrane, as Auchendrane had done to Dalrymple? Were the Master of Cassillis to undertake the task and remove Mure by a simpler method, and a surer, than the processes of justice, he would be guilty of an offence against the laws of the realm, and therefore strictly dependent on his forbearance in not handing him over to the powers that were. The more he thought over the matter the better he liked the idea; so he despatched a messenger to bring his brother to Cassillis.

The Master divined why he was sent for.

"Yes," he said, as he entered the house, "I thought you would send for me. Auchendrane is in the trap at last."

"In the trap, yet not in it," was the Earl's reply, "he is only in it if we put him there."

"Has he not murdered Dalrymple, and is that not sufficient to tie the halter about his neck or bring him to kiss the maiden?"

"How do you know," the Earl asked his brother, "that he has murdered Dalrymple? What proof have you of it?"

"Everybody says he has, and everybody would not say he had if he were innocent."

"That does not follow. He might be innocent as you are of the tragedy, and yet the public might say he was the murderer. There might be every kind of circumstantial evidence to point him out as the murderer, and yet the chain might want completion by a single link. It is no use assuming him the murderer if we cannot prove it."

"Nothing can be easier than to prove it, if all that is said be true."

"Yes, if all that is said be true; but I'd wager that more than the truth is being said. Old wives' fables won't hang him—you may depend on that. The dreams of your cousin in Culzean won't convict him; and as for the spouting of blood when little Marie Mure went forward to look at the body—that is out of the question altogether. No, Hew, you will find that if Auchendrane has done this thing he has laid his plans deep. He is not the man to confess what he has done; no mortal eye witnessed the deed; and if he did do it, it is not to be proved by anything that I have heard. But that was not why I sent for you. We shall let the criminal authorities deal with that aspect of the business if they like— and I shall take care that they do if else miscarry—but, what concerns me more is Mure's assault on Garriehorne, his attempt to murder him in the wood of St Leonards. That relieves us of any obligation towards him, and we can now act as if there had been no treaty with Bargany."

"That has been a cursed treaty in every case," replied the Master, "it has left life in Carrick hardly worth living."

"So it has; but now, with Mure it is a thing of the past. He has lived long enough anyhow."

"Too long, I say. He ought to have been killed long ago."

"Quite right, Hew; but better late than never; and that is why I sent for you."

"Yes, I thought it was," replied the Master, "but wherein am I advantaged by his death?"

"I do not understand you, Hew. Wherein are you advantaged? What do you mean?"

"I mean what I say," replied the Master decidedly. "If Auchendrane is to be killed, and if I am to do it, I want to know what I am to get for doing it."

The Earl was non-plussed. He was not prepared for this matter-of-fact way of putting things. He had not anticipated that his brother would demand a substantial consideration.

"It is no concern of mine," continued the Master, "whether Mure lives or dies. He can do me no harm. The time was when I would have slain him, and that, too, with pleasure, without other recompense than the satisfaction of doing it, and of ridding Carrick of an infernal scoundrel; but I cannot afford to put my neck in danger to benefit you, and to gratify your passion for revenge, without being recompensed for the danger."

"I confess," replied the Earl, "you have disappointed me. I thought that the cause of the Kennedys lay nearer your heart and nearer your honour than it seems to do."

"Well, disappointed or not, I move neither hand nor foot in the affair, unless I know beforehand that I am to be re-compensed for the danger I encounter and for the service I do you."

The Earl did not waste time in persuasion. "What are your terms?" he asked coldly.

"These," was the reply. "I will take two of my men with me, and see to it that you are relieved of Auchendrane, on condition that you bind and oblige yourself to pay me yearly during life the sum of twelve hundred marks, and that, in addition, you take into your service the two men whom I employ. That will be their recompense."

"You drive a hard bargain, Hew," observed the Earl.

"Yes, and for a hard enterprise. These are the terms. Do you agree to them?"

"I agree to them," was the Earl's reply.

"Then write it, and sign it."

"You have my word—is not that sufficient?"

"No, my Lord, it is not sufficient. I want a document on which I can rely; and without such a document, Mure of Auchendrane lives, so far as I am concerned."

In making such a demand the Master of Cassillis was wily. He had no faith in his brother; and in addition to making sure of the money through the possession of the bond, he was not less anxious to incriminate the Earl to an extent that would make it impossible for him to turn to his advantage the knowledge of the premeditated deed. If the Master was to place his life and his liberty in the Earl's hands, he must have a key to the situation too.

The Earl was loath to grant the bond demanded, but necessity and his overmastering desire to see Auchendrane swept out of his path, conquered.

And here, handed down intact to this day, is the iniquitous bond * :—

"We, Johne Earl of Cassillis, Lord Kennedy, &c., binds and obliges us that, how soon our brother Hew Kennedy of Brownston, with his accomplices, takes the Laird of Auchendrane's life, that we shall make good and thankful payment to him and them of the sum of twelve hundred merks yearly, together with corn to six horses aye and until we receive them in household with ourself; beginning the first payment immediately after their committing of the said deed. Moreover, how soon we receive them in household, we shall pay to the two serving gentlemen the fees yearly as our own household servants. And here too we oblige us upon our honour. Subscribed with our hand. "JOHNE EARLE OF CASSILLIS."

---

* Pitcairn's Criminal Trials, vol. iii., page 622.

When the bond had been signed and subscribed, the Master rose to take leave of his brother.

"You had better," observed the Earl, "lose no time with Auchendrane."

"Neither we will," replied the Master. "I know him of old. I hope to be here again in forty-eight hours to claim the first instalment of your money."

"I hope you may," returned the Earl; and with these words the interview ceased.

The Master was not long in making his preparations. All he had to do was to secure his two accomplices; and these were not hard to find. On the following evening he was ready to set about the undertaking. He knew what Auchendrane's habits were, that he was not likely to find him abroad by day, but that after nightfall it was the custom of the old man to take exercise on horseback in the grounds surrounding the Tower. He did not know, however, that Mure had been so severely wounded by Kennedy of Garriehorne, and that he was hardly able to walk, let alone ride.

The Master of Cassillis and his two accomplices reached Auchendrane Tower after sundown, and concealed themselves in such a fashion that "the old fox," as the Master dubbed Mure, could not escape them were he to leave the house at all. Shadowed by the trees, they took up their sentry duty, and waited with all the patience at their command until he should appear. Moments added upon one another became minutes; and the minutes lengthened out into hours. Still he came not. The watchers grew impatient. The Master had too much at stake, however, to desert his post, and he remained where he was, watching the lighted window of the room where Auchendrane was supposed to hold high carnival with the powers of darkness, until midnight had gone.

"We may give it up now, I think," he said with an oath. "He comes not forth to-night."

"Too busy with his devil's work, I expect," observed one

of his attendants, "and he will require all the aid of his master to help him now."

"Devil or no devil," remarked the other, "he can never 'stand the cold steel. Six inches of this blade would tax the power of the best devil that ever lived to prevent him going home before his time."

"Hush!" said the Master, "I hear the sound of horses' hoofs. They are coming this way."

And so they were. From the sound, there could not be fewer than a score of horsemen approaching. The night was still, and though they were still far away, there was no mistaking the direction in which they were travelling. As they were advancing at a rapid trot, the sound rapidly became more intensified, until the watchers, still keeping their gaze fixed on the lighted window, saw it thrown open, and the dark figure of Mure himself projected against the light. He, too, had heard the sound; and conscience told him that it boded no good. Mure had no right to expect that he would escape the consequences of his misdeeds; he knew that the authorities could not let his crimes go unattended by consequences; and thus it was that he read in the approaching horsemen the dawn of the coming judgment.

"A thousand curses on them," he ejaculated aloud, "why have they been so swift? Why did I not leave when I had time? I cannot go now. For whither could I go? Not to the woods, not to the shore, not to the dens and caves of the earth. Trapped, by the Almighty, trapped like a fox! James, James!" he called aloud to his son.

James was in an adjoining room.

"Oh, James," exclaimed Auchendrane, as his son responded to his call, "what can I do? What can I do?"

"Do as I do," replied James, "You cannot escape now, even if you would. Remember this, there is no proof against us, and the only way to make sure work of it is to stay where we are, and brazen it out. That is what I am going to do."

"Naught else is there to be done now," was Auchendrane's answer, as he called his old and stronger self into play. "We must protest our innocence now and for ever."

"To the last," added James. "Remember this, I will never give way. Innocent I intend to be, if I go to the grave for it. But there is no fear of that. Man cannot prove what man neither sees nor knows."

"But Heaven knows," said Mure, though rather to himself than to his son.

"But Heaven won't interfere," replied James. "Where are all your philosophy and predestination now? Look the thing fair in the face—they cannot prove it against us—I tell you they cannot; and there is no retribution unless we are weak enough to court it."

As the conversation went on, the sound of the on-coming horsemen became louder and louder. They swept along the avenue leading to the Tower, and as the Master of Cassillis and his two associates withdrew further into the shade, a troop of soldiers defiled in front of the Tower, and their leader knocked loudly at the iron-studded door.

Mure himself threw the door wide open, and stood on the threshold, not a trace of irresolution or faltering in his demeanour. James stood beside him.

"John Mure of Auchendrane," said the commanding officer in a loud voice, "and James Mure, younger of Auchendrane, I arrest you in the King's name. You are my prisoners."

"On what charge do you arrest us?" asked Mure, stepping forward, and speaking with the most perfect composure.

"For the murder of William Dalrymple and for an assault with intent to kill, committed upon Hugh Kennedy of Garriehorne."

"Have you a warrant for the arrest?"

"I have," was the reply of the officer, as he took the warrant from his breast and held it up in his hand.

"It is an atrocious calumny," broke in James impetuously, "an outrage upon innocent men."

"That may be," replied the officer. "It is not to me you have to answer. You will have an opportunity of defending yourselves elsewhere. Meantime you will come with us."

"We obey the summons," said Mure, in a tone of voice in which dignity and injured innocence were well blended. "We obey the summons as loyal subjects of his most gracious Majesty. We shall accompany you at once."

And without another word Auchendrane made ready for the journey.

"There goes for ever my twelve hundred marks yearly," soliloquised the Master of Cassillis, as the cavalcade, with the Mures in the centre, rode slowly away; "may the devil go with them!"

An hour later Auchendrane and his son passed within the fateful portals of the Tolbooth of Ayr.

CHAPTER XXI.

THE TORTURE IS INEFFECTUAL TO EXTRACT CONFESSION.

THE Tolbooth of Ayr was a damp, cold structure, which stood grim and gloomy in the tortuous High Street of the burgh town. For a week or ten days the Mures were among the wretched tenants of the prison. They were confined in separate cells, had no access to their friends, and were treated with unnecessary rigour. The suffering entailed on Mure was consequently considerable. He was still weak and bloodless; and the method of living to which he had been accustomed made the coarse gaol fare as unpalatable as it was weak and unwholesome.

He was almost constantly alone—always, indeed, except when the turnkey went his rounds or the gaoler came to his cell to see that his prisoner was safe. The light by day struggled in faintly through the barred windows, falling on coarse bed and bedding, on the solitary chair, on the cold walls, on the uncarpeted, unmatted stone floor. Auchendrane could find no solace in religion. He was a fatalist, so far as his ideas of predestination were concerned. What fate had decreed, fate would accomplish; and so, to the eye of the turnkey or the gaoler, he presented an appearance of apathy or resignation. He never bemoaned his fate, save to himself. He knew from experience that it was easier to say than to unsay ; that his words would be used against him ; and that his hope lay in silence now and protestation later on.

It was in the silent watches of the night, when a stray star-glint shone through the bars, or when he caught a glimpse of the moon as she sailed across the dark blue heavens ; when the streets were silent save for the tread of the guardian of the peace, and the monotonous calling of the hours as these slipped bye ; when wretched with cold and hunger, and suffering the agonies of pain still adherent to the wound which Garriehorne had inflicted on him, he lay on the straw mattress and covered himself up with the coarse blankets, and the coarser counterpane, out of which heat could hardly be enticed, that his thoughts most troubled him.

Was this to be the end of it all—of all his warrings and plots, his glories and his ambitions ? Was it thus that the great Carrick feud was to come to an end ? He answered his own questions in the negative. His end was not yet. He would escape from his persecutors once again, a free man, cleared from suspicion, and close his eyes in his ancestral tower by the Doon.

And when he slept, his dreams literally chased one another. Now he was at home, the Doon running past the Tower of Auchendrane, the landscape smiling, the grass and the trees and the sky all beautiful and peaceful and serene. Now he was in the saddle, and he heard the war cries of the Kennedys, and gave them back stroke for stroke and blow for blow, and cheered on his stout retainers to the fray. Again he rode in the raid and foray, and swept aside the pride of Cassillis by the Girvan and the Stinchar, and through Glen-app into Galloway. Or he watched the sun sink over Arran in his blaze of self-begotten glory, and darting his rays into the placid surface of the Firth of Clyde. The pleasant past— for even the past of a wicked life can be pleasant when dominated by the misery of the present—trooped its proces- sion along, and he was ever the foremost feature of the galaxy.

But it was not ever so in his dreamland. Strange, weird shades and spectres came to him by night, and coming, haunted him. The spirits of men long forgotten trooped in and looked at him with hard, stony eyes, and harder hearts ; and then passed away to give place to others worse than themselves. The wood of St. Leonard's rose in view against the gloom, and he saw Sir Thomas Kennedy come riding up in the shadow of the trees. He heard the rush of the armed men, the clashing of the steel, the cries of the assailants, the groans of the Knight. He saw him reel in his saddle and come to the ground, and the red blood flow among the grass, percolating amid the roots, and reddening the sod. Worst of all, he was again on the Girvan sands. Again the piteous appeal for mercy, the pleading eyes, the uplifted hands ; again the crashing blow on the skull, the corpse on the brown shore, the advancing tide ; again that cold wade into the waters with the body that would not go away, for all the while it looked at him, and transfixed him with its hideous stare ; again the loud splash as the waves closed round their victim, and the billows rolled as they rolled before. The dead man rode on the waves as buoyantly as a feather, with eyes still intent on him, unspoken vengeance on its tongue, and raised finger of identification. And behind and beyond them all, in the deepest darkness, and yet painfully visible, stood the scaffold, and on the scaffold the headsman, with axe on shoulder, or the uprights and the cross beam and the cold glittering steel of the Maiden waiting to descend upon his neck.

How he would rouse himself as he was led by the executioner up the steps by the Market Cross of Edinburgh, and protest his innocence, and call God to witness that he was stainless! How he would call out in his dreams until he startled his fellow-prisoners, and made even the unresponsive walls of the Tolbooth vocal! And then he would awake, and sit up in bed, and pass his hand over his eyes in the darkness, and thank Heaven that it was nothing but a dream; and then he would think, and think, and think, until the night was over and gone, and the faint light of morning relieved the gloom of his narrow cell! These nights were a hell to Auchendrane, but they, too, he told himself, would pass into the shadow land.

James Mure's brutalised, phlegmatic temperament was not so wrought. He cursed the gaoler, he cursed the turnkey; he cursed everybody, himself into the bargain. He protested his innocence in the ears of the officials with an earnestness that almost made them believe in him, and sent them out on to the streets to tell the few remaining sympathetic friends of the Mures that they were victims to the tyranny of the Earl of Cassillis.

The town's folk, as a body, would have stood by Auchendrane if they could. But they could not. In fair fight they had fought by his side; and had he been imprisoned for nothing worse than the slaughter of a rival, they would have known why he was thus shut up. His misdeeds, however, were on every tongue, and there was not a man, woman, or child in all Ayr who did not know the character of the offences with the commission of which he was accused, and the precise nature of a dozen different crimes besides, of which he was not accused and which he had never committed.

They waited for the result, professed openness of mind, tarried complacently on the verdict, and, after the manner and custom of the people in all ages, meted out to him his doom ere yet it was pronounced. In reality they believed anything and everything against him, from the murder of Dalrymple down to, or up to, his proficiency in the black arts and his familiarity with the devil.

Within a month Auchendrane and his son exchanged the rigours of the Tolbooth of Ayr for those of the Heart of Midlothian.

The criminal authorities were in a quandary. They were anxious to bring home to Mure the murder of Sir Thomas Kennedy, the murder of William Dalrymple, and the onslaught on Kennedy of Garrichorne in the wood of St. Leonard's. Of the two major charges they had no proof that would hold water; the latter was a paltry, and, as the times went, not on the whole a very serious offence. Many a consultation they had and many a plan they tried to get at the truth; but without result. Their investigations in the west country led to nothing. They could glean no information from Kennedy of Bargany, who point blank refused to appear as a witness, and who availed himself of the opportunity to enjoy a lengthened sojourn in France. Mure of Cloncaird was dead. The Earl of Cassillis surmised, and expressed himself forcibly; the Master of Cassillis swore that he believed him guilty, but his oath of belief was useless. Bannatyne, the tenant of Chapeldonan, had disappeared, and neither man nor woman knew where he had gone. Many hazarded the opinion that the Mures had killed him, but that opinion, like the Master's oath, could not avail in the witness box.

The evidence, indeed, was so weak that a prosecution for murder must necessarily fall to the ground; and the criminal authorities were at their wit's end.

They were loath to proceed on the minor charge, and yet they could not establish the greater. And the minor offence

was bailable! What made it worse was that they felt convinced that the Mures were guilty.

King James took a special personal interest in the matter.
The state of the west country, the contendings of rival factions, the ignoring of law and order, had long annoyed him.
Ten or twelve years ago he had insisted on inter-marriage
between the families of Mure of Auchendrane and Sir Thomas
Kennedy of Culzean, in the hope and the expectation, that
marital bonds would prove too strong for feudal proclivities.
The result had belied his anticipations. For a time, indeed,
peace had settled on Carrick; but only for a very brief time;
and when the peace was broken the conflict had raged with
added 'intensity. The Sovereign was convinced in his own
mind thát Auchendrane was the head and front of all the
offending; and now that his officers had the Mures safe in
durance vile, he was resolved that they should not escape
unless their innocence could be completely established and
made manifest to the world. When, therefore, the Lord-
Advocate was brought practically to a standstill by the
absence of proof, King James insisted on James Mure being
subjected to the terrible ordeal of torture in order to extract
a confession from him which might be used in evidence in the
Court of Justiciary.*

* The torture of James Mure was brought about through the direct instigation of the Earl of Cassillis, whose letter to the King is still preserved in a
manuscript volume in the Advocates' Library, and runs thus:—

MOST SACRED SOVEREIGN,
It may please your Gracious Majesty, I have taken this
boldness, upon the further trial of the treacherous murderers of my uncle the
Laird of Culzean and of the boy who carried the letter of his dyett, committed
by the Laird of Auchendrane and his son; and now further cleared by the
great pains and care of my Lord Chancellor, who has brought them to such
contradictions in their depositions that all indifferent men may be persuaded
of their guiltiness of both these murders. Notwithstanding whereof, they
still continue in ane denial. I would Most humbly beseech Your Majesty
that it might be Your Majesty's gracious pleasure to grant a warrant to the
Chancellor and Council of Scotland to put them to the Boots, wherethrough
they may be brought to a more evident confession. So, most heartily wishing
Your Majesty long prosperity and happiness for ever,—I remain,
Your Majesty's most humble Servant and subject,
CASSILLIS.

After their arrival in Edinburgh, the Mures were not permitted to see one another until they met face to face, each under charge of the officers of Court, in the old Justiciary buildings in the High Street. Two judges sat on the bench; and besides these none were present save the officials, the Lord Advocate and one of his deputes, and the public executioner. No previous warning was given to Auchendrane or to his son that they were to be subjected to a preliminary enquiry; but neither needed to be told what awaited them as they emerged from the dark passage which communicated between the Heart of Midlothian and the Court House. A mutual glance they exchanged with one another, which was all that was necessary to ensure their joint determination to hold fast by the declaration of innocence on which they staked their hopes of life. Mure tottered as he took his place at the bar of the Court—imprisonment having wrought additional havoc on his already exhausted frame; but James stood up stout and bold, and gazed fearlessly around him.

"John Mure," said the presiding Judge, opening the proceedings without further formality," you have been brought here on a warrant, charging you with the crime of murder. What say you, are you guilty or not guilty?"

"Before I answer your Lordship's question," replied Auchendrane, "may I crave permission to know what is included under the charge of murder upon which I have been brought hither?"

"You are charged with aiding and abetting in the murder of Sir Thomas Kennedy of Culzean, and, in conjunction with your son, of having murdered one William Dalrymple on the sea coast of Carrick."

"My lord," replied Mure, "I am an old man and have not long to live. In the nature of things my time is short; and standing on the brink of the grave, it is not meet that I should say other than the truth."

19

Mure was proceeding to speak further, when the Judge interrupted him.

"Stay a moment; take the oath."

Auchendrane raised his right hand, and the oath was administered.

"I swear by Almighty God, and as I shall answer to God on the great day of judgment, that I will tell the truth, the whole truth, and nothing but the truth."

"Now, sir," added the judge, "remember that you have not only taken an oath to God to tell the truth, but that your deeds and your words alike will be subjected to a rigorous criminal investigation. What do you say?"

"I am fully conscious of the responsibility to Heaven which this oath has put upon me; and knowing that I must, in the course of nature, shortly put off this mortal body, I declare my innocence of the charges brought against me. I have already appeared before the Privy Council charged with being actor or art in part in the murder of Sir Thomas Kennedy; and having tholed an Assize for that, and been found innocent, I take it that I cannot again be accused of that crime."

"You have not been found innocent, sir," sternly replied the Judge, "though you were not found guilty. Do you deny in the presence of God and of these witnesses to what you say, that you are innocent of that crime?"

"I do, my Lord, emphatically and indignantly repudiate, and reprobate any and every charge in connection with the death of Sir Thomas Kennedy that can be brought against me."

"Then, what of William Dalrymple?" asked the Judge.

"That, my Lord, is a vile and horrible calumny. I neither laid hands on the lad, nor do I know aught of his death. Why am I so charged? Is it not the case that the man in whose house he lived, the tenant of the farm of Chapeldonan, has disappeared? And yet, thanks to the malicious machi-

nations of my enemies, I stand here accused of his murder.
The Lord on high knows that I am innocent."

" You can sit down in the meantime," remarked the Judge,
coldly, " James Mure," he continued, addressing the younger
man, who rose defiantly to his feet and scowled at the bench,
" you are accused, in conjunction with your father, of having
murdered William Dalrymple. What say you ?"

" By whom am I so accused ?" asked James.

" By me," replied the Lord-Advocate, turning round towards
the dock.

" No, my Lords," said James, " I am only nominally accused
by the Lord-Advocate. The real accuser is the Earl of
Cassillis. It is he that has trumped up this ridiculous charge
against us ; it is owing to his influence that these indignities
are heaped upon us ; it is he who has been at the founda-
tion of this persecution."

" Take the oath, sir," the Judge said.

James did so, in loud, self-confident tones.

" The Court will hear what you have to say to the
charge."

" I have nothing further to say, than that I am in whole,
or in part, innocent of the crime alleged against me. I never
laid a finger on Dalrymple. God knows I speak the truth."

" Does He ?" asked the Lord-Advocate, solemnly.

" He does, sir. You know that He does ; else, why are we
brought up here without Counsel to speak for us, without an
opportunity to defend our cause and our innocence in the
face of day ?"

" Now, sir," interrupted the Judge, speaking with great
sternness of tone, " the Court does not believe in the denials
to which you and your father have given utterance. The law
of the land has given us power to extract confession from
you by torture. It is not our wish that you should be subjected to suffering ; and before we proceed to do our duty—a
duty which we owe to the cause of justice, and to society at

large—I ask you again, whether you still deny the crime
with which you are charged?"

"I do, indeed," was the unfaltering answer, "I cannot
admit that I am guilty of what my conscience tells me, and
of what my God knows, I am innocent."

At a sign from the Lord-Advocate, the executioner advanced to the front of the bench.

"The thumbkins," said the Judge.

James never changed countenance as he spoke again.

"You may torture me, my lord, as you like; but until the
day I die, I shall maintain my innocence before God and
man."

"Do your duty," the Judge said, addressing the headsman.

The grim official produced at once the instrument of
torture named—the thumbkins, and advanced to where James
Mure stood unflinching. He adjusted the infernal irons on
the thumb of the left hand, and turned the screw until the
thumb was tightly compressed.

"Once more," said the Judge, "are you guilty?"

"I have answered," replied James.

At a sign from the bench, the executioner tightened the
screw until the blood spurted from underneath the nail, and
from the point of the thumb. The pain was excruciating, but
never a groan escaped the unhappy man.   Nor did he speak.
Tighter and tighter grew the compression, as the callous
headsman plied his horrible vocation, until the bones
splintered under the pressure, and James Mure grasped the
dock in which he stood for support.   He set his teeth the
more firmly and bore it all.

"Will you not confess?" asked the Lord-Advocate, in one
of the pauses.

"I have nothing to confess," was the firm reply.

Again the pressure, until the screw could turn no longer
and the thumb was crushed out of the semblance of shape.

The agony was fearful; and but for the firm resolution and iron nerves and will of the sufferer, confession must have been forthcoming.

" You may kill me where I stand," he said, as the screw was reversed—for it could go no further—" I can only die but once, but even once I may not confess to a crime that I never committed."

Auchendrane surveyed the scene in silence, his face, if possible, paler than usual, but his lips tightly closed and a look of unutterable determination upon his brow. Once he rose, as if to speak, but a glance from his son, who thought him wavering, caused him to resume his seat.

There was a whispered consultation between the judges and the Crown prosecutors, while the executioner wiped the blood and flesh from the thumbkins, and cleaned them in order to their readiness for the other hand. But they were not to be again in requisition.

"The boot!" said the presiding judge, as the brief consultation closed; and the executioner dragged forward the heavy, iron-fastened uprights, fashioned so as to secure the foot and the lower part of the leg. James gazed at it, and a glance of terror shot from his eyes, but he steeled himself for the new trial.

" Again," said the judge, " I warn you. You know what you have endured. Worse is in store for you. Confess, as you have a soul to be saved."

" Confess," added the Lord-Advocate, " as you hope to win pardon and salvation."

" I am in your hands," was James' reply, " you can tear my poor body to pieces, but you cannot harm my soul," and God will requite this at your hands."

At another sign from the judge the boot was fixed in its place and a heavy wedge placed within, ready to be driven home by the hammer which the executioner held in his hand. The mental torture of the miserable wretch must have been awful. He knew that as the wedge was driven home, the bones of his right leg must splinter, as those of his thumb had splintered, and that from that day onward he must go through life a cripple; but he was willing to go through with it if he could only thereby save his life. So he called his courage afresh to his aid and submitted to the ordeal without a tremor.

Crash, crash! splintered bones, and the boot full of blood; an ear-piercing yell, and James Mure fainted away. His father caught him as he fell and turned appealingly to the Court.

"You see, my lord," he said, "you see that he has borne the ordeal as none but an innocent man could. Is it not enough?"

"Wait till he comes to," was the callous interjection of the Lord-Advocate, "and he will speak the truth."

But no—when James came to, gradually recovering consciousness, he set his face like a flint and appealed to high heaven to testify to his innocence. So earnest were his words that the judges, accustomed as they were to such scenes, looked at one another; while even the Lord-Advocate began to doubt his assurance that the men before him were murderers. There was another hurried consultation, at the close of which the Court adjourned without another word being spoken. Auchendrane was led off to his cell in the Tolbooth, and James carried to his, in the same grim building.

And so the ordeal of torture was a failure. What was to be done now? If in a quandary before, the authorities were between the horns of a dilemma now. They took time to think. A month passed, and still they were thinking. And what was worse, the tidings of the suffering to which James Mure had been subjected awoke the sympathy of the impressionable public; and from Ayr in the west, as well as from Edinburgh itself, demands came pouring in that Auchen-

drane and his son should be set at liberty. These remonstrances were for a time unheeded, but the tide kept on
rolling in until it would take no denial.

But there was one man who would not flinch from the conviction of the guilt of the Mures, and that was King James.
He stuck to his point dogmatically; demands and remonstrances he set aside; and appeals were for a time unavailing.
The devil, he said, had steeled the heart of the ruffian to
resist the torture, and the devil was not to be master in his
realm. If Auchendrane was in league with his Satanic
Majesty, so much the more reason for not letting him go free
to work his incantations and his charms, and to raise a fresh
cloud of dust to cover his guilt. The sovereign's enmity, for
all that, was worse against James. The old man, though
leagued with Satan, could be kept from mischief, strictly
watched, and prevented from the execution of any more of
his nefarious plots; while, as for James, nothing better than
the Heart of Midlothian should be his resting place for the
remainder of his life.

Time did not soften the monarch's asperities; but so loud
grew the tumult that he compromised. He consented to
Auchendrane being released under a heavy bail bond to re-
appear when called upon : and ere another couple of months
had gone, the old baron was once more in his Tower by the
Doon. His son remained in durance vile.

The return of Auchendrane inflamed the Earl of Cassillis
beyond measure. No sooner was he made aware that his foe
had, for the time being at least, triumphed over the officers
of justice, than he communicated with his brother. The
Master was overjoyed to hear that his twelve hundred marks a
year were not yet quite a vanished dream. Mure had escaped
one fate, why should he not be subjected to another ? The
opportunity for vengeance was to hand; and if Auchendrane
had only been to hand with it, the yearly tribute would soon
have been secured; but the wary old baron, alive to every

danger and conscious of the step which Cassillis was all but certain to take, never left the immediate precincts of his house; and even when he did go out of doors he was invariably attended by one or two of his staunch followers, whom neither his reputation for crime nor yet for sorcery could drive from their allegiance. The crime they cared nothing about, the sorcery they had no belief in. The Master watched and waited but in vain, until, losing patience, he renounced the enterprise until he should have a better opportunity to carry out his plans.

The rustics shrank from contact after dark with the proximity of Auchendrane Tower. The devil was more surely there now than ever he was before. Who could have foreseen, they asked one another, that after the long career of crime in which Mure had been engaged, he would have succeeded in baffling both legal and feudal foes? Any other man than he would have gone down in sorrow to the grave. But he, more than fourscore years old, had emerged from the very Heart of Midlothian itself, as the children of the Captivity had emerged from the furnace, without the smell of fire on his garments, It was not fate, it was not luck, it was not the result of policy or strategy. It was owing to nothing but the machinations of Satan himself, to whom Auchendrane—every rustic in the country-side knew it—had sold his immortal soul.

And so the lighted window which shone out through the trees into the darkness of the night, as it sat low upon Carrick, was more shunned than ever. Men spoke boldly enough of Mure when the sun was high, but they lowered their voices when the red peat glowed on the hearth, and the smoke curled through the hole in the roof of their house, and drew closer to one another. Yet there was such a fascination about him that they could not do otherwise than speak of him; and as they did so in measured tones and low, the faces of the listening women and children grew pale and elongated, and they glanced nervously over their shoulder when they heard a noise. It was little wonder that the traveller hasted bye a house where Satanic imperialism sat enthroned—for who knew that he might not be within hearing of voices and words that no mortal might hear, and live? Who knew what frightful scenes he might not witness so hard by such a favourite resting place of the author of evil?

Auchendrane lived only to die. He was weary of his life, and would gladly have laid it down. But he would not take it. He was not a man to play the Roman fool and die upon his own sword; no, he would dree his weird until death should come to him, come when, come how it might. What is to be, must be, and we cannot escape it—that was Mure's creed, a creed he had never known to fail. It had stood him for scores of years and more; on it he hung his faith; by it he would abide to the last. He was ready for anything that might transpire, though as resolved as ever to stem the current of any predestination that might put his neck in jeopardy. It was then that his fatalism failed him; he could not drift with it to his destruction if he could turn it out of its course.

That may have been why, when one of his attendants told him that Bannatyne had returned from Ireland to his farm of Chapeldonan, he roused himself for a fresh enterprise, and sat far into the morning hours thinking, and thinking, and thinking.

CHAPTER XXII.

AUCHENDRANE MAKES ACQUANTANCE WITH THE SPIRITS OF THE PAST.

How the devil drives on his own! He will neither stop for them, nor allow them to stop for themselves. He impels them to work for their hard wages; and, so long as they are under his thraldom, they are as badly off as Noah's dove, which found no rest for the sole of its foot or for its weary pinions. The analogy is not quite complete, for the dove found haven in the ark, whereas they keep drifting on above the waste of waters until they are swallowed up in the destruction.

So it was with Mure. He might have rested. The most searching investigations had resulted in nothing; the most crucial ordeal through which a man could be put, had only served to emphasise the professed innocence of James and his father of the crime with which they stood charged; and, if he had been content to let well alone, his dreams might have been realised, and he might have been permitted to die within the walls of his own old mansion.

But rest he could not. Bannatyne was home again. The tenant of Chapeldonan wearied of Ireland, as Dalrymple had wearied of Arran. He could not leave his conscience in Carrick. It went with him wherever he went; it dogged his footsteps by day; it lay down with him, though not to rest, by night. It chased him from one place to another, from one scene to another. It waited on his arrival, it was present at his departure. Like many another man similarly situated, he returned home, to the very spot where the aroused conscience had its awaking. Bannatyne knew his danger; but the loadstone that drew him to Carrick was within him and he could not resist it. So home he came, back to Chapeldonan, back to the sands of the Girvan shore, back to the same sea that had swallowed up his ill-fated kinsman.

Nothing was changed. The brown sands were as brown and as bare as ever, though no successive tides could take the furrows out of them that Bannatyne saw; the waves rose and fell as they had ever done, though their dead uniformity in calm, and their restless surging in storm, alike failed to swallow up in their embraces the body that he had seen committed to their charge. And the sky, now bright, now lowering, the stars as they twinkled, the moon as she rode silent and solemn, and the sun as he shone in his strength —all had a consciousness in his eyes which he could not drive into oblivion. No water of Lethe ran by the Carrick shore, no river of forgetfulness. Bannatyne was as miserable at home as he had been in Ireland; but home is home, and there is no evading it.

Bannatyne was resolved stoutly to maintain his innocence. Auchendrane knew it, and yet Auchendrane mistrusted him.

For three months Mure led as miserable a life as could well have fallen to his lot. His way as a transgressor was hard. Now he shut himself up in his Tower, and for days remained in the one small apartment brooding over his chances; and when this brooding became irksome and he wearied of it, he skulked away by night like a thief and sought seclusion in the house of some faithful retainer. He was misery personified. He seemed at times like the Wandering Jew, flitting about from place to place, a great guilt upon his soul, afraid of his fellow-men, afraid of Bannatyne, afraid of himself.

His faith in predestination began to break down, for he got too weak to grip it hard as he used to do. Everything was against him, he told himself. He knew that the peasants evaded his dwelling, scared lest some vision of the night should appear to them, lest some restless spirit should come to them, lest the ghosts of the men whom Mure had sent to their last account should cross their path in the mirk midnight. He knew all that, and he trembled to be the off-scouring of all men. He felt that life was slipping from his grasp, that his name and fame were in the balance, tried and found wanting; and that the Fates had decreed his doom. He had indeed been his own fate; his own predestination; he had worked out his destiny—why then should he rail because predestination was slipping from his grasp and marshalling its power to crush him ?

A desperate man, he became more desperate, and rallied himself for one more effort to clear the ground beneath his feet. Only Bannatyne stood between him and salvation. With the tenant of Chapeldonan out of the way, he could lie down and die in peace. Therefore the farmer must be slain !

But how ? Mure could not do it himself. He was too weak. Age and trial had bent his once erect form; weakness had shaken the iron out of his sinews and nerves; and the wound of Garriehorne had left him minus the use of one of his arms. His faculties for the fray were of the past; and, therefore, he must have others do for him what he could not do for himself.

While resolving the situation for the thousandth time, a new obstacle presented itself. He knew a man who would obey his behests, so far as the murder of Bannatyne went— a man named Pennycooke, who was not only a trusty follower of his own, but a mortal foe to the farmer of Chapeldonan ; but, once that deed was done, what of Pennycooke ? He would be in his hands then; and was the change from the tender mercies of Bannatyne to those of Pennycooke worth the risk ? Not, certainly, unless Pennycooke could be put out of the way. Pennycooke, therefore, must die too. And by whose hand ? Here was another opening for the fiend which prompted him, another case for plotting and scheming and resolving. There was only one other man left to whom he could entrust the fate of Pennycooke, and that was his cousin, Mure of Auchmull, who was a cut-throat as reckless as Auchendrane himself, and who, years before, at Auchendrane's instigation, had despatched, with poignard or dagger, a scion of the Kennedy family as he rode leisurely from the valley of the Stinchar towards the capital of Carrick. He could not well refuse to do the deed, for his life was in

Auchendrane's keeping; and he could not inform against him without putting his own life in peril.

It must be done. There was no other way for it. Every avenue was closed. Bannatyne must be slain by Pennycooke, and Pennycooke, in turn, by Mure of Auchmull. And that would complete the links in the last chain he should ever forge. After it was forged, he should have peace, peace of mind, peace to lie down and die, peace to make his peace with God!

To follow the windings which this intended succession of crimes opens up is not necessary. Pennycooke undertook his share in the transaction without compulsion. A staunch feudalist and a follower of Mure, he never hesitated in accepting the terms, and he lost no time in setting about his enterprise.

Bannatyne, however, though he had incurred the danger of returning to Carrick, was quite conscious of the risk he ran. He knew from experience that Auchendrane would stick at nothing in order to effect the remaining purpose of his life. He had threatened him already when they jointly assassinated Dalrymple. True, he had also threatened his own son; but his son was safe enough in prison, and dared not speak. And, therefore, if further vengeance was meditated, it must necessarily be against himself. This knowledge set him upon his guard in a double direction, for while he exercised the most constant vigilance, and never went abroad without some one accompanying him, and while he was continually armed and on the outlook to resist open attack, he was equally alive to the possibility that the Mures might try to get him into trouble through jointly informing against him, or that the authorities might apprehend him on suspicion, and in the knowledge that he had left the country immediately after the commission of the crime now awaiting elucidation.

Bannatyne, though physically a strong man, was not so, mentally. He lived in cares and fears and continual doubts.

He had nobody to consult or whom he could approach for advice. If he had been a wise man he would have bared his secret to some trustworthy friend and obtained extraneous light; but not being wise, he kept his secret, and his counsel, and his misery to himself, and lived in a state of constant terror.

Pennycooke was like a sleuth-hound. He dogged his prey. He hid among the rocks on the shore and in the plantations hard by Chapeldonan; but, while he was quite ready to execute vengeance, he was not by any means ready to put his neck in the halter. And therefore he could not kill Bannatyne, because the suspicious farmer invariably had one or two comrades by him when he left the environs of his home; and that he very seldom did. For a month or six weeks the intended assassin maintained the quest. He never abated his vigilance; and yet, when occasionally he returned to Auchendrane, he could give Mure no satisfaction, and no assurance that his purpose was likely to be soon effected.

Mure grew more anxious as the days passed on. Had he only been a younger man, he often sighed to himself, he would soon have cleared the way; but age and frailties were accumulating on him, and he knew that he had fought his last battle and performed his last active deed.

It was not given to Pennycooke to send Bannatyne to his last account; for one evening while the farmer of Chapeldonan was sitting by the fireside watching the sparks fly up the chimney and musing on his chances, the house was surrounded by a troop of the retainers of the Earl of Cassillis, headed by the Earl himself. Bannatyne would have fled; but ere he had time to do so, the Earl stood beside him. Interpreting the purport of their errand, Bannatyne rose to his feet.

"I know why you have come, my lord," he said, "but it was not I who did it."

"My friend," spoke the Earl, kindly, "I know that. I do

not think, at all events, that it was. I have only come hither to talk over matters with you, and to see whether the upshot may not be to our mutual advantage."

Two or three of the Earl's followers had accompanied him as he entered the house. Turning to these,

"You may leave us alone," said the Earl—"Chapeldonan and I are going to speak on a business that only concerns ourselves." The retainers obeyed.

"Now, Chapeldonan," continued the Earl, "I have come hither on set purpose to question you regarding the murder of William Dalrymple. I do not say you did it. I do not know whether you had anything to do with it or not. I do not even ask you to tell me if you had any connection with it yourself. But I do want to know whether, to your knowledge or not, the Mures of Auchendrane were concerned in the tragedy. Before you answer me, Bannatyne, I warn you well, I believe you know more than you have ever told. If you trust me fairly and openly, I shall be your friend and protector; if you do not, you shall go to Cassillis House with me this very night, nor shall you leave it until you have disclosed what you know, or until you are handed over to the officers of justice. I wish to avoid handing you over to them, if I can ; but the truth I must have, and will have, too, before you and I part. You understand me ? "

Bannatyne did understand the Earl of Cassillis. The situation in which he was now placed was not dissimilar to that in which he had found himself that night on the sands of Girvan. To save himself then, he had participated in the murder of Dalrymple ; to save himself now, must he reveal the details of the murder itself ? Must he incriminate himself ? That was the thought that passed through his mind. He was not so particular about sacrificing the Mures.

"I understand you, my lord," he replied, after a pause.

"Dalrymple was a friend of yours, wasn't he—a relation, or something of that sort ? "

" He was, my lord."

" And he was residing with you at the time of his disappearance ? "

" He was, my lord."

" You and he were on friendly terms ? There was no reason why you should have laid hands on him ? "

" There was not, my lord ; there was no reason under the sun. We were on the most friendly terms. And, as I am a living man, I never laid a finger on him, never touched him, had no hand in his death."

" Perhaps, Bannatyne, like Paul, you were consenting to the death ? "

" No, I was not, Lord Cassillis. I would have saved him had he not been beyond my power. He was done to death without my consent, against my will, but in such like that I could not interfere."

" Now we are getting to business. You say he was done to death against your will ; then you know that he was done to death ? "

" I did not mean to say that, Lord Cassillis," replied Bannatyne hurriedly, and taken aback by the knowledge that he had so far committed himself.

" No, you did not mean to say it, sir, but you said it all the same ; and I rather choose to believe what you say than what you mean to say on second thoughts. Better tell the truth at once, Chapeldonan ; it will save you trouble at the hinderend."

" I cannot say more, my lord, than I have done. It was not I who slew Dalrymple, and even if it had been me, I should not tell you so. No man is bound to condemn himself."

" No, not to condemn himself, especially if he is innocent. That is not what I ask you to do. But you may lawfully, by informing against the actual murderer, or murderers, save yourself ; and that, surely, is worth doing."

"I dare not tell what I know, my lord, for I have sworn to keep it secret."

"An oath so taken, under compulsion, is no oath. But tell me this, was it John Mure of Auchendrane who made you take such an oath?"

"I dare not say that it was."

"Dare you say that it was not, sir?"

Bannatyne hung his head.

"Come, come, Chapeldonan, speak up like a man. I have no more time to spare here just now, and must be gone. If you can say no more than that, you must come with me. I know more than you seem to think. I know the motives which prompted Mure to this deed. I know the incentive. The only solution of it is that he, or he and his son, murdered Dalrymple. Besides, are you not alive to the danger of your existence here?"

"I am, my lord, I am fully conscious of the risk that I am running; but I have an oath upon my soul, and I dare not break it or foreswear myself."

"Very well, Bannatyne. If that is all you can say I must take you with me. We shall see whether your tongue may not wag a trifle more freely in Cassillis House, or in Edinburgh. You have heard what was done to James Mure?"

Bannatyne shuddered. The news of James's torture had filled him with terror.

"Once more, sir," continued the Earl, "before I take you with me, I ask you whether John Mure and his son were not, to your knowledge, the murderers of Dalrymple? Remember this—if you speak out firmly and truly, and put yourself in my hands, no evil can befal you. I shall be your friend. If you witnessed the deed, even, I shall go bail for you that you shall escape punishment."

The temptation was a strong one; and the Earl purposely made it strong. He had spoken as he had done, and threatened as he had threatened, in order to frighten and at

20

the same time to encourage Bannatyne into confidence in himself.   He was loath to carry out his threat and take the farmer of Chapeldonan into captivity, partly because he preferred that Auchendrane should not be convicted so very apparently at his instigation, partly because he feared that Bannatyne might proclaim his innocence and refuse to incriminate himself.   But he could not afford to be balked of his purpose; and unwilling though he was, he had no alternative to taking Bannatyne along with him to Cassillis.

His threats and his encouragement were alike fruitless. Bannatyne would not say more than he had said.   The Earl gathered enough to make him absolutely certain that the farmer held the key to the position, and he was not going to lose the key once he had it in his possession.   And so, when he and his retainers set out for Cassillis House, Bannatyne rode, a down-hearted captive, in the midst of the throng.

Their departure was not unobserved.   Pennycooke saw it, and posted off without loss of time to Auchendrane Tower.

"Well," said Mure, as he entered, "do you bring me good tidings?"

"No, sir, I do not; the worst tidings, rather, that I could have brought you."

"These are?" asked Auchendrane.

"That Bannatyne has been taken prisoner by the Earl of Cassillis, and is at this moment safe and sound in Cassillis House.

"A thousand curses on them all!" broke out Mure furiously, "now, indeed, I am tied to a stake.   Get you gone, Pennycooke, and see my face no more."

Pennycooke was glad to take his departure; for Mure looked uncanny as his eyes flashed fire from their deep-set sockets, and he knitted his brows in fury.   Without another word, he closed the door of the chamber where the brief interview had taken place, and went forth into the night.

Up to this point, though Mure had been living in darkness

and in despondency, he had not been without his gleams of hope shooting through the darkness. Their glimmer was lurid, it is true; but still the glimmer was there. But now, and all at once, hope seemed dead, and he realised to the full the danger of his situation. He told himself that Bannatyne would confess, and, if he did, there could only be one result.

He sat down in front of the fire, drew his chair close to the cheering blaze, and buried himself in thought.

"Has it come to this at last?" he said to himself. "Is this to be the end of it all? Am I to be deserted of friends and of hope itself? Is it for this that I stood by Bargany, and led him on until he could have crushed the power of Cassillis as easily as I could have crushed an egg-shell below my heel? A curse upon Bargany! Had he acted as I bade him, and steeled his heart to the issue, not all the power of the Earl could have prevented his downfall. But why should I repine? It has been a maxim with me, all my life long, that everything that cometh to pass is ordained, and that we cannot stand up against our destiny. Fate! ah, Fate! we cannot resist it. We may try to stem it, to dam back its torrent, but strong though our dams be, it will sweep them away. And yet, how could I have acted otherwise than I have done? Destiny, again. How could I have foreseen this issue—how could I have foreseen that after all my warrings, after all the attempts that have been made on my life, after the onslaughts upon me, and the blood I have seen shed—how could I have foreseen that I should have been spared till eighty summers had passed over my head? Eighty summers, indeed! Eighty times have I seen the leaves grow green, and fall; and there is not a man of all my compeers who dwelt here when I was young, who has not gone to the grave. Would to God I had lain down with them in their silent rest! But no, that is not the way of my predestination. I have been spared—for what? Heaven only knows. Yet I have been a fool, though I was a fool for the best. I should have listened to James' warnings, and despatched him out of hand years ago. I disliked the act, and yet, had I done the deed then, it would have gone to sleep long ago. They say these have a habit of cropping up at the bar of Heaven—I wonder if they do. Will I see Dalrymple there, and Sir Thomas Kennedy, and the scores I have sent there before me? And if I do—great Heavens, I see him now"—and Mure started as if he were face to face with an apparition— "I tried to save you," he continued, cowering, and with gaze intent at the window of the room, "I tried to save you, Dalrymple—you know I did."

The cold sweat broke over his brow. "Get you gone, get you gone"—and his voice had an appealing ring in it—"for Heaven's sake do not come to taunt me before my time! If I must meet you, let it be there, not here—let it be when I shall have cast aside this frail body and stand erect in a new birth. Do not stay so long—why do you stay? Come no nearer—come no nearer. There is not room for both of us. Get thee back into the darkness! Were you in heaven, you would not leave it; why, then, does the devil let you out? Back, back, I say; my time is not yet come. I conjure you in the name of the Holy Trinity."

There was a pause as Mure sank back in his chair, exhausted and faint. For a moment he closed his eyes; and when he opened them, the horrible mental shadow had vanished. "Thank God for that, at least," he exclaimed, as he lighted candles in various parts of the little chamber.

Were it possible to pity Mure, he might be pitied here and now. But grey in crime, as he was, he had not a regret for the past. All he cared for was the future. If he could only escape, all would be well.

During the few days which succeeded the old man gave way to his fancies. The ghosts of the past trooped up to his chamber every night. He knew the hour they were coming, and he was on the out-look for them. Till midnight he had

the room to himself; but no sooner had the clock told the
noon of night than the graves were opened, and he waited
till the ghastly tenants should present themselves.

And they never failed him. They came as surely as the
clock struck, a motley group, men whom he had killed in
battle and in raid, men whom he had never seen in life, some
of them with pale, gaunt faces, and eyes that could see in the
darkness of the sepulchre; the spirits of fair young maidens
whose lives he had ruined, and o'er whose graves the grass
had grown rank, lo, these many years; captives whose bones
were even now rotting in the dungeons beneath his feet—
these all drew near and looked upon him, and he shrank
appalled from the contact. The worst came last—Sir Thomas
Kennedy, whose confidence he had betrayed, and whom his
assassin accomplices had done to doom in the wood of St.
Leonards; and Dalrymple.

Dalrymple was the crowning misery. His eyes were
listless, yet they glowed with the fires of Erebus. The fixed
stare was the stare of a dead man; yet of a dead man who saw
what he was looking at, and would take no denial in the gaze.
Auchendrane felt the piercing gaze in his heart.

The visits were irregular after midnight. Sometimes the
unhallowed troop repeated their gruesome procession more
than once—sometimes they seemed in a hurry to be gone.
To Auchendrane they were a stern reality. And when they
had gone he used to wonder whither they had gone; and,
worse still, whether, when he went to the shadow land, they
would so taunt him through unending ages.

And even when the spectres were not by him, his own
thoughts were, and his dreads; and he lived a life of perpetual
agony and terror. When he left his chamber he slunk along
the passages as if Death were at his heels, chasing him with
his scythe. Yet how welcome the Destroyer would have
been to him, but for the life beyond! And that was a land
of darkness, as darkness itself; and of the shadow of death,
without any order, and where light is as darkness.

To all intents and purposes Mure waited upon events. He read the handwriting upon the wall and he knew what it meant. He would fly no more. Predestination had its meshes about him at last. All that he could do—all that he intended to do—was to protest his innocence to the end.

When the Earl of Cassillis conveyed Bannatyne to his dwelling by the Doon, he had no clearly defined course of action mapped out in his own mind; but he was not long in discovering Bannatyne's weak spot. It was a very natural weak spot, too; he loved his life. He had not the courage to die to save Mure, or to save his own reputation, and he was willing, if worst came to the worst, to sell Auchendrane or his son, rather than go to his death before them. The Earl soon discovered this, and took advantage of it. By imprisonment, starvation, and threats, he bent Bannatyne's will until it was like a reed shaken in the wind. The poor man was in despair when it was announced to him that the Earl had resolved to take his life; and sending for his Lordship, he made a clean breast of it.

The Earl was overjoyed. Here was his revenge to hand at last. Not for a moment had he ever permitted his hatred to Auchendrane to abate. Had he only known it, he could not have punished him more severely than by leaving him alone, a prey to his fears, his conscience, his dreams, his ghostly visitation; but these Lord Cassillis knew nothing about. What concerned him was that Mure had been his arch-enemy, and that, through his instigation, his power as the feudal divinity of Carrick had been shaken. That was an offence that could not be forgiven; and therefore, if he could accomplish it, Auchendrane must die the death.

He was not slow to act on the information wrung from Bannatyne. He made haste to ride to the Scottish Metropolis, and to set the authorities on the right track. He took care that the King should see his zeal in the matter; and lest there should be any doubt on this score, he indited an epistle to His Majesty, setting forth in detail his own exertions for the common weal.

The authorities, set anew in motion, paid a second visit to Auchendrane Tower; and when they left it, John Mure left it with them. He cast one last glance at the strong house which he had held so long; and the next minute it was out of his sight—and for ever.

CHAPTER XXIII.

AUCHENDRANE'S PREDESTINATION IS SUMMED UP.

It is the morning of the 11th of July, 1611. A fair, summer morning, the sun already above the house-tops of Edinburgh, Nature as joyous as if sin had never tarnished her, and as unconscious as if she had all the field to herself!

Round the doors of the Court of Justiciary throng a mixed crowd, composed mainly of the sensation-loving burghers of the metropolis. Mainly, but not altogether. Lords, knights, and squires from the westland are there, men who know the Mures and want to hear for themselves whether they are as guilty as they are said to be; gallants of the town, scions of noble families summering in the city, portly burgesses, civic dignitaries—all crowded together in front of the unopened door.

The door is opened and in they throng. There is no respect of persons. First come, first served—for the body of the Court is open. Every man for himself, straining, struggling, fighting to obtain a good place. They pack the available space in the area, and overflow the gallery; they stand in the passages, in the recesses of the walls, at the doors—everywhere that standing room is to be had. There are more without than there are within; but the Courthouse is small, and is not meant for an amphitheatre. Besides, it is stuffy and ill-ventilated; and ere the day is done it will be hot and oppressive. But what of that to those who are within? Have they not been happy enough to secure places where they can see and hear for themselves all that is going on? The trial is the most sensational of the times, for the fame of the criminals is on every lip.

The officials drop in slowly one by one, the Jurors, the Clerk of Court, the Lord Advocate and his two deputes, the three counsel for the defence, the Chaplain, the City representatives. The Chaplain stands in friendly converse with the Lord-Advocate, waiting to say his say and to be gone.

A blare of trumpets in the street, then within the precincts of the building. A hush falls on the Court, the door is thrown open, and, bewigged and ermined, the Judge advances, the macer carrying the mace before him. The audience rise to their feet, the doors are closed, the Chaplain briefly prays, everybody resumes his seat, the name of the jurors are called over, and all is ready.

"Call the diet against John Mure, James Mure, and James Bannatyne."

Bannatyne there too? Yes, his name is on the indictment.

There is a passage leading from the cells underneath to the body of the Court; the passage is closed by a door which opens from above by an officer who leans over the rail in front of the dock and pushes it in. There is a sound of footsteps. The audience is on tip-toe of expectation, every neck is craned forward, and even the Judge, hardened to such scenes, ceases writing, and looks up to see the prisoners enter.

Auchendrane himself leads the way, more gaunt, more cadaverous, than ever; his high check-bones higher, his nose more hooked, less colour in his cheeks, his eyes shining balefully from out their deep sockets, his hair falling silvery over his shoulders, his bushy eyebrows knitted, his beard resting on his chest. He is bent forward with the weight of trial and trouble, and with the eighty years that furrow him. He is followed by his son James, who walks with a crutch, and carries himself as bravely as he can. His father has fixed his gaze on the Scottish arms above the judge's head; James scans the assemblage, who scan him in return, and mentally take unflattering notes of his appearance and demeanour. Bannatyne comes last, his chin resting on his breast, his eyes downcast, shame and a sense of disgrace and abject misery written on face and demeanour. He leans forward, buries his head in his hands as he sits down, and, as latter-day scribes would put it, feels his position acutely.

There is a tiresome preliminary discussion, which wastes two hours, to the inexpressible disgust of the audience, over the relevancy of the indictment. Technicality upon technicality is interposed, but one by one these are set aside, and the charge is found relevant. The audience are grateful; they are getting frightened lest the sensation should be swallowed up in some abstruse point of law which they do not comprehend.

"John Mure—you are accused of the crime of murder. What say you? Are you guilty or not guilty?"

Auchendrane rises to his feet, draws himself together, steadies his voice, looks the Judge full in the face.

"Not guilty, my lord!"

James gave a similar response in studied, loud, defiant tones; and Bannatyne in a voice which hardly reaches the Judge.

A jury is empanelled, and the case goes on.

Auchendrane thought that all these things which they witnessed against him had been buried deep in an irrevocable past. But no! here they are again, trooping up in damning sequence. Here are men who hid in the woods of Cassillis and of Auchendrane years ago, and who watched the comings and goings of Mure and his confederates ere Carrick rang with the tidings of the death of the Knight of Culzean. Here is one who saw the cavalcade ride away to St. Leonards

early in the morning, but not too early for Providence to
send a watcher to see it; and another who saw the Chief of
Bargany ride back in the afternoon after the deed was done.
The boatmen are there who sailed away from the mouth of
the Doon with Dalrymple, and who left the young lad in
Arran; citizens of Ayr who could speak to James Mure
entrapping the poor scholar a second time, and enticing him
to the Tower of Auchendrane; companions of Dalrymple in
Flanders, who had heard his threats, imperfectly understood,
but whose meaning was wonderfully clear now under the
fierce light of justice; two of the companions of Dalrymple,
who had stood bye while James Mure and he wrestled and
strove together on the street of Ayr, and heard the curse
which James uttered as he flung himself upon his antagonist
and nailed him to the ground in his nervous grip; rustics
from Chapeldonan who had watched Dalrymple in hiding,
and noted how reticent he was, and how obscure he kept
himself: a renegade servitor of Auchendrane, who had harnessed the horses of the Mures on the night when they rode
off for the Girvan shore, and who had stabled the jaded
steeds when the riders returned on the following morning
with their spades and their rope and their firearms; the
fishers who had seen the body of the murdered man cast up
on the beach, and who told with awe-struck countenances
how the blood had sprung from the victim when Mure's
grand-daughter drew near to behold it.

How the coil winds round and round the murderers!
There is only one turn wanting to complete it. And that too
is forthcoming. It is the deposition of Bannatyne. His life
depends on that deposition; had it not been forthcoming
voluntarily, the Thumbkins and the Boot would have extract-
ed it, or to the scaffold he might have gone with his unconfessed sin on his soul. But here it is, in detail, full and
complete; not a word a wanting. It makes the audience
eerie as it is read.

It works a strange change on the Mures. Hitherto they had listened and said nothing. They had watched the chain being forged, yet ignorant that the last link had been so hammered out, and that there is not a flaw in the whole of it; but now that the Clerk of Court in matter-of-fact tones reads out all that took place on the Girvan shore, they can stand it no longer.

The old man springs to his feet and clutches the edge of the dock with his bony fingers. He looks to the Judge, to the Jury. Sternness sits on the Judge's face, and there is no reciprocal pity in the glance of the jurymen who hold his life in the balance.

" God knows, my lord and gentlemen," he ejaculates, as he falls upon his knees and raises his hands and his eyes to Heaven, " God knows that we are innocent! This is a vile, a horrid concoction, my lord, a lie—a lie from beginning to end ! "

There is excitement in Court, a stillness, a great hush compressed.

" It is true, my lord, every word of it," interposes Bannatyne firmly, " it is true to the letter."

" It is a lie," answers James, " a vile, dastardly, cowardly lie. This is a deposition wrung from this man by the Earl of Cassillis and used against us for his own private ends. We are innocent, my lord and gentlemen, we are indeed innocent."

" Silence ! " commands the Judge. The prisoners resume their sitting posture and the deposition is finished.

The tale of evidence is complete ; the Lord-Advocate goes over it, point by point, detail by detail, telling the story as a connected narrative, and fastening on each his share of the guilt. Counsel for the defence follow, the Judge sums up, the Jury retire.

The excitement in Court is intense; and in the interval for relaxation now afforded the auditors hazard their opinions on the verdict. Their opinion, rather—for there is not a man in gallery or on basement who is not convinced that the Mures murdered Dalrymple; that Auchendrane was art in part in the slaughter of Sir Thomas Kennedy, and that Bannatyne technically, if his guilt is not as great as that of his fellow-culprits, is guilty of having shared in the murder of his kinsman.

The Jury return into Court; their verdict is written on their faces.

"Gentlemen of the Jury," says the Clerk of Court, "have you agreed upon your verdict?"

"The Jury," answers the Chancellor, "are unanimously of opinion that the prisoners are guilty as libelled."

Guilty! You might have heard a pin fall in the Court. The Clerk writes out the finding at length, and the grating of his quill as it travels over the paper sounds loud in the gloomy stillness.

Guilty! Auchendrane buries his head in his hands and shakes with emotion. The spasm passes, and he is himself again. James listens unmoved, and Bannatyne hears the dread word as if he were in a dream, and as if some other body were being tried for his life, and condemned.

The Judge leans forward and speaks a few words to the Lord-Advocate, and then assumes the black cap.

"John Mure of Auchendrane, the Jury have unanimously found you guilty of the crimes libelled. I would be wasting words were I to seek to impress on you the enormity of your guilt. I need hardly, I fear, adjure you to make your peace with the God against whom you have sinned so grievously. But it is not yet too late; it never is for the repentant sinner. The thief on the cross was saved at the eleventh hour—why not you? You need have no hope here, you will in a few days have done with earth, and it only remains for me to pronounce the dread sentence by the execution of which the laws of your country will magnify themselves.

James Mure, you have heard what I have now said to your father; and what I have said applies to you as well. Abandon hope here. Seek mercy at the judgment bar of God, before whom you will ere long stand. Bannatyne, it is my duty to sentence you similarly; but the Lord-Advocate, in respect of your confession and of your not being a free agent in the murder of Dalrymple, will make application to His Most Gracious Majesty the King for your pardon. But let this be a warning to you that you will never forget to your dying day."

Ere the Judge has time to pronounce formal sentence, Auchendrane falls on his knees—

"Hear me, my lord; let me speak. I am innocent, I am, indeed!"

"Add not perjury to murder, sir," sternly replies the Judge. "God hears you; upon me your words fall as an idle tale, and I believe them not. Confess to Him and lie not to me."

"I dare not confess, my lord, things whereof I am innocent. God has not forsaken me so far as to let me confess deeds which I never committed."

"Silence!" rebukingly shouts the Officer of the Court.

And the formal sentence follows:—

"The justice, by the mouth of Alexander Kennedy, dempster of Court, decerns and adjudges the said John Mure of Auchendrane, elder, James Mure of Auchendrane, younger, his eldest son and apparent heir, and James Bannatyne, called of Chapeldonan, and each one of them, to be taken to the Castle Hill of the Burgh of Edinburgh, and there, upon a scaffold, their heads to be stricken from their bodies; and all their lands, heritages, tacks, steadings, rooms, possessions, tiends, crops, cattle, inside plenishing, goods, gear, titles, profits, commodities, and rights, whatsoever, directly or indirectly pertaining to them or any of them, at the committing of the said treasonable murders, or since syne; or to the which they or any of them have right, claim, or action, to be forfeit, escheat, and inbrought to our Sovereign Lord's use; as culpable and convicted of the said treasonable crimes.

Which is pronounced for Doom."

Again Mure lifts his eyes and his hands appealingly, but, ere he has time to say more, he is rudely pushed towards the trap stair, which leads to the cells below, and disappears.

And the audience throng out into the streets, weary with excitement. It has been a long day, and the sun is westering, and dropping behind the houses.

The Heart of Midlothian is a dreary dungeon at best; but by contrast, to those within at least, it is doubly so in the long genial days of summer. All the gladness, the life, the light, are without; nothing within the gloomy cells, save misery, crime, wretchedness.

The Mures occupy separate cells. They have seven days to live. Seven suns are yet to rise and set ere they bid eternal farewell to the light; seven short days wherein to atone for a lifetime of crime! It is short enough.

The morning after the trial they are waited upon by two of the reverend fathers of the Reformation. Neither Auchendrane nor his son is civil to them. They are repulsed, their attentions discarded, their counsel slighted. The Mures are going to die as they have lived. The coil of predestination is about them, Auchendrane says; and innocent though they are, they are quite aware that there is no hope. The Judge told them so, and they do not doubt his assurance. Both are wrathful with Bannatyne, and curse him aloud, and the sun goes down upon their wrath.

The ministers of Christ are not to be easily repulsed; and the second day is not far advanced ere they are admitted within the gateway of the prison, and conducted by heavy portals and through long solemn passages to the cells tenanted by the condemned men. They are more respectfully received; but what do innocent men want with confessors? They are

obdurate, and Mure inclined to discuss his favourite theory.
What must be, will be, he tells the clergymen, and there is
no escape from doom. It is predestination that has ruined
him. He could not have acted otherwise all his life long
than he has done; for his deeds were written in the book of
Fate, and they are not his, but Fate's. Every effort to shake
him is in vain; and James scoffs, and rails, and curses his
luck.

The time is getting on, passing, like the swift ships, like a
weaver's shuttle. What, asks James Mure of himself, if
these ministers of the Gospel should be right, and he wrong ?
Why should he die with a lie upon his lips ? Why, on the
other hand, should he die and leave a tarnished reputation
behind him ? His mind is torn between the alternatives.
He would fain win salvation if he could. If he could ! Yes,
but what chance has he of salvation now ? None. And so,
when his daily visitors come, to plead, to beseech, to pray, he
steels himself for the inevitable, and is callous as ever.

Auchendrane has had a bad night of it. Those infernal
spectres have come in through the locked doors and the
grated windows, and wearied and vexed him. Why can they
not let him rest ? Why torture him before his time ? If the
ministers could only pray them away and give him peace !
Peace ! there is no peace to the wicked. Will he not confess ?
Confess ? Confess what ? He has lived an innocent man,
and he will die as he has lived, with protestation on his lips.
He will go to the bar of the Eternal with his protestation !
And so another day goes past, and night sits upon the city.

Another day dawns, the fourth day. Spectre-haunted,
Auchendrane is nervous and timorous until the sun has risen
high and he shakes off the memories of the night. James'
determination begins to waver. Will he not, he asks the
ministers, have a chance in the world to come unless he
confess ? No, they tell him, to die without confession is to
die with a lie; besides, it is his duty to confess and to admit

the justice of his sentence.   Confession, too, is the first
indication of penitence; and so he ought to confess.   The
process goes on working, and as the ministers plead with him,
he breaks down and will tell them all.   At least he will tell
them all to-morrow; meanwhile they must be content with
his admission that his sentence is just.   Will that do?   What
must he do to be saved?   The old answer and the old
assurance.

But no confession can be wrung from Auchendrane.   He
is innocent—innocent—innocent!   The ministers plead with
him.   They do not tell him that James has confessed, for
James has asked them not to do it until he has had time to
tell all.   Another night—time is galloping away—only two
more nights and the murderers will have to lie down no
more, save in death.

James has spent a restless night, when the ministers, on
the morning of the fifth day, find him still stretched on his
couch.   "I am glad," he tells them as they enter, "that I
have confessed.   It has taken a load off my mind."   They sit
down, and he tells them all.   He extenuates, and explains
away, and talks of necessity; he reviles the Earl of Cassillis
as the cause of all his misfortunes; he curses the fate that
drove him on, and ever on, to his own destruction.   And
then he listens while the ministers explain the way of
salvation, and they leave him penitent and prayerful.
Penitent for what?   For having been caught in his wicked-
ness?   Prayerful for what?   That he may escape retribution
hereafter?   Let us not be uncharitable.

Auchendrane is buried in thought.   Daily he is growing
weaker.   His appetite is gone; he is but a shadow of what
he was.   Will he not confess?   Not he.   Still, he has
nothing to confess.   But James, tell his spiritual advisers,
has told all.   Has he?   Then there is no further need why
he should keep silence.   He did the deeds; but was he not
justified in the doing?   Were they not all the natural

outcome of circumstances, the inevitable consequence of feudalism? Will he not seek salvation? No, not he. He is going to die as he has lived. The sentence was just; but there is no time to make his peace with Heaven. Prayers and tears are alike unavailing. "Leave me alone," is his sole response. And he is left alone to think over the inevitable, and to prepare for his nightly visitants. Thank God, they can't come much oftener, at any rate.

Day the sixth, and last. It is a long day for Auchendrane, though, when night comes, it has been all too short. He is still as obdurate as ever, argumentative and discursive. The ministers come and go; they come and go again; and when they leave for the night, he has not given them the faintest point on which they can hang a rag of hope. He has lived too long; his heart is seared as with a hot iron; and he wishes it was all over. James spends the day in listening to his advisers. He says he hopes for salvation through the blood of Christ; and fondly hugging the hope, he lies down to rest.

The last night! What a sad thought for the two poor wretches lying stretched upon their hard beds! The last sun has gone down upon them; never again in this world will the stars twinkle over them, or the moon walk out in her glory. They have all but done with earth. No more for them the rush of the Doon, or the birds singing upon the trees in the bonnie woods of Auchendrane! No more the sun gilding the waters of the Firth of Clyde ere he drops out of sight behind the dark peaks of Arran! No more the brown slopes of Carrick! For others, the raid, the foray, the conflict, the excitement of living! For them——

The last night!

Edinburgh is early astir. Crowds are flocking towards the Castle Hill, and putting in time roaming about the battle- . ments, and feeling strong in the security of the ramparts, the guns, the frowning walls of the historic castle which sits so proudly over the fair city. The people are wrought up to a high state of excitement, for, though an execution is no uncommon spectacle, it is not every day that two men of old family, and whose names have of late been a household word far beyond the scenes of their misdeeds, are to be delivered up to the public executioner.

Besides, this is a state execution. Strangling and the stake are good enough for wizards and witches, the gibbet for common malefactors; but to-day the old Scottish guillotine, the Maiden, stands on the slope of the hill leading to the city, where all may see it, and witness the final earthly scene in the life of the Carrick squires.

The morning is still early when Auchendrane rises from bed, where he has sought to snatch a few hours of repose, and makes ready to meet his doom. He has nothing to do save wait. The ministers of religion are with him by seven o'clock, but he listens unmoved and immovable. Eighty years have seared his soul, his mind is made up for the inevitable, and he will go to the scaffold with unchanged demeanour.

His son avails himself of the ministrations, and listens attentively to the earnest exhortations; otherwise he betrays no emotion. His courage is still of the bull-dog kind, though his counsellors flatter themselves that it is the courage of Christian resignation. To them he is a brand plucked from the burning.

The day wears on till ten clock strikes on the bells of St. Giles. The executioner arrives. Auchendrane's long hair and flowing beard are closely cropped, for it is undesirable that anything should come between the tender skin of the neck and the gleaming edge of the knife. He submits philosophically, for there is no alternative. James's hair, which has grown in prison, is similarly treated. He shrinks not when he feels the rude scissors on his neck. What need to shrink at the first touch of the steel, when the last is at hand !

They are carefully lifted on to a cart; beside them sits the executioner. A company of soldiers come up to the Heart of Midlothian, their war-pipes awakening the echoes of the lofty High Street. As the cart emerges, they fall into position and surround the cart.

The street is crowded, and, as far as Mure can see, there is no end to the throng. On the whole the solemnity begets silence; but there are mutterings which reach the ear of Auchendrane and his son, and by which they know that silence and solemnity are not always the same as sympathy. Rumble, rumble, on goes the cart. The distance is only a few hundred yards. As they advance, the crowds thicken and the excitement grows greater and more intense.

They emerge on the square. The sun is high in the heavens, the sky is blue, the castle smiles in the light; even the Half Moon battery with its frowning guns, and the jagged brown rocks out-jutting in their emblematic strength, seem to be merged in the scene of beauty on which the sun smiles; and the broad Firth of Forth lies gleaming, calm, reflective, in the light, its waters dotted with a spare sail and throwing into relief the coast line beyond. It is a scene on which to dwell.

But scenery and Nature in her fairer guises are out of sympathy with crime. She never withdraws her influences because sin defaces her, but goes on calm and serene, unchanging in her serenity and unaffected by the strifes and the sorrows and the crimes of man !

Through the dense crowd comes the cart with its burden. It halts by the scaffold; and the criminals, as they look up and see the uprights, and the knife waiting liberation, and the basket filled with sawdust beyond, and into which many a head has fallen, require all their ortitude; but they brace themselves to the ordeal, and preserve their composure unmoved, apparently immovable.

Auchendrane is assisted to dismount; James is lifted bodily

out of the cart, for his crushed foot forbids voluntary loco-
motion, even to the scaffold.

They stand upon the scaffold and cast a quick glance upon
the scene.   The immense throng is hushed and silent—
waiting—waiting!

Quickly the executioner seizes Mure, binds his legs together,
and assists him into position as he lays his head upon the
block.

In another instant the old man has gone to the bar of the
final Judgment.

James Mure hears the knife fall.   He has shut his eyes so
that he may not see it; but he cannot shut his ears to the
long sigh of the crowd or to the horrid swish of the knife as
it descends on its fatal message.   Oh for one hour more of
life, for the broad plains of Carrick and the banks of the
Doon!

The executioner turns to him.   He lays his head in the
fatal semi-circle.   The knife, which has been again raised to its
position, but whose clear steel is besmirched with blood, is
waiting for a new victim.

Another moment and it is all over.   The crowds disperse.

THE END.

W. JOLLY AND SONS, PRINTERS, ABERDEEN.

NEW BOOKS AND NEW EDITIONS.

NOCTES AMBROSIANÆ. By PROFESSOR JOHN
WILSON ("Christopher North"). Popular Edition.
Post 8vo. Price 4s. 6d.

In issuing a POPULAR *edition of this remarkable work, the
editor has omitted those portions which were of interest* ONLY *at the
time of original publication, such as matters of merely passing
interest, questions of politics and science, and other affairs that have
now passed out from that stage from which they were viewed fifty
years ago. But there are other matters, the interest surrounding
which is as great as ever—these the editor has been careful to retain.
Especial care has also been taken with regard to the amusing element,
with which these pages will be found laden.*

*THE EARLY PROSE AND POETICAL WORKS
OF JOHN TAYLOR, The Water Poet*, 1580-1653.
Post 8vo. Price 5s.

*A most remarkable man. His writings are highly descriptive of
the manners and customs of the period. In 1618 he travelled on
foot from London to the Wilds of Braemar, and published an
account of the journey, entitled " The Penniless Pilgrimage." In
the Scottish Highlands he became the guest of the Earl of Mar at a
hunting encampment among the hills, all of which he saw and
describes.*

THE LAIRD OF LOGAN: Being Anecdotes and
Tales illustrative of the wit and humour of Scotland.
Post 8vo. Price 3s. 6d.

*A complete, very handsome, and the only large type edition of the
famous " Laird of Logan." This work was compiled by three very
distinguished literary Scotchmen, namely, John Donald Carrick,
William Motherwell, and Andrew Henderson, all of them authors
of works relating to Scotland. This is the only unadulterated
edition, and is here given to the public as it came direct from the
hands of the editors.*

*THE WILD SPORTS AND NATURAL HISTORY
OF THE SCOTTISH HIGHLANDS.* By
CHARLES ST. JOHN. Post 8vo. Popular Edition.
Price 4s. 6d.

*One of the most interesting works published on Scottish field sports.
Its pages are devoted to the author's experience in deer-stalking,
otter-hunting, salmon-fishing, grouse-shooting, as well as with all
the representatives of animal life to be found in the Highlands, such
as the eagle, wild cat, black game, owl, hawk, wild duck, wild geese,
wild swan, seal, fox, etc., etc.*

THE HISTORICAL TALES AND LEGENDS OF AYRSHIRE. By WILLIAM ROBERTSON. Post 8vo. Price 5s.

The County of Ayr is especially rich in story and tradition. In the centuries when feudal strife was rampant, the great county families maintained ceaseless activity in their warrings with one another. And the result of their plots, raids, enmities, machinations, and contests are to be seen in the existing social life in Ayrshire. The volume presents a series of historical tales and legends illustrative of the feudal and early social history of the shire. In every instance the author deals with facts of an intensely interesting nature.

EARLY SCOTTISH METRICAL TALES. Edited by DAVID LAING, LL.D. Post 8vo. Price 6s.

Extremely interesting early metrical tales in the original spelling, with valuable notes by the distinguished antiquary who collected the tales and issued the first edition of the book. The tales are thirteen in number, and comprise such as "The History of Sir Gray Steill," "The Tales of the Priests of Peblis," "The History of a Lord and his Three Sons," etc., etc.

BRITISH TRADE; or, CERTAIN CONDITIONS OF OUR NATIONAL PROSPERITY. By PROFESSOR JOHN KIRK. Crown 8vo. Price 4s. 6d

A companion volume to " Social Politics," by the same author, and now out of print. Regarding the latter volume, Ruskin says : " I had no notion myself, till the other day, what the facts were in this matter. Get if you can, Professor Kirk's 'Social Politics;' and read for a beginning his 21st Chapter on Land and Liquor, and then as you have leisure all the book carefully."—FORS CLAVIGERA, March, 1873.

SPORTING ANECDOTES. Being Anecdotal Annals, Descriptions, and Incidents relating to Sport and Gambling. Edited by "ELLANGOWAN." Post 8vo. Price 5s.

An entirely new and most interesting collection of anecdotes, relating to all sections of sporting life and character, such as horse-racing, boxing, golfing, jockeys, cover-shooting, gambling, betting, cock-fighting, pedestrianism, flat-racing, coursing, fox-hunting, angling, card-playing, billiards, etc., etc.

THE LIFE OF JOHN KNOX. By THOMAS M'CRIE, D.D. Demy 8vo. Stiff Paper Boards. Price 1s. 6d.

A cheap edition of this important work. The life of Knox comprises a history of Scotland at one of the most critical periods, namely that of the Reformation.

*HUMOROUS READINGS FOR HOME AND
HALL.* Edited by CHARLES B. NEVILLE. FIRST
SERIES. Price 1s.

*Humorous and amusing Readings for large or small audiences,
and for the fireside. This series (the first) contains thirteen pieces,
such as "Old Dick Fogrum Getting Settled in Life," "The Bachelor
Feeling his Way," "Mr. Gingerly's Delicate Attentions," etc., etc.*

*HUMOROUS READINGS FOR HOME AND
HALL.* Edited by CHARLES B. NEVILLE. SECOND
SERIES. Price 1s.

*A sequel to the above. The second series contains fourteen readings,
such as "Dick Doleful's Disinterested Motives," "Ferney Fidget,
Esq., in London Lodgings," "A Philosopher Getting Married,"
etc., etc.*

*HUMOROUS READINGS FOR HOME AND
HALL.* Edited by CHARLES B. NEVILLE. THIRD
SERIES. Price 1s.

*The concluding series of Mr. Neville's readings. This issue
contains fourteen pieces, all of a highly humorous nature, such as
"Dandy Nat's Hopes and Fears," "How Billy Muggins was
brought to Terms," "Cousin Jones's Valuable Legacy," etc., etc.*

*HUMOROUS READINGS FOR HOME AND
HALL.* Edited by CHARLES B. NEVILLE. Post
8vo. Price 3s. 6d.

*The three aforementioned series bound in one thick handsome
volume, cloth gilt.*

*THE SCOTTISH BOOK OF FAMILY AND
PRIVATE DEVOTION.* By TWENTY SCOTTISH
CLERGYMEN. Crown 8vo. Price 5s.

*Morning and evening prayers for family and private use for
quarter-a-year. Week day and sunday. Also prayers for the sick,
forms of invocation of the Divine blessing at table, etc.*

*ANGLING REMINISCENCES OF THE RIVERS
AND LOCHS OF SCOTLAND.* By THOMAS TOD
STODDART. Post 8vo. Price 3s. 6d.

*If not the most useful, this is at least the most interesting of
all Stoddart's angling works, of which there are three in number. The above is not to be confounded with "The Scottish
Angler" on the one hand, or "The Angler's Companion" on
the other, though from the same pen. The present work is
colloquial throughout, and teeming with the richest humour from
beginning to end.*

HUMOROUS AND AMUSING SCOTCH READINGS.
For the Platform, the Social Circle, and the Fireside.
By ALEXANDER G. MURDOCH. First Series. Paper
Covers. Price 1s.

*Humorous and amusing Scotch readings, fifteen in number,
and illustrative of the social life and character of the Scottish
people, than which the author believes no more interesting subject can be found. Among other readings may be mentioned,
"Mrs. Macfarlane's Rabbit Dinner," "The Washin'-Hoose
Key," "Jock Broon's Patent Umbrella," "Willie Weedrap's
Domestic Astronomy," etc., etc.*

*HUMOROUS AND AMUSING SCOTCH READ-
INGS. For the Platform, the Social Circle, and the
Fireside.* By ALEXANDER G. MURDOCH. SECOND
SERIES. Paper Cover. Price 1s.

*A sequel to the foregoing, contains fourteen readings, comprising
"Johnny Gowdy's Funny Ploy," "Jock Turnip's Mither-in-Law,"
"Lodgings in Arran," "Robin Rigg and the Minister," etc., etc.*

*HUMOROUS AND AMUSING SCOTCH READ-
INGS. For the Platform, the Social Circle, and the
Fireside.* By ALEXANDER G. MURDOCH. THIRD
SERIES. Paper Covers. Price 1s.

*The third and concluding series of Mr. Murdoch's popular and
highly amusing Scotch readings. This issue contains "Jean
Tamson's Love Hopes and Fears," "The Amateur Phrenologist,"
"Peter Paterson the Poet," "Coming Home Fou'," etc., etc.*

*HUMOROUS AND AMUSING SCOTCH READ-
INGS. For the Platform, the Social Circle, and the
Fireside.* By ALEXANDER G. MURDOCH. Thick
Post 8vo. Cloth. Price 3s. 6d.

*The three aforementioned series, bound in one thick handsome
volume, cloth gilt.*

THE COURT OF SESSION GARLAND. Edited by
JAMES MAIDMENT, Advocate. *New edition, including
all the Supplements.* Demy 8vo. Price 7s. 6d.

*A collection of most interesting anecdotes and facetiae con-
nected with the Court of Session. Even to those not initiated in
the mysteries of legal procedure, much of the volume will be
found highly attractive, for no genuine votary of Momus can
be insensible to the fun of the Justiciary Opera, as illustrated
by the drollery of the "Diamond Beetle Case," and many others
of an amusing nature, such as "The Poor Client's Complaint,"
"The Parody on Hellvellyn," "The King's Speech," "Lord
Bannatyne's Lion," "The Beauties of Overgroggy," etc., etc.*

ST. KILDA AND THE ST. KILDIANS. By ROBERT
CONNELL. Crown 8vo. Price 2s. 6d.

"*A capital book. It contains everything worth knowing
about the famous islet and its people.*"—THE BAILIE.

"*Interesting and amusing. It includes a lively description of
the daily life of the inhabitants, the native industries of fishing,
bird catching, and the rearing of sickly sheep and cattle, and
gives a vivid picture of the Sabbatarian despotism of the Free
Church minister who rules the small population.*"—SATURDAY
REVIEW.

THE PRAISE OF FOLLY. By ERASMUS. *With
Numerous Illustrations by Holbein.* Post 8vo. Price
4s. 6d.

*An English translation of the "Encomium Moriae" which
has always held a foremost place among the more popular of
the writings of the great scholar. This work is probably the
most satirical production of any age. It is intensely humorous
throughout, and is entirely unique in character. This edition
also contains Holbein's illustrations, attaching to which there is
very considerable interest.*

ANECDOTES OF FISH AND FISHING. By THOMAS
BOOSEY. Post 8vo. Price 3s. 6d.

*An interesting collection of anecdotes and incidents connected
with fish and fishing, arranged and classified into sections. It
deals with all varieties of British fish, their habits, different
modes of catching them, interesting incidents in connection with
their capture, and an infinite amount of angling gossip relating
to each. Considerable space is also devoted to the subject of
fishing as practised in different parts of the world.*

TALES OF A SCOTTISH PARISH. By JACOB
RUDDIMAN, M.A. Post 8vo. Paper Covers. Price 1s.

*The deceased author was a person of singular beauty and
originality of mind, and may well be ranked alongside of Wilson,
Hogg, Bethune, Pollok, and other such standard writers of Scottish
tales. The tales are nineteen in all, and comprise such as "The
Sexton," "The Unfortunate Farmer," "The Lonely Widow,"
"The Foreboding," etc., etc.*

SCOTTISH LEGENDS. By ANDREW GLASS. Post
8vo. Paper Covers. Price 1s.

*Four legends, relating chiefly to the west and south of Scotland,
entitled, "A Legend of Rothesay Castle," "The Laird of Auchinleck's Gift," "The Cruives of Cree," "The Grey Stones of Gar-
laffin."*

A BANQUET OF JESTS AND MERRY TALES.

By ARCHIE ARMSTRONG, Court Jester to King James I. and King Charles I., 1611-1637.

An extremely amusing work, reprinted in the original quaint spelling of the period. In addition to the immense fund of amusement to be found in its pages, the work is highly valuable as throwing much light on the social customs and ideas of the period. The author experienced life in connection with all ranks and sections of society, from his own peasant home in the north, to that of the Court of his Sovereign.

AMUSING IRISH TALES. By WILLIAM CARLETON.

Post 8vo. Price 2s. 6d.

A collection of amusing and humorous tales descriptive of Irish life and character. The distinguished author has been designated the Sir Walter Scott of Ireland. The tales are fifteen in number, such as " The Country Dancing Master," " The Irish Match-Maker," " The Irish Smuggler," " The Irish Senachie," " The Country Fiddler," etc., etc. All of them are overflowing with the richest wit and humour.

THE WHOLE FAMILIAR COLLOQUIES OF ERASMUS. Translated by NATHAN BAILEY.

Demy 8vo. Price 4s. 6d.

A complete and inexpensive edition of the great book of amusement of the sixteenth century. Probably no other work so truly and intensely depicts the life and notions of our forefathers 350 years ago, as does this inimical production of the great Erasmus.

There are 62 dialogues in all, and an immense variety of subjects are dealt with, such as " Benefice-Hunting," " The Soldier and the Carthusian," " The Franciscans," " The Apparition," " The Beggar's Dialogue," " The Religious Pilgrimage," " The Sermon," " The Parliament of Women," etc., etc. The whole work is richly characteristic, and is full of the richest humour and satire.

AMUSING PROSE CHAP BOOKS, CHIEFLY OF LAST CENTURY. Edited by ROBERT HAYS CUNNINGHAM. Post 8vo. Price 4s. 6d.

A collection of interesting prose chap books of former times, forming a good representative of the people's earliest popular literature, such as " The Comical History of the King and the Cobbler," " The Merry Tales of the Wise Men of Gotham," " The Merry Conceits of Tom Long, the Carrier," "The Pleasant History of Poor Robin, the Merry Saddler of Walden," etc., etc.

THE DANCE OF DEATH: Illustrated in Forty-Eight Plates. By JOHN HOLBEIN. Demy 8vo. Price 5s.

A handsome and inexpensive edition of the great Holbein's most popular production. It contains the whole forty-eight plates, with letterpress description of each plate, the plate and the description in each case being on separate pages, facing each other. The first edition was issued in 1530, and since then innumerable impressions have been issued, but mostly in an expensive form, and unattainable by the general public.

THE LITERARY HISTORY OF GLASGOW. By W. J. DUNCAN. Quarto. Price 12s. 6d. net. *Printed for Subscribers and Private Circulation.*

This volume forms one of the volumes issued by the Maitland Club, and was originally published in 1831. This edition is a verbatim et literatim reprint, and is limited to 350 copies, with an appendix additional containing extra matter of considerable importance, not in the original work.

The book is chiefly devoted to giving an account of the greatest of Scottish printers, namely, the Foulises, and furnishes a list of the books they printed, as likewise of the sculptures and paintings which they so largely produced.

GOLFIANA MISCELLANEA. Being a Collection of Interesting Monographs on the Royal and Ancient Game of Golf. Edited by JAMES LINDSAY STEWART. Post 8vo. Price 4s. 6d.

A collection of interesting productions, prose and verse, on or relating to, the game of golf, by various authors both old and recent. Nothing has been allowed into the collection except works of merit and real interest. Many of the works are now extremely scarce and, in a separate form, command very high prices. It contains twenty-three separate productions of a great variety of character—historical, descriptive, practical, poetical, humorous, biographical, etc.

THE BARDS OF THE BIBLE. By GEORGE GILFILLAN. Seventh Edition. Post 8vo. Price 5s.

The most popular of the writings of the late Rev. Dr. Gilfillan. The author, in his preface, states that the object of the book was chiefly a prose poem or hymn in honour of the poetry and the poets of the Bible. It deals with the poetical side of the inspired word, and takes up the separate portions in chronological order.

ONE HUNDRED ROMANCES OF REAL LIFE. By LEIGH HUNT. Post 8vo. Price 3s. 6d.

A handsome edition of Leigh Hunt's famous collection of romances of real life, now scarce in a complete form. The present issue is complete, containing as it does the entire hundred as issued by the author. All being incidents from real life, the interest attaching to the volume is not of an ordinary character. The romances relate to all grades of society, and are entirely various in circumstance, each one being separate and distinct in itself.

UNIQUE TRADITIONS CHIEFLY OF THE WEST AND SOUTH OF SCOTLAND. By JOHN GORDON BARBOUR. Post 8vo. Price 4s. 6d.

A collection of interesting local and popular traditions gathered orally by the author in his wanderings over the West and South of Scotland. The author narrates in this volume, thirty-five separate incidental traditions in narrative form, connected with places or individuals, all of a nature to interest the general Scottish reader, such as "The Red Comyn's Castle," "The Coves of Barholm," "The Rafters of Kirk Alloway," "Cumstone Castle," "The Origin of Loch Catrine," etc., etc.

MODERN ANECDOTES: A Treasury of Wise and Witty Sayings of the last Hundred Years. Edited, with Notes, by W. DAVENPORT ADAMS. Crown 8vo. Price 3s. 6d.

The Anecdotes are all authenticated and are classed into Sections—I. Men of Society. II. Lawyers and the Law. III. Men of Letters. IV. Plays and Players. V. Statesmen and Politicians. VI. The Church and Clergy. VII. People in General.

In compiling a work like this, Mr. Adams has steadily kept in view the necessity of ministering to the requirements of those who will not read anecdotes unless they have reason to know that they are really good. On this principle the entire editorial work has been executed. The book is also a particularly handsome one as regards printing, paper, and binding.

THE LITURGY OF JOHN KNOX: As received by the Church of Scotland in 1564. Crown 8vo. Price 5s.

A beautifully printed edition of the Book of Common Order, more popularly known as the Liturgy of John Knox. This is the only modern edition in which the original quaint spelling is retained. In this and other respects the old style is strictly reproduced, so that the work remains exactly as used by our forefathers three hundred years ago.

THE GABERLUNZIE'S WALLET. By JAMES
BALLANTINE. Third edition. Cr. 8vo. Price 2s. 6d.

*A most interesting historical tale of the period of the Pre-
tenders, and containing a very large number of favourite songs
and ballads, illustrative of the tastes and life of the people at
that time. Also containing numerous facetious illustrations by
Alexander A. Ritchie.*

THE WOLFE OF BADENOCH. A Historical Romance
of the Fourteenth Century. By SIR THOMAS DICK
LAUDER. Complete unabridged edition. Thick Crown
8vo. Price 6s.

*This most interesting romance has been frequently described as
equal in interest to any of Sir Walter Scott's historical tales. This
is a complete unabridged edition, and is uniform with "Highland
Legends" and "Tales of the Highlands," by the same author. As
several abridged editions of the work have been published, especial
attention is drawn to the fact that the above edition is complete.*

THE LIVES OF THE PLAYERS. By JOHN GALT, Esq.
Post 8vo. Price 5s.

*Interesting accounts of the lives of distinguished actors, such as
Betterton, Cibber, Farquhar, Garrick, Foote, Macklin, Murphy,
Kemble, Siddons, &c., &c. After the style of Johnson's "Lives of
the Poets."*

KAY'S EDINBURGH PORTRAITS. A Series of Anec-
dotal Biographies, chiefly of Scotchmen. Mostly written
by JAMES PATERSON. And edited by JAMES MAIDMENT,
Esq. Popular Edition. 2 Vols., Post 8vo. Price 12s.

*A popular edition of this famous work, which, from its exceedingly
high price, has hitherto been out of the reach of the general public.
This edition contains all the reading matter that is of general interest;
it also contains eighty illustrations.*

THE RELIGIOUS ANECDOTES OF SCOTLAND.
Edited by WILLIAM ADAMSON, D.D. Thick Post 8vo.
Price 5s.

*A voluminous collection of purely religious anecdotes relating to
Scotland and Scotchmen, and illustrative of the more serious side of
the life of the people. The anecdotes are chiefly in connection with
distinguished Scottish clergymen and laymen, such as Rutherford,
Macleod, Guthrie, Shirra, Leighton, the Erskines, Knox, Beattie,
M'Crie, Eadie, Brown, Irving, Chalmers, Lawson, Milne, M'Cheyne,
&c., &c. The anecdotes are serious and religious purely, and not
at all of the ordinary witty description.*

DAYS OF DEER STALKING in the Scottish High
lands, including an account of the Nature and Habits
of the Red Deer, a description of the Scottish Forests,
and Historical Notes on the earlier Field Sports of
Scotland. With Highland Legends, Superstitions,
Folk-Lore, and Tales of Poachers and Freebooters.
By WILLIAM SCROPE. Illustrated by Sir Edwin and
Charles Landseer. Demy 8vo. Price 12s. 6d.

" *The best book of sporting adventures with which we are
acquainted.*"—ATHENÆUM.
" *Of this noble diversion we owe the first satisfactory description to the pen of an English gentleman of high birth and extensive fortune, whose many amiable and elegant personal qualities
have been commemorated in the diary of Sir Walter Scott.*"—
LONDON QUARTERLY REVIEW.

DAYS AND NIGHTS OF SALMON FISHING in
the River Tweed. By WILLIAM SCROPE. Illustrated
by Sir David Wilkie, Sir Edwin Landseer, Charles
Landseer, William Simson, and Edward Cooke.
Demy 8vo. Price 12s. 6d.

" *Mr. Scrope's book has done for salmon fishing what its pre-
decessor performed for deer stalking.*"—LONDON QUARTERLY
REVIEW.
" *Mr. Scrope conveys to us in an agreeable and lively manner
the results of his more than twenty years' experience in our great
Border river. . . . The work is enlivened by the narration of
numerous angling adventures, which bring out with force and
spirit the essential character of the sport in question. . . . Mr.
Scrope is a skilful author as well as an experienced angler. It
does not fall to the lot of all men to handle with equal dexterity,
the brush, the pen, and the rod, to say nothing of the rifle, still
less of the leister under cloud of night.*"—BLACKWOOD'S MAGA-
ZINE.

THE FIELD SPORTS OF THE NORTH OF EUROPE.
A Narrative of Angling, Hunting, and Shooting in
Sweden and Norway. By CAPTAIN L. LLOYD. New
edition. Enlarged and revised. Demy 8vo. Price 9s.

" *The chase seems for years to have been his ruling passion,
and to have made him a perfect model of perpetual motion. We
admire Mr. Lloyd. He is a sportsman far above the common
run.*"—BLACKWOOD'S MAGAZINE.
" *This is a very entertaining work and written, moreover, in
an agreeable and modest spirit. We strongly recommend it as
containing much instruction and more amusement.*—ATHENÆUM.

PUBLIC AND PRIVATE LIBRARIES OF GLAS-GOW. A Bibliographical Study. By THOMAS MASON. Demy 8vo. Price 12s. 6d. net.

A strictly Bibliographical work dealing with the subject of rare and interesting works, and in that respect describing three of the public and thirteen of the private libraries of Glasgow. All of especial interest.

THE LIFE OF SIR WILLIAM WALLACE. BY JOHN D. CARRICK. Fourth and cheaper edition. Royal 8vo. Price 2s. 6d.

The best life of the great Scottish hero. Contains much valuable and interesting matter regarding the history of that historically important period.

THE HISTORY OF THE PROVINCE OF MORAY. By LACHLAN SHAW. New and Enlarged Edition, 3 Vols., Demy 8vo. Price 30s.

The Standard History of the old geographical division termed the Province of Moray, comprising the Counties of Elgin and Nairn, the greater part of the County of Inverness, and a portion of the County of Banff. Cosmo Innes pronounced this to be the best local history of any part of Scotland.

HIGHLAND LEGENDS. By SIR THOMAS DICK LAUDER. Crown 8vo. Price 6s.

Historical Legends descriptive of Clan and Highland Life and Incident in former times.

TALES OF THE HIGHLANDS. By SIR THOMAS DICK LAUDER. Crown 8vo. Price 6s.

Uniform with and similar in character to the preceding, though entirely different tales. The two are companion volumes.

AN ACCOUNT OF THE GREAT MORAY FLOODS IN 1829. By SIR THOMAS DICK LAUDER. Demy 8vo., with 64 Plates and Portrait. Fourth Edition. Price 8s. 6d.

A most interesting work, containing numerous etchings by the Author. In addition to the main feature of the book, it contains much historical and legendary matter relating to the districts through which the River Spey runs.

OLD SCOTTISH CUSTOMS: Local and General. By E.
J. GUTHRIE. Crown 8vo. Price 3s. 6d.

*Gives an interesting account of old local and general Scottish
customs, now rapidly being lost sight of.*

---

*A HISTORICAL ACCOUNT OF THE BELIEF IN
WITCHCRAFT IN SCOTLAND.* By CHARLES
KIRKPATRICK SHARPE. Crown 8vo. Price 4s. 6d.

*Gives a chronological account of Witchcraft incidents in Scot-
land from the earliest period, in a racy, attractive style.   And
likewise contains an interesting Bibliography of Scottish books on
Witchcraft.*

"Sharpe was well qualified to gossip about these topics."—
SATURDAY REVIEW.

*"Mr. Sharpe has arranged all the striking and important
phenomena associated with the belief in Apparitions and Witchcraft.   An extensive appendix, with a list of books on Witchcraft
in Scotland, and a useful index, render this edition of Mr.
Sharpe's work all the more valuable."—*GLASGOW HERALD.

TALES OF THE SCOTTISH PEASANTRY. By
ALEXANDER and JOHN BETHUNE.   With Biography
of the Authors by JOHN INGRAM, F.S.A.Scot.   Post
8vo.   Price 3s. 6d.

*" It is the perfect propriety of taste, no less than the thorough
intimacy with the subjects he treats of, that gives Mr. Bethune's
book a great charm in our eyes."—*ATHENÆUM.

*"The pictures of rural life and character appear to us re-
markably true, as well as pleasing."—*CHAMBERS'S JOURNAL.

*The Tales are quite out of the ordinary routine of such litera-
ture, and are universally held in peculiarly high esteem.   The
following may be given as a specimen of the Contents:—" The
Deformed," "The Fate of the Fairest," "The Stranger," "The
Drunkard," "The Illegitimate," "The Cousins," &c., &c.*

---

*A JOURNEY TO THE WESTERN ISLANDS OF
SCOTLAND IN* 1773.   By SAMUEL JOHNSON, LL.D.
Crown 8vo.   Price 3s.

*Written by Johnson himself, and not to be confounded with
Boswell's account of the same tour.   Johnson said that some of
his best writing is in this work.*

THE HISTORY OF BURKE AND HARE AND OF THE RESURRECTIONIST TIMES. A Fragment from the Criminal Annals of Scotland. By GEORGE MAC GREGOR, F.S.A.Scot. With Seven Illustrations, Demy 8vo. Price 7s. 6d.

"*Mr. MacGregor has produced a book which is eminently readable.*"—JOURNAL OF JURISPRUDENCE.

"*The book contains a great deal of curious information.*"— SCOTSMAN.

"*He who takes up this book of an evening must be prepared to sup full of horrors, yet the banquet is served with much of literary grace, and garnished with a deftness and taste which render it palatable to a degree.*"—GLASGOW HERALD.

THE HISTORY OF GLASGOW: From the Earliest Period to the Present Time. By GEORGE MAC GREGOR, F.S.A.Scot. Containing 36 Illustrations. Demy 8vo. Price 12s. 6d.

An entirely new as well as the fullest and most complete history of this prosperous city. In addition it is the first written in chronological order. Comprising a large handsome volume in Sixty Chapters, and extensive Appendix and Index, and illustrated throughout with many interesting engravings and drawings.

THE COLLECTED WRITINGS OF DOUGAL GRAHAM, "Skellat," Bellman of Glasgow. Edited with Notes, together with a Biographical and Bibliographical Introduction, and a Sketch of the Chap Literature of Scotland, by GEORGE MAC GREGOR, F.S.A.Scot. Impression limited to 250 copies. 2 Vols., Demy 8vo. Price 21s.

With very trifling exceptions Graham was the only writer of purely Scottish chap-books of a secular description, almost all the others circulated being reprints of English productions. His writings are exceedingly facetious and highly illustrative of the social life of the period.

SCOTTISH PROVERBS. By ANDREW HENDERSON. Crown 8vo. Cheaper edition. Price 2s. 6d.

A cheap edition of a book that has long held a high place in Scottish Literature.

THE BOOK OF SCOTTISH ANECDOTE: Humorous, Social, Legendary, and Historical. Edited by ALEXANDER HISLOP. Crown 8vo., pp. 768. Cheaper edition. Price 5s.

The most comprehensive collection of Scottish Anecdotes, containing about 3,000 in number.

THE BOOK OF SCOTTISH STORY: Historical, Traditional, Legendary, Imaginative, and Humorous. Crown 8vo., pp. 768. Cheaper edition. Price 5s.

A most interesting and varied collection by Leading Scottish Authors.

THE BOOK OF SCOTTISH POEMS: Ancient and Modern. Edited by J. Ross. Crown 8vo., pp. 768. Cheaper edition. Price 5s.

Comprising a History of Scottish Poetry and Poets from the earliest times. With lives of the Poets and Selections from their Writings.

** These three works are uniform.

A DESCRIPTION OF THE WESTERN ISLES OF SCOTLAND, CALLED HYBRIDES. With the Genealogies of the Chief Clans of the Isles. By SIR DONALD MONRO, High Dean of the Isles, who travelled through most of them in the year 1549. Impression limited to 250 copies. Demy 8vo. Price 5s.

This is the earliest written description of the Western Islands, and is exceedingly quaint and interesting. In this edition all the old curious spellings are strictly retained.

A DESCRIPTION OF THE WESTERN ISLANDS OF SCOTLAND CIRCA 1695. By MARTIN MARTIN. Impression limited to 250 copies. Demy 8vo. Price 12s. 6d.

With the exception of Dean Monro's smaller work 150 years previous, it is the earliest description of the Western Islands we have, and is the only lengthy work on the subject before the era of modern innovations. Martin very interestingly describes the people and their ways as he found them about 200 years ago.

THE SCOTTISH POETS, RECENT AND LIVING.
By ALEXANDER G. MURDOCH. With Portraits, Post
8vo. Price 6s.

*A most interesting resumé of Scottish Poetry in recent times.
Contains a biographical sketch, choice pieces, and portraits of
the recent and living Scottish Poets.*

THE HUMOROUS CHAP-BOOKS OF SCOTLAND.
By JOHN FRASER. 2 Vols., Thin Crown 8vo (all
published). Price 5s.

*An interesting and racy description of the chap-book literature
of Scotland, and biographical sketches of the writers.*

THE HISTORY OF STIRLINGSHIRE. By WILLIAM
NIMMO. 2 Vols., Demy 8vo. 3rd Edition. Price 25s.

*A new edition of this standard county history, handsomely
printed, and with detailed map giving the parish boundaries
and other matters of interest.*

*This county has been termed the battlefield of Scotland, and
in addition to the many and important military engagements
that have taken place in this district, of all which a full account
is given,—this part of Scotland is of especial moment in many
other notable respects,—among which particular reference may
be made to the Roman Wall, the greater part of this most
interesting object being situated within the boundaries of the
county.*

---

*A POPULAR SKETCH OF THE HISTORY OF
GLASGOW:* From the Earliest Period to the Present
Time. By ANDREW WALLACE. Crown 8vo. Price 3s. 6d.

*The only attempt to write a History of Glasgow suitable for
popular use.*

---

*THE HISTORY OF THE WESTERN HIGHLANDS
AND ISLES OF SCOTLAND,* from A.D. 1493 to
A.D. 1625. With a brief introductory sketch from
A.D. 80 to A.D. 1493. By DONALD GREGORY. Demy
8vo. Price 12s. 6d.

*Incomparably the best history of the Scottish Highlands, and
written purely from original investigation. Also contains particularly full and lengthened Contents and Index, respectively at
beginning and end of the volume.*

THE HISTORY OF AYRSHIRE. By James Paterson. 5 Vols., Crown 8vo.   Price 28s. net.

The most recent and the fullest history of this exceedingly interesting county. The work is particularly rich in the department of Family History.

MARTYRLAND: a Historical Tale of the Covenanters. By the Rev. Robert Simpson, D.D.   Crown 8vo. Cheaper Edition.   Price 2s. 6d.

A tale illustrative of the history of the Covenanters in the South of Scotland.

TALES OF THE COVENANTERS. By E. J. Guthrie.   Crown 8vo.   Cheaper Edition.   Price 2s. 6d.

A number of tales illustrative of leading incidents and characters connected with the Covenanters.

PERSONAL AND FAMILY NAMES. A Popular Monograph on the Origin and History of the Nomenclature of the Present and Former Times.   By Harry Alfred Long.   Demy 8vo.   Price 5s.

Interesting investigations as to the origin, history, and meaning of about 9,000 personal and family names.

THE SCOTTISH GALLOVIDIAN ENCYCLOPÆDIA of the Original, Antiquated, and Natural Curiosities of the South of Scotland.   By John Mactaggart. Demy 8vo.   Price raised to 25s.   Impression limited to 250 copies.

Contains a large amount of extremely interesting and curious matter relating to the South of Scotland.

THE COMPLETE TALES OF THE ETTRICK SHEPHERD (James Hogg).   2 vols., Demy 8vo.

An entirely new and complete edition of the tales of this popular Scottish writer.

GLASGOW: THOMAS D. MORISON.
LONDON: HAMILTON, ADAMS & CO.

www.ingramcontent.com/pod-product-compliance
Lightning Source LLC
Chambersburg PA
CBHW020938030726
47496CB00005B/1251